Dissonant Song

Other Books by David Hochhalter and Tom Crepeau

Wandmaking 101
Wandmaking 201

Healer's Awakening
Healer's Journey
Healer's Love

Living Song
Dissonant Song

DISSONANT SONG

David Hochhalter and Tom Crepeau

Copyright 2023 David L. Hochhalter and Tom M. Crepeau

All rights reserved.

No part of this book may be reproduced or transmitted in any form by any means—graphic, electronic or mechanical—without permission in writing from the author, except by a reviewer who may quote brief passages in a review.

    This is a work of fiction, not a work of history. All characters portrayed in this book are products of the authors' imagination. Even when a character is modeled and named for a person who really existed, what emerges on the page is a portrayal of a fictional character who did what they did on these pages to create a good story. It is not presented either to praise nor to diminish the actual people. Instead, our characters are used by the authors to present a good story, nothing more, and (hopefully) nothing less.

Cover Design by Briar Banerji, https://theminism.wixsite.com/
Editing by Meredith Bond
Proofreading by The Editing Hall
Formatting by Anessa Books

Published by Anessa Books
Virginia, USA

Prologue

-Terrance-

The Fay woman and I were trying to keep the ship steady in a storm. The two of us took turns adjusting sails while the other held on to the tiller as waves crashed around us. Even with my enhanced strength and agility, I almost fell over the side as a wall of water slammed into me, nearly capsizing the boat. We were taking in water, a few more waves like that, and it wouldn't matter what we did, we would go under. I didn't know how long I could keep this up. I could feel sunrise was almost upon us. Even though the sky was a rolling mass of clouds, keeping the sunrise hidden, would I be forced to sleep again?

I heard the Fay woman shout something, but the howling wind tore away her words. She was doing everything possible to keep the ship angled in the right direction.

"What?" I shouted back while bracing a rope to hold our mainmast in place. "I can't hear you."

"It's going to be okay," she shouted back. "Thank you for showing me the way."

Huh? "The way?" I shouted back. "What are you talking..." Morning was upon us. I felt my body begin to sleep, but I pushed with everything I had and woke back up. During my momentary unconsciousness, the rope had slipped from my hands, and the boat veered starboard. Scrambling to grab the rope, I mentally pleaded with myself; *I am Terrance, I am Terrance.* I didn't want the morning sun to strip away who I had become. If I went below, the boat would likely sink, and the Fay woman who had stayed in my songs all these years would be gone as well. There was no going back for me. I wanted to live, but Terrance was a man who would look death in the face to save others. If I gave up, she wouldn't have a chance.

Just as I got my purchase and hauled the mainmast back in place, a giant wave slammed into the stern and the woman in my songs disappeared. I sprang toward the tiller. Was she still with me? A hand reached out and grasped mine. At the same moment, the last of the wind died down, and with it, the waves receded. Above me, clouds began to break apart, and I felt sunlight on my body.

I was still Terrance!

But more surprising, the person I was grasping wasn't the Fay woman but Lady Elizabeth Navartis.

"I'm here." Her cheeks dimpled. Soaked clothes outlined her body in delightful ways. "It's going to be okay," she said and leaned into me.

I could feel the warmth of her body against mine. Just as I was about to lean down to meet her lips, I heard another voice, urgent and apprehensive.

"Terrance, sunrise is almost here. Can you wake up?"

I knew that voice. Franklin, Darlene's husband. But I didn't want to wake up yet.

Lady Navartis laughed, kissed my chest, then took a step back. Thousands of lights erupted from the ocean and formed into a unicorn. After mounting her stead, Lady Navartis leaned down to kiss me. Just before she did, her image evaporated as I felt Franklin shaking my shoulders.

Opening my eyes, Lady Elizabeth Navartis was gone. Standing over me was Franklin. Camillo was next to him. The inside of the cave was a sparkling red. Sunrise was here.

"Your timing stinks," I said, while pushing with my elbows to sit up. I would swim any ocean to be with that woman. But who was I fooling? She was the pinnacle of womanhood. If she walked into a room full of royalty, everyone would part before her. There was one queen, and she was it. Hordes of nobles would climb any mountain just to be the one to dance with her.

"You wanted me to try to wake you at sunrise," said Franklin. "In another few minutes, the sun will touch you." He looked toward the cave entrance. Darlene, his wife, was sitting on the edge, looking out.

<*"Are you sure, my friend?"*> asked Camillo.

"No, but if I am to lose my memories, I would rather it be among friends." Previously, before I remembered who I was, the sunlight tore at my memories and my strength.

Franklin took his place next to Darlene, and she leaned into him. Both were tired and dirty. Over the course of the night, they had helped to dig out Gerald's body. Currently, it was covered with a tarp. Assuming I survived the next ten minutes, I planned to bring his body to his wife for a proper burial.

I sat down next to Darlene, and she reached out a hand. I took it, and together we watched the sun slowly rise.

Camillo was right behind us, looking out as well. He started to sing and the snow around him sparkled. Well, what do you know? Now that he has a name, he can sing as well. As his song ended, the light was almost upon us.

<*"Did you dream of the Fay woman, my friend"*> asked Camillo.

"She said goodbye to me," I said.

Darlene gripped my hand tighter. "Your name is Terrance."

"My name is Terrance," I repeated, and the sun's rays hit my body.

Chapter 1

If the mirror on the wall saw me before coffee in the morning, it might crack.
-Vivian Hampton

-Vivian Hampton-

Pioneer School

The tickling sensation on the back of my shoulder half woke me up. I had felt the first one the previous day and several times since. It always seemed to portend an event of some kind. But right now, I was in my room, snuggled under warm blankets. What was going to bother me here? Partially opening an eye, I glanced at the clock on my nightstand. I had twenty minutes before I had to get up. Rolling over and pulling the blankets tighter about me, I was almost asleep again when I was bounced into the air.

Was there an earthquake? Had the dragon come again?

As I started to untangle myself from the blankets, Wanda blurted out in indignation, "We got upstaged by the dragons. We're on page three!" She was standing on my bed, probably having jumped up on it. She twisted the newspaper around and showed it to me. "See, page three."

Reminder to self, have a sit down with Wanda about waking me up if it wasn't an emergency. Considering I was just bounced awake and had hair in my face, the only thing I could clearly see was Wanda. I could sort of make out the picture in the paper of me and Wanda standing on opposite sides of Camillo.

Currently Wanda was in her gym clothes and, from the smell, had probably been practicing in the gymnasium for some time. Does my henchman ever sleep? I groaned and turned over. Instead of going away, Wanda began bouncing up and down while reading the article.

"*Missing snowman found,*" she read dramatically and paused. When I pulled a pillow over my head, she bounced again and continued to read. "'Vivian Hampton, a sophomore at the Pioneer school, who created the enchanted snowman, was reunited with her winter guardian last night. At 11:18 p.m., she pricked her finger, blood welled up, and the young enchantress named her snowman, Camillo.

"The exciting story of how the snowman made its way back to Ms. Hampton is only overshadowed by the arrival of not just one, but two dragons. Already, children around town are waiting in anticipation, hoping that the newly minted Camillo will visit them. Can the town's newest member survive the spring thaw? Will Ms. Hampton create more snowmen? There is a rumor the guardian's guild is sending a representative to interview the young lady and examine Camillo. Will Ms. Hampton, who bears a striking resemblance to Lady Cassandra, share her secrets? Indeed, the young lady stood with Lady Cassandra just yesterday afternoon. While there has been some speculation that Ms. Hampton is related to Lady Cassandra, she assures us that is not the case. The rumors persist, however, and one must wonder what other surprises Ms. Hampton has in store for us.

"In eight weeks, there is to be a tie breaking competition between House Duke and House Orozco. Just five days ago, it was unthinkable that House Orozco would even place in the spring game. Now, bars across town are placing them as neck and neck. Will Vivian Hampton repeat her performance, or will House Orozco fall into the shadows?"

I threw my pillow at Wanda. "I had another twenty minutes of sleep."

Wanda has endless energy. She gets up every morning before daybreak to practice in the gymnasium. She was determined to make the sophomore gymnastics team. If she does, she and her teammates would even compete in Avalon city.

Wanda jumped backwards, easily dodged my pillow, and landed on the floor. "Come on, get up," she begged. "I want you to sign the article, so I can send it to Lady Gawain. If I hurry, I can get it out in today's mail."

Groan. Once Wanda had Lady Gawain stuck in her head, she became obsessed. "Fine," I yawned and sat up while pulling hair out of my face. "Do you have a pen?"

Wanda held one up. Of course, she did. She was my henchman.

After I signed the article, I grabbed the three letters on my nightstand and handed them to Wanda.

"Can you mail these for me?" One was to my mother, and another to my father—I hoped he was in the same town. Being a bard, he moved around a bit. Writing my letter to him took three tries before I was happy with it. With the first two, hints of anger kept on creeping into my words. While I was angry at Father for abandoning Mother and me, there was some hope he wanted to reconnect. I didn't want to push him away, even though I imagined screaming at him sometimes. The third letter was to Lord Winton, letting him know I found Camillo and bound him to me. While I could have sent him a message through my wand, I preferred writing.

Wanda grinned and took my letters, then ran out of my room.

Technically, I had another ten minutes before I had to get up, but there was no going back to sleep now. Thank you, Wanda.

I was staring at my empty coffee cup and wondering why there weren't any stories about surviving the next morning. Would Prince Charming still be in love with Snow White after he saw her with tangled hair and bloodshot eyes? I can't remember a single story about the next day. Maybe I should write one? Would anyone want to read it though? Even Mr. Disney would likely laugh at the idea. His stories always seemed to end with a kiss. Somehow, that felt wrong. The song shouldn't just end, but grow and shift. Watching my parents and others, I knew life wasn't always easy. There were the occasional angry chords, but the song didn't just end. It was still there to be played.

Glancing over at Jeffery, he looked ready to take on the day. The spell I use every morning to help braid my hair hadn't worked exactly right for some reason, so Wanda needed to help me braid, then pin it up.

Sigh. Boys have it easier.

Stop it, Vivian, I thought to myself and reached for the coffee decanter near me and sighed again. It was empty. Others around me, including those who normally didn't drink coffee, were on their second cup. Apparently, I was slow on the uptake this morning. Didn't Wanda tell me that High Lady Gawain believed there were coffee gods? If I prayed hard enough, would my coffee mug refill itself? I generally didn't like coffee, but this morning, I had unconsciously reached for it. To redirect my thoughts, I looked toward the freshmen side of the table. It looked like Samantha, Amanda, and Elaine were in a whispered conversation. Were they forming a team? Coming together? I hoped so. It didn't take too much imagination to picture it going the other way. Who would be the queen of the freshman class and all that?

Last night, I bet the freshmen got together and shared stories. Amanda likely hid behind the anagram Thorol, not wanting to share that she was a high noble. Whereas Samantha was from Texas on Earth where her family owned huge amounts of land. I bet they were rich. Also, there was a weak political connection—the new merlin was from Earth as well. Even though the two had never met that I knew of, Samantha may have picked up that she had some clout. And finally, there was Elaine. Of the three, she was by far the least educated and barely able to read. But I heard it had come out that Lady Cassandra Altum was sponsoring her. I wasn't sure if anyone had specifically asked her where she was from and then put two and two together. Her being from Llamrel hamlet meant she came from the lands of Avalon's dragon. Since I hadn't heard any rumors yet, probably not. Being that she felt so out of place here, I was glad Amanda and Samantha were including her in their conversations. It almost looked like they were up to something. That's when I noticed the three of them turn their heads as one and almost glare at me. No, not me, Wanda and Sierra.

"Okay. What's going on?" I asked Wanda, who was pointedly glaring back at the three of them. I swear they were having a stare down.

Wanda sniffed and Sierra grinned. Surprisingly, she looked, well, happy. Uh, oh.

Sierra gave the three of them a quick stare, then looked at me. "They tried to sneak Samantha into the main hall with her hair down. I caught them and then got Wanda. The two of us had a 'talk' with the three of them."

Wanda and Sierra clapped hands together. "I got to be the good constable," remarked Wanda. "While Sierra got to be the bad one. She's good at being the bad one."

Sierra raised her glass of milk in salute. "I like them. They're already working as a team. But they're not good enough, yet."

"No yelling?" I hoped.

The corners of Sierra's mouth turned up. "I may have implied that you needed *volunteers* to examine shaft sixteen for our secret training sessions."

My mouth opened in surprise. "I would never do such a thing." The headmistress had directly stated that no students were allowed to go into any of the mines until the guild master had certified them as safe.

Sierra drained her milk and glanced over at the freshmen again. "Well, we'll never know now, will we?"

"You're a bad influence on my henchman," I grumbled to Sierra.

Mina raised an eyebrow. "And yet, we're the ones who ask Sierra to sneak through the halls at night to get us food from the kitchen. If anything, this is all your fault."

"What? I don't remember giving permission to, well, threaten anyone."

Mina nudged me. "Snowball Queen has been granted great powers. Use them wisely. If I remember correctly, you implied Samantha's hair had to be braided. It got done. Even Lady Daniel from House Thama asked my opinion about something this morning. You have school cred now."

Was that true? Was I, well, elevated—I mean, socially? I looked toward the other side of the table where the upperclassmen sat; a few raised their drinks to me, and I got several "Snowball Queens," directed at me. Okay, maybe Mina was right.

"Fine," I said and looked down at my empty coffee cup again. Then a horrid thought struck me. I whined and leaned into Mina. "I forgot to drop potions, and it's my first class."

"Our first class," she said. "Too bad we can't plug into Wanda. We would have endless energy."

Wanda stuck her tongue out at us, then went back to whispering with Sierra.

"Do you know if the journeyman is teaching it or Professor Vermis?" I couldn't think of why Mina would know, but maybe.

From behind me I heard, "I understand Journeyman Reece will be teaching the sophomore and freshman potion classes, Miss Hampton."

Turning in surprise, I saw there was an older footman placing a large coffee pot on our end of the table. What was more amazing, it wasn't just him; all the footmen and maids were bringing our table seconds. Usually, it was House Duke that got refills first, then Thema. House Orozco was always last. No one was left starving, but to be on time for our classes, we had to forgo second helpings of food, which seemed to hurt the boys more. Some of them were endless pits of hunger.

"Would you be Mr. Walters?" I asked the man as he picked up the empty coffee pot.

"Excellent memory, Miss Hampton," he said while giving me a little bow. Then he leaned down and said, almost in a whisper,

"Would it be possible for us to be introduced to your snowman at some point?"

Wanda leaned across the table. "Absolutely. But the sun hurts him, so how about tomorrow evening, just north of town?"

Mr. Walters winked at us, then turned away. Wanda and Sierra clapped their hands together again. I rolled my eyes. "Head girl here. Camillo should have a say in this. He's not a dog to just order around."

"Oh, come on," protested Mina. "We got served first. Besides, Terrance might come with him," she said wistfully.

"Mina," I said, a bit shocked. "You already have a boyfriend. And besides, Terrance is, well, very different."

She sniffed. "Doesn't mean I can't look."

Before I could pick up the coffee pot, Reg made a grab for it but was too slow. Jeffery got to it first, then pointedly refilled my mug.

Good boyfriend.

"Oh! Boyfriend point," declared Wanda. "Is it one or two points for refilling your mug?"

From the table over, Lord Thomas, Mina's boyfriend from House Coley, said, "Two points, definitely."

Mina shot back, "One point. Someone else brought that coffee to the table."

Jeffery asked a bit hesitantly, "There are boyfriend points?"

"Dude," laughed out Lord Thomas. "Oh yeah, and they can go negative too, so watch out." This brought snickers and a few outright laughs from some of the junior and senior boys up and down both tables.

Sierra had a wicked smile on her face and cracked her knuckles. "If that happens, do I get to hit him?"

"No hitting," I said louder than I intended. "We're House Orozco, not House Duke." Lord Seth from House Duke turned and glared at me. He wasn't wearing a jaw brace this morning. The master healer the headmistress found must really know his stuff.

Before I could think of something else to say, I watched the headmistress stand up from the teachers' breakfast table and walk toward the podium. As everyone turned toward the front of the hall, all the murmuring died away. I knew the headmistress hadn't gotten any sleep the night before last and probably had almost none last night, but she looked rested. I bet she took a potion to offset the effects. If so, she will probably sleep like a rock tonight.

"Good morning," she said, tapping her wand on the podium. "While the last three days have been exciting, I want to remind all of you this is a school. It is possible the dragons may return at some point. Should they do so, it would be *unwise* to meddle in their affairs. Let them be."

At the headmistress's pause, Lord Thomas leaned over and whispered to Mina, "And the dragon likes his meat well done too."

Mina smiled but didn't respond. Others were looking about and whispering as well. From the conversations I picked up in the halls over the last two days, I bet there would be some who would ignore the headmistress's warning and try to meet them. Good luck. I didn't think they would be eaten or taken, but Rupert, our dragon (well, Avalon's dragon), didn't seem the sort to put up with idiotic fans. I could, however, imagine a scenario where would-be adventurers were turned to stone for a few days or teleported someplace horrible like the bottom of an outhouse. Besides, he had a girlfriend, Lady Cassandra Altum. From briefly seeing the two of them interact, I thought the dragon liked strong intelligent women, a person who would push back. If any of the ladies from House Duke or Thama were hit with even a hint of the dragon's power, I bet they would cower in a corner.

The headmistress rapped her wand on the podium to get our attention again. "Silence! Or the professors will begin handing out detentions. For the incoming students, welcome. The Pioneer Academy is the second oldest school in Avalon. Many famous sorcerers, sorceresses, merchants, explorers, captains, duelists, and others were taught here over the seven hundred and thirty-four years of our existence. Some incoming freshmen may not be able to read and write well, but this is not unusual. Extra study sessions are in place to help you quickly master the written word. Music is part of the curriculum and just as important as magic, math, and history. At the Pioneer Academy, you will be pushed. Nothing but hard work, testing yourself, and working together as teams will allow you to pass your first year. For those who stand out, you will be offered positions as guides. The common term for this is 'hero.'

"Normally, we give a one-day grace period where magic dueling is not allowed in the hallways, but this year, this has been extended to the first two weeks. I encourage each of you to read the rules and familiarize yourself with what is not allowed on school grounds. Furthermore, it has been decided that upperclassmen may only target other upperclassmen. There is one exception to this. Should a freshman or sophomore initiate the challenge, then the upperclassmen are allowed to respond in kind."

Sierra snorted. "I bet the seniors from House Duke will ignore that when they think that they can get away with it."

I nodded absently, as did Mina and others. If they had a shot, I bet they would take it.

"Two new subjects have been added this year," continued the headmistress, ignoring the whispering. "Physics, which includes both rune and Newtonian physics. Currently we only have eight signed up for the class, so there is space if this subject interests you. The other was added last night. Lady Mayapple and her apprentice have agreed to teach a class on guardians. They should be arriving within the week. Everyone who is interested, please talk to their head of house for consideration."

The headmistress looked down at the podium for a second, probably to check her notes. Just as she looked up, Lady Aveline's voice rang out from House Duke. "I bet they're going to dissect Snowball Queen's little boy."

Laughter echoed up and down Dukes' table. A few students from House Thama joined them. I could feel my face go a bit red as hundreds of eyes looked my way, and with that, a memory surfaced.

I was seven the first time I stood on stage by myself preparing to sing. My parents and I were in a small town, singing songs and telling stories, hoping to collect a bit of coin before moving to the next town. But then it was my turn. Like now, all eyes were upon me. It was only with my parents' training at controlling my body and breathing exercises which kept my nervousness from taking over. A part of me wanted to cry, to tell them I wasn't ready and to run off the small stage. Instead, I took a deep breath, slowly let it out, and began to sing.

Instead of just coppers, we got a silver talon from one of the nobles that day. My father hugged me, and my mother kissed me on my head. I had done it. I had sung for the first time in front of an audience, and they clapped. After that, I was still nervous every time I stepped up on stage, but it never consumed me. But once I began developing, the apprehensive feelings reared up. I always kept my back straight though and ignored the looks I got.

Pushing back at the feelings which had reared up inside me, I sat up straighter while tilting my head up slightly. I had done it then, and I could do it now. I was Vivian Hampton, an elegant young lady. My snowman was not a thing to be dissected. By refusing to hide my head in fear or shame, I could feel an odd sort of energy expand out around me. Very similar to when I sang in front of an audience and could sense they were caught up in the song. But this was different somehow. Instead of being silent, which was the normal reaction of House Orozco, I could feel a growing annoyance of everyone up and down our table, joined by House Coley. Not directed at me, but Lady Aveline.

Wanda bounced up from her seat and shot right back, "You don't have the brains to last one day in that class, Lady Aveline. I bet the dragon won't give you a second glance either," she sneered out.

Lady Aveline shot to her feet and pulled out her wand. Other Duke students joined her, plus a few from House Thama. Several dozen from our house stood along with some from House Coley as well, including Mina, Jeffery, and Sierra. House Kumar was caught in the crossfire of glares as their table was in the middle of the hall.

The tension in the hall was nothing like I had ever felt before. We were challenging House Duke, and they weren't about to back down. It felt like everything was spinning out of control, and I had no idea how to stop it.

I watched in horror as Lady Aveline began to raise her wand.

"Sit down, now!" rang out the headmistress's voice. At the same time, a wave of white energy blew out from the podium, catching everyone who was standing in the chest; their clothes immediately began to glow. I had no idea what kind of spell she used and from the nervous looks, neither did anyone else. But the important part, the tension in the hall shifted. Everyone was looking at the headmistress now instead of targeting people from other houses.

Professor Malton was glaring at Wanda while motioning for those who were still standing to take their seats. Other teachers were doing the same. Even Professor Vermis looked like he wanted to tear into Lady Aveline.

"That spell I just cast," said the headmistress very coldly, "was a variant used for the snowball fights. If your clothes are glowing, all it takes is for a teacher to add the second part of the spell, and you will be frozen in place until the end of the day. Additionally, you have all earned yourself detention. Meet here in the main hall after dinner. Please enjoy the rest of your day."

Chapter 2

To die, to sleep;
To sleep: perchance to dream: ay, there's the rub;
For in that sleep of death, what dreams may come?
-Shakespeare, Hamlet

-Terrance-

Mrs. Capmond's family cemetery
"I mixed some of Betsy's blood into your tea," whispered Mrs. Capmond while giving me the wooden cup. "Let me know if you like it." Then she handed out tea to the others who were helping to dig her husband's grave; presumably there was no blood in theirs.

Being that the ground was still frozen meant it was slow going. Fortunately, we had Darlene and another who had a wand. Apparently, years ago, someone came up with a spell that helped to shatter frozen dirt. It made an odd sort of sense; people died in the wintertime as well. Short of digging graves during the balmier months in preparation that they were going to be filled for those living this far north, they needed options. The wand Darlene was letting me use wasn't designed to cast anything but basic spells, so I was relegated to being one of the diggers, which I didn't mind. Reminder to self, *Get a better wand.* That was going to take winning some hands of poker where gold talons were in the pot; not happening today. While I took a sip of tea and considered its flavor, I half wondered if there was a gravedigger's guild. Well, the last few days had been a bit morbid for me. Death was on my mind or, rather, living again was.

Camillo moved to the edge of the grave and seemed to peer into it. We had two more feet to go. This far down, it was getting easier to dig. The ground was just cold, not frozen. Currently, I was waiting for my turn to help again.

<*"Do you only bury those who have been good?"*> he asked.

Everyone around stopped what they were doing and looked at Camillo. Having something talk into your mind can take some getting used to. The two down in the hole looked up. Darlene raised an eyebrow. Franklin grinned into his mug of tea.

"Everyone gets buried, but not everyone gets a light," I said and pointed to the lit candle lantern suspended above the grave we were digging. "In Avalon, it is used to show the fallen a path."

<*"So, to help keep their soul glowing?"*>

"Exactly." I took another sip of tea. Okay, goat's blood had a bitter flavor to it, or maybe it was just the goat. Betsy was one of the three goats on Mrs. Capmond's small farm. During the summer months, she apparently used them for weed control in the graveyard and other such places. However, right now, Betsy stood just outside of the old, low fence, glaring at us. Probably trying to decide who it should bite for the indignity of losing a bit of blood.

I could feel that touch in my mind, which indicated Camillo was about to ask another question.

<*"What happens when the candle burns out?"*>

The preacher clutched his bible to his chest. "The Maker takes their soul to heaven," he declared. From his rising pitch, I imagined the man liked giving rousing sermons filled with the evils of sin. From the way he kept on holding his bible like a shield, I suspected he wasn't certain what to make of Camillo and was less certain of me. We were in the shade of a large tree, but my shadow still got to perform occasionally when the wind blew, creating pockets of sunshine between the branches. At the preacher's words, the wind blew again, and my shadow appeared. It knelt down and began to pray. Darlene moved herself between my shadow and the preacher.

Camillo looked at the candle lantern, then to the preacher. <*"Vivian Hampton comes and gets their souls?"*> he asked.

Franklin burst out laughing. So did a few of the others. The preacher's face went red. Whatever response he was about to make was cut off by Gerald's wife. "Why don't you come inside, Pastor? I can show you our family bible. Gerald preferred the New Testament."

Once they were out of earshot, I said to my friend. "Tonight, we can talk about the Maker and about gods." I found it hard to imagine I could be a teacher as it related to the philosophies of religion, but here I was. There had to be a drunk angel looking down at me and laughing his ass off right now.

But my friend's questions were honest. Just as I was about to add on to my statement, Darlene nudged me. In terms I can understand, that meant: shut up, idiot, and close your stupid trap. I can learn, it just takes dying for it to happen. I guess I'm just a bit more hardheaded than others.

"I think, perhaps, you should have Miss Hampton in that discussion, Camillo," declared Darlene. "After we're done here, you can go into Mrs. Capmond's shed to stay out of the light. Once it's dark, head to the school."

<*"Will you stay with me, my friend?"*> asked Camillo.

I was about to say "Of course," when Darlene pushed her heel into my toe. "Terrance needs to meet the headmistress of the school, Camillo. You can meet up with him tonight."

My friend was silent for a few seconds. <*"I will stay under the tree. I want to watch the Maker appear to take Mr. Capmond's soul."*>

What can you possibly say to that? One of the men just shook his head, but dirt started being shoveled again. Once it was my turn again, I jumped down into the hole and began digging. The repetitive actions were therapeutic. They allowed my mind to wander.

Which made me wonder what I believed. I certainly believed there were demons, having seen one myself. But was there a God, an overall Maker?

The old chestnut trees on the east side of the graveyard provided good shade. Camillo didn't like direct sunlight any more than I did for similar reasons. For him, heat was pain. Being a snowman, he associated feeling scared to melting. I honestly wasn't certain if he understood the seasons were changing and it would get warmer soon. I didn't want my friend to pass, but outside of moving north with him, I had no idea what to do short of sophisticated magic. While I was reluctant to meet the school's headmistress, as Darlene had implied, she was a powerful sorceress, Camillo's best chances of survival probably only existed in the world of magic. I knew spells that could cool things down— very handy when you want a cold drink on a hot day, but the kind of cooling crystals required for my friend would likely be one of a kind and something had to power them. Magic didn't come for free as much as some people wanted to believe it did. Could Camillo hang on long enough for something to be made? I hoped so.

For me, though, direct sunlight didn't tear at my thoughts anymore, which was a relief. But it did slowly reduce my strength and cause an odd itching feeling which quickly grew intense. Wearing a long winter cloak with a hood certainly helped. Was this permanent, the new me? I had no idea. I felt like I was building the instruction manual on the fly. Being in the shade was better. I was slightly stronger than a normal person and my shadow was less active.

I made a note to myself to write down everything that was happening to me. I had promised to get my notes over to Dr. Cognitor. Being honest with myself, what I really wanted to do, hopefully, was discuss them with Lady Elizabeth Navartis.

Over the course of the night as we dug out Gerald's body, Darlene and Franklin told me what they knew of Lady Elizabeth. The Navartis family was the last known line of Arthur, and Lady Elizabeth being the oldest female child was, therefore, the highest lady of the land. The general feeling in Avalon was that it was

DISSONANT SONG\23

natural for her to become the new merlin's guide. From the stories, Arthur was essentially raised by Merlin from the time he was a young teenager, so it was Avalon's turn to reciprocate. I could imagine that if Lady Elizabeth ever walked into a bar and asked for a drink, her money would be no good. They would likely immediately make a plaque that said, *Lady Elizabeth Navartis, the merlin's guide, drank here.*

From the way Darlene spoke of her, Lady Elizabeth wasn't merely seen as royalty, but as some kind of passed down echo of Arthur in the body of a woman. Now having met her, I could see it. I wasn't sure what the woman felt about that, but from my brief interaction with her, I suspected she could keep her balance in just about any situation. I hoped she would be willing to sit down with me and go over my notes. Well, I can hope—dream, really.

Two nights ago, I was thinking of visiting the barmaid's daughter from *the Last Pixie* in the hope I would remember what it was like to be with a woman—a memory I could call my own. Now though, well, Terrance had come face-to-face with a goddess, and it was hard to think about any other woman after I had seen Lady Elizabeth. Even though it was ludicrous to imagine she might be interested in me. If I slept around, this far-fetched hope of mine would be buried alive. At that thought, I noticed the grave was deep enough.

The two of us who had finished the bottom two feet of Gerald's grave accepted a hand to climb out, and we dusted off our clothes. Franklin, Darlene's husband, with help from others, had attached ropes to Gerald's coffin in the traditional ceremonial manner, so six people could lower him down. As we waited for Mrs. Capmond to come back with the preacher, Clant, one of Franklin's war buddies, glanced at Camillo, then pointedly looked behind me. I knew what he was doing, staring at my shadow. Maker only knows what it is doing now.

"So, you were cursed. Did it hurt?"

He was asking about the story we told as we walked down the mountain carrying Gerald's body. I originally wanted it to be just me, Darlene, Franklin, and Camillo, assuming he wanted to come. He did, as it was overcast. But I quickly discovered that a private procession was a fool's hope. Teams of people were hiking up the mountain to defend their claims or striking out to make new ones. While I was becoming known in certain parts, Camillo stood out. Besides, we were hauling a body. That always raises eyebrows. People want to be able to pass along a good story. It makes them feel connected. Gore and death attract people like bears to honey.

Before we hit our first switchback, we were surrounded. Apparently, Camillo had fans, and they wanted the experience of talking to Miss Hampton's snowman. Then, the first story Darlene, Franklin, and I put together was told. Gerald was hiking yesterday morning when the dragon came. He hid in a cave, but it collapsed on him. This brought the anticipated "poor guy" and other such remarks. But as expected, the story quickly began to take on a life of its own. People began talking about others who had died up in the mountains too.

The other story was about me. We needed to explain my shadow without having someone try to shove a stake through my chest. It was important to me that we didn't put Camillo in a position where he had to lie on my behalf. He trusted me implicitly, and I didn't want to abuse that. Assuming a way was found for Camillo to continue into early springtime without melting, I imagine he would eventually talk to people who were intentionally lying to him. You can't interact with people for very long and not be exposed to that. But it wasn't going to be me. So, the story that got crafted was that Camillo and I stumbled upon an old curse. It got me, and only with Camillo's help, I was able to get out before it killed me. But the damage had been done, a bit of the curse had taken hold. The base story was accurate if you left off the curse—we did meet an evil spirit, and it fought us. We just added some embellishment to explain my shadow. Once Camillo and I found a way out, we stumbled upon Gerald's body, and now we were bringing him home to his wife for a proper burial.

On the third rendition of the telling, Camillo added, <"*My friend told me to leave without him, but I would not. He is my friend.*">

A friend is someone that stays with you, always. That was my definition of a friend to him a few nights ago. As always, I felt an odd sort of warmth inside me remembering that. Terrance was a man who wanted to live up to his beliefs, not sell them out.

Now that we had dug Gerald out, we were bringing his body back to his wife for a burial. While I got a few nods and pats on the back, Camillo was the star. But every time he was hit with a word or concept he didn't understand, my friend turned to me for help. Terrance, world renowned translator. I can add snowman to my list of known languages. The people we met just assumed the two of us were a team now. My friend and I even got some invitations to meet their children.

At some point, the sun came out from behind the clouds, and my shadow decided to have some fun. It pretended to be drumming on Franklin's shadow's head. Story of my life; last time it was a demon setting me up to be killed. Sometimes you just can't win.

Suddenly, it got quiet, people stepped back, and wands were pulled out. One person even had a silver rune engraved derringer.

"I thought vampires couldn't be out in the sun," said the man with the derringer as he cocked it. The barrel was pointed at my chest.

"You're correct, they can't," said Darlene. "That's the curse. Terrance's shadow got animated."

"That damn warding stone," growled out a younger man and put away his wand. "I bet those archeologists from Earth triggered the curse. Bunch of idiots."

The man with the derringer pointed it at the ground and lowered the hammer. "Well, you best be careful, someone might shoot you anyway, hoping to claim a bounty."

"Agreed," I said. "But if I hide, then people will begin to assume the worst."

Some animals would get you a bounty if you brought in their pelts. These were usually mist wolves and similar large predators; animals that were willing to hunt people. If a Jingo bear wandered into town and someone was lucky enough to kill it without ending up dead, the bounty might get them ten gold talons; for the average person, that could support them for three years. Topping the list of bounties were the undead, zombies, and the like. If someone brought in a vampire, and it could be confirmed as one, they would probably be set for life.

I got some nods at my comment. "Well, we'll pass the word," said the man with the derringer as he pocketed it.

"Much appreciated," I said and took a bite of the beef jerky Darlene had given me last night. It was salty, but it didn't make me want to throw up anymore. See? No vampire here.

The man who had pulled out a wand and then put it away considered me. "Was the curse down in that shaft in which you and Camillo were stuck last night?"

"Yes, sir. We found a crack in the wall some distance down, which led into a natural cavern with odd lights about. That's when I stumbled into it."

He grunted. "I'll let the miner's guild know. They'll probably condemn the mine."

"Please do," interjected Darlene. "We don't want anyone else caught by that curse."

One of the men spat on the ground. "Damn warding stones."

The tallest of the men who hadn't said anything yet asked me, "I hear you drink at the Dancing Pony Inn?"

It was more of a statement than a question.

I nodded. "Darlene and Franklin introduced me to it. I like to play poker there. Occasionally, my luck is good." I looked back at my shadow; it was now acting like it was holding a hand of cards. "Well, sometimes anyway," I said.

He tipped his hat at me. "Might stop by. Thank you for taking care of Camillo. A man's got to have at least one friend."

What should have taken a half hour took two. But the important part was done—stories were told, and we got Gerald's body back home. I might still become someone's trophy hoping to collect a bounty, but at least I had a chance to walk the streets without being killed. I would take it.

I pondered Clant's question, *did it hurt?*

"It felt like a spirit had wrapped its hand around my heart, then squeezed." I wasn't lying, that's pretty much how it felt right at the end before Camillo had the sense to figure out how to stop the spirit. Snowman he may be, but he had more common sense than most people.

Clant tapped his chest, then made the sign of the cross, others grunted. I could tell a follow-on question was about to be asked when Mrs. Capmond came out with the preacher. By now, there were a good thirty other people who had heard the burial was taking place. A few were the usual who just wanted to see the show. The bulk of them likely knew Gerald to some degree. They offered their sympathies to Mrs. Capmond with promises to help her out.

She sniffled and thanked them for their kindness. "Terrance and Franklin are helping to rebuild my roof. But stop by whenever you would like, I could always use the company."

The preacher kept his sermon short, probably at the behest of Mrs. Capmond. Maker only knows the questions Camillo was going to ask about it later tonight. Then everyone took their turn putting a small item on Gerald's body before his coffin was closed and lowered into the grave. One or two didn't have anything but a copper penny, others had something more personal.

I placed the obsidian arrowhead that had killed me on his chest. "Old man," I whispered. "Thank you for giving me a second chance." A part of me wondered what would happen if I died again. Would that be it, or would I reform in Gerald's grave? I had no idea, then snorted. I was hiding from my feelings. This good old man gave me a second chance, and I was afraid of not being worthy of it. "I hope you can look down at me and be proud old man," I whispered and turned away so the next person could add their own prayers.

Chapter 3

"Wait! Wasn't it toe of a frog? Uh oh. Run."

Experimenting with potions should be done in warded circles.

-Chapter one of Potion's Guild Safety Pamphlet

-Vivian Hampton-

Pioneer School

Everyone was quiet as we filed out of the main hall. Once around the first corner, Wanda grabbed me from behind and screamed in excitement: "That. Was. AWESOME!" She wasn't the only one energized. Instead of acting chastised, my friends seemed to treat having been tagged by the headmistress's spell as a badge of honor. Honestly, it wasn't just them. Others from House Orozco who were glowing were acting as if getting in trouble was, well, righteous. Normally, we would be quiet now. However, they seemed to want everyone to know that they had faced House Duke and would do it again.

Was I being used as a symbol of hope, a person others could rally around? At that thought, I felt an odd cool pulsing sensation on my back left shoulder. Stretching out my arm a bit, it went away. I was about to crane my neck to try to look at my back but was stopped by Mina's nudge.

"What's up?" I asked.

"Look at Elaine," she whispered. "Should we step in?"

I could hear the compassion in her voice, that motherly aspect of Mina which helped keep me focused last year instead of screaming in frustration. Amanda and Samantha were flanking Elaine. She was partially bent over, back to the wall, and hugging herself. I thought her knees might be shaking too.

All three of them were glowing. I bet when Amanda and Samantha stood up to challenge Lady Aveline, Elaine instinctually had as well and got caught in the spell.

I wondered if Elaine's apprehension might be partially cultural. She grew up living on the dragon's lands. There were lots of old stories about what the dragon would do to you if you annoyed him. Personally, I thought most of them were ludicrous. But they did make for good storytelling. However, for those living on his lands, were some of the stories real or perhaps had substance to them? If so, I could imagine the hamlet developing strict social rules. I was also a little intrigued; it could make for an interesting song. But the real issue in front of us was what should we do about Elaine?

Amanda and Samantha were quietly talking to her, probably trying to calm her down. The three really did seem to be forming a team.

Sierra rolled her eyes. "No one helped us when we were freshmen."

"Sierra!" I said in frustration. "Just because it was that way then, doesn't mean it has to stay that way." But I also remembered what Lord Nathan said a few days ago, "It's a rite of passage for every freshman." Would I have stepped forward and become the head freshman of our house if we hadn't been hung out to dry last year? Mina was very motherly. She would have been the obvious choice if we didn't have to develop coping strategies so as not to get hit by a spell. Some days last year, I felt like a general planning out stealth raids just to get everyone to their next class safely.

"Wanda," I said, making a quick decision. "Put together a team and check up on all the freshmen later today. See how they're doing. If you think someone in House Orozco needs help, come and get me."

Wanda grinned. "As the Snowball Queen says. One commando team coming up." She and Sierra clapped hands together again.

Commando? I was about to ask what she thought I meant when Lord Seth and Lord Keith veered toward us. Their henchmen followed. "Wait until my head of house gets done with her," whispered Lord Seth threateningly, then walked past us ignoring the rest of my friends completely.

"Don't," said Mina to Sierra.

I agreed with her. While a part of me did want to have them expelled, if we started the fight, their retaliation would be legitimate defense, and we would be punished. Currently, they were in a two-week detention. If they stepped out of line during that time, the headmistress would expel them. I bet that's why the no targeting rule had been extended to two weeks. It felt unfair to the rest of us, but I bet Professor Vermis had demanded it. As much as I wanted to push them, the whole point of detention was to understand that you did something wrong and hopefully learn to not do it again. At that thought, that same odd cold sensation came back for just a second, then faded.

Jeffery and Reg came over. "What did Mr. Glass Jaw want?" asked Reg.

Wanda giggled at the "glass jaw" comment. Others heard him as well. *Uh, oh.* I bet Lord Seth just got a new nickname that he would blame us for.

I bit my lip. "I think he has asked his head of house to make a formal complaint against Elaine for hitting him."

Reg looked like he wanted to throw his backpack at the snit.

"Let's get to our first class," I said and turned away. It wouldn't surprise me if I was back in the headmistress's office later today standing next to Elaine. Not the day I was looking forward to.

I stopped and stared. For a second, I thought Wanda and I had entered the wrong room.

I had never seen the sophomore potions room this clean before. All the various stains on the tables and floor were gone. Even the small cauldrons we used were neatly arranged on the back shelf and looked like they had been scrubbed. Every pair of workbenches had been pushed together making for a larger one. Each pair was placed around the room's one large etched ring in the center of the room. It took me a second to notice all the odd smells were gone as well, replaced with a lemony scent. Even the paintings about the place seemed to be fresher as if they had been cleaned. Where had Professor Reece found the time? He only arrived at school two days ago. At that thought, I heard his voice. He was standing just to the right of the largest chalkboard.

"Come in," he said, with a smile. The man was vibrating with excitement. "Find your name tag and we can get started."

Name tag? That's when I saw them—he had assigned everyone a seat. This was very different from last year.

Wanda grumbled, "To our left, bug number two is here."

She was right. Lord Keith and his henchman were seated at one of the workbenches, and they didn't look happy. The reason was obvious. Seated at the tables as if they were equals were freshmen, and not all of them from Duke. Last year, the freshmen had sat in the back of the room while the sophomores sat in the front, and everyone got to pick their own tables.

Well, at least Professor Vermis isn't teaching our class, I thought to myself and started looking for my name tag.

I was glad Professor Reece hadn't separated heroes and henchmen. Wanda sat just to my right. I hoped Mina and Sierra would be at our table, but I quickly learned there was only one sophomore team per pair of tables. Sitting with us were eight freshmen, three of them from my house: Samantha, Landon, and Henrietta. I wasn't sure if the professor had intentionally put Henry at a separate table or not, being that he was Henrietta's twin brother. Of the other five freshmen, there were two from House Kumar, two from House Thama, and one from Duke.

I wished Jeffery was taking sophomore potions with me, but he said his head of house wanted him to take accounting instead. Just thinking about him made me remember last night. *We had sat by the fire together holding hands. He kissed the top of my head and ...*

My happy memory was broken by Wanda's whisper, "No one is saying anything."

Quickly looking around, she was right. Professor Reece had mixed freshmen from different houses together, and no one was saying anything. *Well, I'm Vivian Hampton*, I thought to myself. Let's try cashing in on that social credit Mina implied I had now for something good. At my thought, that same pulsing sensation came from the back of my shoulder. Ignoring it, I looked at the freshmen around my table. "Hi. I'm Vivian Hampton, Lord Winton is my sponsor, and this is my henchman, Wanda Hine. Both of us are in House Orozco."

At the mention of Hine, the taller of the two boys from House Kumar, whose name tag read Alton, snorted and looked away.

"You can at least be polite," I said, trying to maintain a smile on my face.

Wanda's house was very young, a bit less than two hundred years old. They were the Igors to the risk takers of Avalon—usually explorers, guides, or miners hoping to strike it rich. No one in their house had any magic that I knew of, but they were considered very trustworthy and dependable. Recently, the Hine name had risen a bit as two of the explorers hiring them had struck it rich. One had been Wanda's uncle. He was paying for her to go to school. Without Wanda, I would be pulling my hair out. She keeps everything organized for me and pushes me when I need it—sometimes more than I want, but that was Wanda. I had just gotten used to it. Once we graduated, I was going to ask Lord Winton to sign a letter of recommendation for Wanda to her house elder.

But for many of the arrogant nobles, if your lineage didn't go back to the time of King Arthur or before, you weren't worth talking to.

Samantha immediately shot back with, "Little proud, are you? I bet your daddy broke his arm patting himself on the back."

What an odd insult. Was it a saying from Earth?

Wanda cocked her head, obviously parsing it out, then giggled.

"He wouldn't need to, unlike *some* families, he has servants for that," sneered Alton.

I sighed. Well, we weren't off to a great start. My attention was caught by the thin, young man from House Duke. His name tag read *Quade*. He seemed to shrink in on himself. Curious, I would expect anyone from House Duke to have an ego twice the size of a normal person. Yet, he apparently didn't want to engage. I was about to ask him who his family was when Professor Reece tapped the chalkboard to get our attention.

"So, who can tell me why the potions guild is considered below the main sorcerer's guild?"

He had listed the top ten guilds on the blackboard: wandmaker's, bankers, healers, sorcerer's guild, potion's guild, and so on.

Henrietta's hand shot up, as did that of her brother, Henry. A few others did as well. Wanda's was practically reaching for the sky. I raised my hand as well.

"Lord Henry," he said, pointing to Henry.

"A potion maker can't project their magic through the air, they must maintain physical contact with what they are attempting to imbue. While a sorcerer can project magic through a wand to cast a spell."

"An excellent textbook answer, young man." Professor Reece smiled and tossed him a small item. Henry caught it, then held it up for his sister to see. It was a Raven's mint, or at least I thought it was. But the wrapping was copper foil, not silver or gold.

"You may enjoy it after class," said Professor Reece and pulled another from his desk. "I made them myself. I hope you like what appears. But some very famous potions makers were sorcerers as well." He almost bounced to the other side of the chalkboard where he had drawn a graph, and a few inches away, a simple pictograph of a person with a wand and a rock. With my Sight, I could tell he had imbued a bit of magic into the drawing.

"Consider," he said, pointing to the drawing of the person holding a wand. "Casting a spell is a near-immediate event. Magic is focused into runes, essentially a set of equations. This magic is held together for a short time and either focused through a wand or otherwise projected by the caster." He moved his finger to the rock. "Then, it flows toward the intended target. The equation laid out in the runes becomes a projected spell." He tapped the chalkboard, and the drawing moved. Runes appeared around the wand, sank into it, and were shot toward the rock. The rock rose and hovered, then fell to the ground. "But the point is, it's an immediate event. Depending upon the ability of the caster, his or her wand, and a few other things, there is an upper limit to the amount of magic in play."

"But for potions," he said and stepped back. "What can you do with a potion that you cannot do with a wand? Anyone?" he said with excitement.

As he talked and moved, I felt like I was looking at a male version of Wanda—he had endless, bouncy energy. While Wanda was fifteen, the same age as me, Journeyman Reece, well now Professor Reece, was probably in his early twenties, but he had that same infectious attitude as Wanda. It was hard not to like him. I bet all the cleaning in the room had been done by him.

Henrietta, Henry's twin, slowly raised her hand.

"Go ahead Lady Henrietta," said Professor Reece.

Lord Keith's henchman snickered under his breath. "Commoner." Making it sound like an insult.

"Yeah?" shot back Sierra from another table. "And so are you."

Professor Reece tossed the mint he was holding into the air, then catching it. "And so am I, young man. But you still must address me as Professor, even though I am only a senior journeyman. I suspect Professor Vermis will agree with me in this."

He said it as an implied question. But there was a hint of a threat in his words too. I remember back a few days ago when the headmistress said to him, "*Should you fail to live up to Professor Vermis's expectations....*" Professor Vermis was very stern. He gave those in his house a break and treated the other houses as inferior, but he didn't like losing control either. I bet Professor Reece picked up very clearly from the man that you are the professor and must maintain control.

There was silence in the room.

"I am waiting, Mr. Jordon," said Professor Reece to Lord Keith's henchman, "for the correct inflection."

Lord Keith nudged his henchman, who didn't look happy for being called out. He gave Sierra a nasty look, then said formally, "She's not a noble, Professor."

Professor Reece's dark mood suddenly disappeared, and he tossed a mint to Jordon. "Thank you, Mr. Jordon."

He smiled at Henrietta, "I stand corrected. So, to reiterate, what can you do with a potion that you cannot do with a wand?"

She gave me a quick look, and I nodded at her. It was almost as if she was looking for my permission to speak up.

"Making a potion does not need to be just an immediate effect," she said. "By continuing the connection with the cauldron, additional energy can be added to the mixture."

"Exactly," Professor Reece said with enthusiasm. He tossed her a mint. "The most obvious examples are core potions. Even the basic ones must be imbued with tremendous amounts of energy. That is something which cannot be done by a spell alone."

Samantha looked intrigued. "What's a core potion, Professor?"

"Is it Ms. or Lady Samantha?" asked the professor. "I am afraid I don't know the Republic's layers of nobility."

"Um, technically I'm a lady," she said.

I think I blinked. She had never brought that up before. By now, I knew her grandmother was from Avalon, but I didn't know if that was where her title was from. Did her father have a title too?

That odd cool sensation on the back of my shoulder came back. I looked behind me, Lord Keith was almost glaring at her. *Why?*

Mina was a low noble but still a noble. Other than the normal, I'm from House Duke and you're not, Lord Keith wouldn't give Mina the time of day. He acted like she was beneath his notice. So, why did he seem to care about Samantha?

Was that sensation of mine I felt behind my shoulder this morning a sort of sixth sense or something else? I had no idea. But now was not the time to figure it out.

Professor Reece gave a small bow to Samantha. "Lady Samantha then. A core potion can permanently alter a person's physical attributes. Each is made for a particular person and takes days, if not longer, to imbue properly. The most common ones are hair restoration potions, followed by ones to adjust the eyes to see better, straighten your teeth, and so on. They are tremendously expensive and only a second-degree potions master is allowed to brew them. But a sorcerer cannot focus that kind of power into one single spell. Also, there is no known wand which can handle such a surge of magic."

He shook his head and gave out a weak smile. "The potion's guild is very rigid about rules. Were I to try selling a core potion, I would likely be standing in front of a Sorcerer of the Realm within a day."

Lord Keith said with a touch of heat, "I bet Professor Vermis could make one." And then he added on reluctantly, "Professor."

"As Professor Vermis is only a first-degree master, I suspect he understands the rules even better than I do. Knights of the Realm are very unforgiving about some things."

I cocked my head. "Sir, Professor Reece? What about imbuing an item with a spell, such as the light spell on a rock? If the runes are attached to something we are holding, more energy can be added."

Professor Reece rubbed his hand together. "Lady Vivian, correct?"

"Yes, Professor, but it's Ms. Vivian. Lord Winton is my benefactor."

He nodded his head slightly and tossed me a mint. "You have stumbled upon the homework assignment for the sophomores, Ms. Vivian. What are the differences and similarities between imbuing, brewing, and enchanting?"

He raised his voice at the groans from the sophomores around the room. "It's important to master the distinction. I want a summary of each and examples as well. Turn in at least three pages in total. It is due in two days."

Wanda nudged me. "Thanks a lot," she said under her breath.

"For the freshmen," said the Professor, ignoring the continuing groans. "I understand some of you may not be able to read well. Therefore, I, along with the other professors, will be holding reading and writing sessions during your breaks and after school. They aren't mandatory, but we are here for you. However, in two weeks, I want a list of the ingredients that go into a light potion. Then write down and turn in the basic steps on how to brew one."

I felt that odd pulsing sensation again and looked toward Elaine. She looked ready to cry.

♪♪♪

Professor Reece tapped the chalkboard. The drawings and words shifted to become the ingredients and basic recipe for making a light potion. "Sophomores," he said, "this should be easy for you. Once all of you have the foundation of the potion ready, you will have five minutes to imbue as much energy into it as you can. Then, we will trigger them and set them aside. Whoever's potion shines the longest gets to choose the next five illusions I will brew into my chocolate mint mixture. Henchmen, after you're done helping your hero prepare their potion, I want you to support the freshmen who have magical ability, so they can attempt to brew one. I'm not expecting success from everyone. Treat this as a learning experience."

Wanda grumbled as the two of us gathered ingredients, tools, and a cauldron. "What a low blow," she murmured. "I get to help a bunch of freshmen who were born with a silver spoon in their mouth."

"Wanda," I whispered back. "I think it's a good idea. We get to learn about each other."

Wanda glared at me. "Fine. I promise not to accidentally dump Alton's potion in his lap. But if he makes another snarky remark, I'll do it on purpose."

Ignoring Wanda's threat, I said, "See if you can learn anything about Quade. He seems very unsure of himself."

Wanda grabbed our last ingredient, dried lighting bugs. "Got it," she said in apparent understanding. "We can try to turn him to the light, then make him our spy into House Duke."

I rolled my eyes but didn't correct her. A part of me almost agreed with her.

Wanda and I kept up a running commentary about how we were preparing the ingredients and why I was mixing them in a certain way and what changes I was looking for after completing each step. Like last year, I found it relaxing making a potion and somehow this was even better. It felt soothing being a guide to others as well. I wondered if that was what the professor was hoping from the sophomores, to help the freshmen.

Samantha and Landon were taking notes. Henrietta had probably made this before, but she seemed interested. Surprisingly, the young man from Duke was taking notes as well. The others were listening but not engaging. Well, Wanda and I were trying. I wasn't going to start jumping up and down to get their attention. It was on them to participate.

Once I had it all mixed into the right paste, I began slowly stirring in the base, watered-down maple syrup. This wasn't a healing potion, so the syrup didn't need to be fresh. Once done, I looked up at the professor for the signal to begin. Mina was ready to go as were most of the other sophomores.

"Lord Keith, are we almost there?" asked Professor Reece.

He growled back, "Yes, Professor. I'm ready now."

Wanda whispered in glee, "His henchman accidentally put in too much ground charcoal. They had to start over again."

Ah. Wanda was very proud of being dependable. But another thought struck me, *the young man had helped Lord Keith before, and they had made this potion last year. Why was he having a problem now?*

Professor Reece started counting down. "Five, four, three, two, and one. Heroes, you may begin."

I put my hands on the two handles of the cauldron, which was really a split wand, and began pushing in magic. I was a little nervous as the spell I tried to cast this morning hadn't worked correctly, probably because I was so tired. But I was awake now, and my fears were unfounded. Magic began flowing from me into the cauldron, and the mixture rolled and twisted in a way I expected.

Professor Reece walked around the room to see how each of us were doing. At about the ten second mark, I could see my potion begin to magically glow with my Sight. Okay, not bad. A new record for me. I really did want to win the competition, so I pushed harder. Then I felt that odd pulsing sensation again and angled my head slightly just in time to watch Jordon, Lord Keith's henchmen, toss a pebble at me. Since I still had my sight on, I could tell there was some magic bound to it as well. Maker knows what it was supposed to do if it touched me. Instinctively, I cast the runes for a shield spell, centering it behind me, all the while forgetting I was also sending magic into the cauldron.

Professor Reece saw what was going on and shot a spell at Lord Keith's henchman which completed the second part of the headmistress's spell from this morning, and he froze in place. However, the pebble was already in the air heading toward me. But what surprised me even more, the shadow of Jordon didn't freeze immediately as well. For a moment, it looked like it had morphed into a wolf. I blinked and his shadow was back to normal. Had I imagined the whole thing?

Then the spelled pebble hit my shield.

Chapter 4

Everybody is a genius. But if you judge a fish by its ability to climb a tree, it will live its whole life believing it is stupid.
　-Albert Einstein

-Vivian Hampton-
Pioneer School, Physics Room

As Wanda and I walked into the physics room, I immediately felt a drowning sensation: four of the five chalkboards were covered with equations featuring runes and equations I had never seen before.

Why in the world did Lord Winton think I could pass this class?

Aside from Professor Gass, there were only eight in the class, and this included Wanda and me. Apparently, no one else decided to sign up for it. That's when I noticed we were the only women. Also, the other six were all seniors, and none of them were from House Orozco. Elaine and I were probably feeling the same sense of drowning right now. She needed to learn how to read and write better, while I felt the same way in this class.

At our entrance, all the seniors turned to look at us. What felt strange was that I didn't get that awkward sensation of being examined as a woman when I walked into a room full of men. No, I did a little, but there was something else too. I wasn't sure how I felt but just standing here felt silly.

Unlike the potions class, Wanda and I got to sit wherever we wanted. Unfortunately, the professor indicated the two open places in the center of the front row. Being the youngest, I wanted to sit in the back, but apparently the professor wanted everybody up front. As we were sitting down and taking off our backpacks, Wanda whispered to me, "This is a senior's class. Are you sure we should be here?"

I shrugged. "There's only one physics class offered and Lord Winton told me to take it." But Wanda was right. This had faceplant time written all over it.

Around the sides of the room, there were intricate mechanical contraptions in rune-etched glass cases. What was more astonishing was what looked like frozen spells encased in silver mesh on pedestals along the back wall. Also, there were four books in the back row, each with their own glass covers. Were these bound books, essentially their own living matrix? I had only seen one before, in the public library in Avalon city during a field trip last year. *Wanda and I have stepped into the unknown.* That sinking feeling in me grew bigger. Faceplant time might become full body splat.

Professor Gass was an older man with a head of white hair. I had seen him in the main hall a few times but had never spoken to him. From the little I could deduce; I thought the other teachers bored him. During meals, he was usually reading or making notes in a book instead of engaging with others.

"Good morning," he began. "I know most of you are tired. But the day progresses, and we will get through it. The sun will set and rise again. But let's make sure we have the room calibrated first."

Room calibrated? I had no idea what he was talking about. A few of the other students glanced my way. Why were they looking at me?

After grabbing an old walking stick with a crystal mounted on the top, Professor Gass stood up. "Lord Grayson," he said to a Duke senior. "I understand you passed your admission tests for a reserve Realm Knight. Well done. Therefore, I want you to be my Gluck for today."

Gluck?

It took me a second to associate the word with an old song. Before I could stop myself, I asked, "A magic diviner, Professor?"

The man leaned against his walking stick, cocked his head slightly toward me, and I thought I saw a hint of a smile. "Well, you might do after all, Ms. Vivian. You're up first. I suspect the room will need to be calibrated around you. I understand in your last class, an aspect of the link with your snowman came into being?"

I think my mouth hung open. We had just come from that class; how could he know?

Everyone was looking at me now. I blushed slightly but kept my head up. "Yes, professor. I, er, well, cast a shield spell while I was imbuing a potion, and it was unexpectedly intense."

The professor tapped his cane on the ground. "I assume there was a reason why you tried both at the same time, young lady?"

"Yes, Professor. Jordon, Lord Keith's henchmen, tossed an imbued pebble at me, one of those silly ones where bubbles would come out of your ears. Just before it touched me, I cast a shield spell, and suddenly, I was surrounded by swirling snowflakes."

Lord Grayson rolled his eyes skyward. "What an idiot. I assume he's frozen in place now?"

Wanda raised her hands in celebration. "Yep. It was awesome!"

Something wasn't right. Lord Grayson was in Duke, but he wasn't acting like I was beneath his notice. He seemed almost nice.

"Ms. Wanda," said the professor pointing his cane at a smaller chalkboard, "Since you were a direct observer, please draw out the patterns of energy you saw surrounding your hero. As detailed as you can."

Wanda lowered her arms. "Um, okay. Why?"

Professor Gass raised an eyebrow. "Would you like to try that again, young lady, or would you prefer detention?"

I whispered to Wanda, "You forgot to call him professor."

Her face went red, and she gulped. "Sorry, Professor. It won't happen again."

"The drawing Ms. Hine. We are waiting. Lord Grayson, would you please use the number three jar?"

I was interested in what Wanda had seen. I had never been able to cast a shield that covered me before and it all happened very fast.

♫

Once I had dropped my shield spell in my last class, I expected all the energy to disperse. Instead, it was sucked into my light potion. I honestly wasn't certain what had happened.

After order had been restored, Professor Reece pressed the white crystal on his desk to reach Mrs. Rousseau, the headmistresses' secretary. He asked for two students, so they could drag Lord Keith's frozen henchman to her office. Then, he turned to Lord Keith.

"Young man, I am aware that if you step out of line in the first two weeks, the headmistress will expel you. Therefore, I will assume, only temporarily, that it was your henchmen who instigated this. However, you are responsible for him. Once you are done imbuing your potion, please report to Professor Vermis for punishment."

Lord Keith looked mad, and I thought he might say something awful. Instead, he said, "Yes, professor," and went back to imbuing his potion.

Three minutes later, the professor began counting down. At his zero, I took my hands off the cauldron. Mina and the others did as well.

"Please carry them into the warding circle," said the professor. "Place your name tag next to it, then I will activate the spell."

I was a little nervous as I wasn't sure what had happened to my potion. But it still had the color and constituency of a light potion that hadn't been activated. I wasn't sure, but with my Sight, it looked like there were little snowflakes swirling around in my potion that I had never seen before. After putting it down, I put my name tag next to it.

That's when I noticed everyone was looking at me. I could feel Wanda's excitement as she knelt down to examine my potion. "You're the best hero ever," she whispered. "Go ahead, let's see what happens."

"What if it... well, explodes or something?" I whispered back.

Professor Reece chuckled. "I don't think we need to worry about that. However, safety first. All of you out of the ring, and I will activate them myself."

He charged the circle once we were all out of it. Then began tapping each potion with a silver rod starting with Lord Keith's and worked clockwise. Mine was the last. All the other potions were glowing. I bet Mina's would last a good five hours before it went out. From the way its magic flowed inconsistently, I didn't think Lord Keith's would last more than an hour or two. He seemed to sense this and muttered under his breath.

Professor Reece had an impish grin as he tapped my cauldron with his silver rod. The potion began to shine brightly. I watched Mina's eyes go wide. Wanda gasped and then jumped up and down. Glowing snowflakes began to rise out of my potion and hovered for a second before falling back into it. More snowflakes rose as the effect continued.

I didn't know what to say.

Professor Reece rubbed his hands together. "I suspect Professor Vermis and I will see if we can reverse design your potion, Ms. Vivian." He stood up and bowed to me. "What do you want to name it?"

Wanda squealed and hugged me. A little devil in my mind hoped Jeffery hugged me later tonight when I told him about it.

♪♪♪

Wanda began drawing out a design on the chalkboard while Lord Grayson pulled down a large glass jar and began sprinkling what looked like a fine ground silver mixed with something else on the inside of the room's one warding circle.

As Wanda's design grew in complexity, I swear I had seen it before. But I couldn't put my finger on it, yet. She stopped and looked at me. "Could you turn sideways? I was watching you from that perspective."

I did and she tilted her head back and forth slightly, then made a few more additions to her drawing.

It was there, a pattern. But I couldn't place it. It was like snowflakes had connected with a matrix of energy.

Professor Gass went to stand on the other side of Wanda's drawing. "You have a good memory, young lady." Then to the room at large, "Five points to the first person who can tell me the three main intersecting points."

Intersect points? What was he talking about?

The other students wandered closer to the blackboard as if they had understood what the professor was talking about. I don't think I had ever been in a class where I felt this lost before.

By now, Lord Grayson had put away the jar and was wiping his hands with a cloth. He came over to look at Wanda's drawing too.

Conflicting emotions arose in me. First, I had an odd sort of frustration at being ignored. But it was also refreshing as well. Normally, when I was in a room full of men, at least a few of them would be looking at me. But not with this group. Wanda's drawing of my shield held all their interest. These students were very focused. They were two to three years older than I was, but they seemed even more mature. The second was my annoyance at being left out. I felt like they were talking about me and not bothering to include me in their conversations, treating me as if I was just a silly woman. I had seen other women take this posture: smile, look pretty, make sure everyone had food and drink, then laugh insipidly at questions directed at them. I half wondered if some women were trained to do that from birth.

One of the young men tapped out three points on Wanda's drawing, two of the others rolled their eyes. The taller of the two said, "It was a three-dimensional shield. You can't build the energy matrix like that."

The professor tapped his cane. "Agreed. Anyone?"

The young man from House Kumar suggested to Wanda, "Was the pattern any different higher or lower?"

Wanda slowly tapped the chalk on the board. "I don't think so," she said at last. "But everything happened fast. So, I'm not certain."

The boy nodded at her. "Fair point. Good memory."

Wanda blushed at his compliment. I was astonished. He was from House Kumar and treating Wanda like a human being. Was I still in the same school?

Lord Grayson put down the rag he was using to clean his hands. "Ms. Wanda, was any of it a different color?"

Wanda considered his words. I could also tell she was enjoying being the center of attention. "I think so, but only at..." and her voice trailed off. "At three points," she concluded excitedly, and added three small circles on the drawing.

Lord Grayson stepped back. While still peering at the drawing he asked, "Ms. Wanda, I'm serving my Realm Knight responsibilities this weekend. My henchman is out due to a family emergency. Would you be willing to step in to help?"

I think I blinked. Was he trying to steal Wanda away from me? I had to serve detention this weekend, so I was going to be busy anyway. But Wanda's *my* henchwoman!

Wanda's mouth opened in astonishment. But before she could say anything, Lord Grayson turned to Professor Gass. "Professor, are you assuming it was only a single layer shield?"

Professor Gass grinned. "Five points, young man. I think our next steps should be some testing."

I couldn't take it any longer. I know I wasn't a noble, but I was proud of who I was. I got my friends to work together, built a snowman, and even Lady Cassandra was going to work with me.

Through all that, Wanda was by my side. "Do I get a voice at being an experiment, Professor? Or am I just the silly woman in the room?"

It came out snarkier than I had intended. Wanda stared at me, then frowned. Was I jealous that the men were talking to Wanda and not me? Maybe, a little. But I was also annoyed at being treated like a thing they wanted to experiment with.

It was like clockwork. All eyes swung to me. A little part of me wanted to shrink away from this sudden scrutiny. Also, one of the young men suddenly seemed to notice I was a woman and blushed. Another stammered out an apology and put his hands in his pockets.

Sigh. I bet I just became the bitch. Not what I hoped to accomplish.

Professor Gass tapped his cane on the ground again. Then with what I thought was a hint of a smile, he added, "Your point is well taken, Ms. Vivian. I know and respect your benefactor. I also think he would agree with your statement. You are not merely a test subject, and it was not my intention to make you feel that way. I apologize."

I wasn't sure what to say. A professor just apologized to me. And he knew my benefactor. "Um, thank you, Professor," I said. "What do you need to calibrate for?"

He turned to Lord Grayson. "Young man, expand on my thoughts."

Professor Gass certainly seemed to like Lord Grayson. A part of me was reluctantly liking him too, even if he was from House Duke. And the other part was that he asked Wanda for help. I was grudgingly happy for her. Since Lord Grayson's request wasn't a school activity, she had better be paid. But if he tried to steal her again, I would have my snowman hand him a piece of charcoal.

Lord Grayson bowed to me. "I apologize as well. I should have asked your permission before I asked your henchwoman for help."

Just the fact he recognized the distinction between henchman and henchwoman made me respect him more.

Wanda gave me a pleading look. She really wanted to do this. Sigh. "Thank you. If Wanda wishes, of course she can help you. What do you need her to do?"

Wanda grinned and moved a step toward him.

Lord Grayson's voice darkened a notch. "I was instructed to travel to the next valley and help settle any disputes that might come up. I'm only staying the weekend. Also, while I'm there, I have been ordered to start mapping out the area. That's what I really want Ms. Wanda's help with. Being a Hine, I expect she knows how to map an area?"

Wanda rolled her eyes. "Of course. I helped my father before the war..." her voice trailed off and she looked down. "I know how to do it."

At the mention of the war and the implication of the loss of her father, there was silence in the room. So many people died in the war. Wanda had told me she was seven the last time she saw him alive.

"Please make sure Wanda stays safe," I said to Lord Grayson. Lady Cassandra said all the trees had been knocked down and all the predators had run away. But had they?

He bowed again. "I will. But I didn't mean to be discourteous. What Professor Gass wants to do is confirm you have three magical ground states. One from you because of your inherent magic, another to Lord Winton due to your oath, and the last pointing at your snowman. For any complex magical equations, we test out in this room, we need to account for everyone's ground states. That way, there is less of a possibility of any spells we work with behaving unexpectedly."

I followed that. "Thank you," I said. "So, what do you need me to do now?"

He grinned at me. "Step in the circle, and we will activate it."

Oh.

Okay, this is interesting. After Professor Gass activated the circle with me in its center, all the ground silver began to rise in the air. I felt like I was in the center of a snowstorm.

Professor Gass walked around the outer edge of the spell circle while studying the effect. He wore a set of spectacles with multiple-colored eyepieces he could raise or lower on little gears. After lowering a blue eyepiece into place, he said to Lord Grayson, "Please walk counterclockwise around the circle slowly. There's another link I believe."

Lord Grayson held a diviner's rod in both hands. But instead of a forked wooden stick, this one was made of silver, and the tip had little colored glass balls dangling from it on thin silver threads. Each ball was of a different color matching the professor's unique glasses. As Lord Grayson slowly moved around the circle, he kept the tip pointed at me. I noticed every few steps that the glass balls would change how they were attracted to the circle. When that happened, the professor would raise or lower some of the gears on his odd glasses. I had never seen anything like them before and wanted to know what they were. But the professor probably wouldn't appreciate the interruption right now.

"Interesting," murmured the Professor. "I stand corrected, you have four ground states, Ms. Vivian. I assume the third one is your snowman. But the fourth?"

Chapter 5

If you want to find the secrets of the universe, think in terms of energy, frequency, and vibrations.
-Nikola Tesla.

-Vivian Hampton-

Pioneer School, Physics Room

As I stood in the circle, that same odd sensation of feeling like an experiment came back. Most of the fine silver mixture now formed layered circles. The outermost one was about two feet from my body. But some of the silver rose higher to create four thin lines which extended from me to the inner edge of the main circle.

Wanda and others were staring at the effect. "Um, Professor..." I started with. I had no idea of what I was looking at.

But he answered before I could finish. "Any person with magical abilities would have the silver mixture gather in circles around them, Ms. Vivian. Generally, the more circles, the stronger their magical ability. Considering I can see five distinct layers, perhaps six, you are able to focus a great deal of magic, should you wish to do so."

Lord Grayson moved toward the fourth line and all the little glass balls on his divining rod were pulled toward it.

Professor Gass murmured, "Now that was interesting. Lord Grayson, do another circuit."

As he did, Wanda followed him. "What do you think it is?" she asked.

Keeping his magic divining rod steady, he replied, "No idea, but Vivian should really get a better wand, it's only a matter of time before she accidentally destroys the one she has."

Conflicting emotions rose in me again. I felt a twinge of jealousy as Wanda followed him around. She was my henchwoman. The other, Lord Grayson honestly seemed to care about me too. He seemed, well, nice.

"What are those four lines, Professor?" asked Wanda. Like everyone else, she stood just outside the main circle. Like her, the others were studying thin lines of floating silver intently.

"The left one is her oath to Lord Winton. The second is her magical ground, the third is likely to be your hero's snowman. The fourth, I'm not sure. However, whatever it is, it is very complex." Then tapping his cane on the ground, he addressed me, "Ms. Vivian, let's start with the third link. See if she can reach out to the creature."

Creature? I didn't like him being described like that. It felt like he was describing my snowman as a mindless animal.

"Professor, he can talk to others and has a name too," I said with a bit of heat.

Professor Gass raised his glasses slightly to look at me. Instead of being annoyed, he had a smile on his face. "Point taken, Ms. Vivian. Since this class is all about studying Newtonian physics and runes, I have a habit of describing things as objects. Your rebuke is appreciated."

I could feel my face go red a bit. "Um, thank you, Professor. Do you want me to reach out to Camillo now?"

"Yes. Lord Grayson, please take a step back. I suspect there will be a bit of magic bleeding out of the circle when Ms. Vivian does so. I want the divining rod to be able to interact with it."

The others, including Wanda, took two steps backwards, making me feel a bit nervous as if the professor had declared I was contagious. But no one was looking at me apprehensively, merely with interest. Lord Grayson was mature for his age. He treated me like a person. Mother had told me men generally get better as they get older. Was she right? I was grudgingly beginning to like Lord Grayson.

I focused on my connection with Camillo. The moment after I named him while pressing a drop of my blood into his chest, an icon of a little snowman formed in my mind. When he was close enough to me, about two hundred feet or so, I could sense the icon brighten a bit. Once that happened, I could see out of his eyes if I wanted to, and we could talk to each other. Now, it just floated there and faintly pulsed now and then. I wasn't certain why standing in this circle would help me reach out to him as he was probably too far away right now, but I did what the professor asked.

Several things immediately happened. The icon in my mind lit up, and I could see through his eyes again. Second, some of the silver mixture at my feet rose higher in the air and followed the third thread of energy.

Wherever Camillo was, I recognized Terrance, Mr. and Mrs. Thorough, plus Mrs. Capmond. Along with them, there were about another fifteen or so watching a coffin being slowly lowered into the ground.

<*"Camillo,"*> I asked. <*"Who is being buried? And where are you?"*>

From the surprised expressions on the faces of everyone just outside the circle, they apparently could hear me speak to my snowman as well.

"Lord Grayson," said Professor Gass sharply while lowering another colored glass into place. "Move three paces to the right. Everyone else move back another step."

<*"Creator? I can't see you. Are you here to take Mr. Capmond's soul?"*>

Well, I knew who was being buried now. I had never been on Mrs. Capmond's little homestead in the mountains but had seen it from a distance. I bet this was her family's graveyard. Then my mind caught up with Camillo's question. Take his soul? I'm not a god. Then an uncomfortable realization struck me—from Camillo's point of view, I was. I had created him.

Swallowing and thinking fast, I thought back as calmly as I could. <*"God will come and take his soul, Camillo."*>

<*"My friend said the same thing, Creator. What does God look like? May I stay here until nightfall? I would like to watch Him come."*>

Oh, my gosh. Wanda's eyes had gone wide. Some of the young men had similar reactions. Another snickered, and I gave him a frustrated look. This wasn't funny. But it was Lord Grayson who whispered out a suggestion, "Faith can't be seen."

I gave him a quick smile in thanks. <*"God works through faith, Camillo. Faith cannot be seen, but we feel it in our heart. However, you may stay by the grave until nightfall. Please come to me at the school then."*>

<*"Yes, Creator."*> And suddenly I felt the connection with Camillo go back to a slow pulse in my mind, and I was no longer looking through his eyes. All the floating silver making up the scene slowly fell to the ground.

Wanda bounced up and down. "That. Was. Awesome," she shouted.

Several of the young men seemed to be looking at me differently. *Okay, why?* They had to have seen Camillo last night when I had named him.

Lord Grayson put down the silver divining rod. "Thank you for giving Camillo the opportunity to question reality." Then his voice darkened a notch. "I dislike having someone else shove their version of religion down my throat."

Professor Gass took off his unique glasses and pondered me. "As interesting as that discussion was, you two, this is a class on physics. I believe I now have the data to properly create a grounding bracelet for you Ms. Vivian, at least for that link. You only need to wear it while you're in my room."

"Thank you, Professor." Then I asked nervously, "But will it break my connection with Camillo?" I wasn't going to wear it if it did.

"Not at all young lady, it will just create a ground point for the connection instead of it shifting all over the place. Now let's discuss this other link of yours."

♪♪

"Yes, Professor. I honestly don't know...." And my voice trailed off. Now that I was looking at Wanda's drawing from farther away, I recognized where I had seen the pattern before—in the headmistresses' office when Lady Cassandra was arguing with the two dragons. Her fitted shields had briefly appeared, Wanda's drawing was almost identical. Was the shield spell I called this morning being augmented by Lady Cassandra?

"I suspect you just had a moment of revelation, Ms. Vivian," suggested Professor Gass. "May we be enlightened?"

I bit my lip. "Um, Lady Cassandra offered to work with me a bit too. She offered to help me with gathering magic while singing."

Wanda knew this, but no one else in the room did. A few of the young men sucked in their breath. Lord Grayson cocked his head. "But that wouldn't create a link unless..." He stopped in midsentence.

Professor Gass pondered me while tapping his glasses. "Unfortunately, this ring is not designed for that kind of power. Tomorrow, we will convene our class in the basement, to use the school's master ring. With luck, we will get the information we need. Once we have that data, Ms. Vivian, I will see if a second bracelet can be crafted. Lord Grayson, please break the ring and we can proceed with the others."

"Sir, Professor Gass?" I asked while stepping out of the ring. "Will my benefactor be responsible for covering the cost of these two bracelets?" I never got a hint that Lord Winton was disappointed in me or felt I was abusing his resources, but making these bracelets sounded expensive.

"No, Ms. Vivian, the expense will come from the school's budget."

Like me, the others took their turn in the ring. Every one of them had magic to some degree or another. The silver mixture moved to form circles around them. The smallest was only two circles. But like me, Lord Grayson had five distinct circles. He also had three trails of silver floating in the air touching the main circle's edge, versus only two for the other students.

"As I expected, Lord Grayson," said the Professor. "The first is of course the oath to your house, the second is your magical ground link, and the last is your oath as a junior reserve Realm Knight. Like Ms. Vivian and the others, I will have a silver bracelet constructed for you."

Then he turned to Wanda. "You're up, young lady."

"But I don't have any magic, Professor," she protested, while looking uncertainly at the circle.

I felt that odd pulsing sensation on my shoulder again. Was Wanda embarrassed? It occurred to me she rarely talked about herself when magic was discussed.

"Hey, you're the best henchwoman ever," I said using the same phrasing Wanda used to describe me. "I wouldn't know what to do without you."

Wanda's face reddened briefly. She gave Lord Grayson a hesitant smile, then took a tentative step across the ring. Once in the center, she sighed. "Go ahead."

Wow. What was wrong with Wanda? Her normal glass half full personality had been replaced with resignation. I never knew not having magic frustrated her this much. I cocked my head as she hesitantly smiled at Lord Grayson again. Then she clasped her hands nervously, sighed, and broke eye contact to look at the ground. Was she infatuated with the man? Admittedly, I was grudgingly beginning to like him too. But was Wanda afraid he wouldn't be interested in her once we confirmed she had no magic?

There were magic rings or charms she could wear. But each was imbued with a single spell and very expensive. I knew some of the wealthier students had one or two. Then there was amulet magic, like Sierra in the Mole clan or Mia in the Great Forest clan. They had many spells encoded in them, but then you were committed for life in the clan's structure. Not a path I would want to take. But would Wanda?

While I pondered this, Lord Grayson charged the ring. As expected, none of the silver mixture circled around Wanda. She sighed, and then her eyes went wide as a bit of the mixture slowly rose and made not one but two faints link from Wanda extending to the edge of the ring. The second one touched the edge of the circle, right in front of me.

Professor Gass put his glasses back on. "The first is your house oath Ms. Hine, but the other...Ms. Vivian, please move clockwise around the ring."

I slowly moved as he asked.

The second thread of silver followed me.

Wanda's eyes had gone wide. "What does this mean, Professor?" she said, and bit her lip.

Ignoring Wanda, Professor Gass pondered me. "Have you felt anything odd over the last day or so young lady?"

"Yes sir. An odd pulsing sensation on the back of my shoulder. It started yesterday, but it's more intense today."

"And was your henchwoman near you when you felt the first pulse?"

I had to think about it for a second. "Yes, sir," I said slowly. "I first felt it when I named Camillo. Wanda was standing right next to me."

"You mean I could cast magic through Vivian?" exclaimed Wanda.

Professor Gass turned slightly and cocked his head, apparently waiting.

Wanda blushed and added, "Professor."

"That is one theoretical possibility," suggested Professor Gass. "However, more experimentation will have to wait for another day. Regardless, I will need to account for your ground state as well, young lady. Like your hero, I will have a silver bracelet made for you."

"Professor?" asked Lord Grayson. "Why didn't we see the link when Ms. Vivian was in the circle?"

"Good question, young man. One possible explanation is it somehow tied to one of the other links. However, more data will be gathered tomorrow. For now, please take your seats, and we can begin."

After we found our seats, the professor pulled off one of the glass cases to reveal a small but very detailed waterwheel. "Let's start with some basic Newtonian mathematics," said Professor Gass and pulled out his wand. "This is a miniature of the waterwheel I designed for Lord Winton. You can find a similar example on page five of your physics book."

As Professor Gass talked, he tapped his wand to various points on the waterwheel, then equations began writing themselves out on the board. While I understood the concepts, he was moving so fast, I quickly became lost.

And this was chapter one. None of the seniors appeared confused at all. A few almost looked bored. Faceplant time. Why in the world were we in this class?

Wanda gave me a pleading look. She probably felt the same way I did. More than anything, it was her uncertainty which gave me the courage to raise my hand.

"Yes, Ms. Vivian," said Professor Gass. The current equation appearing on the chalkboard froze.

"Professor, we're just sophomores. Is there a study period where we can come in for help?"

"Sir," chimed in Lord Grayson. "I need to account for my training hours. Would you allow me to tutor them?"

Professor Gass briefly looked at something on his desk, probably a scheduler of some kind. "The room is available an hour before dinner." Then glancing at me asked, "Does that work for you two?"

Wanda and I both nodded and Professor Gass began again. It just got harder from there. Wanda and I were doomed. I couldn't see how either of us could pass this class. What in the world was Lord Winton thinking when he asked me to take it? For her part, Wanda almost seemed angry for some reason. Trying to keep up meant all my attention was focused on the equations.

Chapter 6

The most valuable trade resource Avalon has is our ladies.
-Lady Venessa Navartis, former Lady of the Land.

The old Avalon sees women as a trade negotiation. My attempt to change that backfired spectacularly. To save my friend from an ugly marriage, I ended up negotiating a marriage contract for her with another family, whose head of house happened to be a fey guardian dragon.
-Lady Petra Abara of Gawain

-Vivian Hampton-

Pioneer School

Wanda was oddly quiet in our next class, choir. It was really a combination of singing and musical theory with a bit of history of songs thrown in as well. Lady Petrushka, our choir instructor, taught the class last year as well. She had been a touch stern, but she got me. Her ear was excellent, and if I wavered in control at all, she picked it up at once. Then the dreaded violin would twang—that was her way of letting us know we were off. She would pluck at it and demand, "Again."

Personally, it worked for me, but some of the other students hated it. After we found our seats and went through the normal introductions to the freshmen, she asked me to come up and sing a series of scales and triads, basic ones. Then she had each freshman come up and try to reproduce what I had done. Some of them were horrible. Samantha, especially so. Surprisingly, Elaine wasn't bad.

Amanda was amazing. After hearing her, Lady Petrushka told me to sing a chromatic scale and hold the last note. Amanda did an okay job. She had some potential.

"Very good all," said Lady Petruska. "Some of you are better than others, and this is to be expected. We will work hard, and you will improve. For now, I want the sophomores to sing for me, so I know who has been practicing and who has *not*," she said in a threatening tone, amplified by the twang on her violin.

"We will start with the *Lacrymosa*. Ms. Vivian, I would like you to start."

I was in my element and loved it. Singing always made me feel happy. I felt like I was reaching out to the world, sharing the song with the rest of the universe. As I sang, memories surfaced of all the nice things that had happened over the last few days. My nervousness just faded away; there was just me and the song. Suddenly, I felt energy wrapping around me, and my eyes went wide. I blinked my Sight on. Translucent shimmering runes began appearing on the walls. I immediately stopped singing, and they faded.

"Why did you stop, young lady?" demanded Lady Petrushka, tapping her violin. "Your time elements were perfect."

I could feel myself blush. "Um, I think I was accidentally calling magic to me while I was singing. I, well, could feel it beginning to gather."

Lady Petrushka played out an F on her violin. "I am glad you had the sense to stop. We will work on that Friday afternoon." Then she pointed to another sophomore. "Now, begin."

I moved to stand by Wanda and sighed. This was the class I was really looking forward to, and now I couldn't sing. About twenty minutes later, the sophomore henchmen and henchwomen had their turn. Wanda did a decent job of it. She must have been practicing, and I told her so.

She just looked away from me.

"Did I say something wrong?" I asked her.

For an answer, I got silence.

The Thought

The thought in the ground sensed a gathering song. Before the magic could take shape, the song stopped.

It tried to triangulate from the one warding stone which had been exposed and was now gathering light. Without another stone uncovered, it could only get a rough idea of where the song had come from. It had more energy now, not much, but enough to reach out through the warding stone. Instead of answering back, the humanoid creatures went away. Was there a pattern to their movements? It could not detect one. But through its warding stone, it could also look down from the mountain and see the valley where the song had likely come from. Memories of long ago surfaced. The stone buildings were different now—wider and taller. With more energy available, it also pushed a tendril of energy toward the crack in the wall where it sensed a trickle of light.

Was its new master there?

Each day, more sunlight was collected and brought into the lower chamber.

While it continued to wait, options were considered. Two of its buried warding stones were under the tallest structure in the valley. Could energy be sent to them?

It was very patient as it tried out ideas.

-Vivian Hampton-

Wanda was still silent as we headed to the gymnasium. It was our break period, but she liked practicing on the balance beam while I sat on the bleachers and did homework. There wasn't a class being held in the gymnasium right now. Other than the two of us, the place was empty.

I was almost done working my way through the first physics problem when I noticed Wanda had come over. She was looking down at me, hands clenched.

"Did you do that on purpose?" she demanded.

Huh? "Do what? What are you talking about?"

"Lord Grayson. He asked *me* to help him. Then you come along and set up *a study session* with him," she said, making air quotes, implying I might have other motives.

What? "Wanda, he set it up and volunteered to help us. I don't..."

But Wanda cut me off, almost shouting at me. "So maybe I could have some magic, but it's only through you, Miss Perfect?"

Miss Perfect? My life was a mess. I felt like I was barely hanging on most days. But what really caught my attention was Wanda's eyes. They were getting moist. "Wanda, I'm not..."

"Can't I have a boy like me too?" she yelled. Now tears began to trickle down her face. "I don't have any magic. I don't have a body like yours. I can't sing like you. You're smarter than I am. All I wanted for once was maybe to have a boy like me. But you come and take that away too."

A body like mine? Half the time I was nervous about how I looked. "Wanda, your singing was great. Why..."

"I walk into a room, and no one notices me," she said, tears starting to fall to the ground. "You walk into a room and boys are drooling over you." Wanda clenched her fists and seemed to get herself under control. "Why do I always have to be in the background?"

She fell to her knees in front of me and openly cried. Between sobs she got out, "Why can't I have a choice?"

I didn't know what to say. Wanda had never gotten mad at me before. She was always so upbeat and positive. Always pushing me forward. Sometimes more than I wanted. I replayed that thought. Wanda running into a room while screaming in excitement, jumping up and down, pushing me to get others together. Was that her way of trying to get boys to notice her?

"Wanda, I am so sorry," I said softly and laid my hand on top of hers, then kissed her forehead. "You are one of the most amazing people I know. I wouldn't know what to do without you."

Wanda gulped for air and grabbed on to my hand. "You're so perfect. Next to you, I'm flat and boring," she whispered out. "I know boys are sort of stupid, but Lord Grayson was different. I wanted him to look at *me* that way." She sniffled. "You know, as a woman. Before I have to..." and her voice trailed off.

I pulled Wanda toward me, and she collapsed on the bench to lean against me. "I'm sorry," she said softly, then rubbed at her face. "It's not your fault that you're perfect and I'm not. I guess I really am just a Hine."

She said her family name like it was a curse.

"Wanda, my parents divorced because of my magic. My father believes my mother had to have been unfaithful. When I walk into a room, I can feel some of the boys staring at my chest, and I want to slap them. If someone made a potion that made them smaller, I'd probably take it. Lord Winton has me, us, taking physics, and I am so lost. We're probably going to get our butts kicked in eight weeks when we square off against Duke again, and it will all be because of me."

As I talked, I could feel my own eyes getting wet. "I'm barely holding on, and the *only* thing keeping it all together is you. A Hine." I leaned my head against hers. "Wonderful Wanda Hine."

Wanda leaned into me. We didn't say anything for a few minutes.

"You would really take a potion to make your chest smaller?" asked Wanda, sitting upright.

"No hesitation. It's very awkward."

Wanda looked down at her own chest. "Why can't I get boys to notice me?"

I was silent for a few seconds. "I think you are beautiful the way you are. Have you ever let any boys know you might like them in that way?"

Wanda shook her head, then said very softly, "What if my uncle pulls me out of school?" She suddenly emulated an older man's voice, "A Hine is supposed to work hard, be focused, and always pay attention. No dalliances for you."

"Did your uncle really say that?" I asked, appalled.

"Exact words," sighed Wanda. "He's not my eldest, but he is my benefactor. I appreciate that he is paying for me to go to school, but I feel like I'm trapped too." Wanda gave me a weak smile and reached for my hand. "I wish I had a nice benefactor like yours."

I was trying to organize my thoughts. Just the fact someone else thought my life was perfect was so odd. Admittedly, I did like Lord Winton as a benefactor. He never made me feel uncomfortable, he seemed interested in how I was approaching problems at school, and, other than physics, he allowed me to take the classes I wanted. Now that I had met Lady Kiera, I felt very accepted by them. But Wanda obviously felt trapped. I remembered her words from before, "Why can't I have a choice"—then almost in the same sentence—"before I have to."

Trapped. I remembered back to something Lord Winton said while we were walking around the school grounds and talking about Jeffery. *Let me know if it becomes more, and I will reach out to his eldest.* He was giving me freedom to choose my own path. But did Wanda have that option?

When we occasionally talked in the Orozco common room about our futures, Wanda had always been very vague. I knew her parents weren't alive anymore, and she had lived with her uncle before coming to school. Did he have a specific plan for her? One she didn't want. Then the pieces started to fit together.

"Wanda," I asked softly. "Does your uncle have plans to marry you off once you graduate?"

She gave me a sideways glance and nodded.

I cautiously asked, "Do you like him?"

For an answer, Wanda burst out crying and leaned into me again. I wrapped my arms around her as she sobbed.

I had no idea Wanda's family was this dictatorial about her future. I was aware she was the only female Hine of her generation. My apprehension that Lord Winton might choose my husband had lessened now that I had met Lady Kiera. But Wanda apparently wasn't allowed that freedom.

Wanda's crying turned to sniffles, and I pulled my arms back.

"I don't hate him," began Wanda looking at the ground. "Kyler is a year older and can barely read. He's the eldest son of a man who owns three small inns. My job would be to keep the books while having children. Kyler told me he wants at least seven. My uncle thinks this is a great opportunity to expand our house."

I was appalled. Not that her benefactor was selecting her husband or that she would be having children. But that he had no idea of Wanda's capabilities and was thinking so small. I relied on Wanda for everything. She had so much potential. Before I could think of what to say, Wanda glanced at my notebook. "You did the first physics homework problem?"

I squeezed her hand. "Without the book's examples, I couldn't have done it." I remembered Wanda's infatuation with high nobles. Was part of that imagining she could escape her uncle and live a life of her own? An idea began to take shape in my mind. "Didn't you say Lady Gawain never dated anyone until she was nineteen?" I asked. "Then slapped her boyfriend, now her intended, in public?"

I could feel Wanda's grin. "That's the story. I heard half of Avalon City was betting on who would give in first."

"The spring dance is coming up in ten weeks," I said. "You're a gymnast, maybe you could offer some dancing lessons to boys you might like. Hopefully, you won't need to slap them though. It's a school event. I don't think your uncle would disapprove if you danced with a boy then."

Wanda giggled. "Or more than one." Then she leaned into me and asked softly, "So, Lord Grayson. Are you interested in him?"

"I'm warming up to him, but we just met. Besides, I have a boyfriend. *And*... I really do like Jeffery." Jeffery still didn't have his head of house's permission to date me, which worried me a little. I hoped he got it soon. I had never kissed anyone before and wanted to experiment. All the songs made it sound very passionate. But more importantly, he was supportive and fun.

Wanda gave my hand a quick squeeze in return. "I can tell you're thinking about Jeffery. You have this faraway look."

I stuck my tongue out at her.

"Would you like a suggestion?" I asked.

"Maybe."

"If Lord Grayson really does hire you to help, and he is happy with you, ask him to sign a letter of recommendation for your head of house. If he learns there are lords willing to hire you, maybe he will recognize your potential and have a talk with your uncle." The head of house had legal authority over all the other members of the house, and this included any contracts.

At my idea, I could feel Wanda's energy slowly returning. The Wanda I knew was coming back.

"We still have a little time before our next class," I said. "Why don't you show me the routine you're working on for the competition?"

Wanda was hoping to get on the school's sophomore gymnastic team.

She bounced up, "Sure I—"

We both turned at the sound of the far door slamming open. Then I cringed at the angry shout. Male and very annoyed. Two boys were coming into the gymnasium, and they looked like they were ready to battle each other. Their wands were out. I didn't recognize the boy who was pushed through the door as his back was to us, but I could make out the taller one. Lord Grayson.

What was going on?

"Wanda," I hissed. "This might be dangerous. Let's hide."

We scrambled to the edge of the bleachers and crouched under them, peering out.

"You little asshole," shouted Lord Grayson, making a sweeping motion with his wand. His opponent flew backwards, sliding on the ground. That's when I recognized the other person as Lord Seth.

Lord Seth scrambled to his feet and cast a spell. Red energy flew toward Lord Grayson, who contemptuously cast an angled shield. The spell ricocheted away. "I'm a reserve Realm Knight, you little shit. Do you know what's about to happen?"

"That you're about to do something nasty to me," growled Lord Seth. "Big bad Realm Knight picking on sophomores."

"You are that stupid, aren't you?" hissed out Lord Grayson, who cast another spell. An illusion appeared of Elaine. "Your head of house made a formal complaint. Do you want to know where the complaint ended up?"

"What the hell is wrong with you?" shot back Lord Seth. "We're both in House Duke. You should be supporting me." His wand arm was vibrating, I bet he was ready to cast another spell.

"Who is Elaine's benefactor?" demanded Lord Grayson.

Lord Seth cast a spell. It ricocheted away again. "She's a country bumpkin, a liar," he spat out. "There's no way her benefactor is Lady Cassandra."

Lord Grayson shook his head. "I just received orders by Senior Realm Knight Bardot to report to the headmistresses' office in five minutes. Not only is Lady Cassandra Elaine's benefactor, but she's also apprenticed to Sorcerer Petotum on the Wizard's Council. There's a law that states that, if a formal complaint is made against a Council member, it must be immediately reviewed by the entire Wizard's Council. That happened two hours ago. Your bleeding head of house is about to be met by Sorcerer Petotum."

Lord Grayson sheathed his wand, turned away, and then stopped after opening the door without turning around. "I guess you really are that stupid. I hope your entire family likes spending time as frogs."

He let the door close behind him.

Lord Seth just stood there for a moment. I couldn't see his face, but Wanda and I heard his scream of frustration. Then he ran for the door.

Wanda and I stared at each other.

"What's going to happen to Lord Seth's family?" whispered Wanda.

"I have no idea." This could get bad. Part of me did want Lord Seth expelled, but his family elder coming to the attention of the Council? That couldn't be good for them.

So much was happening, I forgot what time it was. That's when I realized if we didn't run, we would be late for our next class.

Chapter 7

No good deed goes unpunished.
-Any pessimist.

-Terrance-

The Pioneer School

A Sorcerer and Sorceress of the Realm escorted me through the school. Trailing just behind were Darlene and Franklin. I could hear the chatter of students from a distance. As we turned a corner, other Realm Knights reopened the hallway for general use again. Since the school's halls were lit by permanent globes of light, my shadow was very evident and enjoying itself.

A few of the animated paintings on the wall noticed my shadow moving. The older man, in a suit that was out of date two hundred years ago, hid behind the chair in his painting. Another, that of a rotund lady dressed in a flowing opera gown, shrieked in alarm. My shadow mooned her. It has no sense of decorum.

"Sorry," I said to the two Realm Knights. "My shadow thinks it's funny."

The older of the two Realm Knights, the one with wide gold trim on her collar, snorted. Her name tag read Commander Bardot. "We visited the cave this morning and found the crack in the wall. Whatever's down there is something powerful. You're lucky to have made it out."

"Without Camillo's help, I wouldn't have." Then growled at my shadow, "Stop that." It was trying to goose the Realm Commander on the bottom.

My shadow shrugged and looked away. Nothing to see here.

Yeah right. Apparently, I have been cursed. My shadow, for all the world, acted like a thirteen-year-old boy with no manners.

"The snowman," she said. "A representative from the guardian's guild will arrive in a few days. We want her opinion before we decide what to do about it."

I could feel myself bristle at the thought they might mean him harm. "He is my friend. Should you mean him ill intentions, you best consider what I might do to you first."

The younger Realm Knight, barely a man, glanced at me. I could hear his heartbeat pick up.

Commander Bardot said deadpan, "I'll keep that in mind."

From behind me, Darlene spoke up. "Who are we meeting besides the headmistress?"

I suspected the arrival of the Realm Knights had surprised her.

For an answer, we got silence.

Waiting in what had to be the secretary's office was an interesting experience. My shadow winked out of existence when I crossed into her office. I doubted my luck was such that it was gone for good. The protection spells weaved into this room had to be amazing.

Instead of treating me like a threat, the secretary offered me a bowl filled with silver wrapped mints. I obligingly took a piece, unwrapped it and popped it into my mouth. See? No vampire here. A small dragon appeared, wrapped itself around my left wrist, gave out a small puff of illusionary fire, then disappeared.

"Very nice dear," smiled the secretary. "Those are very rare."

It was hard not to like her. I bet she treated everyone in her office the same regardless of age.

Standing against the wall were two other Realm Knights. The two that had escorted me here took up position blocking the doors. Message very clear: move and you won't like it. Darlene and Franklin sat next to me, and both turned down the offer from the secretary for a piece of candy. From the way they talked, I could tell Darlene and the secretary knew and liked each other. Five others were already sitting in chairs when we arrived. Three of them had to be miners from the looks of their clothes. Another was introduced as Mayor Bircham, and the last was an ancient man who had a leather case at his feet. Not a lawyer, I suspected, but someone who knew the law.

I thought the general nervous energy I could feel was about me, then I heard someone blurt out in fear. The sound came from the headmistresses' office. I am very good with placing people based on how they talk. The inflection suggested an older man, educated, arrogant, and now, suddenly very afraid.

I raised an eyebrow and asked the secretary, "A noble who's getting a spanking?"

Darlene had painted the headmistress as a powerful sorceress. Was she staring down a parent or head of house whose little darling decided they didn't have to play by the rules?

The corners of Realm Sorceress Bardot's mouth turned up. She was standing at attention in front of the headmistress's door.

"He's an idiot," she said.

Ah. The little darling must have been very bad indeed for a senior Sorceress of the Realm to become involved. A male voice responded, different from the first speaker. Calm, extremely educated, and direct. But what really surprised me was the power in this man's words. Whoever he was, he had a mastery of magic which only true experts achieve. They had brought in a heavyweight.

Realm Sorceress Bardot stepped aside just before the door opened. Stumbling out were two, who had to be lawyers, quickly followed by an older man with thinning white hair. The last was a young man. From the resemblance, he had to be the older man's grandson. All four of them barely noticed us and quickly left. From their horrified expressions, I believed they knew something bad was coming their way.

"Please escort our guests in, Commander Bardot." It was the same voice that had chastised the four who had just left. I didn't know who the speaker was, but from Darlene's open-mouthed expression of surprise, she did. By her deep curtsy when she entered the room, I knew I had better give the best bow I could. After straightening, what caught my attention was the young lady standing to the left of the sorcerer.

"Let me introduce my apprentice," said the sorcerer. "I understand some of you have met Lady Cassandra Altum already? Please, take a seat."

The other occupant of the room was an older lady who had to be the headmistress. Darlene and Franklin went to sit by her.

"Sir, Sorcerer Petotum!" said Mayor Bircham with enthusiasm. "It is an honor to have you in our town."

From the way the man spoke, I bet he was hoping someone had a camera with them. If he could hang the picture in his office, his local political power would increase just by having met this man.

Sorcerer Petotum tilted his head. "Your town is a beehive of activity. Already teams of explorers are crossing the mountain to reach the next valley. But what I want to address first is what Terrance discovered deep within the mountain. My apprentice has already made a full report to the Council."

The mayor blurted out, "Is it a curse released from the warding stone?"

The eldest of the three minors rubbed his hands along his thighs, as if cleaning off something nasty. "We don't know what it is, but we found the crack in the tunnel. What's beyond is odd, sparkling lights." He gave the two other miners a nervous glance. "I've never seen its like before, and whatever it is, it's slowly extending tendrils of light toward the crack. No one has gone in or out. But there are enough people up on the mountain who now know that something's down there. Keeping them out will be hard unless we collapse the tunnel."

Franklin snorted. "The stories are spreading through town like wildfire. Come nightfall, you're going to have waves of people hoping for a glance."

The mayor banged his fist on the arm of the chair he was sitting in. "Is it related to the warding stone?"

Lady Cassandra glanced at her master before speaking. "Short answer? Yes."

"Collapse the tunnel then," demanded the mayor. "And we can rebury that damn stone."

Sorcerer Petotum steepled his fingers. "Who owns the mine?"

"Mr. Terry Hotckins," spoke up the old man with the leather briefcase. "I believe his grandson just arrived in town a few days ago to begin working it again."

"Blond hair, looks about seventeen, five-ten, and currently broke?" I asked apprehensively. Apparently, no good deed goes unpunished.

Sorcerer Petotum smiled slightly. "I understand he tried locking horns with you over a poker game Terrance—and lost."

I sighed; everyone seems to know what I've done in this town. I should just wear a sign saying, *follow me*. "Yes, sir. He's got a nasty attitude and thinks the world is his for the taking. Afterwards, we exchanged words on the matter."

"How much is the mine worth in its current condition?" asked Sorcerer Petotum to the older man.

He rifled through his briefcase and pulled out a piece of paper. "It was purchased six years ago for fifteen gold talons. Current rate, it would probably sell between seventeen and twenty gold talons. More if another seam was discovered."

Sorcerer Petotum tapped his chair. "Offer him a new site of comparable value. If he pushes back, tell him the Council has authorized the demolition of his mine, and we would pay him a quarter of its current value, but the Council wants it." He turned to look at the oldest miner. "Impenetrable within the day. All work required will be paid for by the Council to the local miner's guild."

The mayor relaxed and the miners nodded. What's better than having a problem? Having a problem someone else will pay you to make it go away. I bet that bill will be huge and no one will complain.

"Now, let's discuss the warding stone," said Sorcerer Petotum. "Avalon does have an agreement with a university from the Republic that they are allowed to dig here."

"But it's releasing curses," whispered the mayor. "We should dig it up and dump it in a river."

Lady Cassandra coughed. All eyes turned to her. "That would be very unwise. The best bet would be to rebury it."

From the way the headmistress looked at Lady Cassandra, I could tell they had met before. And the headmistress wasn't entirely happy about something. "How long," she asked, "will it take for the warding stone to settle down after it's reburied?"

I could tell Lady Cassandra was considering her words carefully before answering. "Without further data, I couldn't say."

"And your boyfriend," asked the headmistress with a hint of annoyance. "What is his opinion?"

Boyfriend? She didn't seem to mean Sorcerer Petotum, who could answer for himself. The mayor's eyes sparkled at this sudden tidbit of social news. Several of the Realm Knights standing around the room had cocked their heads in curiosity as well. They were greatly interested in who this individual was.

Sorcerer Petotum stood up. "Mayor Bircham, thank you for coming. The Council will have a decision within a week of what we will do with the warding stone." Then to the miners he said, "The Council wants the tunnel collapsed by tomorrow. We will pay well if it is done sooner."

The mayor was reluctantly escorted from the room. The miners and the older man departed as well. Before the door closed behind them, I could hear the three minors discussing the best method to collapse the tunnel.

"Now, Terrance," said Sorcerer Petotum. "Let's talk about you."

And here it comes. Turns out every guess of what they wanted was wrong.

"You want me to do what?" I asked, not sure if I'd heard the man correctly. Sorcerer Petotum had one of the Realm Knights bring in a stack of folders to hand to me.

"Unsolved cases, Terrance," repeated Sorcerer Petotum with a sunny smile. "Just in and around this town, going back some twenty years. It was my apprentice's idea, but I liked her recommendation."

"I am not going to sign on as Realm Knight," I said.

"We don't want you to," said Lady Cassandra. "But it will give you something to do, and with your unique past, I think the job will be a good fit."

I gave her a direct stare while crossing my arms. "Camillo needs me. He relies on me to explain the world to him."

"Just think how interesting your conversations are going to be now," said Lady Cassandra with a grin. Ignoring my continued insolent stare, she added, "Junior Realm Knight Lord Grayson just took his vows. He needs a guide."

"I would be honored to work with someone who fought their way through the curse," said the young man, stepping forward and holding out his hand to me. "Lady Cassandra has said you have a great deal of experience in examining the clues at the scene of a crime."

She was making me out like I was a detective—that sneaky woman.

Darlene pursed her lips and snickered. "Sherlock Terrance. We can even get you a deerstalker cap and a pipe."

"It's not funny," I said.

Franklin broke out laughing. "Does that make me John Watson? I'm not sure if that's a promotion or not. Afraid my healing skills consist of handing over a bandage though."

Probably to cut off my next line of attack to try to get me out of this, Sorcerer Petotum said, "I understood you had the opportunity to meet the Iron Dragon and the Merlin's guide. What were their orders?"

The room's atmosphere suddenly changed. The young Realm Knight who was still trying to shake my hand stood up straighter, if that was possible. I swear there was suddenly some hero worship going on with him now as well. I bet Sorcerer Petotum did that on purpose. Now this kid will stick to me like a bear to honey.

"To pay attention, look for clues, defend the area, and call them if things got bad."

Sorcerer Petotum patted me on the back. "We're just making it official."

I turned back to Lady Cassandra. "I hate you."

"Learned it all from the Iron Dragon," she said, dimpling. "You never know, if you do a good job, Lady Elizabeth might enjoy comparing notes with you. If you think you're feeling put upon, imagine trying to be a guide to the new merlin. It used to be my unofficial job, so I can imagine there are days she will want to scream."

I recognized a carrot when I was hit over the head with one. "Fine," I growled out and shook the young man's hand. "I prefer working at night," I said, hoping it might deter his enthusiasm.

He bowed. "As I am still taking classes here, that fits in well with my schedule."

Need to try harder then. "I like poker too. Does that get in the way of your vows?"

"I will politely watch, sir. I might learn a few things."

They not only saddled me with a kid, but a nice, polite kid at that. What did I do to deserve this?

While we talked, Lady Cassandra pulled out a small silver jewel encrusted case. It took me a second to notice the jewels had been cut into the shape of runes: very small ones.

"What's this?" I asked. "Please tell me it's not the second arrowhead."

The young man grinned. "I look forward to your stories, sir."

"Nope," said Lady Cassandra. The smile slid off her face. "I don't know if this is a good idea or not. If you ask me to take it back I will, and I'm only letting you borrow it. The ring is beyond expensive."

For her to say it was beyond expensive meant something. Realm Knight Grayson watched in wonder as I slowly opened the silver case. As Lady Cassandra implied, there was a single ring inside. *Made of...* and my thought trailed off. "Is it made out of orichalcum?" I whispered. Just an ounce of the stuff was worth, well, whatever you asked for.

My new junior partner stared down at it. "What does it do?" he said in wonder.

"I borrowed it from a vault at the Houser Bank," said Lady Cassandra. "Among other things, it might help your undignified friend be a little more cooperative."

My mind caught up with the other part of her statement. Camillo was anything but undignified.

"You mean my shadow?" I asked.

"Yes. Now let's talk about the stick."

Déjà vu. "I take it you're going to step in when the Iron Dragon becomes unavailable due to her condition," I said sarcastically. I felt like Lady Cassandra must have been taking notes from that woman. The Iron Dragon was pregnant with triplets. I couldn't imagine she would be acting in the field for much longer.

Sorcerer Petotum said in a commanding voice, "That information should not leave this room. Now, the stick."

The headmistress took a step forward and looked me directly in the eye. "You're tall, handsome, and mysterious. An enticement for many a young lady at this school. If you cross that line with Ms. Hampton or any other young lady here, I will hunt you down and make sure it hurts."

Lady Cassandra added, "and I will ask my boyfriend to hunt you down. He won't miss. Burning to death is a painful way to go."

Oh.

Burning to death? Was her boyfriend a dragon?

Turning back to the young Realm Knight who was staring open-mouthed at Lady Cassandra, I said, "Let's go hold up somewhere and talk, before little Miss Iron Dragon here adds on any more conditions."

Darlene and Franklin followed us out. Franklin was still chuckling.

"Oh, shut up," I said.

Chapter 8

While fun to visit an oracle, making sense of their visions often requires a great deal of interpretation.
-Guide to Avalon, 4th printing.

-Vivian Hampton-

Pioneer School

Wanda and I were late for our next class, English composition, but so was just about everyone else. Entire halls had been blocked for several minutes, then some reopened, so getting to class took a bit of navigating. One difference in the classroom from last year was the small simple printing press at the back of the room. I had never seen an actual one, only pictures. As Wanda and I were looking at it, Jeffery came in with Reg, immediately followed by Mina and Sierra.

Professor Rittlehouse, like last year, let us sit wherever we wanted. So by silent agreement, all the sophomores who were taking the class sat near the front while all the freshmen were at the back. On each desk were three books; I was excited to see that one of them was *The Tears of Avalon*. The other two were textbooks of classical literature.

As other students filed in, Professor Rittlehouse chatted with us and asked how we were doing while introducing himself to the freshmen and making sure he was pronouncing their names correctly. He had been an easy-going, likable professor last year.

From the way he was talking, he was taking the same approach this year.

Fifteen minutes later, he waved at the door, and it closed. "I am sure other professors have said this already, but it bears repeating. We don't expect all the freshmen to be able to read well when they first start. Our door is open during study periods and after dinner for any who want. Please, stop by."

"Each of you has three books. Regardless if you are a freshman or a sophomore, you will be reading them. For the first week, sophomores are going to take turns reading out loud, while the freshmen follow along." He pointed to Wanda. "Ms. Hine, your enthusiasm has served us well in this class. Please step up and read the first poem from *The Tears of Avalon*. Then we're going to discuss what each of you think it means."

Wanda popped up and walked to the podium.

It was fun to watch her read the poem. It was a long one, and she was very animated and obviously enjoyed acting out the parts. She even got some laughs.

Then I sucked in my breath. The room faded away to be replaced with a wooden entranceway. Where did the classroom go? I tried to move, but it was like my mind was disconnected from my body. Did someone shoot me with a spell ball of some kind? I didn't know of any kind of spell that could do this.

At the edge of my field of vision, I watched a man walk right through me. It felt for all the world like my insides were being tugged at and my field of vision moved forward with this man. Scared, I tried to get his attention, but nothing I did seemed to make him notice I was here.

He stopped in front of a low counter. Behind it was Wanda! But this wasn't the Wanda I knew. She was a bit older, very pregnant, and there were two small children in a crib behind her. How could she be this pregnant when the younger of the two was less than a year old? What was more distressing was the absence of her inner light. Wanda's voice and movements were almost mechanical. Not cold, but she wasn't trying to make a connection either. Greetings done, she had the man sign a ledger, then handed over a key. As the man turned away, whatever this was began to disintegrate around me, and suddenly, I was back in the classroom. Almost no time had passed; no one seemed to notice anything odd. Everyone was looking at Wanda reading out the poem. The only difference was that I was gripping my desk.

What just happened?

Mina leaned over and nudged me, "Are you okay?" she whispered. "You sort of blanked for a second."

I let go of the side of my desk and gave her a weak smile. "Just tired."

I refocused on Wanda as I tried to get some bearings about me. Then the realization of what I just saw hit me. Was that vision of mine about Wanda real? Her future? The Wanda reading to the class was nothing like that vision. A growing despair grew inside me thinking what I just saw could become real, her future. She had so much potential, *has* so much potential, I corrected myself - to be turned into a baby factory, doing a job requiring almost no brain power, day after day? While I fully expected to get married and have children, I hoped Lord Winton expected me to do something that would expand his house. Not something that slowly bled the color of life out of me. Now having met Lady Kiera, I firmly believed I would have some autonomy of who I chose as a partner, and a voice in what I wanted to do.

However, Wanda was the only female of her generation in her family. Once she completed school, that is, hopefully completed school, she would be traded away to the eldest child of a man who owned three small inns.

Suddenly I got it. Her uncle hoped to bring their operation into the Hine house. Wanda would be turned into a baby factory so her children could grow up and manage their own inns. Her uncle was thinking long term, but at the expense of Wanda. She was just a pawn in his plans. To play her part, she would produce child after child as fast as she could until there was nothing left of my henchman.

My henchman. I could feel my anger beginning to simmer that someone thought so little of her. *How dare he!*

My eyes went wide as I felt a presence touch my mind. This was the same woman from the other night. Very powerful. Lady Cassandra said she was the voice of this woman. I still didn't know her name.

<"What you just witnessed was a possible future, Vivian. Additionally, that spelled pebble tossed at you this morning was indicative of an immediate one, think crux point; letting you know reality could go one way or another.">

I bit back my anger. <"So, Wanda is destined to follow that path?">

<"It is one of many futures. Currently the most probable one. Destiny usually doesn't exist. Everyone has free will, but what you saw is the likeliest path your friend will walk down. Think, ruts in reality. However, like anyone, the more Wanda can visualize a different reality, the likelier it will be that she can climb out of her current rut and move to another path.">

<"Did I, well, did I help Wanda when I suggested she get a letter of recommendation for her head of house?">

<"Most likely, a little. Things like this can't be measured, and there is no certainty. Don't treat any vision you get as absolute. The ripples change all the time. Having free will means everyone else has it too. You could get lost trying to see the totality of it. Even I can. My recommendation is to support whom you choose. But it is up to them, indeed anyone, to have the strength and wisdom to make a leap to another path. However, to make a leap comes with risk. No one can escape that, not even me. You cannot have change for free.">

I was silent for a second. <"Ma'am, what is really going on? I mean, why me?">

<"Wanda is almost done reading, so we have only a moment. The visions are because you have the sight. It is tied to the bardic voice. I have no part in what you see or don't see. I am merely acting as a guide. However, as your world expands, it is possible you may see things that may be of interest to me. While I am very powerful and can predict likely futures, it does not mean I see them as you do. If you are willing to share with me, I am willing

to continue being your guide. But fair warning, I am offering guidance only. I cannot reach across and help you without a service being demanded. Talk to Cassandra about it. You are under no obligation whatsoever to continue this arrangement.">

Then she retreated from my mind, and a moment later, Wanda finished the last part of the poem. Multiple feelings were bubbling up inside me. I was glad that I got some understanding of what was happening to me. A small part of me had wondered if something was wrong with my body. I was also happy that I might have helped Wanda at least a little. But if my latest vision had any substance, Wanda was going to need more pushing. Mostly though, I was feeling lost and wished I could talk to someone about this. At that thought, an idea formed in my mind.

Professor Rittlehouse started calling on freshmen to talk about what they thought the poem meant. He was a firm believer that you stood up before you talked. When he got to Samantha, she stood up and blushed. "The poem talks as if Excalibur had a soul, and it was sad Arthur was getting old and had to go to sleep. Could it really talk to people like that?"

She got some cold stares and at least one nasty comment from a sophomore in House Duke. That's when I noticed neither Lord Seth, his henchmen, nor Lord Keith were here. Then I remembered the argument between Lord Seth and Lord Grayson. Had things gone badly for Lord Seth?

Professor Rittlehouse clapped his hands. It was his favorite method to redirect the classroom. "We hold Arthur and Excalibur dear to our hearts. This poem is about how it makes you feel. None of us were alive then. That was over six hundred years ago."

Elaine started to say something, reddened, and stopped.

"Ms. Elaine," said Professor Rittlehouse, "everyone gets a go. Stand up and tell us what your thoughts are."

She reluctantly stood up and gulped. "Well, the new merlin has a staff that can talk into our minds too, so I suppose Excalibur could as well. I think the poem is very beautiful. Did I say something wrong?" she whispered as she sat back down. Everyone was staring at her. The room had gone silent.

Amanda, who was sitting right next to her, asked in wonder, "You met the new merlin? How come you didn't say anything?"

"Well, I was afraid to talk to her, but her staff was very nice. It liked to float around and talk to people."

The reactions across the room ranged from disbelief to wonder.

Professor Rittlehouse looked like he wanted to ask his own question, then clapped his hands again to get our attention. It didn't work, everyone was still focused on Elaine and questions were being thrown at her. Amanda stood up to stand beside Samantha, the two of them flanking Elaine who was looking very flustered. They were sticking together as a team. *Go House Orozco*, I thought to myself.

A Duke freshman snorted. "Really," he sneered. "And, my dad can fly to the moon too. You're nothing but a braggart."

That got some chuckles from his fellow Duke friends.

Professor Rittlehouse clapped his hands louder. He was ignored.

Elaine shot back with, "Well, my wand was made by..."

But whatever she was about to say was drowned out by Professor Rittlehouse's shout. "Everyone sit down, NOW!" The tip of his wand was touching his throat.

All eyes turned to him. I had never seen such fierce intensity from the professor before. He was always so laid back.

Once seats were taken again, he smiled at us and lowered his wand. "A good poem will touch the emotions within us. Love, excitement, fear, sadness, and other equally important feelings. It's important to feel them, but it's equally important not to be carried away by them." Professor Rittlehouse glanced at me. "Being from a family of Bards, Ms. Vivian can probably recite countless stories and songs of what happens when one lets their emotions consume them. It always ends in disaster. One of the most famous being Romeo and Juliet."

I bit my lip and nodded.

The professor picked up two piles of papers from his desk and gave us a small bow. "To help calm everyone down, let's talk about homework."

That got the expected groans.

"These are for the freshmen," he said and asked the sophomores to pass them backwards. "And these," he said with a smile, "are for the rest of you."

Then the professor held up *The Tears of Avalon*. "Freshmen. On page nineteen, you will find a copy of a letter written by one of Sir Gawain's children to Arthur. It's very basic, the best understanding we have is that the child was nine at the time. The paper which was just passed to you is the exact same letter." He pointed to a Coley freshman and said, "Please tap the first letter of the first sentence on the paper."

He did, and we could all hear the first sentence of the letter. It was monotone but understandable. "The magic imbued in the paper will only last a day or two. Your homework assignment is to practice writing out the same letter, then write a second one, changing it any way you want. This assignment is due in two days."

The expected groans occurred. The professor let it go on for a few seconds.

Wanda whispered to me, "Here it comes."

"Sophomores, your homework assignment is to read the last letter in the same book. I want at least two pages which detail your interpretation of the letter. This includes how it makes you feel and what memories it strikes up in you. Due tomorrow."

Wanda banged her head on the table. Jeffery, Ken, and some of the other sophomore boys groaned. Discuss feelings. I bet they would rather be in a duel to the death.

Ignoring Wanda and the continued groans, he pointed to the small printing press. "Now, for the extra credit assignments," said

Professor Rittenhouse with enthusiasm. "This project goes through the semester. That machine in the back is a simple printing press with very few moving parts, so it should have no issue functioning. Your goal is to experiment with the ink. Could a different infusion of magic create a better talking paper or even a moving picture? The Avalon newspaper guild is sponsoring this. For anyone who wants to consider putting together a team, please pick up an entry pamphlet from my desk which lists out all the rules."

The professor looked up at the clock. "Since we don't have enough time to go over the next readings, the next ten minutes are yours, then head to lunch."

Elaine was mobbed. To control the questions, Samantha and Amanda stepped in to manage the crowd.

Wanda grinned at me. "I bet it's true considering where she's from. I read an article saying that Lady Cassandra and the new merlin were in that area helping about six weeks ago. Wouldn't it be amazing if the new merlin came here to say hi?"

"It certainly would," I said absently.

Looking over at Elaine again, it was interesting watching Samantha and Amanda manage the torrent of questions directed at Elaine. With her friends helping her, Elaine was doing a good job of staying calm. Samantha and Amanda might have a run for their money over who would be the freshman head girl.

Wanda asked, "What does it feel like not being the center of attention?"

"Surprisingly nice." To change the topic, I added, "We do need to get the freshmen and sophomores together to talk about the competition in eight weeks. When and where do you want to have it?" I thought it unlikely the mining guild would certify any of the shafts as safe anytime soon.

Wanda pulled Sierra over. They had a quick discussion, then both turned to me and smiled.

Uh-oh.

Chapter 9

Keeping someone else's secrets is the mark of a good friend.
-Lady Gawain.

-Vivian Hampton-

Pioneer School

Sierra paused right before passing through the entrance to the main hall. A translucent shimmering field filled the opening that hadn't been there this morning. When students in front of us passed through it that had been glowing from the headmistresses' spell, there was a brief pulse of energy and the glowing faded.

Mina teased her, "I can ask Landon to hold your hand."

Sierra gave her a dark look and stomped through. Heads turned her way as the spell, which made everything glow on her, came apart with a flash. Sierra seemed surprised at the sudden applause from those already at the House Orozco table; instead of her normal glower, she curtsied. Will wonders never cease.

Wanda handed me her backpack and bent her fingers backwards. Uh-oh.

"What are you..." I asked, but Wanda had already started running forward. Right before hitting the shimmering field, she dove forward, hit the ground with her hands and did some kind of handspring while spinning in the air. The spell on her blew apart as her body touched the field making little dots of energy expand out from her for a second. Wanda finished it all off by landing on her feet.

There was a moment of silence from those in the main hall. Then thunderous applause. Even a few people from House Thama began clapping. Quade, from the Duke table stood up, probably to applaud as well but was pulled down by the two sitting next to him.

I just smiled and walked through the field carrying my backpack plus Wanda's. A few "Snowball Queens" came my way, but it was Wanda they cared about right now. I just took my seat and watched as a few boys came up to talk to her. *Go Wanda,* I thought to myself as I sat down next to Mina.

♪♪♪

Over lunch, Wanda leaned toward me and held up two fingers. "I took your advice. Dancing lessons."

Sierra nudged herself away from Wanda while grumbling, "You're heading toward the dark side."

Wanda ignored her and asked me, "Do you think Professor Malton could teach you that spell the headmistress used this morning? I would look really cool during gymnastics if I could glow like that when I was on the beam."

"Um, what happens if someone tags you in midjump with the second part of the spell?" I suggested. "Wouldn't you freeze in place?"

"Good point," said Wanda while craning her head to look over at the Thama's table. "We could try experimenting on Alton until we got it right. Who knows," she said hopefully, "maybe we can turn him into a bug."

Mina giggled, but I didn't take the bait. There was no love lost between Alton and Wanda.

"Some good news," declared Wanda, still craning her head. "Bug number two and Lord Keith aren't here."

I followed Wanda's gaze. She was right. And, neither was Lord Seth or his henchman.

While selecting food for my plate, I glanced at Jeffery. He was erasing a few words from a letter he was composing. Reg was next to him, talking out the side of mouth while eating. "Tell him you're going to ace your classes and can handle the distraction."

Jeffery bit into a sandwich. "I don't think he understands what ace means, how about class leader?"

Reg nudged him. "Good idea. Makes it sound like you're the head student without being one."

I was about to ask them who they were writing to when Lord Thomas and Nathan came over. "Got your letter," Nathan whispered to Wanda. "We got Professor Malton and Professor Holtin to give you the basement spell chamber every Tuesday and Thursday evening for the next seven weeks so the sophomores can practice with the freshmen."

Professor Holtin was the head of House Coley. She was an older woman who used to be a Realm Knight in her time. She had retired from that job some ten years ago to work here.

Mina leaned over and kissed Lord Thomas. "I hear a but coming."

Nathan's face darkened. "Yea, well, Professor Vermis is allowing Duke to use it every Monday and Wednesday. I bet they're going to leave spell snoopers all over the place to spy on us."

Wanda grinned. "Or we spy on them instead."

"Beat them at their own game," said Nathan. "I like it." Then he cocked his head. "I heard a rumor you're working for Lord Grayson."

Sierra and Mina stared at Wanda. From the other side of the table Reg said, "What? But he's from House Duke."

"He's a reserve Realm Knight," shot back Wanda. "He's not allowed to show favoritism."

Wow, Wanda was willing to defend him. I wondered if she was taking my idea to heart—of asking him to sign a letter of recommendation for her head of house.

Lord Thomas looked dubious. "Once a Duke, always a Duke," he intoned deadpan. "Better be careful. He might be trying to spy on us."

Wanda looked like she was about to make a snarky remark.

"I trust him," I said, jumping in. "Give Wanda a chance. Who knows? He might decide to help us."

"That will be the day," I heard from Jeffery.

Wanda stuck her tongue out at him. "Vivian believes in me. You're her wanna-be boyfriend. It's your job to support me."

There was a short silence. Okay, Wanda was really pushing back.

"Let us know if you need to be rescued," said Lord Thomas and gave Mina a kiss on the top of her head. "Good Luck."

After the two of them left, Sierra turned to look Wanda up and down like she was suddenly diseased. "You're serious," she said incredulously. "He's a *boy*, a senior, a lord, and a reserve Realm Knight." She enunciated "boy" like Wanda had stepped in something nasty.

"Don't forget good looking," grinned Mina.

"I heard that," laughed out Lord Thomas just before sitting down at Coley's house table.

"If you kiss him," declared Sierra, "you'll have boy cooties forever. I hear they never wash out."

Reg rolled his eyes. Jeffery went back to working on his letter.

As I ate, I started on more of my homework. Time management saved me last year, and I was going to need every drop of it this year. After chatting with a few others, Wanda did the same. About ten minutes in, she nudged me. "We're getting served seconds before House Duke again. I bet they're angry," she said happily.

Looking up, I could see she was right. I caught the eye of Mr. Walters, the footman I had talked to this morning. He came over and I whispered to him, "I reached out to Camillo. He should be here soon after the sun goes down. You can meet him tonight if you want."

He gave me a quick smile and a small bow. "Thank you, Ms. Vivian. I will pass the word."

Jeffery, Reg and just about every boy up and down our table made a grab for the seconds. I rolled my eyes and went back to my homework.

Hearing the headmistress tapping her wand on the podium, I looked up. So did everyone else.

"I would like to inform you," she said with a hint of a smile, "that my secretary lost a bet to me. She believed ten or fewer students would be frozen by lunchtime. There were seventeen. Since her office was filling up with temporary statues, I decided to end the spell early."

Wanda giggled, then said under her breath, "Too bad Lord Keith wasn't frozen as well." Reg laughed out loud, and a few others joined him.

"I am sure those of you who were caught in the spell this morning are eagerly awaiting to know your punishment. It is to help Professor Vermis and Professor Reece sort through the potion supplies which have arrived from Avalon City. You will report to them at eight this evening."

The headmistress raised her voice to be heard over the groans. "For the seventeen who decided not to heed my warning, please report to Lady Farsh at 8 p.m. The horse stalls need to be cleaned, scrubbed, and fresh hay laid down."

A freshman from House Thama raised his hand. "Does this include the freshmen too?" he asked incredulously.

"I am sure you meant to say, does this include the freshmen too, *Headmistress*, Lord Andrew," she said looking down from her podium.

The young man gulped. "Yes, Ma'am, that's what I meant to say."

"Excellent then, Lord Andrew. I imagine you will learn a new skill tonight—how to work with others to get a job done."

"Now, on to the next part of the day. Freshmen, if you brought a wand, representatives from the Wandmaker's Guild will be in your magic class to identify and register it. For those that don't have one, if you have any magical talent, a beginner's wand will be assigned to you based on your affinity. All testing is done by a certified Wandmaking Guild master. Sophomores will be evaluated as well. If the Wandmaker's Guild believes a better wand is warranted based upon your growth, one will be provided."

She held up her hand. "Juniors and seniors, if you believe you should be re-evaluated for a better wand, please ask your head of house if they agree testing is warranted. Now, Professor Lessnara would like to make a few announcements."

The short, older woman walked up to the podium. "I will be running the scavenger hunt in eight weeks to settle the tie between the Duke and Orozco sophomores. Any freshmen who wish to participate may, but they must have a signed letter from their parent, sponsor, or guardian to do so."

She leaned forward slightly. "While I am sure there are some who hope to see fights in the streets, knowledge, intelligence, intuition, and planning will win the day. The headmistress and I will be keeping track of all the students. Some of the items we are asking you to locate will have simple magical traps near them. If a student gets tagged by one, they will be frozen for ten minutes. Then, they will be able to rejoin the game."

Hands shot in the air across the hall. Professor Lessnara ignored them all. "Six weeks from now, the official rules will be posted. Moving on, there are some who are not able to be with us today because of family emergencies."

"Mr. Anton, Lord Grayson's henchman, had his head of house pass away and will be with his family for the funeral, then transfer of power. We hope his new head of house will allow the young man the opportunity to complete his senior year. Also missing are Lord Seth and his henchmen along with Lord Keith and his henchman. All four families are being audited by the council. I am sure each house will pass without incident. Any letters of encouragement you wish to send will be delivered by the school free of charge."

"Yeah, a cursed one," Reg murmured under his breath.

Professor Malton made a shushing motion to Reg.

"The final announcement is to ask you to please introduce yourself to Lady Bell. She is a transfer student from Notir University. Her family had to make some financial adjustments but wanted her to finish school and graduate. To fill a missing gap, she has been placed in House Thama."

Lady Bell briefly stood and curtsied to all of us and sat back down. She looked a bit older than me, very pretty, with black hair done up in the traditional braids. I wasn't certain, but it looked like she was wearing an emerald choker. That had to be expensive. I bet her family came from money.

Reg exclaimed in a low voice, "Wow, you never know..."

But I didn't hear the last part. I was having another vision. The room faded away to be replaced by a forest. Like in my vision before, I couldn't move. Suddenly a large wolf ran by me at tremendous speed; in less than a second it was gone.

And I was back. What in the world?

... "I could show her around town," finished Reg.

Jeremy nudged him. "Never going to happen."

I rolled my eyes. At least Jeremy wasn't drooling over her like Reg. But I secretly wished I had her poise.

Wanda leaned into me. "Reg doesn't stand a chance. I bet she's from serious money."

Amanda and Samantha caught up to Wanda and me in the hallway as we were heading to our next class.

"Do you know where Elaine is from?" asked Amanda, keeping her voice low.

I felt that odd sensation on my shoulder again.

I looked at all the people in the hall. "Let's go find a corner," I suggested. Once we had a bit of privacy, I lowered my voice. "Wanda and I met Lady Cassandra. We do know where she's from. Is there a problem?" Considering the number of people who were trying to chat Elaine up, I was sort of surprised that where she was from wasn't common knowledge by now.

"Elaine is drowning," said Samantha. "Amanda and I are trying to help, but she seems surprised that anyone would think she's important. Apparently, she's the only one in her family who can read."

That matched up with what Lady Cassandra had told me and Wanda. "I'm still not sure what you're asking me," I said.

Wanda glanced around to make sure we were still alone. "What do you need?" she whispered.

Samantha glanced at Amanda. "Well?"

Amanda took a deep breath and seemed uncomfortable. "When Elaine told me where she was from, I had this odd feeling pushing at me. Not anger, but a desire to, well, put her in her place. I've never felt anything like that before and that's not me."

Samantha bit her lip. "It's real. I watched magic forming around both of them that almost looked like rolling fire. It was weird."

Immediately I had another vision, but this one was just a flash, lasting less than a second. In it, Amanda and Elaine were each surrounded by a sparkling outline of an outraged dragon. Surrounding Elaine was Avalon's dragon, and around Amanda was her head of house, a huge gold and silver dragon, but slimmer than Avalon's. The two swirling energies were preparing to fight each other. Then I had another flash, and the scene changed. This one showed Amanda and Elaine holding hands while standing together on a hill and raising something in triumph. The difference between the two visions was obvious. If Amanda and Elaine didn't support each other, they would battle each other for supremacy. However, if they became friends... well, would that somehow feed back to the actual dragons? I knew what future I preferred, and it didn't involve dragons battling.

Wanda poked me. "Vivian, are you okay?"

I shook my head to clear it. Okay, what did Samantha know? Wanda knew Amanda was a high noble, but she didn't know about the ring. "Samantha," I said, "could you and Wanda give us a minute?"

I was glad Samantha and Amanda were coming to me for guidance. Last year, as freshmen, we had been abandoned by Lord Howard, the then-sophomore head student of Orozco at the time. He didn't come back after doing poorly on his finals, and no one missed him. I vowed I would never abandon anyone like that if I could help it. The freshmen had to try to figure out things for themselves as well. But if they came to me for help, I would offer it.

"Come on," said Wanda. "The big girls need to talk. Let's go over here." And they walked a few feet away.

Turning back to Amanda, I asked, "Does Samantha know you're really a high noble?"

Her mouth opened in astonishment. Well, I guess not.

Her eyes narrowed. "How did you find out? Did my father tell you?" she asked, accusingly.

"No. Neither Wanda nor I will tell anyone either. It's your story. But that annoyed feeling you described likely isn't coming from you but from the ring your head of house gave you."

Amanda crossed her arms. "My half sister gave me this ring. She said it was a gift from my father."

"From your father or from your head of house?" I asked carefully while watching Amanda's face.

"Um, my head–" and she stopped. "What's going on? Do you know my half sister?"

I shook my head. "I think you and your half sister need to talk. It's not my place to say anything. But I bet Elaine has the exact same thing happening to her. She's probably even more confused than you. Please try to be her friend instead of fighting her."

"What is really going on?" demanded Amanda as she twisted the ring on her finger. The longer we talked, the more I could see the high-noble in her rising to the surface. In a few years, she was going to be something to see.

What to say? "Amanda, the only thing that's important right now is that you and Samantha keep on supporting Elaine. Also, do you trust the two of them enough to tell them who you really are?"

"Maybe," she said, looking away. "I want to talk to my father first."

"That's a good answer. I wish my father had stood by me." I bit my lip and made a quick decision. "If you and Elaine want to experiment with what you two sensed, grab Samantha and come find me. I know what it is."

"How come—"

But I shook my head. "We're going to be late for class if we stay here much longer. Talk to your half sister first."

Amanda gave me a frustrated look but nodded and left with Samantha for their next class.

"So?" asked Wanda. "Is Amanda going to spill the beans to Samantha?"

I grinned at Wanda as we fast-walked to our next class. "Oh henchman, your insight is amazing."

Wanda stuck her tongue out at me. Just before we entered the gymnasium, she asked, "What do you think that rolling magic was?"

"I'll tell you later."

Welcome to P.E. This was the class I hated the most. Wanda loved it. It wasn't that I didn't have any balance, rather I still felt like a stranger in my body.

Wanda, as expected, worked with the gymnastics instructor. For the first fifteen minutes, she helped the freshmen on the balance beam, high bar set, and the rest of the equipment. Then, Wanda began practicing with her teammates. I was secretly jealous she had such balance and control but would never say that out loud. That was just who Wanda was, and I was glad she was among friends who shared a common passion. When it was her turn, she jumped off the balance beam with one twist in the air and made her landing.

Go henchwoman.

Me, though... well, I decided to go for fencing. Very quickly, I learned holding a fake sword and mock fighting in a play didn't translate into fighting with one in real life. By the end of the class, I decided that I might be slightly better than horrible.

Chapter 10

We recommend not starting a conversation about wands while visiting Avalon. First, you will quickly discover that many are very passionate about certain wand houses, and the second, the more alcohol imbibed during the discussions, the more likely you will end up in a duel.

-Guide to Avalon, 4th printing.

-Vivian Hampton-
Prittle expansion wing, Pioneer School

Our next class was magic. While walking there, I tapped my sheathed wand—a twelve inch stick of carved hickory. Along its length were carved musical symbols inlaid with silver. Even though it was considered a senior apprentice's wand, I was surprisingly attached to it. It was the most expensive thing I had ever been allowed to have. The school let me borrow it, by way of the Wandmakers Guild. The tuition Lord Winton paid on my behalf covered the insurance for the wand. Without that, well, thirty gold talons is a lot of money. I dreaded to think what the wand I was about to get would cost. Best not to think about it.

The brass plaque on the left side of the double doors to the Prittle expansion wing read: *Dedicated by Randolph Prittle*. He was a well-known Realm Knight who had graduated from our school over eighty years ago. One of his grandsons had died recently in Avalon City fighting a necromancer. The school's flag had been at half-mast for a week to honor the young man. Mina told me our headmistress's mother was his cousin.

Each stone block of the foundation of the large room was rune carved. Eight marble pillars were in one long row supporting an arched ceiling some eighty feet up. Along the rear wall, four sets of glass double doors opened onto a wide, covered, open-air training area with dozens of rings carved into the stone floor. That's where we practiced last year as freshmen. Now as sophomores, I hoped we would be allowed to practice casting magic indoors. The professors insisted that all freshmen must practice their magic outside.

"What's wrong with Ken?" I asked Jeffery. Reg and Franklin were standing next to him, each with a hand on his shoulder. Ken was staring at his wand on the table in front of him. Had he been crying?

Those three were a triumvirate of trouble. Of the three, only Ken could cast magic, but I couldn't tell you who had egged on who last year. Whenever I got called by Professor Malton to hand out punishment, half the time, it was one of these three.

"He's saying goodbye to Goliath," said Jeffery.

I looked at him in surprise.

Mina giggled out. "He named his wand?"

Jeffery blushed. "Sure. I mean, of course."

I had to ask, "Did you name your wand too?"

"Ken's very attached to his wand," said Jeffery without answering my question. "It's a boy thing. You wouldn't understand."

"I bet you named your wand Pectus," teased Sierra.

Jeffery rolled his eyes and went over to his henchmen, who was patting Ken on his shoulder.

Sierra shook her head. "Boys," she said in exasperation.

"Vivian," Mina said slowly. "Look around."

It took me a second. It wasn't just Ken and Jeffery. Other sophomores seemed, well, sad. Maybe it mostly was a boy thing.

Professor Malton came over, Amanda was with him and looking apprehensive. Uh-oh, did she get herself in trouble?

"Ladies," said Professor Malton conversationally, "I need to pull Vivian away. If you don't mind, please help the other teachers while they work with the freshmen."

Wanda raised her eyebrow at that but left with Mina and Sierra.

"Is something wrong, Professor?" I asked, intentionally not looking at Amanda. If she did do something wrong, I would have to administer justice as head sophomore of our house. That felt uncomfortable as she was really a high noble. If Lord Lohort learned about my judgment and disagreed with me, I bet he could make life miserable for Lord Winton. A small part of me hoped Professor Malton would hand out punishment if it was needed. But darn it, I said the words last year and became head freshmen, now head sophomore. Either Amanda would respect that or not.

"Not as such," replied Professor Malton, and I relaxed slightly. "But an unusual financial matter has come up, and we need a decision made. The headmistress should be down in a moment."

Huh? What was he talking about?

"I, well," began Amanda. "Haven't decided if I should tell Samantha and Elaine who I really am yet."

"Okay?" I replied. "Glad you're considering it. What's the financial matter?" Was there a disagreement between her father and her head of house about who should pay the school's tuition. If so, why was I involved?

Amanda blushed. "I just learned the wandmaker guild representatives must certify any wand a student brings with them to school. If they don't, I'm not allowed to use it while on school grounds."

Still confused, I said. "So?" Mina's parents had bought her a wand before she came here last year, and she had gotten it certified. I shrugged and turned toward Professor Malton. "Doesn't everyone who brings a wand to school have to get it certified?" I was vaguely aware it had something to do with the school insurance policy. While I didn't come to school with a wand, I watched members of the wandmaker's guild examine and certify every wand a freshman brought with them last year. From the looks of it, they were going to do the same this year as well.

When someone started talking about their wand and which house made it, invariably it would kick off a heated discussion about who had the better wand. If there was one thing Avalon cared about, it was wands. However, just about everyone agreed on two things: the Darci Wand House made the second-best wands out there, and the Retorian House made the best. From what anyone knew, nobody in the school's history ever owned such expensive wands. Currently, there are about twenty or so active wand houses. But I didn't know the names of all of them.

Professor Malton coughed. "You are correct. However, the school insurance can't cover Lady Amanda's wand."

Amanda nervously rolled her wand between her palms. "I don't want the guild to certify my wand where others can see it."

"Amazingly lost," I said as the headmistress came into view. "How are those two connected?"

Amanda blushed and held up her wand so I could see the house marking. "Dad got it for me as a present after the courts elevated me. It's a Darci wand."

Oh. My mouth hung open in astonishment.

I think I blinked. "You want my opinion if Amanda is responsible enough to have her wand at the school?" I said incredulously.

The headmistress had escorted Professor Malton, Amanda, me, and an older Realm Sorceress into a small office. Her nameplate read Bardot and from the width of the gold trim on her collar, I thought she was a senior Realm Knight. Once inside, the Realm Sorceress cast a complicated spell whereupon a large translucent bubble of energy surrounded us. Then she introduced herself as Realm Sorceress Commander Bardot. Even Amanda seemed nervous being next to this imposing woman. It made me feel like I was standing in the headmistress's office and being glared at, even though I hadn't done anything wrong. I hoped. Then her question made my jaw drop.

Realm Sorceress Bardot smiled briefly. "Legally, you took an oath when you accepted the position as head student last year. You are an officer of the school. Think 'voice,' admittedly a junior one, but recognized as such by the school's board. Since Lady Amanda is in your house, your vote counts. If either yourself, Professor Malton, or the headmistress don't think Lady Amanda is responsible enough to have her wand on the school's grounds, I won't sign off on the insurance clause."

Oh. I never really thought of myself as, well, an officer of the school. But I did take the oath. Moreover, now I understood Amanda's concern. If Samantha or Elaine learned she had a Darci wand, they would put two and two together. Well, Samantha might, I doubted Elaine would understand the significance. There was no way Amanda Thorol could afford such a wand, but High Lady Amanda Lohort was another matter.

I had to calm myself down at the enormity of the question. I doubted if Lord Winton could afford a Darci wand. "If I said yes," I cautiously asked, "and something happened to the wand, would Lord Winton be financially responsible for it?" While I thought Amanda was responsible, I didn't want my benefactor to be on the hook for an enormous sum of money.

"Not at all," replied Realm Sorceress Bardot immediately. "The decision ultimately falls on my shoulders. However, if something did happen to the wand, the headmistress would have to answer to the board of directors, and I would expect the school's insurance premiums to go up significantly. Your voice in this is about Lady Amanda's character only."

Amanda gave me a pleading look. It was an odd feeling knowing that I had power over her. I bet there was a little devil just waiting to whisper in my ear about how much of an advantage I could demand from Amada before saying yes. Personally, I wondered if Lord Seth and some others did that, making sure they received as much as they could, either for themselves or their house, before agreeing to anything. I pondered that thought. Would Lord Winton want me to do that? Would I? Just thinking about it in those terms made me feel a bit ill. If I kept on down that rabbit hole, it might be hard to get out. The only important thing to me was that Amanda was trying to help Elaine instead of pushing her away.

"I think Amanda is responsible enough," I said to the Realm Sorceress. "But Amanda, you can't hide the maker of your wand for long. The moment you pull it out and someone who knows gets a good look at the symbol, everyone's going to know it's a Darci wand."

Amanda bit her lip. "I know. But I want another day or so. I've already contacted my father. He and my half sister are coming here to talk to me. I don't want to tell my friends until I do that."

That made sense to me, and I was glad she was taking my suggestion to heart. Reminder to self, don't tell Wanda that Lady Julia Lohort might be stopping by. If I did, she would probably try to do something absurd to meet her.

Realm Sorceress Bardot pointedly looked at Professor Malton. He bowed slightly. "I agree with Vivian. Lady Amanda is responsible enough to have it. I dare say her father would be a might annoyed if she lost it."

That left just the headmistress. She nodded her head slightly. "I agree."

Amanda let out her breath. "Thank you."

"I will countersign the insurance rider," said the Realm Sorceress. "Let me see it, so I can certify it."

After Amanda handed her wand over, the Realm Sorceress studied the wand from several angles. Then she cast a spell on the engraved signature. Immediately the Darci house symbol appeared in the air above the wand with a string of symbols underneath it. Then the symbols faded away.

I was curious. "Nobody did that last year to my wand. What were those symbols?"

Commander Bardot smiled briefly and handed Amanda her wand back but addressed me. "No one is going to encode magical cyphers into a beginner's wand." Then turning to Amanda, she added, "I certify your wand is a Darci wand, young lady. You don't need to present it to the guild members out there."

Amanda breathed a sigh of relief.

Commander Bardot almost smiled. "You might have the most expensive wand this school has ever seen."

Almost under her breath, the headmistress mused, "I can't wait for the subject to come up at the next board of directors' meeting." Then she suddenly smiled while looking at Professor Malton. "John, it's about time you had a turn talking to them. Besides, this young lady is in your house after all."

He was about to reply but was stopped by Amanda's sudden interjection, "Ma'am, that might not be correct."

We all turned to her.

"What do you mean, young lady?" said Commander Bardot sharply. "I doubt if anyone has a Retorian wand out there."

Amanda blushed slightly at the sudden scrutiny, then bit her lip as if she was deciding if she should add anything to her statement. "Well," she gulped. "Elaine's wand is likely more valuable than a Retorian wand. She told me it was made by…"

But whatever she was about to say was cut off by the urgent knocking. Realm Sorceress Bardot dropped the bubble of energy around us and opened the door. "What's the problem?" she asked of the Realm Knight who was standing there.

"Lord Ninebart, the representative for the Wandmaker's Guild, is a bit upset. I think the headmistress needs to take over."

I just assumed the headmistress wanted me and Amanda to follow her. As we neared the back of the room where all the tables had been set up, we could hear the shouting. "If you try to take her wand again, I will hog tie you!"

There was only one person with that unusual twang. Samantha was annoyed.

Like last year, the tables were stacked with books. I knew what they were—the history and registry of wands. Every year, wand manufacturers would publish the wands they built. Some wand houses went back thousands of years. My wand was made about twenty years ago by Crescent Pomodo. I even got to meet her when we visited the Pomodo shop in Avalon City on a field trip.

Near the tables were large wooden cases which had been brought in from Avalon City escorted by a platoon of guards. Six Realm Knights were guarding them. Inside these cases were wands. My wand would probably either end up back in one of the cases, or I hoped, be passed down to one of the new freshmen. All the Realm Knights were paying attention to the shouting but seemed reluctant to leave their posts.

Amanda groaned out. "I should have warned her."

"Warned who about what, young lady?" asked the headmistress as we turned the corner and stopped. A crowd of people were surrounding a round table. On one side sat Elaine, looking very afraid. Standing right next to her was Samantha, obviously annoyed. She was leaning forward with both hands on the table and glaring at the old man across from her. Flanking him were three thinner men who, if anything, looked older if that was possible.

"I can wrestle a calf to the ground in ten seconds," she growled out. "Try taking her wand again, and I'll kick your chair out from underneath you."

As she talked, Samantha's twang got worse. But something else caught my attention as well: Wanda. She was bouncing up and down while repeating what sounded like S.M.M.C. over and over again. I don't think I had ever seen her this excited before.

"Lord Ninebart, what seems to be the problem?" As all eyes turned toward the headmistress, Amanda pushed her way through the crowd to stand on the other side of Elaine. Well, I guess Amanda and Samantha were taking my plea to heart. They were defending Elaine.

The man stood up. Okay, he was even older than I thought. It looked like a breeze might blow him over. He pointed to Elaine's wand while wheezing out, "This wand is from an unregistered house, Headmistress. The Wandmaker's Guild cannot certify it. It must be confiscated."

Elaine snatched her wand back and held it protectively against her chest. "My lady made it for me. You can't have it."

My lady? Then it dawned on me who she likely meant. Her benefactor, Lady Cassandra Altum. The rumors suggested she knew how to make wands.

The headmistress walked over to Elaine. "Young lady, why don't you and your two friends go for a walk with Professor Malton? Let me handle this." Then turning to Wanda, she sighed. "Ms. Hine, while we all appreciate your enthusiasm, please stop bouncing up and down. Go with Professor Malton."

"But Headmistress," protested Wanda. "S.M.M.C.," she said and bounced again.

"Now."

Wanda grumbled but turned to leave. I was about to go with her when the headmistress indicated I should stay. Okay, why?

The headmistress sat down where Elaine had been. "Sit down, Lord Ninebart." Her voice was very cold. Like Amanda had done, Realm Sorceress Bardot stood to the left of the headmistress and crossed her arms.

"That young lady—" began Lord Ninebart.

"Ms. Elaine Haylen," corrected the headmistress. "Whose wand you just threatened to take, is a student in my school."

One of the three behind Lord Ninebart urgently whispered to him. Lord Ninebart reluctantly sat down. "Fine," he wheezed out. "Ms. Elaine Haylen's wand is not from a registered house.

Therefore," he said and thumped his wrinkled hand on the table in satisfaction. "The Wandmaker's Guild cannot certify it."

"Does the wand have a maker's symbol?" asked the headmistress.

Lord Ninebart swung the large book in front of him around. On the left were hand drawn symbols, then the name of the wandmaker's house. "S. M. C," he said. "Obviously sloppy work, there's a two above the M. Who knows what an unregistered wand could do?"

A memory bubbled up in the back of my mind. Listening to Wanda as she happily talked to me about nobles and other people who had caught her attention.

A lot of the information had just gone in one ear and out the other. But not this. Besides, she was jumping up and down just a moment ago and repeating S.M.M.C. "Um, sir? Lord Ninebart?" I said taking a step forward. "That's not a misprint, sir. I believe it's meant to read S, then M squared, then C."

"Who is this young lady?" demanded Lord Ninebart. "Is she our culprit?" His tone implied I was the wandmaking criminal who should be arrested now.

I bit my lip and looked at the headmistress for help. I still didn't know why she wanted me here.

"Go ahead, Ms. Hampton," said the headmistress, while keeping her gaze firmly fixed on the old man across the table. "I believe I know where you are going with this and devoutly wished Lady Cassandra had mentioned it to me."

At the mention of Lady Cassandra, one of the three men standing behind Lord Ninebart opened his mouth in astonishment. I bet he just got it.

I swallowed. "Well, sir, S.M.M.C is short for the Sunshine Mystery Magic Club. It's the club the new merlin set up." Then looking at the headmistress, I added, "Lady Cassandra Altum, Sorcerer Petotum's apprentice, is said to be a club member as well. For all we know, the new merlin helped to make that wand."

Lord Ninebart looked stunned. The man who had opened his mouth, closed it. He reached down to swing the book around, then stammered out, "Merlin's tooth! She's right."

The headmistress leaned forward. "Now, Lord Ninebart," she said flatly. "You have one of three options. I can contact the Council for you. Second, I know someone who can get a message to the new merlin, whereupon *you* can tell her she isn't allowed to make any more wands. Or, if you're very polite and apologize to Ms. Elaine Haylen, maybe she will allow you to examine her wand."

The headmistress leaned forward a bit more. "Choose carefully."

Realm Sorceress Bardot snorted. "There's a fourth one. He could challenge the new merlin to a duel."

Chapter 11

Annoying a known witch is a very bad idea.
-Guide to Avalon, 4th printing.

-Vivian Hampton-

Prittle expansion wing, Pioneer School

My wand was on the table right in front of me. I wanted to snatch it back and clutch it to my chest just like Elaine had done. Mrs. Brandysmith, a nice older lady with the Wandmaker's Guild, was having me try out other wands. I felt squeamish. As if I was cheating in front of my old wand.

Wanda leaned over and touched the second wand of the four Mrs. Brandysmith had brought out.

"That one is made by House Beret, young lady," smiled Mrs. Brandysmith. "Their house is only a few hundred years old, but they have a good following at the street level. Nothing like Darci of course, but some very good street sorcerers use Beret wands."

The wand in question was made from birch and didn't have any musical symbols engraved in it. Just the Beret family symbol—that of three ovals superimposed on each other.

As my queasiness increased, I wondered how Ken and Jeffery were doing. I bet Ken had tears trickling down his face. Jeffery, well, I didn't know, but he seemed to like his wand. He had even let me try it out on occasion.

I could imagine my old wand whispering to me in a pleading voice, "Don't leave me."

I wanted to run out of the room and throw up.

"It's okay, young lady," said Mrs. Brandysmith soothingly. "I can tell you're sad. Most are when the time comes to say goodbye to their wands."

Wanda sat down and cupped her chin with her hands. "Too bad I can't have your old wand. I could try channeling magic through that link with you."

I turned to stare at Wanda and my sad feeling shifted to excitement. "Wanda, you are amazing."

♪♪♪

Professor Malton sighed. "It is just an experiment, Mr. Rosland."

Mr. Rosland had taken over for Lord Ninebart after he left with the headmistress so he could apologize to Elaine. Word that Elaine had a wand with the new merlin's symbol was spreading through the school like wildfire. I could imagine the reaction Amanda would get if she pulled out her wand and shouted out, "I have a Darci wand."

Now no one would care.

I heard a rumor someone from the Retorian House was sending a representative to the school in hopes of examining Elaine's wand. If true, good luck with that; they would have to get past Amanda and Samantha first. The friendship between the three of them seemed to be strengthening by the hour. I know it wasn't all because of me, but it made me feel good that I might have nudged them that way, just a little. Now, I just needed to keep on nudging Wanda. She was my henchman and very important to me.

"My benefactor is Lord Winton," I said, trying to push the idea along of Wanda having my old wand.

"Your idea is a very unorthodox one," sniffed Mr. Rosland. "However, if the school is willing to provide insurance against the wand, I will allow the young lady to keep it for six weeks."

Wanda let go of the seat she was gripping, jumped up and squeezed me tight while grabbing my old wand. I felt like I was in a vice. Considering this was the third time she hugged me, my waist was probably an inch thinner now. Apparently with Wanda, nudging translated into being squeezed.

"What happens after six weeks?" I asked.

Mr. Rosland handed over three books along with a notebook. All but one had the Wandmaker's Guild symbol on them. "You will follow all guidelines and safety instructions laid out in these guild manuals, young lady. You will write down every experiment, all the methods you used, and all results, be they good, bad, or simply strange."

I tentatively opened the largest book. It was called *Experimental Wand Testing* and was over three hundred pages long.

"Um, sir? But my old wand isn't experimental. I used it over the last year. The Wandmaker's Guild certified it and everything."

Mr. Rosland gave me a flat stare. "Do you want me to agree to this test or not?"

I felt a drowning sensation engulf me.

I looked over at Wanda. Her face was glowing in excitement. I didn't want to disappoint her. "Yes, sir," I sighed. *Where was I going to find the time to read these books*? Then I remembered he hadn't answered my question.

"Sir, six weeks?"

"If Ms. Hine has developed a proficiency with the wand, and you have properly followed the guidelines, Professor Malton and I will talk again. Otherwise, the guild will take the wand back."

Wanda clutched my old wand tightly and gave me a pleading look.

What have I gotten myself into? How come trying to nudge the universe translated into more homework? Sigh. *Put a smile on my face*. Without Wanda, I would be drowning. I owed her a chance to try to make this work.

"Mr. Roseland," I asked, holding up the third book he had given me. "This isn't about wand testing." Or at least I didn't think it was. The book was obviously new, the paper runner sealing the book hadn't even been broken. Across the top of the book in silver lettering was *Training Techniques and Testing Standards for Calling Magic*.

Professor Malton coughed. "It's the headmistress's idea. We were going to talk to you about it earlier, but obviously things went sideways. Get yourself situated with a new wand and we can go over our proposal toward the end of class."

"Okay?" Hopefully, this wouldn't involve more homework on my part.

Well, I could dream.

"Now, Ms. Hampton," said Mrs. Brandysmith while pushing the four wands toward me again. "Let us get you properly equipped with a new wand. Any one of these are considered acceptable to a beginning journeyman. In fact, all of them have been used as such before."

I don't know why, but none of these wands excited me. They were all plain looking. Well, most wands were. After I had cast a few spells through each, I could sense they were all better than my old wand. The runes focused quicker, and I was able to push more energy through them as well. During each test, Mrs. Brandysmith kept a smile on her face while giving me a running commentary about each wand. Which house had made them, and who had owned them before. She was a walking encyclopedia of wands.

"Ma'am," I asked hesitantly. "Am I allowed to look through the case?"

She had pulled out the four wands from a wheeled case, which one of the Realm Knights had pushed over. While the front was open, I could see there were about fifteen other wands inside. Once Mrs. Brandywine had pulled out these four, the Realm Knight had closed it again.

She hesitated for a second, then nodded at the Realm Knight. He moved a silver engraved wooden disk over the front and with my Sight, I saw magic pull back. A second later, there was an audible click.

"You're not allowed to reach in and touch any of them," warned the Realm Knight. "If you want to try one, only someone from the Wandmaker's Guild may pull them out."

"Yes, sir," I said.

"What happens if we try to take one?" blurted out Wanda in excitement.

"I arrest you," the Realm Knight said bluntly. From his tone, I could tell he wasn't kidding.

"Wanda!" I said, admonishing her. "Leave him alone."

Squatting down in front of the case, I made sure I didn't reach into it. I could see incredible magic traps woven into the wood; traps so complex that I had no idea what they did. More importantly, I didn't want the case to bite my hand off—or worse.

While mentally trying to reach out to that sensation I felt over the last day, I looked from wand to wand. There were sixteen of them. On the fourth one down, I got a twinge and a brief vision of me being blown backwards and landing in mud.

Okay, not that wand.

At the ninth one down, I got another vision. I was having a spell fight with a girl from House Thama, but I couldn't make out her features. It was like parts of her body were occluded. What was even stranger, it looked like her shadow was that of a wolf. This was the third time today I had a vision about a wolf. Was there a connection? Each vision was very brief. But one thing was certain, that positive feeling I was getting from this wand increased. So, maybe?

As my eyes moved to the last wand, I felt that same prickling sensation on the back of my shoulder again. I turned to Mrs. Brandysmith and pointed at that wand. "Can I try that one?"

"I'm sorry, dear," she said. "That one is for demonstration purposes only. It has a core."

I tilted my head, "Sorry, a core?" I didn't know what she was talking about.

The Realm Knight standing next to the case grinned. "Meaning, it can't be purchased."

"Oh. But I don't want to buy it, just use it while I'm at school. Are there rules against that?"

The smile fell off Mrs. Brandysmith's face. "Dear, I'm sorry. But your school doesn't have that kind of insurance. Why don't you pick another wand?"

I was about to tell her Amanda had a Darci wand, and Elaine had a wand likely made by the new merlin and stopped. *Vivian Hampton*, I thought to myself. Lord Winton was my benefactor. I hoped he would fund the expense to help Camillo, and I didn't want to push my luck asking for a wand that would likely cost a fortune. If it was either a wand or Camillo, Camillo won. Vivian Hampton stood by her friends.

"Okay," and I pointed to the ninth one from the top. "That darker wand with gold runes engraved into it. Can I try it?"

Mrs. Brandysmith held a forced smile. "Of course, my dear. But it's a very temperamental wand."

I wasn't sure what she meant by that, but that good feeling grew stronger as she pulled out the wand and handed it to me.

Wordlessly, I moved to one of the spell circles about the place, charged it, and slowly took a deep breath. Letting it out, I imagined the runes around the wand for the spell I wanted to cast. They formed quickly, and I cast the spell. It worked perfectly. Where the other wands she had me try were good, the spell structures I imagined were almost pulled into this wand even as I thought about them. Wow, I had never felt anything like that before. Deciding to push it a bit, I focused more energy into the runes I was imagining. Then, held them in place for a bit as I infused them with more energy before casting the spell. My spell shot from my wand impacting the spell circle. Cracks appeared in the air around the spell circle where my spell impacted. I guess I should use a stronger circle next time. Glancing down, I noticed the golden runes engraved into the wand had shifted a bit. *What did that mean?*

Mrs. Brandysmith chuckled. "Well, the wand certainly agrees with you, Ms. Hampton. But you will need to have Professor Malton's permission before you can have it."

I tilted my head in thought. Something was missing. On all the other wands I tried, Mrs. Brandysmith happily kept up a running commentary about them. Her only comment about this wand had been that it was temperamental.

"Ma'am," I asked. "Who is the maker?"

"Let's talk to Professor Malton first."

"Okay?"

"Technically, your school's insurance can cover this wand," Mrs. Brandysmith said to Professor Malton. "But it wouldn't surprise me if Ms. Hampton needs to exchange the wand within the month."

"You said it was temperamental," said Professor Malton. "Why?"

Mrs. Brandysmith chuckled. "Nothing horrible. It's not cursed, if that's your concern. Just, it's rather unique."

After flipping through one of the more recent history books on wands, Mrs. Brandysmith looked up. "Here it is. The wand was originally commissioned as a bet. Apparently, someone ticked off a witch, not a good way to start one's day. Anyway, Scarlett Lister, the witch, teamed up with Luna Pomodo to create this wand, and they won the bet. My understanding is that this wand is partially enchanted."

I was entranced. "What was the bet about?"

Wanda peered at my wand. "Probably something horrible," she said excitedly.

Mrs. Brandysmith chuckled again. "I have no idea. It's not listed in any of the books. Anyway, the wand was put up for sale through the Pomodo shop and carries their family symbol. But no one bought it. So, it's been passed around for the last thirty-odd years from student to student in the loaner program."

"Well, I like it," I said.

"Is either of the two ladies still alive?" asked Professor Malton.

"Luna Pomodo is, but she's rather old now. I have no idea about Lady Lister. But the family has become a bit more well-known of late because of—"

"Lady Sebine Lister!" said Wanda with enthusiasm. "She's Lady Gawain's right hand. I bet Lady Sebine's great aunt is the witch who made the wand." She turned to me. "You have to keep this wand."

"Wanda, it's not really mine."

Professor Malton contemplated me for a second, then eyed Mrs. Brandywine. "If Vivian decides she needs a different wand, is there any cost to exchange it?"

"If you have her come to Avalon City, none. If you want us to pay for the Realm Knight's time to bring additional wands up here for her to try, quite a bit."

Wanda was jumping up and down.

"Professor Malton," I asked. "I would like to try it."

He sighed and nodded.

After Mrs. Brandywine left to help another student, I asked Wanda to check up on the freshmen—specifically Elaine and her friends. "Please remind Samantha to, well... not threaten anyone from the Wandmaker's Guild again."

Wanda snorted and rolled her eyes but left at my behest. This left me alone with Professor Malton. "Sir, would there be some time I could talk to you privately?"

"There is. May I know the nature of the conversation so I can be prepared?"

"Yes, sir, well..." and I gave him a short summary of what the lady said to me and the odd pulses I was feeling now and then. I knew he wasn't my father, but Professor Malton felt like he was somewhat taking on that role. He was always so understanding, patient, and never turned me away.

He was silent for a few seconds. "You should be aware that the headmistress is quite annoyed with Lady Cassandra right now. Whomever she is the voice of, she didn't consult with the headmistress prior to contacting you. To make matters worse, Lady Cassandra's tactful omission about Elaine's wand has just increased the headmistress's frustration."

"Oh." My stomach flopped. "Am I in trouble, Professor?"

"No. Just the opposite. Rather, you have to look at it from the headmistress's point of view. She is ultimately responsible for all the students and feels as if this woman has usurped her authority. She is taking her anger out on Lady Cassandra, even though that is likely unfair."

My mouth went dry as I imagined the headmistress and Lady Cassandra squaring off against each other. "What do you need me to do, Professor?" I felt like my world was beginning to crumble. I didn't want the two of them to fight because of me.

"I think at some point, it would be beneficial if you were to ask this woman to make an appearance. The headmistress would like to ask her some questions."

"Professor Gass has asked me to stand in the school's main ring tomorrow, to see if a grounding bracelet could be made for this link. I have no idea if she will appear or not."

Professor Malton tilted his head. "I will let the headmistress know. Regarding a time to talk privately, I am available right after dinner."

I bit my lip. "Could we talk while heading to the edge of town? Camillo should be coming down about then."

"It will be my pleasure, Vivian. Now, regarding that third book. The headmistress and I will explain why it was given to you toward the end of class. You are in no way obligated to say yes."

"Okay?" I said.

Chapter 12

Magical dueling is very popular in Avalon.
-Guide to Avalon, 4th Printing

-Vivian Hampton-
Prittle expansion wing, Pioneer School

Ken and Jeffery were circling each other in one of the larger spell circles, those reserved for dueling. Each had their wand out. These two loved to duel, but now they sported new wands. It was like a switch had been thrown. Thirty minutes ago, Ken was practically in tears about giving up his old wand, and now, he was excited and happy about testing his new one out. Meanwhile, I still imagined my old wand was looking at me and feeling sad at being displaced.

Boys are so weird. I don't understand how they can be sad one minute and then happy the next.

It wasn't just those two. Just about every dueling circle was being used, all by boys. Teachers acted as judges, making sure the rules were being followed. There were only about fifteen spells freshmen and sophomores were allowed to use for informal dueling challenges.

The onlookers, mostly other students, were cheering their friends on. Others were holding the money for the various bets. I still found it amazing that the headmistress allowed betting inside the school. There were some rules, including no student could bet more than a copper talon. Some students came from prosperous families. She probably didn't want a student beholden to paying money they didn't have.

I felt obliged to watch Jeffery, so Wanda and I walked over to the dueling circle.

Wanda said happily, "I bet a copper talon on Ken."

"Wanda!" I said with exasperation. "You're betting against my boyfriend. Shame on you."

"Oh, come on." Wanda bounced. "Ken's faster. Besides, Jeffery doesn't have that killer instinct. He's from a family of merchants."

Ouch. But Wanda was right. While Jeffery was obviously enjoying himself, Ken was faster. Two minutes later, Jeffery got sideswiped a third time, and the teacher declared Ken the winner. Both bowed, then shook hands.

"Not bad," said Reg while pounding Jeffery on the back. "You almost had him when you dove to the left."

Ken bowed to his fans and, with a little flourish, pointed his wand in the air. He got some applause and a few giggles from some of the girls watching the fight.

"Anyone?" he asked. "Want to have a go?"

The school's informal rules allowed the winner to compete again if there was a challenger. Samantha stepped forward, twirling her wand between her fingers. "You're not bad. Are freshmen allowed to duel sophomores?"

Professor Malton coughed. "The head student would have to give permission. Since a freshman head student has not been selected yet, that responsibility falls on Vivian for now."

All eyes turned to me.

"I don't mind," I said. "Providing you go over the rules with Samantha and limit yourself to spells you *both* know that are on the approved list."

Samantha and Ken were quickly surrounded. "Okay, rules," said Ken. "This is informal dueling, meaning nothing nasty and either player can bow out at any time. The person who hits their opponent three times with a spell is considered the winner, and shields don't count. Part of the job is to get past a person's shields. Oh, and the last part, you can't bet against yourself or have agents who bet against you."

"Okay, simple enough," remarked Samantha. "I recognized two of the spells you used. What are the others?"

After a quick back-and-forth, it was determined Samantha only knew three of the spells on the approved list. Which didn't surprise me.

Ken cracked his knuckles and winked at her. "So, are we betting?"

"Absolutely," said Samantha with a mocking curtsy. "What's the fun if we don't? But not money. If I win, you take me out on a date."

Ken's mouth fell open in astonishment.

I immediately stepped in. "Not going to happen. You're on Avalon now. You need your head of house's permission before you can officially date someone."

Samantha rolled her eyes. "Fine. A walk through the town this coming weekend. You can show me around."

Ken bowed. "And if I win, you play Spells, Swords, and Dragons with me and my mates."

"Deal," said Samantha.

With my Sight, I could see a faint swirl of magic flow around the two of them. They made a pact and were now bound to honor it.

Ken's grin got wider. "So, you think you can take me?" he said while taking his place in the spell circle.

"I'm not Miss Liquid Lightning, but I can hold my own."

"Sorry?" asked Ken.

"Amanda. She's fast. Way faster than me."

Something in Ken's eyes changed, it was as if he stopped seeing Samantha as just a girl and focused in on his opponent. His shoulders loosened up, and he bent his knees a bit, mostly likely so he could shift quickly if he needed to. Wanda was right, Ken had the makings of a duelist.

I whispered to Wanda, "Are you betting on this one?"

She shook her head. "Samantha is fast, but I have never seen her duel before."

Professor Malton raised his arm. "I will be the judge on this one. If either wants to step out of the ring at any time, they are allowed. That will end the duel. If you hear me blow my whistle, the duel immediately stops. Understand?"

Samantha and Ken nodded, then went back to studying each other intently.

"Go," shouted Professor Malton and stepped out of the ring.

Ken pulled his wand and got off a spell, a shimmering bolt of energy rocketed toward Samantha. I recognized the spell, one of the splatter effects—if it hits you, it leaves a big red donut shaped splotch until it wears off in a few minutes.

Instead of pulling her wand, Samantha dove to the side. Then she ran forward and slid between Ken's legs while pulling her wand in one smooth motion. "Gotcha," she shouted in excitement as she released her spell. She couldn't miss. A big red splotch appeared on Ken's rear end.

Laughter erupted from the onlookers.

Ken's face went red. He spun around and got off a shot. But Samantha rolled away, Ken's spell just missing her by an inch. I had never seen anyone move like that before. Most people just slowly moved around the circle, occasionally turning to the side but not using speed and athletics as a weapon.

To Wanda's point, Ken was fast. Just as Samantha jumped up into a crouch, she got hit by Ken's spell on her leg. Ken tilted his wand upward slightly and smiled. Samantha saluted him with her wand and grinned right back.

I could tell the two of them were having the time of their lives. Samantha was quick on her feet, but Ken could cast spells faster than she could. A minute later, it was two to two. The number of people watching the duel grew. There had to be a good fifty people now.

The freshmen started shouting, "Samantha, Samantha..." While the sophomores chanted, "Ken, Ken..."

I watched as more bets were placed. There had to be upwards of thirty copper talons in that pile.

Ken concentrated, and a decent sized shimmering field appeared right in front of him. It didn't cover his entire body, but it would be hard to get around. He tilted his wand upwards again. "Now we separate the men from the little girls," and cast two spells in quick succession.

Not bad, to hold a shield like that while casting took excellent concentration. Samantha dove to the side, got a much smaller shield up, and got off a spell which collided with Ken's shield. However, she didn't have the training to keep her shield up for long while casting. It flickered, then faded. Ken used that moment to cast another two spells. Samantha twisted sideways, both spells just missed her.

"Not bad," murmured Wanda. "I bet she's going to try out for gymnastics."

Ken's eyes narrowed, and he dropped his shield. Some of the people who had bet on him groaned, but I knew what he was doing. This freed him up to fully concentrate on casting spells. Ken feinted to the right, then dodged left: three spells rocketed toward Samantha. Her eyes went wide, and she got off a spell while twisting away and rolling to the ground. But her accuracy was off, her blue spell was angled wrong and went too high, while Ken's third spell hit her in the arm.

Professor Malton stepped into the ring. "The duel is over. By three to two, Mr. Kenneth Anderson is the winner."

"You almost got me." Ken grinned and offered a hand to Samantha. She took it and jumped to her feet.

"You're going to need to teach me the rules of that dragon game," she said.

"How about later tonight?" He grinned.

I rolled my eyes, then whispered to Wanda, "Let me know if Ken bends the rules and tries to turn it into a private study session," I said. While I trusted Ken, sort of, I remembered back to Jeffery and me holding hands last night and hoping he would kiss me. I got the feeling Samantha could take care of herself, but she was from Earth, a freshman, and liked pushing against the rules. I wanted her to know that she had to follow my rules, which meant Avalon's rules. At that thought, I got a sense of why the headmistress was mad at Lady Cassandra.

"Oh, I'm going to put Sierra on the job," Wanda said gleefully.

Of that I had no doubt. That girl knew how to hide. I could imagine her popping up between Ken and Samantha if they started to snuggle while shouting, "Surprise!"

Ken declined to duel again and gave up the circle to another person. I went over to Jeffery and nudged him with my hip. "How's the new wand?"

He grinned at me. "Great! I can cast faster with it. I can't wait to write to my dad—" then his face fell.

"What's wrong?" I asked.

"I've written a letter to my head of house about you. Dad told me I didn't need the distraction of dating right now. He said our family was counting on me to do well, so our house can be expanded."

"Oh." I felt myself deflate. So that's what Jeffery and Reg were talking about over lunch. It made sense now. I bit my lip and asked, "Do you want me to write him a letter introducing myself?"

Jeffery looked uncertain. "Thanks, but no. Your benefactor is Lord Winton. Gramps would probably think I was going above my station."

I think I blinked. Going above his station? But I'm not titled. There's no "lady" in front of my name. I'm just Vivian Hampton. "Okay," I said, trying not to show my uncertainty. An odd sense of feeling in-between surfaced, like I really didn't belong anywhere. I didn't feel comfortable in my body yet, my family was a mess even though both of my parents seemed to be finding a way of moving forward, redefining themselves. But who was I?

Jeffery must have picked up on my sadness. "It's going to be okay, Vivian," he said and touched my hand. "My grandfather is great. I'm still planning on going out to dinner with you on Friday."

I gave him a smile and remembered back to when we held hands, then Jeffery kissing my fingers and—*Stop it Vivian*, I said to myself. Just a few moments ago, I had to remind Ken and Samantha they had to follow the rules. So did I. But a part of me didn't like having to either. Sometimes it sucks being the head girl.

Jeffery bounded off to talk to some other friends.

Wanda came over and grinned. "So, no kiss?" she teased. "Only winners get a kiss?"

I stuck my tongue out at her. "His dad said no. Jeffery is writing to his head of house to see if he can date me."

Wanda looked like she was about to make a snarky comment when both of us heard Professor Lessnara's voice behind us and turned.

"Hello, Vivian. Has Professor Malton explained why I asked for you?"

The short, older professor had pushed a cart full of books over to the dueling circles, then called me and Wanda over. She was one of the magic teachers for the upperclassmen, so I wasn't sure why she was here right now or wanted to talk to me; the upperclassmen always described her as "tough, but fair." Years ago, the woman had been a well-known duelist, and it was rumored her family owned several dueling clubs in Avalon city. Was that why she was here, to watch the up and comers? A little devil on my shoulder hoped she would recruit Samantha. It would be nice to see the surprised reaction on the boys' faces as they faced off against a young woman; maybe even get beaten by one.

Did it bother me that dueling seemed to be a boys-only club? Maybe, a little.

Putting a smile on my face, I shook my head. "No, ma'am, things got a little hectic."

"As I heard. I'm still waiting my turn to examine Ms. Haylen's wand. However, let's discuss your henchman. You can blame her for your involvement in the offer I am about to propose to you."

"Me?" exclaimed Wanda. "What did I do?"

Professor Lessnara picked up one of the books on the cart and handed it to Wanda. Now that I was next to the cart, I could tell every book was the same: *Training Techniques and Testing Standards for Calling Magic*. The book given to me earlier.

"Ma'am?" asked Wanda.

"Break the paper runner, young lady."

Wanda pulled it off and gasped. At the bottom of the book was the author's name. *High Lady Petra Abara of Gawain*. Then underneath, *volume 0 (pre-publication)*.

Wanda's mouth opened in astonishment.

"Your henchman," said Professor Lessnara with a chuckle, "wrote to Lady Gawain and asked if there was anything she could do to help. Apparently in the same letter, she suggested that her hero, one Vivian Hampton, was the best hero ever."

"Lady Gawain wrote back?" squeaked out Wanda in excitement.

"To the headmistress," replied Professor Lessnara. "She received Lady Gawain's proposal this morning."

"Wanda, what have you done?" I said feeling apprehensive. I knew she wrote to Lady Gawain on occasion and had even received a letter back. But I was sure it had to be from her secretary, not the high lady herself.

"What does she want Vivian to do?" Wanda asked breathlessly. "Whatever it is, the answer is yes."

"Wanda!" I said in exasperation. "You can't volunteer me for something without asking me first."

"But it's Lady Gawain," squeaked out Wanda.

Oh God.

"Ma'am?" I asked Professor Lessnara, "can I say no?"

Wanda hit me on the arm with Lady Gawain's book. "Vivian!"

A hint of a smile touched the edges of the professor's mouth. "Certainly, if that is your wish. However, would you like to hear the proposal first?"

I sighed and took a step away from Wanda. "Yes, Professor." I didn't want to be hit by a book again. That hurt.

"As you probably know, Lady Gawain is in the Great Forest Clan. She wants the clans to follow consistent training standards which lead to levels of certifications. What you are holding is her pre-publication manual. She asked three schools if they would vet her suggestions and provide feedback before final publication. Due to your henchmen's letter, Lady Gawain asked the headmistress if the Pioneer Academy would like to participate in the vetting. Personally, I think it's a good idea and long past due."

I think I blinked. "You want me to run this?" I asked cautiously.

Wanda bounced.

"Not at all, young lady," replied Professor Lessnara. "I will, but I am looking for an assistant."

"But, ma'am, neither Wanda nor I are in a clan. And I still don't understand what you are asking me."

"True, you're not. But you have the bardic voice, which means, in theory, you can call magic too. If the stories are correct, with training, you should be able to call amulet spells and cast as well. You will work with me twice a week helping to push the students who are also in a clan. We would follow the guidelines in Lady Gawain's book and see how it works, then provide feedback to her. Very much like what you're about to do with your henchman and experimenting with a wand."

I was stunned. Me, assisting a teacher in magic? But I could barely keep up with my homework as it was. "Ma'am," I started to say but was cut off by Wanda's excited, "Vivian says yes."

"Wanda," I said, now annoyed. "You have a voice, but so do I. I'm barely holding my own. If my grades start slipping, what would Lord Winton think? He's paying for me to go to school."

"Oh, come on, Vivian," she pleaded. "You're the best hero ever. You always figure it out."

The professor seemed amused at our interplay. "You are under no obligation to say yes, Vivian. However, as a teacher's assistant, you, or rather your head of house, would be paid for your time. It isn't much, but I also think this would be a good experience for you."

I bit my lip and thought about it for a second. Wanda looked like she was ready to hit me with the book again if I pushed back. "Three conditions," I said. "I want Lord Winton to agree to it. Second, if my grades start slipping, I want the ability to back out. And, finally, I'm not doing it unless Wanda is by my side," I stressed, "and she gets paid too."

Wanda's eyes went wide, and she hugged me again. I think that was the fourth hug today. Then we both looked at Professor Lessnara.

"Agreed."

Wanda shrieked and hugged me. Okay, fifth time today.

"What?" Sierra said indignantly and crossed her arms. "But my Lodge Leader sets the training rules."

It wasn't just Sierra. The headmistress had passed the word that all the clan members from the sophomore and freshman class to gather up—all fourteen of them.

"Let's try that again, young lady," said the headmistress with a hint of force.

Mina shot Sierra a pleading look.

"Ma'am," concluded Sierra.

"This is a school. My school. Which you all attend. One of the subjects is magic, of which this is the class. New training standards are coming out for the clans. Therefore, you will follow them, and we will test you, or rather Professor Lessnara and her two assistants will—and this includes homework."

Mia raised her hand slowly.

"Go ahead, young lady," said the headmistress, pointing to her.

"But all I can do is barely call light. And even then, it only sometimes works."

"And that is what testing, homework, and pushing yourself is for," replied the headmistress in a dry voice. "I repeat, this is a school. Since the group of you seem put upon, you are welcome to write to Lady Gawain and complain. She's the one who has written the new training standards." The headmistress's mouth twitched. "However, I don't think you'll get much sympathy from her."

Sierra grumbled, "Fine, but my lodge leader will probably complain. Who are the two assistants?"

"Vivian Hampton and Wanda Hine," replied the headmistress.

Sierra's head swung around to glare at Wanda. "I'm going to get you for this."

Sometimes you just can't win.

Chapter 13

It is terrifying when you realize others are shaped by your actions.

-Lady Gawain.

-Terrance-

Library, Pioneer School

I rubbed my face. "Three? That's it?"

"Terrance, he's barely eighteen," admonished Darlene.

The four of us were sitting at a table in the back of the school's library. A long bookcase hid us from view. It didn't take too much imagination to suspect this was a make out spot for the young and infatuated. What's better than a clandestine meeting? Being able to say with a straight face, "I was at the library."

However, right now, it was useful for hiding my shadow from prying eyes. Currently it was pouting and leaning against the wall. When giggles or whispers of the opposite sex came near us, my shadow strained at some invisible force to try to peer around the corner. Apparently, it can hear or pick up sounds through me. Who knows what it would do if it got the opportunity to perform in front of a bunch of teenagers.

On the table were some twenty older magic books which had a good index of runes. The problem was that half of the runes on the little box holding the ring weren't in any of the books in front of us. We needed older or more esoteric books. More importantly, I didn't recognize them either, and that's saying something.

The "kid," as I thought of him, reddened. "Sir, I am a quick study. What other languages do you want me to learn?"

I looked up at the ceiling in frustration. He was so damn polite too. I sighed and glanced at Franklin, Darlene's husband, who was reading through the folders that minx, Lady Cassandra, had handed to me. She was beautiful, poised, confident, polite, and I wanted to squish her face into the mud. Hand me a kid as a partner and then sort-of draft me. I reminded myself to do something nasty to her. I just hadn't figured out what yet.

Franklin looked up from the folder he was reading and glanced at the kid, then me. "Terrance," he said softly, almost compassionately, "have you considered your anger might really be resentment?"

I grunted and crossed my arms. "What are you talking about?"

Darlene nodded slightly. "I hadn't considered that," she said, and leaned over to kiss her husband.

The kid looked between Franklin and me in obvious confusion, then his eyes widened slightly. "I'm sorry about your loss, sir," he stammered out.

"What are you talking about?" I demanded. Whatever they were implying went right over my head.

The kid looked at me with compassion. "The loss of your son, sir."

Franklin's mouth opened in astonishment, then laughed. "I was talking about Camillo, the snowman. Believe me, Terrance doesn't have any children."

Now it was the kid's turn to look confused. "But I thought—"

"I am not resentful," I growled out and stopped myself from shouting at the kid.

But was I? I let out my breath and looked away. That true innocent found me. Me. And he'd wanted help. He could have chosen anyone, but he chose me. And now I had to share him with this kid who didn't know anything.

Darlene leaned forward and put her hand on top of mine. "Terrance, either Camillo has his own voice, or he's just a thing. He doesn't belong to you."

"But he found me," I emphasized and stopped myself again.

Without Camillo, would I have chosen another path? Given into the hunger? Without him, I certainly would have died when the spirit attacked me.

He was my only friend when I felt like the universe wanted to abort me.

My friend. A feeling so intense grew inside that it verged on pain. Caring. Not an emotion I had experienced much before, outside of the thrill of the chase. I remembered earlier when I told the Realm Knight Commander that she had best worry about me if she meant harm to my friend. I meant every word of it. If this kid was going to survive the upcoming storm, someone needed to care about him, and it was apparently going to be me.

"It's Lord Grayson, right?" I asked the kid.

"Yes, sir."

"Fine. Maybe you'll do. I expect Camillo will be coming down to meet her around sunset. Once they're done, we can do some reconnaissance of our own. There are some things I want to check out. Till then, what are your obligations?"

"I only have classes in the morning, sir. So, other than tutoring two sophomores before dinner, I am free." He tilted his head and asked, "Her?"

"Lady Vivian Hampton," I said. "She's the one who made Camillo."

Something like surprise briefly crossed the kid's face. "I wasn't aware Ms. Vivian was a titled lady. I was under the impression her benefactor was Lord Winton."

"Ever met the cursed knight?" I asked.

The kid sucked in his breath. "No, sir!"

"Well, if you do and suggest to him that Ms. Vivian, as you call her, isn't a lady, I'd give you even odds that will be the last thing you ever say."

The kid looked like he wanted to ask me a thousand questions. Before he could open his mouth, I turned to Franklin. "How are you holding out?"

He and Darlene hadn't gotten much sleep last night. They had taken turns helping me dig out Mr. Capmond's body. Being close to sixty, the two of them had to have been exhausted. But they were staying with me, which I appreciated. My list of friends was small but growing. It made me feel connected to this town in a way I wasn't certain how to describe.

"Exhausted," said Franklin. "But if I go to sleep now, I'll wake up in the middle of the night. Darlene and I will probably stay to meet Camillo, then head home."

"Well, we have a few hours until the kid here needs to play tutor. I'm not even going to think about putting on the ring the little witch gave me until I know what all these runes are. There are quite a few I don't recognize, and I thought I knew every rune in existence. We need better books."

Darlene put down the book she was reading down and stretched. "I can get you into the restricted section. But I need something to eat first."

She and Franklin left, promising to bring back something for the kid and me. Once they were out of earshot, Lord Grayson said, "Sir, witch? Are you referring to Lady Cassandra? She's Sorcerer Petotum's apprentice!" The kid's voice had a hint of anger to it, like he was ready to accuse me of desecrating his mother's tomb.

Good. He was starting to push back.

"Yes, but that young lady has ulterior motives. I don't like being someone's pawn." I pointed to the stack of folders Franklin had been reading through. "There's either something in here she wants or wants solved. But it goes both ways. If we can figure out what it is and get it, then we have some leverage."

The kid obviously hadn't considered that before. "Sir, you're speaking as if there are layers of misdirection with Lady Cassandra."

I stood up and stretched myself. "You're thinking too narrowly, Lord Grayson. Remember back to what Sorcerer Petotum said to the mayor, *the council will have a decision about the warding stone in a week*. They could have had it buried today. Why put it off?"

Then I started raising fingers. "I remember seeing nine Realm Knights. There are probably more hiding about. You would know better than I. But the point is, my money is on that some of them have been given orders we know nothing about. Then there's the Lady Cassandra, who can walk into a Houser Bank vault and pull out a magic ring made of orichalcum. She's likely taking over for the Iron Dragon. I don't want to get caught between her and her primary target. We need to find a trail of breadcrumbs, so we know when to duck."

The kid just stared at me for a few seconds. "Sir, primary target? Who are we looking for?"

I gave him a thin smile. "*What* we are looking for, you mean."

"Sir?"

I ignored his confusion and countered with, "Back to our trail of breadcrumbs. Possible trail one, Sorcerer Petotum said a Republic University had been granted the rights to dig here. Who gave them the idea? Likely, someone or something whispered in their ear. Tomorrow, I want you to interview those archeologists from Earth. Your status as a reserve Realm Knight should give you the legal sway to ask. Pay close attention to their pupils and listen for word pattern shifts."

"To see if any one of them has been enthralled," he said, obviously getting it. He leaned back while whistling under his breath. "Sir, you're acting as if Sorcerer Petotum and Lady Cassandra are expecting you to do this."

I grinned at the kid. "They are. But you won't likely be the only one interviewing them either. Realm Knight Commander Bardot likely knows part of the story. Watch your back."

He swallowed. "Sir, she's a legend. Are you implying Realm Commander Bardot may have ulterior motives?"

"Unlikely," I said, and the kid relaxed. "But consider this, would a Realm Knight's oath be something on the order of 'to protect and defend the realm'?" I asked.

"Yes, sir," said the kid. "I took it myself."

"And who do you report up to, ultimately?" I asked, waiting to see if the kid started to get where I was going with this.

"The Wizard's Council, sir."

"And do you trust all of them?" I asked.

The kid's silence was confirmation enough.

"Cow's blood?" I asked after taking a bite of my sandwich. The thinly sliced meat was rare and delicious. The tomato added flavor. Lettuce in my opinion was only there to keep the bread from getting mushy. I paused and considered that thought; all those memories were from my doppelgänger. Taking another bite, I took stock of my hunger. It enjoyed the cow's blood, fed it, gave me strength, but compared to human blood, it was cheap red wine. Could I go for days, or longer now, without drinking human blood? Well, we were going to find out.

Franklin looked up after pulling several pickle slices from his sandwich. "The kitchen staff is making blood pudding for dessert tonight. Darlene grabbed a dollop."

The kid stopped eating and watched my shadow for a second. It was playing a game with the bookcase. Extending a hand, then jumping back. Every time it got close, a small curl of energy would reach out from the bookshelves and try to tag my shadow's hand. While my shadow was playing, the spells woven into the bookcase weren't. I vaguely wondered what would happen if my shadow got hit by a strong curse. Would I feel it?

The kid looked down at his sandwich, then asked nervously. "Sir, one of the other Realm Knights said you might be a vampire. But... well, what are you, sir?"

Darlene and Franklin looked at each other. "Do you want us to give you some privacy?" asked Darlene.

I shook my head and looked at the kid. "Lord Grayson, I'll do what I said. Teach you what I can and try to keep you safe, but this isn't a game. I don't think I am a vampire, but I don't know what I am," and extended my hand across the table. "Count my pulse."

The kids' eyes went wide as his fingers pressed into my wrist. "What are you, sir?" he asked in a whisper.

"The Iron Dragon has asked for my notes about what I can do. You're welcome to read them as well. But I want to make something clear," I said, staring into the kid's eyes. "Those who I call friends didn't turn me away. They gave me a chance. If someone makes a run at them, they had best consider me first. I have already died once. And for my friends, I'll do it again."

The kid pulled his hand back. "Sir, who are we hunting?"

Franklin got up and looked around the bookshelf. "No one's around."

"We are hunting a smart demon and its agents," I said. "Our job is to find its agents, call in the big guns and then hope we can duck fast enough."

"Oh."

The kid went back to eating his sandwich. Life for him just got very real.

♪♪

"Will you stop that!" I said in exasperation. Twenty minutes ago, my shadow had started playing the "touch me game" with the library's built-in protective spells and had never stopped. It seemed to give him endless amusement. I felt like a parent hearing, or in this case seeing, a pair of children doing the ever entertaining *don't touch me game,* which every parent with more than one child knows about. I'd only had my shadow for a day, and

I already wanted to put him up for adoption. It amazed me humans hadn't gone extinct yet. After dealing with the first child, why in the world would anyone want a second?

My shadow gave me "the finger," while trying to touch the shelf again without being tagged. As before, a translucent blue hand reached out from a book and almost got him.

I rolled my eyes.

With my Sight, I could see the outer layer of protective wards woven into the wooden shelves. Focusing in on the spells, I was able to look deeper. There were fire and water protection spells in place as well.

I pointed to the bookcase which hid us from the rest of the room. "How do the active spells get recharged?"

Darlene twisted her head around. "The library is one of the grounds for all the spell circles in the school."

Ah. The magic must go somewhere. It was likely shunted through the sections with silver imbued runes.

I pointed up. "Spell crystals?"

The kid swallowed the last of his sandwich. "Rubies in the gargoyle eyes, sir. They're not true guardians, but they can animate for a short period of time to defend the school. The spell crystals are overflow points when there's a magic surge. The sun provides a little extra energy too."

The basics of energy-magic transfer. I had seen the gargoyles on the roof as I was escorted to the school. Eight were on the front, there had to be more. The total amount of magical energy they could absorb was likely staggering. A frontal assault would get you killed. I vaguely wondered if it would be possible to steal one of the gems and re-etch a spell in it to help keep Camillo keep cold.

I drew out a rough sketch of the school and pushed it to the kid. "In your spare time, ask the question, how would you break in? Assume Lady Vivian or one of her friends is the target and work from there."

Lord Grayson asked uncertainly, "To kill her?"

"No, to seize her. Figure her abductors are expensive but expendable. They're unimportant. It will be the ones paying them, or the layer above that, we care about. Anyone else is a cutout."

His mouth twitched. "Sir, so you are aware, I have been ordered to travel to the next valley over this coming weekend to help map it out. Ms. Viv—Lady Vivian's henchwoman is coming with me."

I leaned back and considered the young man. "Funny how things turn out not to be coincidences. Sounds like I will need some camping gear. Let's go to the restricted section."

"Well, that brings our unknown runes down to five," I snorted.

We had been down in the library's restricted section for more than two hours, and I was beginning to feel as if this was a waste of time when Darlene found an old tome of a book buried under some ancient scrolls. The dust covering it suggested no one had touched it in years.

"What language is that?" asked Darlene.

The faded hand-drawn characters weren't written in ink; sometimes it's best not to ask. The book didn't have its own will, but close. My bet was Darlene wouldn't have found the book if we hadn't drawn out the runes we were looking for. An odd sort of protection charm: *If you don't need to know, I'm not here* kind of spell.

"Archaic Chinese," I absently replied. "Some believe a dragon lived there for a time some eight thousand years ago or so."

"You can read that?" the kid said, leaning over the large book.

"Some," I said while copying the notations which described the rune. "A job I took exposed me to the language."

"So, what does the rune do?" asked Darlene. "And how did this book end up here?"

"Well, if I am reading the notations correctly, and that's a big if, it's a sort of yin and yang connection point to other runes."

I was roundly stared at. I sighed. "Think inverse but equal, one can't exist without the other type of thing."

Franklin leaned forward and used his staff to stand up. The man was getting tired. After stretching, he asked, "You're suggesting there's another layer of runes?"

"Probably," I replied.

Darlene blew hair out of her face. She was tired too.

"How do we see them?" asked the kid, in wonder.

"Worst case?" I replied. "Put on the ring first. But don't you have a class to tutor soon? We're not going to solve the mystery of the ring today."

The kid muttered out a "damn." He had forgotten the time. Then his eyes opened wide. At the same time, Franklin hissed out while adjusting the grip on his staff. Gone was the old man. He saw a threat.

"Darlene," he whispered, "behind you."

She and I turned around to stare at a shimmering floating apparition of an old woman.

"Gerald has a message for you, Creature," said the apparition. From her tone, she wasn't trying to be scary, more curious. She was studying me intently. Her gray hair was up in a tight bun and held in place with several hairpins. It took me a second to recognize what they really were—wands. What an unusual woman this was. It wouldn't surprise me if there were other wands hidden about her in places one wouldn't normally look. I bet she had been something to see when she was alive.

"Sir, what do we do?" asked the kid in a terrified whisper.

Without turning around, I said, "Don't ask it a personal question. It's a spirit."

"What is the message you were asked to deliver?" I asked the apparition. I got the feeling this one was powerful. More so than the one Camillo and I had fought, which just reinforced to me that whatever was below, was vastly powerful. Spirits cannot exist without something very powerful keeping them in place. To power this spirit? Well, I had no idea.

She pondered me for a few more seconds before answering, "His message is this. 'Thank you for bringing my body home.'"

I stood up, and the old woman floated backwards a few feet.

"What manner of creature are you?" she asked.

Interesting that she asked me a personal question. If it was the other way around, I would be bound to her until I had fulfilled a service.

I bowed. "Madam, I don't know." Then cautiously added, "If one wanted to talk with you again, what would you request?" Always good to be polite with strange spirits who held multiple wands as hairpins. The spirit I fought before was unhinged and wanted to use Camillo's body to leave his imprisonment. This one was likely stronger, but she didn't seem to be mad at anyone.

"I will consider your question, Creature," she said and began to fade away.

Well, my instincts had been right. You find resources in the oddest of places.

The kid's face had gone white. "Sir, I need to leave for my tutoring."

"Go ahead, kid. I'll see you later."

As we walked up the stairs, Franklin pulled out a copper talon. "Up for a bet?" he grinned. "I say you scared him off."

Darlene sighed, and I heard her say "men" under her breath.

♫

"I can't get rid of you, can I?" I said to Commander Realm Sorceress Bardot.

She snorted. "What did you think of Lord Grayson?"

Franklin and Darlene were trailing as the Realm Knight escorted me to a newer wing of the school. "Franklin thinks I scared him away," I said. "My money says he's going to stick it out."

"You have a habit of not answering questions, don't you?" said the Knight Realm Commander.

I glanced at her. "You show me yours, and I'll show you mine."

She gave me a glare. "We're not playing games here, Terrance. We lost two Realm Knights recently when they picked up a trail. Before we could get them reinforcements, they were dead."

Darlene sucked in her breath. "That wasn't in any of the newspapers."

"And won't be," growled the Realm Commander. "Without a breakthrough, it's going to get worse."

"Is the kid supposed to be your sacrificial lamb?" I asked. "And to answer your question, I grudgingly like him. Why did you pair him up with me?"

"Honestly? An oracle," she replied. "We're grasping at straws. You're the only one we know of who encountered the demon and lived, well, wasn't destroyed. We're hoping lightning strikes twice."

"I don't know what you think is going to happen," I said angrily and turned to her. "It's a demon. A smart one. I died. I already told the kid we're looking for breadcrumbs, and if we're lucky enough to stumble across a lead, we call in the big guns and then duck." I took a step toward her and growled out, "Are you setting the kid up to die?"

He was just a kid but wanted to learn and was paired up with me. I felt that odd feeling again of caring about something again. With it, came a sudden understanding—to care meant I had a responsibility toward him.

Commander Bardot looked away for a second. "Look, the job comes with hard choices. I lost my younger brother to a necromancer. He didn't die well. So, I'm sorry if you're a little squeamish."

I took another step toward her. We were nose to nose now. "I repeat. I'm not a Realm Knight, and I didn't sign up to be one. I play by my rules, so stop being a prick." Then in a low voice I asked, "Did the oracle have anything to say about Lady Vivian Hampton?"

"Above my paygrade," she replied, not blinking. "I honestly don't know."

Through our arguing, I could hear the steady beat of her heart. The rate never changed. Either she wasn't lying, or she was just that good or both.

Franklin tapped his cane on the ground. "Absolutely fascinating listening to the two of you bicker, but why are we headed toward the dueling rings?"

Realm Commander Bardot turned ninety degrees and resumed walking in the direction we had been heading. "Because Sorcerer Petotum wants Terrance here to show the wand guild how someone might break through their wards. In return, he gets to borrow any wand in the case."

I blinked. Well, then, let's go have some fun. Out of the corner of my eye, I watched my shadow jump in the air and do a little jig.

While continuing to walk forward, Realm Sorceress Bardot reiterated, "Borrow."

I smiled. You always need to put conditions on these things. One might borrow a wand for a very long time.

"That's not possible," wheezed out the old man. His eyes had almost bugged out, and from listening to his heart, it skipped a few beats too. "It can't be done!"

Funny how people say that when their world gets turned upside down. The wards and traps within the chest holding the wands were good, very good. But I was built from a master thief, one of the best out there. Heck, even that damn demon needed me. People are always amazed when they discover that, to break through their traps, great power isn't needed. On the contrary, sometimes a simple silver dusted feather can do the trick. It's not the size, but how you use your tool.

"How did you do it?" asked a Realm Knight in a strangled voice. He had been watching me the entire time.

"Arrest him," wheezed out the old man and pointed a trembling finger at me. He gulped for air and that's when I heard it. His heart made an odd shuddering sound. That couldn't be good.

I turned toward the other five people from the Wandmaker's Guild—all old men—but compared to the one next to me whose face was turning white, they were practically young whippersnappers. "Does the school have a healer? Your friend here needs help."

♪♪♪

Once Lord Ninebart, as I heard him called, was tended to, I turned back to the Realm Knight who asked the question. "Commander, Realm Sorceress Bardot said, and I quote, 'to show the Wandmaker's Guild how someone might break through their wards.' In return, he gets to borrow any wand in the case."

I tucked the feather behind my left ear. "I showed you. Now I'm going to choose a wand."

The wand on the bottom felt very interesting indeed. I could sense it had a core—the wand maker essentially made a very powerful wand, then hollowed out the center. Then they inserted a page from a living book inside and resealed the wand. Depending how philosophical you are, when you use the wand, the rest of the book supposedly has dreams about what you are doing. I couldn't be certain, but I bet the wand was here for a reason. When I pulled it out, the room went silent. Realm Sorceress Bardot snorted and handed over a silver talon to Sorcerer Petotum.

I bowed to the room. "I'll let you know when I'm done borrowing it. Please excuse me, I have a meeting with a snowman."

I wasn't sure who had more fun in there, me or my shadow. I wondered if the little minx of an apprentice set this up or not.

Darlene and Franklin followed me out. Franklin was chuckling to himself.

Chapter 14

The rules for magically linking a sentient being to you are weird and not easily undone.
    -Lady Gawain

-Vivian Hampton-

Physics Room, Pioneer School

"Okay spill," said Wanda. "What's going on between Amanda and Elaine?"

The two of us were in Professor Gass's classroom, but Lord Grayson wasn't here. I was sure he said today. Were we too early? I didn't think so, but I also didn't want to answer Wanda's question. She didn't know about Amanda's head of house, and it wasn't my story to tell, so I redirected her.

"The basic safety rules for wand testing says the tester must be in a warded circle," I said.

I had already read through the first chapter of the three-hundred-page book called *Wand Testing*. We only had six weeks to try to make this work. Considering classes, homework, Camillo, hopefully a boyfriend, preparing for the scavenger hunt, and a wedding, there wasn't much free time in there. Oh, and let's pile on being a teacher's assistant to a subject I knew little about. There weren't enough hours in the day.

A wedding. I sucked in my breath. Wanda and I needed new dresses. I didn't want to show up at Lord Winton's wedding wearing a plain dress.

At my surprised exclamation, Wanda twisted her head to try to look at her back. "Did I get tagged with a note spell?"

Note spells were one of the simpler curse spells. Unless you felt the faint tingling, they were hard to detect. Then glowing letters would appear on your back. The spell only lasted a few minutes, but the attacker usually had something silly or obnoxious spelled out. *I'm with stupid*, was a common one. The spell only allowed for twenty letters and those included spaces.

"No. I mean Lord Winton's wedding. We need new dresses."

Wanda rolled her eyes. "Henchwoman here. Sierra visited the local Blind Buttonhole for me and gave them our measurements. They're going to have some samples for us to look at this evening."

Oh.

"Wanda, you're amazing."

Instead of bouncing in excitement, which was Wanda's normal reaction when talk turned toward nobles, she blushed and looked down at the ground for a second. Then I heard her say, in a small voice, "From my winnings, I have eight copper talons now. Can I put it toward the dresses with your money too?"

Suddenly I could feel the apprehensive Wanda in the room with me, the one that had emerged during our break earlier today. I cautiously asked, "You want a better dress?"

Wanda looked up and nervously rolled my wand, now her wand, between the palm of her hands. "I like your idea of winning my head of house over. If I had a nicer dress, maybe," she said wistfully, "if I could get a picture of myself with Lord and Lady Winton, then send a copy to him."

Wanda was taking my idea to heart. Time to fan the flames. "I think that's a great idea. I haven't spent much of Lord Winton's extra money he sends me. How about I match it with whatever extra you throw in?"

For that, I got another squeeze of death. Number six.

"So, what am I supposed to do now?" asked Wanda.

My redirection worked. Wanda didn't bring up the subject of Amanda and Elaine again. She had moved to the room's one spell ring with my wand. Sigh, her wand. I still imagined it was looking at me while muttering, *you abandoned me* in a mournful voice.

Focus. This was Wanda time now.

I looked down at my own journal notes. Step one, build the runes for light in your mind and mentally imbue them with energy. At my question, "Do you know the runes to make a light spell?" I got another eye roll.

"Duh. Seen you do it about a thousand times."

I wrote down on the next line in my journal, *ignore snarkiness*. The man from the wandmaker's guild had said to write down everything. "Okay, imagine as if those runes were floating around the wand. Then send them energy."

Wanda concentrated. Nothing happened.

"Aren't you supposed to be doing something too?" suggested Wanda. "Like turning on the magic tap?"

"No idea," I said. "Um, how about I stand on the ring itself?"

Wanda shrugged, "Maybe, but—"

"Have you tried encoding the spell into the wand?"

Both Wanda and I turned. Lord Grayson stood just inside the classroom now. I had no idea how long he had been standing there.

Wanda blushed and performed a curtsy. "Sir, you think Vivian needs to encode the spells into my wand?" she asked, while holding up her wand higher.

He walked forward, stopped, and did a quick bow to the two of us. That was odd, why bow to me? "You don't encode spells into your wand, Lady Viv- Ms. Vivian?" he asked.

There it was again, he almost called me Lady Vivian. Was there some obscure rule I was missing? Lord Winton and Lady

Kiera get married and now I'm somehow a low noble in their house. I doubted it. After shrugging, I said, "Let's try it."

Wanda hopped over the edge of the circle to stand by me. "How come you're late?" she asked Lord Grayson.

"Wanda!" I said in annoyance. "His business is his business, besides he's a Realm Knight. It was probably something important."

Lord Grayson seemed to relax. Now he had a lopsided grin, making him somehow seem cute. "Ms. Vivian, you're correct. I was performing my duties as a Realm Knight," he said, then almost laughed. "Believe it or not, I saw a spirit in the restricted section of the library."

Wanda bounced and asked enthusiastically, "Did it try to curse you?"

"Actually no," he said, and Wanda's face fell. "But before we get into the physics homework, why don't we try encoding the spell?"

I held out my hand and Wanda looked at me blankly. "I sort of need my old wand back to encode it."

As I mentally reviewed the procedure for encoding a spell, Wanda asked, "How come you don't encode any of your normal spells? Mina, Ken, and the rest who have wands do it."

"It's a crutch," said Lord Grayson before I could. "Lazy spell work. If you can hold the runes in your mind while imbuing them with energy, then you're more likely to be able to cast higher-level spells and add more power. Without that, it's a two-step process. Step one, focus and find the spell you want to cast within the wand, then imbue the runes with energy which are held in place by the wand. Then cast. And all wands have a limit to the spells they can hold. The most complex spell they would likely be able to cast would be third degree spells. Even then, their wands could probably only hold one, maybe two spells." He shrugged. "Obviously the better the wand, the more spells it can hold."

Wanda cocked her head. "So encoding is sort of like amulet magic, except with a wand, so you can adjust which spells are in there?"

I stared at Wanda. That was amazingly intuitive.

Lord Grayson blinked. "A very good analogy, Ms. Wanda. I can see why Ms. Vivian likes you so much."

Wanda blushed and didn't seem to know what to say next.

I cleared my throat. "What Lord Grayson just said. It's lazy, slower, and I like being able to adjust my spells on the fly if I need to." I blushed and added, "And Lord Winton said the same thing to me last year. I didn't want to disappoint him, so I practiced casting without encoding. Now, it's second nature."

Wanda rubbed her hands together in excitement. "So, when two people are dueling, if one of them uses encoded spells, they are likely to be a little bit slower? I have an edge in my bets. Silver talons, here I come."

Lord Grayson broke out laughing and bowed to Wanda. I couldn't help but grin at Wanda's enthusiasm and Lord Grayson's acceptance of her. The man was just so nice. With only the three of us here, it was easy to forget he was a lord. *Careful Vivian*, I thought to myself. *Remember Jeffery. Also, Wanda hoped the man would give her a letter of recommendation if things worked out.* I didn't want to get in the way of that. And let's face it, he was a senior, and I was a sophomore. Seniors didn't date the lower classes. Socially, that wasn't done.

I finished encoding the light spell into Wanda's wand, forcing myself to think of it as Wanda's wand, then handed it back to her. During this, Wanda appeared fascinated as the simple rune matrix slid up and down the wand, then sank into the wood. As a senior apprentice's wand, it could probably hold about fifteen beginner's spells or about eight first-degree ones.

"Well, give it a try," I suggested.

Wanda stepped into the spell circle again. I stood alongside Lord Grayson, a few feet just outside of the circle, and tried to imagine the link we saw earlier today. Suddenly, I felt the oddest sensation, almost like a bell vibrating. I wasn't sure, but there was something.

Wanda took a deep breath, looked at Lord Grayson, then me, and let out her breath. "Here goes."

♪♪♪

At first, Wanda didn't think anything worked, but I saw faint energy form with my Sight: barely there. Lord Grayson pointed toward the main globe of light in the room and clenched his hands. All the lights went out. The room was in total darkness except for a faint ball of light which had formed around the tip of Wanda's wand. So faint, you could barely see the outline of Wanda's outstretched arm.

Wanda shrieked in excitement and began to run around inside the ring, then somersaulted. After about a dozen of them, all the while still shrieking, she started writing out words in the darkness.

Lord Grayson chuckled. "She's a never-ending battery. We could power the school if we figure out how to tap into her enthusiasm."

I rolled my eyes. "Being Wanda has evolved to become a verb in my mind. I had to deal with it every day."

I could hear him shift in the darkness. "Do you feel a drain?"

"Maybe," I said. "At first, I felt a vibration. Now there is just a faint pull, but it's very small."

Wanda did one more somersault, then bounced to a stop. I was honestly glad she did. For whatever reason, it was making me a bit nauseous watching Wanda move and twist like that without being able to see the rest of the room.

"Try stepping on the spell circle," suggested Wanda in excitement. "Let's see if I can make the light brighter?"

"Let's not push the experiment that far yet" came Lord Grayson's voice. I could almost make out the outline of his body. Was he a little closer to me?

"Okay? Is there anything you want me to try instead?"

"Encode the wand with a few more basic spells. Let's see if Wanda can select the one she wants."

"Makes sense to me."

Lord Grayson gestured to the main globe of light. It, and the other globes, immediately turned back on. I had to shield my eyes against the sudden brightness.

"What do you want me to do?" asked Wanda, still bouncing in the middle of the charged spell circle.

Wanda didn't know how to safely break a spell circle while inside one, so I found the ground energy point and tapped the small spell crystal embedded in the floor. The faint energy defining the ring fell apart. "If you can stop bouncing for a few minutes. I need to write down the notes from our experiment."

I wanted to get it all down before it started to become all jumbled in my mind. Once I wrote something down, I could recall it again. Lord Grayson pulled out a chair and sat down to my right. Wanda right next to him.

"As a recommendation," suggested Lord Grayson. "On the left page write down what occurred in detailed steps. While on the right page, write down how you felt and things you think you observed."

Wanda nudged him. "Vivian's really smart, if she says it happened, it happened."

"And that's lazy thinking," said Lord Grayson, nudging her right back. "From your point of view, it's called acceptance by authority. Vivian's the authority figure in your mind, so if she said it's true, then in your mind it becomes fact. The other is Vivian's. It's easy to accept something as true until you do more experimentation and others review your work to prove it's true."

Wanda nudged him again and laughed. "Does your authority figure just want you to accept things without question? Professor Vermis is like that, he's an annoying—"

I cut off Wanda before she finished that sentence. Lord Grayson was in House Duke. Professor Vermis was his head of house. Let's not create enemies where we don't need to.

"Wanda and I were in the gymnasium when you and Lord Seth, um, talked to each other."

Lord Grayson was quiet for a few seconds. "Sorry you had to see that. He's an obnoxious bug."

I was glad he said it and not Wanda. "What's going to happen to his family?"

Wanda used her hands to begin a drum roll on the table.

"Wanda! Stop that," I said in frustration. "This is about his entire family." Having my own family fall apart, I knew all too well the horrible sensations of feeling scared and powerless, trapped, like I had no voice.

"Sorry," she said. "It's that people like Lord Seth don't seem to care about people like me."

Lord Grayson gave me a look which I translated into, "What's going on with Wanda?" I flipped a page and wrote out, *tell you later.* And made sure the opposing page was raised so Wanda couldn't see it.

His mouth twitched, and he turned to look at Wanda. "Worst case, their families will be stripped of their title and the Council will appoint another noble to their lands, and that includes their siblings."

"Oh," said Wanda in astonishment and gulped. "All of them?"

"Worst case," reiterated Lord Grayson. "Another possibility is that the head of house is reprimanded and loses his seat in the lower chambers for a time or permanently. This is assuming the Council's audit finds something wrong. If they pass, probably nothing."

"So," I said to redirect the conversation. "Here are my notes. What do you think?"

"I didn't mean to do that," Wanda said in frustration and stomped her left foot on the ground.

Now that there were three basic spells encoded into my old wand, Wanda was struggling to cast the one she wanted. Adding to the light spell, I had encoded a breeze and ghost-sound. Breeze was very useful when I wanted to dry my hair faster; it created a steady breeze of air in a small space for a minute. Ghost-sound, only because you had to add something to the spell, essentially pick the sound from a list you wanted it to make and then project it to the destination. It was the first variable spell which first years learned. Nothing bad happened if you got it wrong, except the sound wasn't what you wanted or where you wanted it to be, if it went off at all. The sound only lasted for a few seconds in any case. Last year, when I figured out how to add additional sounds to the list, Ken took my idea and added a fart sound to the spell in his wand. I think he is intentionally trying to set the record for most detentions.

Lord Grayson grinned. "I remember my first three months of learning to cast. Mum's still mad at me for breaking one of her vases."

Wanda stomped her foot again. "It's not funny!"

"Yes, it is," I shot back. "We all had to go through the same thing. Now, it's your turn."

"Yeah, well, I bet you didn't have an audience laughing at you," demanded Wanda and moved to the far side of the circle. A small ball of light appeared at the end of her wand.

Lord Grayson raised his voice. "Was that the spell you wanted?"

"Shut up," said Wanda. "This is hard. Go write up some more notes or something while I practice."

Lord Grayson gestured to the table with my notes, and I took my seat. After taking his, he inquired politely, "So, Wanda?"

I didn't want to go into detail without her permission. "She's the only female of her generation in the Hine house. Her uncle, who is also her benefactor, has plans to marry her off once she graduates to essentially become a baby machine." I leaned back slightly to make sure Wanda was still on the far side of the ring.

"She's hoping you might write her head of house a recommendation if you're happy with her."

Lord Grayson leaned in closer to me. "Ah. That story has been written a thousand times. I take it that this other family has a little money for a dowry."

"The dowry is three small inns. My understanding is that part of the deal would be to bring this new house under the umbrella of the Hine house. They hope Wanda's children would become innkeepers themselves. Her uncle wants to expand the house, but at the expense of Wanda. He expects her to have as many babies as possible as quickly as she can." I sighed and watched Wanda in the spell circle for a moment. "Wanda would become a baby factory. But she has so much potential! It's important to me that my friends are taken care of."

Lord Grayson turned to watch Wanda as well. "My new master is just like that." Then he focused in on me. "Vivian, it will be my honor."

"Thank you, Lord Grayson." And I was suddenly aware of how close the two of us were sitting to each other. I nudged my seat farther away from him. His smile, laugh, and willingness to help Wanda made me really like him. He was also very handsome. Then I felt that pulsing sensation again, and like with my other visions, I was somewhere else.

Lord Grayson and I were dancing together at a school venue. I wasn't certain about the occasion, but it was formal. Then spells began flying from the shadows. Screams surrounded us and ricocheted around the room as students and teachers began pulling out their own wands even as they took cover. Lord Grayson and I made our way over to an upturned table, both of us had pulled out our wands. A shadowy figure emerged across the room, laughing maniacally. He threw something toward me. It landed with a sickly splat sound and rolled to a stop in front of me. Wanda eyes were looking at me, but no one was home anymore. My brain froze up. Wanda.

"Vivian, are you okay?"

That was Lord Grayson's voice. But he was right beside me. Why did he sound so far away?

Wanda died. She can't die.

"Vivian," and with his voice, I felt a tug on my arm. The last remnants of my vision faded away, and I was back in the physics class. I didn't know what to say. Was that going to happen? That voice, I knew it, but I couldn't remember. Who was it? I had to know. Arg, brain, think! But it was so hard to focus when Wanda's dead eyes kept on staring at me.

"Vivian does that occasionally," came Wanda's voice from a distance. "I think she might be getting a vision."

I blinked a few times. "Sorry, I'm a bit distracted." I was more than that. That vision was so clear. The lady said these were possible futures. I just needed to figure out the voice. I let out my breath in frustration. That's when I noticed Lord Grayson had his hand on top of mine.

"What did you see, Vivian?" he asked, his voice full of concern.

"Can you tell me how to ground out the spell circle properly?" demanded Wanda, almost shouting.

I stood up, letting Lord Grayson's hand fall away. "Of course, Wanda. Here's what you need to do."

♪♪♪

Wanda looked up from all the equations. "I still don't get how that can turn the waterwheel. It has got to be extremely heavy."

"True," remarked Lord Grayson. "But the wheel is balanced, and the axle is surrounded by ball bearings, so there's very little friction."

At Wanda's blank look, he added, "Ever help replace a wagon wheel?"

"Sure, when my dad and I—. Oh, I get it now. Like those bearings around the wheel axle."

"Exactly, except the waterwheel's bearings are much larger, and the axle is very thick."

Wanda wrote out another part of the equation and turned to me. "So, what was the vision?"

I swear the two of them were working as a team to get me to tell them what I had seen. Wanda or Lord Grayson would sneak in the question halfway through a conversation.

I stuck my tongue out at Wanda. "I want to discuss them with Professor Malton first."

"Aha," shouted Wanda in triumph. "So, they are visions! Are they about me winning a magic duel? If you and I teamed up together, we could make bucket-fulls of talons."

Lord Grayson made a shushing motion at Wanda. "Vivian, I've met an oracle before. Untrained, the visions can be all over the place. Do you need to take a break?"

I made a quick decision. "There's sort of a person helping me. She says they are crux points, showing possible futures. They don't reflect reality, but a *possible* reality, and I could get lost trying to see the totality of it."

"Oracle," announced Wanda. "I knew it."

"Thank you for telling me," said Lord Grayson. "How about we break? It's almost dinnertime anyway. Regroup tomorrow at the same time?"

I countered, "Wednesday? Wanda and I have history tomorrow."

"Wednesday it is."

I had my coat, mittens, and hat on as I waited for Professor Malton near the school's large main doors. Wanda had already gathered up the footmen and maids who wanted to meet Camillo, promising we would be down in a bit. From my link with him, I could sense he was almost down the mountain pass and about to enter the edge of town. Too far away for communication, but I thought our link was getting stronger. I still wasn't sure why I could talk to him when I was in the spell circle.

"Ms. Hampton, thank you for the invitation to talk."

I turned and smiled. Professor Malton had come up from a side door. The cold air was making his breath condense. He gestured toward the town, and we began walking together. I was still sorting through ideas in my mind and a bit apprehensive. I trusted Professor Malton, but the more I did, the more I felt like my father was slipping away. While another part of me wasn't sure who I was anymore.

"I'm getting visions sometimes," I said, deciding just to dive in. "The lady who talks to me, Lady Cassandra's sponsor, tells me that they are crux points, possible futures."

Professor Malton nodded at me to continue.

"Well, the lady says it is because I have the bardic voice. I can see the flow of possibilities like an oracle, but that it's very easy to get lost, and she said not to treat any vision as absolute. Some of them have been very helpful, immediate things. The rest of them have been about others I am in close contact with and weeks or even years in the future." I gulped and added quietly, "One of them was horrible."

We walked in silence for a few steps. "I don't know a great deal about augury, Ms. Hampton. But I think a better question is, do you feel if you are being led or pointed in a particular direction?"

"Professor?" I wasn't sure what he was implying.

He looked away for a second. "Ms. Hampton, what I—we—are all concerned about, is that someone is trying to use you for their own goals."

I snorted. "Even Professor Vermis?"

"I think Professor Vermis has larger problems at hand. Please don't repeat this even to Wanda. But there is some speculation he may have influenced Lord Seth and Lord Keith toward asking their head of house to make that formal complaint."

"Oh," I wasn't sure what to say. Mixed emotions bubbled up in me. I never expected to feel sad for Lord Seth or his band of troublemakers.

"So, goals," repeated Professor Malton. "It is always important to keep yours in mind. Whomever this individual is, she is obviously very powerful and likes to stay in the shadows. That rings alarm bells for all of us."

Most people wanted their privacy. I did too, and I was a firm believer every person had a right to their own secrets. "I'm not sure I understand."

"While I doubt that this person is a necromancer, the Realm Knights had to fight one some five months ago. A vastly powerful person waiting in the shadows, teasing Lady Gawain. Does that strike any similarities? You can see how we might be a bit apprehensive."

I scrunched up my nose. "I can't see Lady Cassandra getting involved with a necromancer. And whoever this is, the dragons know about her. Besides, she's done nothing but try to help."

"Agreed. However, the headmistress and I don't like unknown visitors mentally reaching out to our students and bypassing the school's wards. As you might imagine, it raises some concerns."

I pondered his comment. "I can see that," I said. "Thank you for listening to me."

He stopped and bowed to me. "And thank you for trusting me, Ms. Hampton. I will see if we can get an oracle to work with you. If nothing else, to provide some guidance on these visions."

It was pure reflex. I reached out and hugged Professor Malton. He was being so kind. I felt him stiffen, then pat me on the back. I jumped backwards. "Sorry, Professor."

He smiled and looked up. Snow flurries had started to dance in the air. Winter was trying to hold on for a few more days. I bet that made Camillo happy. At that thought, a gnawing fear bubbled up inside me. "Professor, the Guardian Master who will be arriving in a few days. Can we trust her?" If she had an agenda to dissect my snowman, he and I were going to run for the hills.

A smile touched Professor Malton's lips. "From what I have been told, she is a force of nature. Even Realm Knights are intimidated by her. I suspect the correct question is, can she help Camillo before it's too late?"

♪♪♪

As we waited for Camillo, an odd thought crossed my mind. "Professor, sometimes you call me Ms. Hampton, other times Ms. Vivian and occasionally Vivian. I can't see a pattern."

Professor Malton bowed slightly. "Ahh, I see your point. Out here, I referred to you as Ms. Hampton. You and I are, well, not alone, but in an open, semi-private social setting, unchaperoned. Perhaps I am being a bit too old-fashioned, but I think it is appropriate to maintain certain boundaries. While in school, you become Ms. Vivian or Vivian if we are among those we know well. If you were not the head sophomore student of my house, then I would not call you by your given name without the proper inflection."

Oh. That made sense. I was about to ask him another question when I felt Camillo's connection strengthen in my mind. He was almost here. Then my mouth opened in astonishment.

♪♪♪

I wasn't sure what to say. Camillo had apparently become the pied piper of children. There were about thirty of them following him as he flowed toward me. Beyond them, maybe another hundred or so adults, probably their parents. Even before he talked to me through our connection, I could feel his excitement.

Seeing me, he turned and pointed at the short brown-haired little boy to his right—<*"This is Daniel. He wants a new ball for Christmas."*>

Before I could respond, Camillo began pointing to the other children around him and telling me their names followed by what each wanted for Christmas. I didn't know what to say. I did the only thing that made sense to me: I hugged him. "Thank you, Camillo," I said, after stepping back. "I need to write all that down. Can we talk about it tomorrow?"

"Already got it," said an amused man's voice. "I was his first victim."

"Terrance," I said in delight. "I'm glad you're still here." That's when I noticed the three others with him. Mr. and Mrs. Thorough and—"Lord Grayson? How do you know Terrance?"

Camillo looked between us. <"*My friend introduced me to Lord Grayson, Creator. I like his glow.*">

Lord Grayson blushed. "He's my new guide. I'm helping him solve old cases around town."

Oh. To cover my surprise, I turned to Professor Malton. "Sir? Professor Malton, let me introduce you to Camillo." While I know he had seen Camillo the previous night, I didn't think the two of them had been formally introduced yet.

Professor and the snowman contemplated each other.

<"*Are you going to be with my Creator, Professor Malton?*">

All the children around us giggled. Professor Malton raised an eyebrow. Terrance and Mr. Thorough broke out laughing while Lord Grayson's mouth opened in surprise.

Why in the world would Camillo think that? I could feel my face go red in embarrassment. Professor Malton was a father figure to me.

Professor Malton settled for bowing to Camillo, then adding, "It is an honor to meet you, Camillo. Thank you for thinking I am worthy but no."

Terrance got his laughing under control. "My friend. I don't think any of us here are worthy of being with Lady Vivian."

<*You sing about being with a woman often, my friend. It is important to you. I want to see the person's glow who my Creator will be with.*">

There were more giggles from the children around us. Even a few of the parents who were close to us laughed. I bet this would make its way to the Pioneer Press somehow: *Camillo, Matchmaker of Snowmen.*

I gave Terrance a frustrated look that I hoped conveyed: *age-appropriate songs from now on*. Camillo was only a few days old.

Putting a smile on my face and trying to keep some dignity about me, I said, "I haven't found the right person yet, Camillo. But thank you. Would you come with me to meet some others at my school?"

<*"Yes, Creator. I like meeting new people. Do you think they will want a toy for Christmas too?"*>

"Kid," said Terrance to Lord Grayson, "that's our cue to leave. Camillo, when you're done, the kid and I will be up on the mountain pass."

From my link with Camillo, I heard him say, <*"Creator, what is dancing?"*>

Like always, our conversations weren't private. I still had no idea why. People near us could hear our mental chatter as we talked back and forth. I made a mental note to see if there was a way of building a private mode between us. Sigh. More things to work on. Sleep was becoming a distant dream.

After Wanda and I had introduced Camillo to the maids and footmen, we headed toward the Blind Buttonhole.

Camillo followed and told me about his day as we moved through the town. It took longer than I expected as children seemed to pop out from everywhere to meet Camillo. Since it was important to him, he learned their names and what they wanted for Christmas. Wanda and I were late for our appointment.

It had only been a day, but I sensed Camillo's vocabulary had grown. He didn't need to have concepts explained to him as often. Also, I picked up that his memory was likely eidetic.

But everyone has their own point of view. When a "friend" explained something to Camillo, it became fact in his frozen mind. He had no ability to understand that there might be nuances. To Camillo, there was God, his Creator (me), friends, of which Terrance was the first friend, then children and everyone else.

Once we turned down Threadneedle Street, I saw Mina waving at us. Sierra was right next to her. "How come they're here?" I asked Wanda.

Wanda sniffed. "You're sort of stingy with money. Mina's afraid you'll choose something plain. So, she's here to be your guide."

It was true I didn't like spending money if I didn't need to. "Fine, but there better not be any feathers." For whatever reason, feathers had come in style about a month ago. Personally, I thought it was ridiculous.

♫

Because we were late, the four of us had to wait a few minutes. During this, Camillo watched us through the main shop windows. By now, there were almost thirty children around him who took turns peering in at us. I'm not sure how it happened, but at one point, the children formed a ring around him and began dancing. Several buggies pulled by horses slowed to watch. With the snow flurries, Camillo, and the children, it was a beautiful site.

Then I blinked at the bright light. That cameraman was across the street and had just taken Camillo's picture. If the reporter was around, I bet he would try to ask Camillo questions. Who knows what my snowman would say, and Terrane wasn't here to protect him. "Sierra," I said, scanning the street for the reporter, "would you be willing to go outside and guard Camillo?" I bet between looking at dresses versus guarding Camillo, Camillo would win.

A smile formed on Sierra's face. "As the Snowball Queen says," and she headed for the door. Just before it closed behind her, I heard, "Okay kids, we're going to make some snowballs and have target practice."

Mina giggled.

♫

Mina looked at color swatches while the two seamstresses took our measurements. A small part of me felt like I was a mannequin.

Apparently, what I wanted was inconsequential. As I stood there feeling frustrated, Mina, Wanda, and the older seamstress discussed dress options. Didn't I get a vote in any of this?

"How come I can't pick out the colors?" I asked Mina.

Mina ignored me and held up a light blue swatch. "That's the one."

"Of course, Milady," said the seamstress. "Now, let's discuss the venue."

"Mina," I said in exasperation. "I'm right here."

The younger seamstress looked at the floor.

Apparently, I was doing something wrong.

Mina sighed. "Vivian. Outside of school, who is the highest noble you have ever met?"

I shrugged. "My benefactor. Why? It's his wedding."

Wanda just shook her head.

"Okay, what am I missing?"

Mina sat down in a chair and let out her breath. "Vivian," she said softly. "You're going to meet Lady Gawain, Lady Tartenille, and likely Lady Elizabeth Navartis, the merlin's guide. If I don't dress you and Wanda appropriately, my mother will disown me. Heck, it's possible the new merlin might be there."

The older seamstress turned slowly toward me. "You're going to meet Lady Elizabeth Navartis?" There was awe in her voice.

Wanda said excitedly, "Lord Winton is marrying Lady Kiera who is Lady Gawain's new sister-in-law, so she's got to be there. And Lady Gawain is Lady Elizabeth's right hand. So, absolutely."

The older seamstress suddenly curtsied. "Please excuse me, milady. I will be back in a moment." She grabbed the younger seamstress's hand and pulled her into another room.

"Mina, sure, they might be there, but come on, Lady Kiera isn't going to introduce me to them. They're *the* high nobles, and I'm just Vivian Hampton. Wanda and I will be at the party and hopefully get a picture together with Lord Winton and Lady Kiera, but that's it."

From the look in Wanda's eye, she obviously thought differently. "We need to add on a feather," she declared.

"Darn right," declared Mina. "If I sent you to this wedding without one, my mother would send me to a nunnery."

I sighed in frustration. "Fine. But only one feather."

"Aren't they coming back?" I asked Mina. The two seamstresses had been gone for over three minutes.

"They're probably getting some fabrics in the color I picked out," suggested Mina as she held up two feathers next to me. "The red one, definitely."

I was back to being a mannequin.

Within my mind, I heard Camillo's mental touch.

<*"Creator, what are drums?"*>

I mentally replied, happy that I had something to do. <*"They are musical instruments to make a beat. Like a beating heart. They give a song a cadence. Why?"*>

<*"Timothy wants a set for his birthday. Am I allowed to give presents on birthdays too?"*>

Uh oh. <*"I think that is something we need to talk about later."*> Then a thought occurred to me—Mrs. Capmond might like some company. <*"Would you stop by Mrs. Capmond's house after I go back to school? You could ask her what she thinks. And when you find Terrance, ask him as well."*>

Hopefully, it would help Camillo understand different people see things in different ways. Besides, Mrs. Capmond had to be lonely.

<*"Yes, Creator. May I stay and watch to see if God comes to take Mr. Capmond's soul?"*>

<*"For a time, if Terrance comes. Stay with him, please. Even if you don't see anything, Camillo. Don't stop believing it happens."*>

<*"Yes, Creator."*>

You never know, but I doubted it was God who came down. All the stories had angels which shepherded the fallen. Who knows, maybe Camillo will see something. If he did, it would be interesting to write a song about it.

As I pondered the structure of such a song, the far door opened, and a tall, very tidy man held open the door for an older woman with long white hair in an elaborate blue dress.

I immediately curtsied. "Lady Huntington." I had seen her about town on occasion and she liked listening to me sing. But I had never been formally introduced to her.

She nodded her head in acceptance of the curtsy. "Ellie tells me you will be attending Lord Winton and Lady Kiera's wedding?"

"Yes, ma'am. Wanda and I were just looking at some dress sketches."

"Young lady, you are representing the Pioneer Academy, the town, and, more importantly, me as I am the highest noble here." She looked down at the sketches on the table and sniffed. "These will not do." Then indicating the neat man who held open the door for her, she said, "Victor, take over."

Victor bowed very low to us. "I have the pleasure of serving as Lady Huntington's modiste. Let us get a proper dress designed for you two. One that will say 'I am a proud, confident, and dignified young lady. Do you dare to dance with me?'"

He took a step back. "Ms. Wanda, let us consider you first."

As the man drew on the canvas with a charcoal pencil, I could tell Wanda was enraptured. Even Mina seemed fascinated by what the man was creating.

I edged my way toward Lady Huntington. "Ma'am, thank you," I said in a whisper. "But between Wanda and me, we only have four silver talons."

The etching of the flowing dress taking form for Wanda was stunning. I didn't want to take that away from her, but there was no way I could afford it.

Lady Huntington sniffed. "Young lady, you have provided a spark of hope to this town. Any noble who doesn't see that, isn't worthy of their title. The two dresses are a gift from me."

Oh. "Thank you, Lady Huntington." I wasn't sure what else to say, but just to make conversation added, "I've seen you watching me sing. Do you like the songs?"

She tilted her head slightly. "I heard a rumor that you have the bardic voice. Is the rumor true?"

I bit my lip. "Yes, ma'am. My training starts with Lady Cassandra this week."

Lady Huntington twisted her head ever so slightly to look at me. "Lady Cassandra Altum, Sorcerer Petotum's apprentice."

"Yes, ma'am."

Lady Huntington's mouth twitched into a smile. "A noble will likely be appointed by the council to administer the new lands beyond the next range. It will be interesting to see who they pick."

I didn't know why she was bringing me into that conversation. "I don't know, Lady Huntington. I imagine it would be someone who lives here as well."

"Indeed Ms. Vivian, and now I think it is your turn in front of Victor."

Mina had her hand to her mouth as she looked back and forth between me and the sketch Lady Huntington's modiste had drawn out. "You're going to look like a queen."

♪♪♪

We met Sierra and Camillo outside. More children had come, but Sierra had gotten them organized into groups. Some were making snowballs, while others seemed to be standing guard, ready to throw. One of the older children approached me and bowed. He was a brown-haired boy, maybe nine years old. "Anton, ma'am," he said excitedly. "Sierra knighted me. I'm now the commander of the Snowball Queen irregulars." After a quick salute, he threw the snowball in his hands at the reporter across the street. It just missed the man. The reporter, for his part, grinned and seemed to be enjoying the game. The cameraman, on the other hand, had a scowl on his face.

"Second volley," shouted Sierra and eight more snowballs streaked across the street, three of them hitting the cameraman. Sierra had formed an army.

Wanda broke out laughing.

Mina nudged me. "The Snowball Queen has been given great powers. Use them wisely."

I couldn't help but smile. Then I curtsied to Anton. "Good job, my knight. May you always strike true."

And I heard the oddest bell in my mind again. Very similar to what I heard when I handed my old wand over to Wanda.

That night as I drifted off to sleep, I had warm bubbles in my mind as I imagined dancing in that dress. Then that vision popped into my head again of the attack and of Wanda being killed. It wasn't during the upcoming wedding but some other time. Also, I was wearing a different dress—nice but not that masterpiece. With effort, I was able to replay parts of the vision and eventually noticed a detail. This was a party at our school. Was this the upcoming dance in ten weeks? But Jeffery was supposed to take me there, not Lord Grayson. It took me some time to fall asleep as I tried to think up ways of discovering the crux points that led to Wanda's death. Just as I was falling asleep, I almost imagined a shadowy wolf running away.

Chapter 15

Finding the devil lies in the details.
-Any good detective

-Terrance-

Mrs. Capmond's Roof

"Damn. Sorry."

I had to control my strength. Now that the night had returned. So had my exceptional strength. My hammer shot the nail right through the shingle into Mrs. Capmond's small kitchen.

Mrs. Capmond looked up at me through the hole in her roof. "Missed me by six inches. I'm not ready to melt yet, young man."

I smiled at the word *melt*. Camillo had described her husband's funeral as a "melting party." Those attending laughed, jokes were made, but more importantly, they accepted my friend. I bet the term "melting party" was quickly going to spread through town.

I looked down at her. "Let's get enough shingles in place tonight so it doesn't snow into your kitchen. Tomorrow, I can expand from there."

"Thank you, young man. Do you think your apprentice would like some more hot tea?"

It was still snowing a bit. Enough had fallen that it covered old tracks. Perfect for what I wanted. Darlene and Franklin had gone back home. I wished them a good night and hoped to see them tomorrow. Franklin was making noises that he was willing to help the kid and me with the cold cases. I suspected he felt that thrill of the chase rising to the surface. I had to remind myself he was old. While he could take care of himself, one good hit, and Darlene might lose her husband. I didn't want to tell that good woman her husband had died following me. I don't think my heart could bear it.

I leaned backwards slightly and watched the snow fall and felt, well, warmth spreading inside me. I had friends who wanted to keep making a difference, and they saw me as someone who could help make that happen. Camillo firmly believed people had souls—their own song. A small part of me was beginning to believe it as well. I still wondered what Camillo saw inside me. Every time I was happy, he described my light as getting brighter.

I was about to grab another nail when I felt a subtle difference. There was another person next to me, and she hadn't been there a second ago. Her sudden appearance hadn't made a sound, and I could have heard a pin drop three rooms away. If she ever turned her mind to it, the woman would make an excellent thief.

"I heard you met Lady Cassandra."

I put down my hammer and twisted to sit down next to Lady Elizabeth, the merlin's guide. She still wore a green dress, but it had somehow shifted to a much darker green. The moving runes had changed as well. Now they looked like muted white dots, almost like snow falling. With the actual snowflakes around us, I bet it would be almost impossible to spot her from a distance. If she was cold, she gave no indication of it. I bet that dress of hers was nearly indestructible.

"I have. She's a sneaky little minx. Not sure if I trust her yet. How are you holding out?"

I didn't think the woman just appeared to talk. My troubles were likely nothing compared to hers. But I was glad she came. That urge in me to be next to a woman surfaced. But you didn't bed this woman—she chose you, and I bet the list of possible candidates was short, and my name was likely not on it.

"Frustrated. There's something happening in the background and somehow Lady Cassandra is wrapped up in it. I personally think she's terrified and is trying to decide if she should ask for my help, which would bring in Sarah if I allowed it."

"Sarah?"

Lady Elizabeth leaned back to look up at the falling snow. "The new merlin. I sense the Iron Dragon, her mom, has forbidden Lady Cassandra from asking Sarah or her friends for help."

I leaned backwards as well. It was surprisingly therapeutic watching the snow fall. Made the world feel at peace. Before I could offer my opinion, a voice from below reminded me the two of us weren't alone.

"Who's up there with you?"

"The merlin's guide, Mrs. Capmond," I replied. Then turning to the beautiful woman by my side. "Do you want any tea? Mrs. Capmond is dying to feed another cup to someone."

Lady Elizabeth dimpled. "No, thank you. I only have a few minutes."

At her smile, I almost fell off the roof. It was like looking at the sunrise and hoping it would never end. Mrs. Capmond's stern voice brought me back.

"No smooching on my roof, young man. Treat the lady with some respect."

Lady Elizabeth laughed and punched my arm.

"Mrs. Capmond," said Lady Elizabeth, turning to peer down. "Could you give Terrance and me a few minutes?"

"Fine. Reckon I'll bring some warm tea to that young man. He's handsome too. Might do my own smooching."

I shot back with, "Your husband's grave is barely cold. Do you have no shame?"

"Sorry, didn't hear you over all the smooching above me."

Once the front opened, then closed, I took a chance, "Care for my thoughts?"

It was probably my imagination. But I thought she moved closer to me a bit. "Yes."

I pushed down my own desire to move closer to her. "If what you say is true, maybe the little minx is trying a runaround. She handed me a ring earlier today. A ring a dragon would want in its hoard."

I felt her look at me and wait.

"It's made of orichalcum. There are runes on it I've never seen before, and at least one layer hidden from me."

"I take it you haven't put it on yet?"

I snorted. "Every thief in existence would come after me if they knew about the ring. Likely dragons too. I bet she's hoping to draw you into it without breaking her promise to the iron dragon. I'm just her pawn."

The two of us watched the snow fall for a bit.

"You're more than a pawn, Terrance. You're finding a way. I really need that too."

Now it was my turn to tilt my head to look at her and just wait. When she didn't say anything for a bit I asked, "How's the moppet?"

She turned her head to look at me and dimpled. "Sarah?"

God, she was beautiful. I had no idea why the snow wasn't melting when it touched her. A part of me wanted to dust it off her face just so I could nudge myself closer to her. That would also be the wrong thing to do.

Instead, I nodded.

She laughed and looked back up at the falling snow. "Sarah and Nenet are at war with each other. It's like two queens battling it out for who will have domination of their school. Jonnie and Lady Cassandra just stay out of the way and expect me to referee. If it wasn't for Captain Calvit, I would have a harder time managing Sarah."

I asked. "Nenet?" I knew who Captain Calvit was. His name was bandied about from others I had met. The Lady of the Lake had appeared and presented him with a sword of power. There were some in Avalon who thought Guinevere's circlet should be passed down to his wife. I heard the discussion got a mite testy in some of the more colorful bars in Avalon City.

"She's the Lady of the Lake's apprentice. Sarah and Nenet are frenemies. It's like watching two dragons circle each other for domination. Trying to provide some balance to Sarah when she gets focused on something is like trying to turn a hurricane. I personally don't understand how her friends did it before I came along."

I leaned backwards. "I take it getting the two of them to focus on an external problem as a team would be difficult?"

"The Sunshine Mystery Magic Club back together again," Lady Elizbeth murmured then snorted. "I don't want Sarah involved in what lies below, lord knows what she would do with it."

"I take it you're ready to pull your hair out?" While I said it partially as a question, I felt like this woman really was hoping for some good advice. What little wisdom I possessed got me killed in my last life. I still wasn't sure what she saw in me.

Lady Elizabeth sat up and dusted herself off, then looked straight ahead. "I never thought I would see the day when a dragon got frustrated."

"Need some history here. That little mop of a kid who splattered me into my next life has a dragon for a master? I sort of thought you were it."

Lady Elizabeth leaned into me, and I froze. "I thought I was the smart one until I encountered Sarah. Think of me as the big-sister-slash-referee. I step in when Sarah's not in a training session with her master, at school, or with her family."

I reached into my pocket and pulled out the ring case. "Up to you."

She straightened up and took the box from me. With my Sight, I watched very subtle fields of magic extend from her hand to wrap around the box. The gems, cut to represent runes, glowed, and the box opened. Inside was the ring.

"Where did she get this?" Lady Elizabeth whispered.

I lightly bumped her shoulder with my fist. "Our little minx implied she got it from the Houser Bank. It's possible you and I are being played."

There was one job my doppelgänger never took. Someone asked him to break into the Houser Bank. The astronomical pay offered was doubled, then doubled again. He just shook his head and walked away. The Houser Bank was rumored to have been established by a family of four elf brothers, hence the full name of the bank was Houser, Houser, Houser, and Houser. Its unofficial name was the bank of the dead. If you didn't have a vault, you didn't come back out. Elder Dragons were rumored to be on the board of directors—at the low end of the table. It was the place where self-aware books were stored. Rumor has it, a Cthulhu attempted to break in and was destroyed. And our little minx just tap-dances in, opens a vault and hands over a ring made of orichalcum with runes I have never seen before. I believed her story. But I bet she was in deep, and the ring was her attempt to either bribe me or drag Lady Elizabeth into the problem. I knew who my friends were, and Terrance stood by his friends.

Lady Elizabeth slowly closed the case and handed it back to me. "Let me think about it. There's something happening here which I don't understand and that worries me."

"Amen."

The two of us sat in silence for a bit. I knew the woman had to leave, but every second with her was precious. With my enhanced vision, I could see Mrs. Capmond pulling her coat tighter as she walked back toward the house. I suspected the kid was thankful for the warm tea.

"Ma'am," I asked. "Why me?"

Why was this incredible woman coming to me to talk things out with me? From the stories, she had a legion of friends, powerful ones. Her best being Lady Gawain who, from the stories, possessed deep wisdom. I was just a duplicate of a master thief. The only wisdom I learned came from lots of pain.

"You're finding a way, Terrance. It's hard to see a way forward, and a small part of me is terrified of what I could become."

A strong urge to put my arm around this queen bubbled up inside me. Very akin to my bloodlust, just coming from a different spot. I pushed it down.

"Without Camillo, I wouldn't be here," I said softly while looking straight ahead. "Seeing a true innocent ask me for help felt like looking into the maker's eyes. I never want to forget that feeling."

The two of us watched the snow fall for another minute. While it stuck to me without melting, it started to swirl away from this woman. I bet she was preparing to leave.

"Terrance, thank you," I heard from beside me. When I turned, she had vanished without a sound.

Mrs. Capmond peered up at me and snorted. "Well, you're learning how to treat a woman with respect. Will wonders never cease?"

"Ma'am," I said. "I've got to start somewhere, and with you hounding me, I reckon I might get it right eventually."

"Well next time, how about you take her for a walk? Women like it when a man can share the world with them."

I picked up another nail. "Might do that."

She walked into her house and looked up at me through the hole in her roof. "Thank you, Terrance," she said and pulled on a second coat.

Come hell or high water, it wouldn't be snowing in her kitchen by the end of the next hour.

♪♪♪

"What did you spot?" I asked the kid as the two of us headed back to town.

After dusting more snow off his cloak, he said, "You were right. I saw one of the Realm Knights. A Jingo bear poked its head out of a cave, snorted, and went back in. A couple of foxes playing. But the last animal was odd."

I had instructed the kid to find a spot where he could hide and let the snow cover him. Some creatures can sense heat, and I wanted him near invisible to just about every sense. Fifteen minutes in, and even I had a hard time spotting him. The kid has some talent.

"Sort through the memories. Talk it out when you're ready." Rule number one, don't push recollection. The unconscious mind sees more than you think, but if you push too hard, it will shift memories around to get to something it understands. Once that happens, the background information is harder to tap.

We walked in silence around a switchback. My enhanced vision noticed the Realm Knight following us. He probably thought he hadn't been spotted. Important to help him believe that. If you control the perception of reality, then it's possible to sometimes nudge it when you want to. All sorts of interesting things fall out of the metaphysical branches when you do that.

"There was a big wolf," the kid started out slowly. "Not surprising up here, but I didn't see a pack. Maybe it was displaced from the valley over being flattened."

"Maybe," I suggested. "What made you think it was odd?"

The kid was silent again. My grudging acceptance of the kid was growing. He wanted to learn, had some skills, knew they needed to be upgraded and was taking the concept that not everyone was what they seemed in stride.

Time to try a different memory tactic. "What are your thoughts on Lady Vivian?"

The kid blushed and looked away.

"It's okay to appreciate a good woman when you see one. Do you want to date her?"

"Sir, my head of house has five ladies he wants to introduce to me."

"You're quite a catch in certain circles, aren't you? You will likely enhance the family of the woman you choose. It's okay. That's how the world works in Avalon. What do *you* want?"

The kid continued to look away. "Ms. Hine, Lady Vivian's henchman, feels trapped. Her benefactor wants to marry her off to become a baby machine. She hopes I will write her head of house a letter of recommendation after this weekend."

"Noble of you," I said. "Will you?" The kid was changing the topic to get away from the original question.

He nodded, then said without looking behind us, "The Realm Knight is following us, isn't he?"

I grinned, g*ood boy.* "He thinks we don't know. Let's keep it that way."

"Sir, who was that woman on the roof with you? She just appeared. Whatever magic she was using was amazingly subtle. I couldn't detect it."

"Lady Elizabeth, the merlin's guide." Now let's see if the kid was going to push back.

"Oh." His mouth twitched, and he put his hands into his coat pockets. "Do you want to date her?"

I smiled. Yep, the kid was pushing back. Good. "Women like her pick their partner themselves, kid. I doubt if I will ever be on the list. But to answer your question, I would. A man's got the right to dream. Keeps him going when the world almost turns black."

The kid kept his hands in his pockets as we rounded another switchback. Then he stopped. "Son of a bitch," he whispered.

"Keep walking," I said immediately. "Don't let those following us suspect we detected something. Give me the details."

"Yes, sir. The wolf had a gem attached to a choker around its throat."

Good, now that he was sorting through his memories, I bet more will pop up in his dreams or at odd times now that his conscious mind has a path to them. Out loud I said, "A wolf wearing a gem could mean a werewolf, a controlled wolf, an illusion, or something else. As you go through the evening, see if any other details emerge."

After the final switchback, the kid took a quick look behind him.

I sighed. One step at a time. If we were going to be attacked, it would have happened already and that Realm Knight following us would likely have been taken out first.

"Sir, you said 'those.' Do you think there's more than just the Realm Knight following us?"

"Kid, I would bet money on it. Now, let's go play some poker." The game of cat and mouse was a long one. If one was very careful, sometimes the mouse had the opportunity to hunt the cat.

I thought the Dancing Pony Inn would be less busy. My mistake. People were streaming into town to make the trek across the mountain to the valley beyond. They needed a place to stay, and the Dancing Pony was good without being pretentious. Just the right place to stay if you had a bit of extra money to guarantee your safety and privacy. Adventurers were taking up a third of the seats in the main hall, talking and drinking. Fifteen I recognized from the previous night, likely regulars. I had played poker with a few of them the previous evening. Then another ten or so I had met on the trails.

At our entrance, a few mugs of beer were raised. That gesture was used worlds over to say we know you, like you, and we welcome you back into the herd.

The kid whispered to me, "Can you drink beer, sir?"

"I might take a sip now and then. Order some food for yourself."

One of the barmaids whispered to a large man at the bar, the one who reinforced the rules the other night. He nodded at her and came over. "Welcome back, Terrance. There's a bet going on whether the curse is real. Total pot is over eight gold talons. Before you step over to the bar, I need to ask you formally if you have any agents who have participated in this bet."

I bowed. "On my oath, I have not bet or have knowledge of any agents who have bet on my behalf."

Eyes turned to me. A few also glanced at the kid. Probably wondering how he was involved in all this. Some of the adventurers leaned over and asked others what the bet was about. As words were shared, their eyes went wide.

"Fair enough. Well spoken. Do you want to settle the bet now or leave it hanging for a while longer? Officially, I set the rules that all betting was closed once you entered."

"Not one to leave things hanging," I replied and stepped over to the bar. Above the bar was a permanent globe of light. My shadow immediately began to animate. It twirled around, did a bow and "sat down" on a barstool, seemingly interested in the woman on the next barstool.

There were some groans, likely from those on the losing end of the bet. Table thumps and more than a few laughs—the winners. But what I was looking for was the narrowing of eyes or some industrious wannabe monster hunter shooting me with a crossbow. One or two spat on the floor and made the sign of the cross.

I didn't pick up any immediate threats. Being that I was the center of attention, these people wanted my story. They took me in last night, laughed, and shared stories. Now it was my turn.

Everything I told them was the absolute truth. I just left out the detail of the merlin apparition. I concluded with, "I met Sorcerer Petotum and his apprentice earlier today. Apparently, if you're lucky enough to break free from what lies below, then you should be drafted."

I pointed at the kid. "They saddled me with this kid. He's a junior reserve Realm Knight who apparently might show some promise. They want us to look at some cold cases around town. See if we can make anything of them, and maybe I'll teach the kid a few things." I concluded with, "Apparently if you succeed at something, someone comes along and hands you more work."

Got some grins and nods at that statement and one burp from a miner. His buddy next to him raised his mug in salute. I bet they were part of the crew which had collapsed the tunnel today.

Pointing at my shadow now pretending to drink a whiskey, "I'm hoping it goes away. But it doesn't seem to care what I say."

For an answer, it gave me the finger again. When I started edging away from the bar, my shadow made a grabbing motion as if he was trying to hold on to the bar while waving at the woman. Once I stepped back ten feet, it faded away again. That's when the laughing started.

I raised my voice a bit. "Thank you for not shooting me full of pointy things. Am I still allowed to drink with you?"

Heads turned toward the stairs. A middle-aged woman showing her first wrinkles was leaning against the barrister. My guess, she was the owner of the inn or the wife of the owner.

"Reckon you can stay, Terrance. I didn't detect anything false in your story, and you told it at my inn. Round of drinks are on me in celebration for the slightly dinged idiot surviving a curse."

I couldn't help but laugh as people cheered around me.

The kid joined me at a table. Once a waitress came over, I ordered three drinks. "The kid here is on the job. He's not allowed to drink. But I'll take one for me and give the other two to those miners. I suspect they saw some things they will wish to forget."

After drinks were brought over. The broader of the two miners came over and sat down to my left. "We saw it," he said after blowing off some foam. "Sparkling and pulsing, growing like a snake. Some say it's from a dragon's dream. And that it is waking up."

"Is the tunnel collapsed now?" I inquired and took a drink myself. The taste would be better if there was some blood in it. Experimentation for another day.

"We did it. Nothing's getting through. But don't know what's going to happen when that dragon opens its eyes."

I raised my glass and clinked it against his. "And considering how long dragons live, let's hope that's a very long time from now."

"Truer words, my friend," said the miner and stood up to go back over to drink with his friend.

A few others came over and hoped for more of my story. I gave them a few tidbits, telling them how scared I was and of Camillo's bravery. Once we had a few moments alone, the kid leaned over. "Sir, what's really down there?"

"Merlin only knows, kid. Still have those old cases with you?"

"Yes, sir," and he pulled the folders out of his backpack. "Which one do you want to start with?"

I stood up and motioned toward the poker table in the back of the room. "I'm going to play poker. You're going to sit near me and read us the particulars on the most recent case as we play. You find nuggets of truth in the oddest of places. Let's see if the other players want to help."

The kid opened his mouth, closed it. Then he followed me as I took a seat near the back of the room.

♪♪♪

The heavy-set man to my right lowered his cards and took a pull on his cigar. After blowing out a smoke ring he said, "Timing's wrong. Mrs. Pearlson was seen by her friends near the center fountain at ten in the morning." He leaned back and looked at the kid. "My wife was there."

Lord Grayson looked up from the notes he had been reading us. "Then either someone's lying, or Mrs. Pearlson was in two places at the same time."

The man who had pointed a derringer at me this morning was sitting across from me. Fortunately, he held five cards in his left hand instead of a gun. He glanced at the kid. "One of them could have been an illusion. But it would have to be a good one. Someone who knew the woman's mannerisms." Then he pushed two cards to the dealer, two more were handed over.

I grunted as his heartbeat picked up a notch. I was going to lose my two copper talons. I leaned my chair backwards and asked the kid, "Who are the woman's neighbors? And do any of them own a wand?"

The kid rifled through his notes. "Sir, I don't know."

The barmaid who had been listening to our back and forth handed over another whiskey to the man on my left. "I do know. Three years ago, Mr. Headon's grandson was kicked out of the Pioneer Academy for thievery. They live two doors down from where Mrs. Pearlson lived."

The man with the likely winning hand put his cards down. I threw my cards down in disgust and grunted. While I knew I was going to lose, I played out the hand anyway. Best to keep up appearances. The rest of the table echoed my frustration. Then I leaned back in my chair again. "Well, what are you waiting for? Go interview Mr. Headon's little family thief. If he's the guilty party, you owe the patrons a drink."

The kid put all the papers back in their folder. "Sir, aren't you coming?"

I threw my ante into the center of the table. "I'm not a Realm Knight. I'm just your guide. On your way there, pay attention for a large wolf."

The man to my left downed his whiskey and raised his eyebrow.

"Someone doesn't want one of these cases solved," I said. "We were trailed coming down from Mrs. Capmond's house."

The man across from me stood up. "I'll walk with you, kid. Let's see if my good luck holds."

I watched him palm his derringer.

Kid was beginning to learn. I looked down at my beer and wished for about the tenth time that I could slip some blood in it.

♫

I won the next two hands and decided to call it quits. Wandering over to the bar, my shadow came back.

"Too bad you can't really slap him," I said to the young lady dressed to pick up a partner for the evening. My shadow had leaned over and had tried to "kiss her." Her palm went right through my shadow, distorting it for a second. Then it leapt backwards and pretended to dance.

After apologizing again, I watched the woman eye me, probably considering if I might keep her warm for the night. I bowed. "Camillo and I are sort of bunking together until we can figure out what to do next."

Before she could respond, I turned to the owner behind the bar. With so many extra people, she had been helping make drinks. "Do you have any more of those glass mason jars?"

Along the right wall were eight mason jars with a name on each of them. Patrons the bar liked who needed the extra money for something. A person could toss in a coin if they were of mind. Three of them had a fair number of pennies, another one a handful of copper talons. It was an old Avalon tradition: take care of your own. I couldn't see any magic protections about the jars, but they had the best protection in town. If you try to take one of these jars, many angry patrons will hunt you down. My bet is no one would ever find the body, and no one would ask any questions either.

I liked this place.

"Is this for you or the kid?" she asked after pulling a mason jar from under the counter.

I smiled to myself. Lord Grayson was forever going to be known as "the kid" in this bar.

"Neither," then took the offered red pen. I wrote out *Camillo*, then under it, *Kids' Christmas list*. Then dropped his list I wrote down into the jar.

She leaned back and considered me. "Is there a story here?"

At her words, the place quieted down. I turned around and held up the jar. "Just about every kid in town found my friend today and told him what they wanted for Christmas." I dropped in a silver talon. "Whether my friend makes it through summer or not, this is for the kids who believe in him."

The place had gone quiet. This wasn't the kind of story they were expecting.

"You're a good man, Terrance," said the owner. She dropped in a silver talon too.

I was completely surprised when she leaned across the bar to kiss me on the cheek. Then with a wink, she laughed. "If you ask me out to dinner some night, you might not get slapped."

Before I could reply, she placed Camillo's jar next to the others. "Okay, you nitwits," she announced. "This is for the kids."

My bet, before the night was out, a few more coins might end up in that jar.

I was still feeling warm from sharing my stories with those inside when I saw the kid turn the corner.

"Well?" I asked.

"It was him. Believe it or not, the idiot was wearing one of her rings."

I snorted. The little thief wanted to show off his trinket to commemorate the murder. I bet they were going to find stolen items which he hadn't sold yet in his room.

"Sir, what now?"

"I'm heading back up to find Camillo. I figure that after today, he's going to have about a thousand questions for me. I am going to stay in a cave with him during the day. See you tomorrow night?"

"You can't get rid of me that easily, sir."

"Kid," I said, and he turned back to me. "Whatever you think you saw, there's going to be more. We need to find that trail of breadcrumbs."

"Yes, sir."

I pulled out my wand, the good one. "Do you know the gather point spell, kid?" Spells often had different names. The gather point spell had about a dozen that I knew of. It was a low-level spell two or more people could cast on their wands linking them together to pass messages. Range was only a couple of miles, and it had no real encryption. But if you talked into your wand while that spell was active, the others who were linked could hear you.

There was a moment's hesitation from the kid. Good, keep on asking who you trust. Finally, I got a "yes, sir," and we tapped wands together. There was a faint pulse of blue light and that was it. The spell only lasted a day.

"Sir," he said after sheathing his wand. "I'm not sure if the spell will extend beyond the school's wards."

"Kid," I said, before he turned away. "Maybe not. But with the wand I have, it just might. Don't hesitate to call if you need to."

I watched him turn the corner, then turned away myself to head back up the mountain.

♩♪♩

<"My friend. I am confused.">

"Well, that just means you're alive." Camillo and I met up at Mrs. Capmond's. I think she wanted to adopt my friend. We said goodbye to the woman and headed back up the mountain to find a suitable mine. Our previous one had collapsed. Hopefully, the new one we chose wouldn't be cursed.

<"My friend, can you help me? One of the parents told me I will melt soon. Do you think that is true? While I don't want to melt, if I do, will I go to my creator?">

Oh. This was going to be a long night. The question of the ages: will God come for me, does He think I'm worthy? Etc... I cocked my head and turned the question around. Did God approve of Terrance? I remembered all the things the kid and I did today. Meeting Lady Elizabeth again, the warmth and acceptance from the patrons and owner of The Dancing Pony, my annoyance at Lady Cassandra. Now that I had a chance to step back, I remembered Lady Elizabeth's comment about Lady Cassandra. "We try not to bother her too often." The cursed knight's statement to me was, "She's the power behind the throne." There was something to that which had to be associated with being able to walk into the Houser Bank.

I suspected if Lady Cassandra brought her power to bear, I would be a gnat. What game was she playing and what throne? If she was recruiting, I wasn't enlisting. I made my choice, perhaps not altogether willingly, but I had signed on with Lady Elizabeth already and wasn't about to change allegiances.

I shook my head to clear it. The only thing that was important tonight was Camillo. He was this odd messenger of hope. Getting people to look at life in a different way—especially me.

"Camillo, I can guarantee Lady Vivian is very happy with you. Let's find a cave, and we can talk some more."

<*"My friend?"*>

"Yes, Camillo?"

<*"Thank you for being my friend."*>

I could feel Camillo's relief I was here and his hope I could make it all better. I looked up at the stars before stepping into the cave. "Maker, thank you for giving me a second chance."

<*"Are you talking to my creator, my friend? I am too far away. I can't hear her."*>

"Camillo, let's talk about faith."

As we talked, my words came from a place within me I hadn't known existed until recently.

Chapter 16

Every so often, two Jingo Bears will fight. Rule number one: You get as far away as fast as possible. Rule number two: They can teleport, so if the other animals around you are still running, you better run faster.

-Attributed to the old saying: Never bother a bear in its place of power.

-Vivian Hampton-

Pioneer School

I wove across the dance floor, feeling exhilarated. My amazing dress seemed to flow with me as I moved to the song. For the first time, I felt not only comfortable in my body but beautiful. My hair, instead of being in one long braid, was in eight, and they intertwined together down my back.

This part of the school dance was fast but formal. The idea being everyone got a chance to dance with others. Every ninety seconds, the musicians would slow the tempo, and the dance would stop; the women would curtsy to their partner, the men would bow in return, then the men would shift to the left, and the dance would begin again.

My current partner was Lord Tomar, a junior from House Kumar. At the pause in the song, he stepped back and bowed to me. He honestly seemed disappointed he had to shift to another lady. What was even better, Lady Aveline, from House Duke, stared daggers at me every time she got close. At one point, she whispered out, "I'm going to show the school what a pretender you are during the competition."

I ignored her and wove away. I felt like Vivian Hampton was beginning to spread her wings, and instead of a moth, what was emerging was a butterfly.

The competition she mentioned was for the women heroes who had magic, sophomores to seniors. The winner would be crowned queen of the dance for the night. Usually only titled ladies participated, but there was no school rule restricting others. Earlier, Wanda had pushed me into signing up.

After a break where I could catch my breath, I got to mingle with Jeffery, Lord Grayson, and others. While I enjoyed the attention, men seemed to gravitate to me for some reason. If I stayed in place for more than a few seconds, I felt a bit like a fox being hunted by a pack of dogs. I liked feeling beautiful, but I wanted space to breathe too. Fortunately, Wanda, Mina, Gail, and others provided distractions, so I could escape.

As I stood in the large circle along with twenty other girls, most of them ladies, I felt both uncomfortable and a little embarrassed. While I had sung in public many times and enjoyed it, now I felt as if I was in a beauty pageant. The rest of the school's students made a wide circle around me and the others who decided to participate in the competition. The musicians started up, and we began a formal but complicated dance. The difference was that we had to add magic to our movements. Missing a step or failing to get your illusion off meant you were out. You could make whatever illusion you wanted, but the idea was it should wow the audience. A part of me recognized this was a mating ritual from long ago: Was your prospective mate healthy enough to keep up a dance and possessed enough magic and control to be worthwhile? I decided to make an illusion of Lucille, the dragon, but much smaller of course. She jumped around me as I danced. From the crowd's reaction, I thought they liked what I did.

Lady Aveline, the senior from House Duke faltered on her second illusion. She was out. By the end of the long dance, there were only two of us left. Lady Bell, from House Thama. She was the transfer student finishing up school. I didn't know her well, but some of the illusions she cast were amazing. The two of us curtsied, and I took in the thunderous applause. Even if I didn't win, I was Vivian Hampton, a beautiful young woman, and no one would take that away from me. I looked around for my friends, Mina, Jeffery, Lord Grayson, Sierra, and—but where was Wanda?

As I turned in place to try to find her, the audience began a clapping beat. This was the elimination round, which one of us would win the audience over. Lady Bell twirled, and her emerald choker glowed with light. It erupted and the light flowed down her dress, shifting colors as it went, looking very much like the first rays of sun. But her illusion wasn't done, the light reformed into a large, black wolf which circled around her. I grudgingly admitted to myself that her spell and control was awesome. The audience oohed as they clapped. All eyes turned toward me. I could feel the anticipation around me: would Vivian Hampton soar or crash to the ground? Jeffery gave me a thumbs up, Mina was shouting, and even Sierra even looked excited. Lord Grayson's mouth was open in surprise. But I still didn't see Wanda.

Letting out my breath, I focused my magic, twirled in place and before my illusion could take shape, I was woken from my dream by a pillow hitting me on my stomach.

Wanda was staring down at me. I felt like I almost had a full night's rest. Glancing out my window, I could tell the sun hadn't risen fully yet. Well, at least she wasn't jumping on my bed this time.

"What's wrong?" I asked. I didn't hear any alarms or other noises which would indicate there was an emergency.

"I don't know. But Professor Malton tried to call you through your old wand and got me. He says it's important."

I pulled the covers off and sat up. "Give me five minutes."

While dressing, I pondered my dream. I was pretty sure it was the same venue from my other vision—the one where Wanda was killed. But I wasn't certain if my dream was another vision, just a dream, or something else? But that wolf kept on appearing. What did that mean? As I pondered other aspects of my dream, I thought about Wanda. She was there before the competition dance started, but I didn't see her after that. Was that the window where someone grabbed her? As I cast the spell to braid and pin up my hair through my new wand, an idea suddenly hit me. The dress in my dream—if what was made for me was the same dress, then I bet my dream was a vision. My sudden insight made me want to sneak into the Blind Buttonhole this evening to look at the gown being made for me.

Professor Malton was waiting for Wanda and me just outside the Orozco's main door. But so was someone else. "Gail?" I said in surprise. She was standing against the wall, looking afraid. Why was she out of bed? Was she the emergency? That's when I noticed her appearance—her hair was down, and her blouse wasn't buttoned up properly. A memory from the other day, when the dragon had arrived, surfaced. Gail had blurted out, "I'm not a virgin," thinking the Dragon might be looking for a new harem. I bet her secret lover was in our school, and the respective families didn't know anything about their involvement.

Wanda snickered out, "I bet it's an upperclassman from House Coley. It's their week to patrol the halls. Whoever he is probably gave her a pass ward."

Gail opened her mouth in surprise. "Please don't say anything. Lord Abner is waiting for the right time to talk to his head of house."

I held out my hand. "Hand it over," I demanded. Gail silently pulled out a silver pin and dropped it in my palm.

"Vivian," said Professor Malton. "While Ms. Magnoli's activities need to be addressed, she's not the emergency. The headmistress contacted me and asked me to get you."

"Oh."

Didn't Mrs. Rousseau, the headmistress's secretary, ever sleep? It was half an hour before the morning bell, and she was at her desk looking ready to take on the day. She had to be at least sixty. I was fifteen and really wanted that last hour of sleep I was currently missing.

Professor Gass was there too, sitting in a chair and nursing a large mug which I presumed held coffee. Some of the professors seemed to be addicted to the stuff. After yesterday, I could see why. At our entrance, he raised his mug in salute. "Apparently, sleep is a frowned upon activity at this school. Why are we here?"

"At least you had time to get coffee," teased Professor Malton. "I had to deal with an errant student."

"It wasn't me or Wanda," I said, so Professor Gass didn't assume it was either of us.

Professor Gass harrumphed. "I would be surprised if either of you were. You two don't act like hormonal infused addlebrained idiots."

Wanda giggled at his comment. But I had the same question as Professor Gass. "Sir, Professor Malton, why are we here?"

The headmistress secretary put a finger to her lips. "Apparently Ms. Thorol took your advice, Ms. Hampton. She is currently in a discussion with her father and others. Parts of it have been rather loud. The young lady seems frustrated at being excluded from certain family matters. Which ones, I cannot say."

Oh. I bet she contacted her father on my advice.

Wanda's eyes went wide. "Lord Lohort is in the headmistresses' office?" she asked in excitement.

Professor Gass raised an eyebrow at her comment and took a sip of coffee. After a moment, he tilted his head forward in apparent understanding. "Ah, an anagram. But I repeat my earlier question, why am I here?"

"Professor Gass," said Mrs. Rousseau. "The headmistress asked me to call you here. I have no idea. But considering who is also in the room with them, I think it behooves us to wait."

I put a hand on Wanda's arm to stop her likely explosion of questions. "We wait."

She pouted, then reached for the candy bowl and fished out a mint.

♫

We sat in silence which just added to my nervousness. I kept on going back to my dream. I was sure my earlier vision and my dream were of the same dance at our school, and my mind froze as I recognized another obvious connection. Lord Grayson, Jeffery, Mina, Sierra, and others—their clothes were the same as well. It had to be the same party. So, Wanda was likely taken just before the last dance ended and the competition dances began. But I still wasn't sure if my dream was just a dream and nothing more than a fantasy of being a beautiful woman.

I inwardly snorted. I had two minds about the competition dances. I had watched them before last year and even before at towns after I had sung. They were essentially beauty contests for eligible women who could cast magic. Men, and some women, would gather around. Usually, bets would take place on who would be the first to fall, the last one standing, and so on. There was an old song that was effectively an auction, each stanza getting faster until there was only one lady left. At the end of the song, she became the wife of the local lord, and they lived happily ever after. The woman had found her prince and true love had won again.

Being honest with myself, I enjoyed the thought that I could be beautiful and powerful. Even though it was only in my dream, it was the first time where I felt like I could hold my own as a woman. A part of me liked it and wanted more. But was this a trap? Another little devil trying to push me into becoming the social queen, a dictator of sorts? People like Lady Aveline, the senior from House Duke, certainly seemed to be like that. I am the queen, and all other ladies shall bow down before me. I wondered how Lady Bell felt about her. Toward the end of my dream, it was Lady Bell who was my final competition. Did that mean anything? I made a mental reminder to talk to her. Being that she was a transfer student, I don't think we had said two words to each other yet. Personally, I hoped she hated Lady Aveline and maybe even squished her face into the mud. Sigh, there were so many little devils in the world.

My thoughts were redirected by Wanda's nudge.

"What?" I asked quietly. She was miming something with her index finger, touching the ring finger on her right hand. Whatever she was implying went right over my head.

"Gail wasn't wearing a contraceptive ring," whispered Wanda. "Do you think she and Lord Abner were... you know?" And her voice trailed off.

It never occurred to me Gail might take their secret relationship that far. I hoped not. She wasn't a noble, while Lord Abner was. If she was trying to get pregnant, that was just idiotic. The child would be considered a bastard, and as much as I thought Lord Abner was a nice enough person, Avalon was very strict about such relationships. The best outcome Gail could hope for would be to become his unofficial mistress. One of those people Lord Abner's house funded but kept very quiet. Besides, I doubted she would be able to stay in school. Gail's benefactor would likely be rather upset if that happened.

I bit my lip. "I hope not," I whispered back to Wanda, while I inwardly cringed about how to start the conversation with Gail. I wasn't sure if this was part of my job as sophomore head student to advise her or sit back and watch the train wreck happen in front of me? As I pondered options, the headmistress's door opened, and she stepped through before closing the door behind her.

The headmistress adjusted a chair and sat down to face me. I couldn't read her expression, but she looked like she hadn't gotten as much sleep as she hoped for. I was a little nervous. Why was she focusing on me like this? I hadn't done anything wrong that I knew of. "How is Amanda, ma'am?" I said just to say something.

"Lady Amanda is a bit annoyed with her father at the moment," replied the Headmistress dryly, still maintaining eye contact with me. "Fortunately, the shouting has stopped. However, I would like to discuss a larger issue… with you, Ms. Hampton."

"Ruth," said Professor Malton. "What is this about? You're scaring Vivian and, honestly, making me nervous."

Without breaking eye contact with me, she ignored Professor Malton's comment. "Professor Gass," she said. "Aside from the dead man's switch, is there a way of reinforcing the school's main spell circle?"

Professor Gass took a sip of coffee, then looked up in apparent contemplation. He seemed completely unperturbed by the headmistress's intensity, while I felt as if a nest of pixies had taken up residence in my stomach. What did I do?

"We could create a second ring around the main ring which would encompass the dead man's switch," suggested Professor Gass after a moment. "But we would need to tie it to the older ground points. It would help if I knew what type of magic we needed to test. Then I could adjust the secondary ring appropriately."

Still staring at me, the headmistress said slowly, "Vivian, Lady Amanda told her father and half sister that you told her that if she and Elaine wanted to experiment with the rolling magic about them, they should come and get you."

Wanda let out a little gasp. Half sister. That likely meant Lady Julia was in the room too.

I gulped. "Yes, ma'am, I did. I asked them to work together as a team and come get me if they wanted to experiment. I was planning on borrowing one of the circles in the dueling arena."

Professor Malton leaned his head backward and groaned. "Oh, maker. That would have been a disaster."

I looked between Professor Malton and the headmistress in frustration. "What am I missing? I just wanted to help them." What was wrong with that? But Professor Malton was acting like I might have blown up the building.

Wanda bounced up and down in excitement. "What's this about? I know Elaine is from the dragon's lands and Amanda is..."

"Lady Amanda's head of house is another dragon, Ms. Hine," said the headmistress, cutting off Wanda. "Who is apparently in a political battle with our dragon. If those two young ladies were put in the same circle, I suspect aspects of the dragons' power would present themselves. Think, avatars."

Coffee blew out of Professor Gass's mouth. "You want me to design a secondary ring capable of withstanding dragon magic!"

"But you always tell us to test everything in a grounded spell circle," I said, a bit confused and honestly a little angry. They seemed to be saying there was another set of rules, which I knew nothing about. "Even the wandmaking testing book says the same thing. I was just following everyone's guidelines."

The headmistress put her hands to her face and let out a sigh. She sounded so frustrated. Pulling them down, she said very quietly, "The dueling rings likely cannot contain any form of dragon magic, even channeled through avatars."

Professor Gass's face had gone white. "I have no idea if the main ring in the basement could withstand that magic either."

The headmistress reached out and put her hand on top of mine. "I'm not angry at you, Vivian. I'm glad you stepped in. It was my job to have foreseen this. My frustration is really at myself. But I find myself in a very tough spot."

"Ma'am," I asked, still confused. "Amanda and Elaine are just freshmen. They have beginner wands..." and I stopped myself in my tracks. No, they didn't! Elaine had a wand made by Lady Cassandra or even the new Merlin. I had no idea of what it could do, and Amanda had a Darci wand. At the same time, a word the headmistress said was getting bigger in my mind. "Avatars ma'am? As in, they might be able to channel the dragons' magic?"

"That's what I am afraid of, Vivian," said the headmistress. "I suspect, this fourth magical link that I've heard you have, likely goes to this visitor of yours. I am hoping she appears so that we can ascertain she has your best interests at heart. Lady Cassandra suggested this individual was politically stronger than the dragons, but can she, also through this link with you, contain any magic that Elaine and Amanda could channel as the dragons' avatars? If I am not reassured or think this entity is not forthcoming, my only other option may be to send one of the young ladies to another school."

Wanda blurted out, "Can Vivian and I go meet Lady Julia?"

"No," said the headmistress immediately. "We will all go to breakfast. When I left them, the shouting had stopped. Let's give them some space."

Chapter 17

There are three core rules in Avalon. Breaking any of them is a death sentence: outright slavery, mind control, and necromancy.

-Guide to Avalon, 4th printing.

-Vivian Hampton-
House Orozco Dormitory, Pioneer School

I had just enough time to wash my face and brush my teeth. What I didn't have was my privacy.

"I want a wand too."

Déjà vu. I felt like we were repeating the day. I spit toothpaste into the sink. Sierra was leaning against the wall, arms crossed, arguing with me. Didn't we do this yesterday? Hopefully the dragon wasn't coming again.

"Take it up with your magic teacher," I said. That should put her off for a while.

She snorted. "Don't you remember? You're it."

Oh. Drat. She was right, sort of. "Actually, Professor Lessnara is running the class."

Sierra countered with, "It's unfair I have to take a magic class now. Wanda has a wand. I should have one too."

I cocked my head as I parsed out her statement. "Sierra, that makes no sense. You say you're annoyed at having magic homework now, and in the same breath, you want a wand.

Wanda's probably going to have magic homework as well. You can't escape it."

"Wanda and I are partners," declared Sierra and partially turned away.

I sort of saw them that way as well. Wanda was my henchman, but she included Sierra in just about everything they did together, outside of gymnastics. The partnership started soon after Mina and I clicked early last year. But where was Sierra going with this? "Okay, I agree—"

I was about to agree that they were partners, but Sierra obviously heard something else. She spun around and gave me a hug. "I knew you would understand," she said in a very un-Sierra like manner. She almost sounded, well, happy. Then she stepped backwards. "I'll let Wanda know," she said and left the bathroom humming to herself.

What just happened? I gripped the side of the sink and looked at my reflection in the mirror. I felt like the person looking back at me was losing control of, well, everything. "Vivian Hampton," I said out loud. "I'm a butterfly spreading my wings." But why did this butterfly feel like the wind was blowing her in every direction but the one she wanted to go? I made a mental note to write a letter to Lord Winton today letting him know about the class I was helping to teach. Within it, I hoped to nudge the idea along that Wanda was part of this too. It was a secret goal of mine to have Lord Winton talk to Wanda's head of house on my, or rather his behalf. I know it was a longshot, but for Wanda, I would take it.

Out of the corner of my eye, I watched Gail sit down next to me at the breakfast table. I was almost done with my math homework and really didn't want the interruption.

"I'm listening," I said without looking at her. Whoever came up with trigonometry was either a genius, or a madman, or both. I kept on having to refer to my math textbook to finish the problems.

"Can we have some privacy?" asked Gail quietly.

I think I blinked and looked up. "We're at the breakfast table," I said incredulously. "The entire school is here. If you want privacy, talk to me this evening."

"What's this about?" asked Mina, leaning forward.

"Did anyone from Duke or Thama spell tag you?" asked Sierra almost hopefully. "Wanda and I can sneak up on them. She's got a wand now."

Oh. My. Maker.

"Gail, really," I said in exasperation. "What do you think is going to happen? You're not in a song where you ride off into the sunset together."

"Oh," said Mina, her eyes widening slightly in excitement. "Who is it?"

Sierra rolled her eyes. "Boys," she said in frustration. "It's better if you just hit them."

Wanda said quietly, "Lord Thomas might be able to help."

Mina vibrated with excitement. "Okay, it's someone from House Coley. Do you need my boyfriend to make the introductions? Who is it?"

"It's your story," I said to Gail. My bet, she was wishing she hadn't brought it up at the breakfast table. Too bad. The only thing she could hope for now was containment. Girls, and I am including myself in that category, loved talking about who was dating who. I don't understand why, but there's a mind itch that needs to be scratched sometimes, and talking about relationships seems to do that.

It was common knowledge by now that Jeffery was trying to date me. From a certain perspective, I understand that meant I was either off limits to other boys, or it became the other extreme. I should be examined closer; sort-of, if a boy is interested in her, she must be worth dating. So far that hadn't happened yet, and I wasn't sure if I wanted it to or not. Other than the fantasy of Lord Grayson who popped up in my head occasionally, I felt safe with Jeffery. He was kind and smart without being pushy. Listening in on conversations from other girls, when talk turned to boys, it seemed like their brains sort of froze up. I didn't want to go there; my schoolwork was too important to me. But the fantasy of kissing Jeffery still bubbled in my mind more often than I wanted to admit.

Gail leaned forward. "Well," she said, picking up on Mina's excitement. "Lord Abner and I met…"

It was like a switch had been thrown. At the mention of Lord Abner, Mina's excitement evaporated. What replaced it was a commanding attitude; Lady Mina was here with us now. "Are you crazy?" she hissed out. "His head of house is Lady Pinetress. The woman's under a great deal of political stress right now."

Wow. Mina's transformation was almost instantaneous, but what was even more surprising was her domineering presence; I-am-a-lady-and-you're-not type of thing. I think I can count on one hand the number of times Mina pulled the Lady card last year. Her motherly instincts toward those who needed help was what had made me like her in the first place. Now, I felt like I was looking at a stranger. What was going on?

More importantly, with Mina's new attitude, I felt very protective toward Gail.

"Mina," I said. "I know Gail's not a noble, and she's probably making a mistake. But she's come to me, us, for help. We should help her." While I meant it, I was still annoyed at Gail and wanted to tell her off too. But I didn't like pushing people away or making them feel smaller. I get enough of that from House Duke and Thama every day.

Mina looked down, and she let out her breath. "Gail, I'm sorry. But, no. There's something big happening right now. Every noble who has a seat in chambers is being pushed hard. Low, middle, and high."

"What's so important Babe?" said Lord Thomas. He had come over from the House Coley table to stand next to Mina. The two of them were an item and had been for the past six months. I had visited Mina's home once. Her family was a low noble, well liked in the area, but they didn't have a seat in chambers; Lord Thomas's family did, and he was her intended. If they followed through and got married when they graduated, Mina would be marrying up.

Gail looked like she wanted to shrink in on herself. I bet she was wishing she hadn't brought up the topic in the cafeteria where others could hear her. I cocked my head and replayed my own thought, *Was this that itch, which even I had sometimes?* The one that pushed everything else aside to think about boys and stopped solving problems? I had even met some older women who were like that: they became a trophy in their husband's house. Unable to function on their own. I didn't want to go there. Whatever Lord Winton had in mind for me, it involved using my brain too, and I was glad of it. Even though I felt like I was now drowning in physics and math.

Mina leaned backwards to look up at Lord Thomas. "The Reece's Racoons full vote. It's in two weeks."

Lord Thomas leaned down and kissed Mina on the head. "All three Chambers are in turmoil over it," he said. "The votes are going to be close. Money and favors persuading people to vote one way or another is intense. What does this have to do with Gail?"

Wanda's mouth was hanging open. "Really! Why would anyone vote no? That's just stupid."

Lord Thomas rolled his eyes. "Welcome to politics. A lot of the more conservative nobles don't think the Reece's Racoons should have any rights. My dad told me he heard fights broke out in High Chambers when Lady Gawain invited several Reece's Racoons to speak on their behalf. Last I heard, the vote in all three chambers was going to be close, especially lower chambers. But I repeat, what's this got to do with Gail?"

Mina kept her gaze on Gail but answered Lord Thomas's question. "Apparently she has gotten involved with Lord Abner."

Lord Thomas tensed up and looked over at Lord Abner, who was sitting at the upper end of the Coley House table and talking to his friends. "How involved, Gail?" he asked bluntly.

Gail's mouth opened, closed, then she looked down. "We love each other," she said softly. Tears started rolling down her cheeks.

"How long ago was it when he approached you?" asked Lord Thomas. "This is important."

"Oh," said Mina and put a hand to her mouth in surprise. "Would someone really do that?"

"What are you two talking about?" I asked. Whatever they were implying had gone right over my head. But I also felt an odd sort of relief: the world didn't revolve around me.

"Did someone slip Lord Abner a love potion or put him under a mild compulsion?" suggested Lord Thomas. "Someone who doesn't want his head of house to vote in favor of the Charter. This individual quietly suggests no one needs to hear about Lord Abner's tryst with a commoner if their house just votes 'no' to the Charter."

Gail burst into tears and ran out of the cafeteria.

Chapter 18

Betting is a culture all is own in Avalon, and there is no age limit.

-Guide to Avalon 4th printing

-Vivian Hampton-

Pioneer School

After checking up on Gail, I gave her my permission to skip classes that day but got her promise she would visit Healer Frenzia in the infirmary after I left. Even though I could cast the locate spell to know where Gail was, I didn't want her to be alone right now. Before leaving for my first class, I promised we would help her figure out what we needed to do next: I had no idea what that was going to be. When I left, she was still lying in her bed, clutching a pillow.

I fast walked to my potions class pondering how in the world do you ask a Lord if your affection for someone was real or engineered? Just asking the question felt like it had *wrong* all over it. I needed help, I just didn't know from who yet. Vivian Hampton, butterfly. But that wind pushing at me felt stronger than ever.

Quade got my attention before I sat down in potions.

"What's up?" I asked, trying to keep a smile on my face. My first class hadn't even started yet, and I already felt like I had lost control of the day.

"Can you check my homework for me?" he said and handed over several sheets of paper.

"Um, Quade. You're a freshman. Your homework isn't due until next Friday. But sure."

I scanned the first page. His handwriting was neat, and he got the basics right. "Have you considered being a tutor for some of the other freshmen?" I suggested as I turned to the second page. And stopped.

There were just six words written on the page:

Can I transfer into your house?

He didn't want anyone else to know what he wrote. I replayed that thought. *He didn't want anyone from House Duke knowing he asked me.*

Thinking fast, I said, "You're missing a key point. Hang on." I wrote down under his message, *I will ask Professor Malton* and put his first sheet back on top before handing them back.

I had never heard of anyone wanting to transfer *out* of House Duke before. It was a badge of honor to be there. Houses and guilds competed against each other to recruit you during your senior year. If you excelled, even during your junior year. Why would Quade want to transfer out?

Then a thought occurred to me, *did Quade expect to be in House Orozco? Then got placed in Duke to make room for Elaine or Amanda*? I had no idea. If he was in our house, considering his obvious education and ability to cast magic, he would likely be in contention for Head Freshmen.

I gave him a reassuring smile and took my seat.

As the rest of the other students arrived, I looked over at all the potions we made yesterday. Two of them were covered; mine and

Lord Kazmuk's from House Thama. The others were exposed and dark—the magic had faded.

On the side chalkboard were names ordered by time, how long the potion had glowed before fading. The top two slots were empty.

I felt a bit proud at beating Lord Keith. His name was near the bottom. Then I noticed he and his henchman still weren't here. I felt an odd pang of sympathy in my chest for them. Those two likely got caught up in the repercussions from the pushback initiated by Lord's Seth's head of house. There was a little part of me that hoped Professor Vermis didn't persuade Lord Seth to file that formal complaint. He was a teacher and as much as I disliked him, I wanted to believe he had the best interest of the students in mind.

During this, Wanda kept up a running commentary on my—correction—*her* wand. The tests we conducted, what worked, and what didn't. Instead of being embarrassed at the litany of things that didn't work, Wanda was enjoying laughing with others who could also cast magic. It was like an extra light was shining in Wanda now: she was transforming, I wasn't sure into what, but there was something blossoming inside her now.

My happy feelings dimmed a bit at seeing Mina and Sierra come over from her table with Mia in tow. Just about the entire school had watched Gail run out of the cafeteria, and I sort of blamed Mina for that. Maybe she was right, but the way she and Lord Thomas came down hard on Gail in an open setting had embarrassed her.

"What's going on with Gail?" asked Mia. "We were supposed to sit down at breakfast together so she could go over my homework. But it looked like you got angry at her. Did she do something wrong?"

Was everything my fault now?

"Stories are beginning to circulate about Gail," said Mina. "Everything from her benefactor is pulling her from school to she tried challenging you for head girl."

"Well, whose fault is that?" I said, a bit exasperated, then realized I should probably lower my voice. Quade and everyone else at my table obviously wanted to hear what we had to say.

"Lord Thomas and I aren't wrong," demanded Mina. "This could get ugly. Do you have any ideas on what we should do?"

Argh, even when it wasn't about me, it felt like it still ended up in my lap. "Can we meet up in the gymnasium during our free period? It was mostly empty the other day. We could strategize there."

"You're getting better at being sneaky," grinned Wanda. "I like it."

Sierra sniffed. "When am I getting my wand?"

I rolled my eyes. "I'm not an endless battery, Sierra. And, I have no idea if my link with Wanda can be reproduced. But we need to talk Professor Malton into it first in any case."

I felt like I was barely treading water with everything happening around me. Without Wanda, I would have sunk already. She's a treasure. My thoughts were brought back to the present by Professor Reece waving at the classroom door to close it.

"In the spirit of betting," Professor Reece said excitedly. "We have Ms. Vivian of House Orozco against Lord Kazmuk of House Thama. Both potions were still glowing last night. No one has checked since." He held up a bag of his mints. "Everyone gets a vote, those that pick the winning team get to pull a piece from the bag. Let's go around the room. Place your bets."

Professor Reece certainly knew how to get the room engaged. However, most of the bets followed loyalty to a house. When it got around to Quade, he said "Lord Kazmuk." Then he looked down. Wanda threw a wadded piece of paper at him. "You're at our table. Show some loyalty."

She was roundly booed from those around the room in House Duke and House Thama. I felt like the political rivalry was more intense than last year.

Professor Reece ignored the interruption and kept on going. At the end, I had six more votes than Lord Kazmuk.

"Recount," someone from House Duke shouted out. "Never put beauty before brains."

What did he just say? I felt a little apprehensive at all the eyes suddenly on me.

Wanda shouted out, "Vivian's got more brains than anyone in House Thama."

Uh oh. Wanda was openly challenging them. This could get ugly.

Before I could ask her to stop, Professor Reece clapped his hands to get everyone's attention again and moved into the spell circle.

"And the winner is!" he said excitedly while pulling off both covers at the same time.

♫

As potions class was breaking up, Professor Reece came over. "Congratulations on winning, Ms. Vivian. If you don't mind, please let me know the five illusions you want me to brew into my next batch of mints by the end of the week."

My potion was still shining at the end of class. But it had lost some of its brilliance from yesterday.

"Thank you, sir, I will. Last class you mentioned you and Professor Vermis were going to attempt to reverse engineer the light effect. Is that still going to happen?"

His face momentarily darkened. "Professor Vermis has been unavailable for guidance. However, the headmistress granted me an alternative. If I can get another professor with potions experience to join me during our class on Friday, for those who want to make the attempt, students are allowed to experiment—

but sophomores only. Freshmen are, of course, allowed to provide ideas if they wish."

That sounded like fun, and I said so.

"Excellent, then we will have at least one table giving it a go this Friday," smiled Professor Reece. "Hopefully more."

Wanda chimed in. "If we can reproduce it, does Vivian still get to name it?"

"That is an excellent discussion you should take up with the headmistress," said Professor Reece and handed Wanda another mint.

Wanda took the mint but rolled her eyes. "Sir, it was Vivian's potion."

I nudged Wanda to be quiet. "Sir, the homework?"

He had given us even more homework. I wasn't the only one that groaned.

"Of which I am sure you will do an excellent job, Ms. Vivian."

Wanda was still grumbling as we left for physics; I made a few comments of my own. It was only our first class of the day and that feeling of treading water had already become more pronounced. At this rate, I wasn't certain I could survive the year.

Chapter 19

There is complex mathematical proof which suggests that three-dimensional reality can be a bit fluid for those with more than three magical ground states. Since the person who drafted it was, to put it politely, insane, no one has yet determined a method to verify the equations or how to apply them. However, attempts continue. Since this generally requires a great deal of alcohol to get the mind into the correct state, it has become a rite of passage for some of the students at our university. Most of them recover—eventually.

-Professor Genard, Notir University.

-Vivian Hampton-
Main Magic Ring, Pioneer School

Wanda and I were about to walk down the last set of stairs which led to the school's main ring when I turned to face her. "No way."

"Think of the money we could make."

Wanda had brought up the subject of signing me up for one of the school's dueling clubs, which I thought was ludicrous. First, I didn't have the time. Second, outside of the occasional spell shot at me in the hallway, I didn't have any formal training at dueling. And third, well, I felt a little uncomfortable imagining groups of people watching me as I dodged spells. Singing in public was different and so was wearing a dress and dancing. I couldn't tell you why, but it was.

"Still no," I replied. "Why is this suddenly so important to you?"

Wanda pretended to cast a spell. "You don't encode any of your spells, so I bet you're faster than most of those pretenders in House Thama and Duke. If Sierra and I play it right, we might get three-to-one odds when you duel them. Besides, don't you want to take them down? Imagine the story, 'Snowball Queen Wins the Dueling Trophy'," she said with excitement.

I rolled my eyes. "I'll make a deal with you. For whatever reason, Sierra wants a wand now too. If you can get her to call magic like you're doing, I'll try out." Immediately, I wanted to take it back. What that really meant was even more homework for me, assuming I could get Professor Malton to agree to it at all.

Wanda hugged me, and I felt a faint magical shroud encircle us. I knew where that came from—I offered a deal, Wanda accepted, and now we were bound to it. Why in the world did I open my mouth like that?

I turned and continued down the stairs. "She's your problem," I stressed. "I'm only involved in this during my free period."

"Absolutely," agreed Wanda. "You know," she mused after a few steps, "we could put your curves to good use. I'll get the seamstresses at the Blind Buttonhole to make a dueling outfit for you that's form-fitting. I bet half of your competitors would have their brains fall out of their ears when they saw you. You wouldn't even need to raise your shields. Three spells and done. The duel would be over in thirty seconds."

It took me a second to realize what Wanda had just suggested. "No."

"Come on, Vivian," she whined from behind me. "We might even get our picture in the paper again."

"Not going to happen," I said without turning around.

"I bet I can get the younger seamstress to sketch out an outfit for you."

I continued to walk down the stairs while Wanda suggested idea after idea. How in the world do you stop Wanda being, well, Wanda? There didn't seem to be an "off" switch.

"Lord Grayson tells me you had some success with your link to Ms. Hampton," Professor Gass said to Wanda after we found our way to the school's main circle in the basement.

I had only been in the room once before during freshmen orientation early last year. The room was still large, cold, and damp. I wish I had worn a sweater over my school uniform.

The only real difference was with the master ring. It was a single circular rut etched into the floor that had been filled in with silver. From the stories, the ring predated the school. However, today, sandbags were suspended from the ceiling toward the back of the room. A large eye ring had been screwed into the farthest section of the silver ring. An attached rope extended straight up to a pulley on the ceiling and over to another pulley which connected to the sandbags. A single rope dangled from the farthest pulley. The creaking noise from the tension in the rope made me nervous. Why was this here? But what caught my eye was Lord Grayson. He was inspecting the area around the sandbags. Wanda waved at the man, and he waved back.

"It's the dead man's switch," I heard from behind and turned around to see Professor Malton approaching us.

I was glad he was here, but my nervousness increased a notch at his dead man's comment. "Sir, you think something bad might happen?" I wasn't sure if I wanted Wanda or myself in that ring if there was a danger.

"I know it sounds a bit ominous, but the design has been safely used for years. Essentially, if someone pulls the release rope, the sandbags fall, which in turn lifts a small section from the ring, thereby breaking it." He winked at Professor Gass, "And the reason I am here is to offer support and make sure you don't end up as one of Professor Gass's experiments."

Professor Gass harrumphed but smiled. "Point taken. Other than learning more about your link with Ms. Hine, we are hoping your guide might make an appearance, that's all. To provide some perspective, we use this apparatus when testing out new spells and other events which could produce unknown results."

"Will Lord Grayson be manning the release?" I trusted him.

"Yes. A word of warning though," said Professor Malton. "If the spell being tested has a lot of energy to it and we break the ring, it can leave those in this room charged a bit. There's a secondary delayed effect, especially for those that have complex ground states. This may leave them feeling lightheaded until the effects fully fade."

I bit my lip. "Like me?"

"Like you, Ms. Hampton," chuckled Professor Gass. "No one knows why, but the prevailing theory is the extra energy gets funneled through the links as well. If you're willing to intentionally experiment, there are several people I know at the Notir University who would like to see the results. I can…"

Being an experiment? Ugh. The thought made my stomach flop. Before I could tell Professor Gass no, Professor Malton did.

Professor Malton sighed. "Frank, not now. Vivian is not one of your experiments. This is precaution only."

"Oh, come on," protested Wanda. "If you cast a powerful spell and we break the ring, maybe I'll get magically charged too. I might be able to cast stronger spells until it fades. We could even try the experiment with Sierra too."

Wanda was hit by two no's—mine and Professor Malton's. However, Professor Gass rubbed his chin in apparent thought while pondering out loud, "That would make for an interesting premise for an experiment."

"Firm no," I replied. "I am Vivian Hampton. Butterfly, not an experiment." I could feel myself go red in the face realizing I described myself as a butterfly.

Wanda giggled. "Men do follow her around. It's funny to watch."

Professor Malton tilted his head. "I suspect Vivian is referring to the famous quote from a boxer on Earth. Float like a butterfly, sting like a bee."

Professor Gass looked like he was trying not to laugh. "I didn't know you liked dueling and boxing, Ms. Hampton."

I think I blinked. What was boxing? Professor Malton must have noticed my confusion. "It's a sport on earth, essentially dueling, but with your hands."

Oh.

"Vivian's going to join the school dueling club," announced Wanda proudly. "I'm designing her outfit."

What in the world.

"Well done, young lady," said Professor Gass, bowing to me slightly. "There have been a few well-known female duelists who graduated from this school, Professor Lessnara was our last one. I wish you success."

I didn't know what to say. Somehow it felt like Wanda's idea had taken on a life of its own. Before I could think of a way of tactfully suggesting I still wasn't sure, Professor Gass handed over two small wooden boxes. One for me, the other for Wanda.

Inside my box were four rune-etched bracelets.

"Sir," I said. "I thought you still needed to calibrate some of the links?" The etchings on the third bracelet were very detailed—to the point I couldn't make out some of them without a magnifying glass.

"True. But since you also have a link to Ms. Hine and your snowman—"

"Camillo," I immediately corrected, "Sir."

Professor Gass gave me a brief smile. "Camillo. Then it is likely two links may be affected by the fourth one. It is an experiment to see how the ground states shift as Ms. Hine draws upon your magic. I expect adjustments will be necessary."

Wanda held up her two bracelets, then put them on. The runes etched into the second one looked almost identical to my first bracelet.

"So you want me to have a go first?" Wanda asked excitedly.

I put on all four of my bracelets and felt a bit embarrassed. I'm not a big jewelry girl. "Sir," I asked Professor Malton, "where are the other students from the physics class? Also, didn't the headmistress want to be here?"

"The headmistress wants to keep the meeting with this individual as private as possible. The other students normally in this class are substituting for me."

I looked around, the headmistress wasn't here. "Sir?"

Professor Malton put a finger to his lips. Professor Gass glanced toward Lord Grayson. "Can you give us a few minutes, young man?"

Lord Grayson nodded and stepped out the back door. What was going on?

Once the door was closed, Professor Malton asked. "How is Ms. Magnoli?"

I cocked my head, what was he really asking? Gail was skipping her classes today, but I knew where she was, as I was her head girl. Professor Malton, being our head of house, had to know too. I bet Gail was sad, angry and.... I put another thought together: why did they ask Lord Grayson to leave? And suddenly I understood. He was a reserve Realm Knight.

"Upset, Professor. But do you really think Lord Abner might be under the influence of a spell?"

Professor Gass grunted out, "*politics*," making the word sound like a curse. "Ms. Hampton, there is no official reason to suspect it. However, if he has been magically nudged in some way, there might be trace energy left on Ms. Magnoli. This would allow certain individuals to quietly take the man aside to examine him. Without that, we would need his head of house's permission to inspect him for such spells. Considering how tense the political situation is right now, things might spin out of control if this isn't handled delicately."

"Professor?" asked Wanda, looking to where Lord Grayson had left. "You really think it might be mind-control?"

Professor Malton sighed. "Vivian, Wanda, with the elevation of Lady Gawain, the power structure is beginning to shift. Let's say someone did nudge Lord Abner. It wouldn't surprise me if similar things are happening in many other places. Certain factions are afraid of losing control and the Realm Knights are stretched thin as it is. History has proven that those in power will go to great lengths to remain so."

Professor Gass put a finger to his lips implying a need for secrecy. "If it became common knowledge that someone did push Lord Abner, the Realm Knights will have no recourse but to step in and that would remove them from other important duties. Also whispered accusations would likely turn to duels. Deadly ones. Politics has made things very tense right now."

Oh. Another thought crossed my mind. "Would Terrance be able to help? He's working with Lord Grayson, but he's not really a Realm Knight." I bit my lip and added, "And he's, well, very different."

Professor Malton and Professor Gass looked at each other. It was obvious by their expressions they hadn't thought of that.

"I'll run it by the headmistress," said Professor Malton quietly.

Wanda bounced once. "Vivian's the best hero ever."

"I'll let Lord Grayson know that he can come back in now," said Professor Gass.

"Vivian," said Professor Malton. "Thank you, but please do not whisper this to anyone else. Not even Ms. Magnoli. Wait until we have had a chance to talk about it."

The door opened, and the headmistress slipped in. "Good," she said. "Thank you for waiting. I was on a spell call with the council."

Wanda practically exploded in excitement. "Is Lord Seth going to be expelled?"

"I believe that should earn you detention, Ms. Hine," said Professor Malton dryly. "I don't remember it written in any of the school's Charters where the headmistress reports to you."

"Lord Seth and Lord Keith along with their henchmen will be back at school soon," said the headmistress, pointedly looking at Wanda. "I will not share the tribulations of their family's turmoil with you. I hazard you wouldn't want yours or Ms. Hampton's shared either."

That stopped Wanda in midbounce. "No, ma'am."

"Are we ready?" asked the headmistress.

"In a moment," said Professor Gass. "Ms. Hampton, your notes."

I handed them over and while Professor Gass added some comments, Lord Grayson came over to stand by me.

"Have you ever used the dead man's switch before?" I asked him. I was still a little nervous hearing the creaking from the rope.

"I have, twice," he said. "It's an excellent design."

That made me feel better. I pointed to the chalk outlines on the floor under the sandbags. "Do not step zones?" I asked.

"Yep," grinned Lord Grayson. "The story I heard was that once a person forgot the sandbags were there and stepped under them. So, the chalk outlines got added."

"I bet," I said and giggled.

Giggled? I don't giggle.

Wanda stomped on my foot to get my attention. Her action was obvious, I'm your henchwoman, but I want Lord Grayson to pay attention to me. You've got Jeffery.

Lord Grayson ignored my giggle and Wanda's not-so-subtle hint. "So, do you have any idea who this woman is?"

I shook my head. "Only that Lady Cassandra is her voice, and I trust her. She's never pushed me to do anything other than think."

Professor Gass handed my notes back. Red comments had been scrawled in the margins on the first page. I flipped a page and the next one. I kept flipping, he'd added comments on the next four as well.

"Sir, I'm trying my best," I said. Considering the number of his comments, I felt like he must be disappointed in me.

"Believe me," he grinned. "With the Wandmaker's guild, more is better. They live for detail. Best get used to it now. Now, let's get your henchwoman," he stressed, and Wanda saluted him with her wand, "into the circle. Then we can begin."

Lord Grayson moved to the back of the room and wrapped the release rope around his hands.

Wanda hopped into the circle, and Professor Malton charged it. With my Sight, I could see it glow. There was a lot of magic swirling around this ring.

Wanda bounced happily while gripping my wand. "Sir, I can't seem to figure out how to select the spell I want."

"And that is what practice is for," remarked Professor Malton. "By the way, your detention will be to spend your evening helping me at the dueling rings."

"Aha," she said with enthusiasm. "You want me to spy on Vivian's competition. Very sneaky. I like it. Can I invite Sierra?"

Professor Malton sighed. "Ms. Hine, a spell please."

Wanda concentrated. Nothing happened, no light, no breeze, no sounds. She shook her wand. "Something is wrong," she said. "It's not working."

Wanda pointed her wand again, no spells.

That was odd, I couldn't see any magic form either. Also, I didn't feel any kind of drain. Was something wrong with our link?

Wanda bit her lip and gave it another go, nothing.

Her hand slowly lowered. "It's gone," she whispered. "That feeling."

I could feel an emptiness grow inside Wanda. The wand fell from her fingers and clattered to the floor. Her face said it all;

Wanda was terrified, terrified it was really gone. Not just the magic, but that spark of hope. Less than a day, and it was stripped away from her. She was back to being a person unworthy of leading her own way.

Feeling Wanda's despair, it triggered a memory within me when I watched my father walk away. I felt so powerless. Empty. As if all the good memories I had with him when I was younger were no longer real; that they had never been real. While the memories were mine, I was sharing the emotion with Wanda.

The emotions! I was feeling Wanda's emotions. Our link was there, but something was blocking the magic.

Lord Grayson let go of the rope and walked over to Professor Gass, who was rubbing his chin while looking down at his own notes. "I was sure I was right," he said.

Professor Malton opened a notebook and compared notes with Professor Gass. "I agree with the design of the rune structure, this should work."

I took a step toward the ring. I was never going to give up on Wanda. I mouthed to her, "It's going to be okay."

"Your equations match what I saw, Professor," said Lord Grayson and pulled a notebook out of his back pocket.

Professor Malton grunted. "Maybe you got an edge wrong? You did have to curve the runes a bit."

None of them were feeling Wanda's fear. The three of them were engrossed in comparing notes.

I took another step forward. "Wanda, they're going to figure it out. Just give them a few minutes." By now I was standing just outside the circle.

"Vivian, it's gone," she wailed. "I can't feel it anymore." She wrenched the bracelets off her wrist. "Nothing!"

"It's not really gone, Wanda. My magic is still here, you're going to get it back." I took another step toward Wanda. My feet were at the edges of the ring.

"Sir," suggested Lord Grayson. "What about Campton's Mnemonic frequency? Could that be in play here?"

"Unlikely," grunted Professor Gass. "That's entirely based on Quiray's function groups."

"You'll get it back, Wanda. I promise," I said and removed the bracelets from my wrist as well. I felt that emotional connection with Wanda pulse, but something was still blocking the magic. The bell in my mind, I thought to myself. When I imagined Wanda pulling magic from me the other day, I heard a bell in my mind. I bet we just needed to reset the link.

Wanda glanced at Lord Grayson. He was absorbed in the discussion with Professor Gass and Professor Malton. "Vivian," she whispered. "What if it doesn't come back?"

I could feel her despair turning into hopelessness. I was feeling a fear from her that can only be described as a candle that had flickered out on a dark night. When it vanishes, the beast comes out to play, and you're the food. Gone.

Professor Malton tapped an equation group on Professor Gass's notebook. "Why rotate that rune? Of course, sorry."

Wanda looked terrified. Alone. "Wanda, we just need to reset the link," and I took a step forward while trying to get to that place in my mind where I heard the bell before. It dinged, but oh was it loud this time. That's when I realized what I had done. My foot was touching the ring.

"Ms. Hampton," I heard from the headmistress just behind me. "What are you doing?"

Out of the corner of my eye, I noticed Professor Gass, Lord Grayson, and Professor Malton look up from their notes.

"Vivian don't!" shouted Lord Grayson.

But my foot had already touched the ring. A half second later, all the silver making up the ring lit up.

Okay, what did I just do?

♫

"What happened?" I whispered to Lord Grayson. A second after the second silver ring glowed, it went out, then the walls and ceiling of the room went away. Everyone was still here, but beyond the stone floor, it looked like we were in a smithy but one sized for a god.

"Vivian?" said Wanda as she slowly turned in place. "Where are we?"

It might have been my imagination, but I thought Wanda was glowing a little too.

"Whatever you do, young ladies," commanded the headmistress, "don't move."

"Wasn't planning to," I said, and I could feel my apprehension edging toward fear. I reached out a hand and Lord Grayson took it. That made me feel better; I wasn't alone in this. With his touch, I could feel his amazement as well. But more importantly, within myself, I could feel that emotional connection with Wanda, and more importantly, the magic was flowing again.

Wanda was still spinning around and like the rest of us, staring. "Vivian," she said in wonder. "I can feel your link again. But what's going on?"

"No idea."

On one side of us were rows of rune etched hammers. The smallest likely weighed more than I did. Swirling around each was magic like I had never seen before. To our right were other smithy tools—tongs and other things. Like the hammers, each was covered in runes. Behind us was a furnace. But whatever was inside wasn't heat, or only heat, but something that glowed an intense blue. But the most amazing thing was at the far end of this stone building.

Three huge, odd beings were looking down at two pieces of a sword; the tip had been sheared off. As odd as these creatures were, they acted for all the world just like Professor Gass, Lord Grayson, and Professor Malton had. They were engrossed with the sword. The rest of, well, everything, was unimportant to them.

The oddest of the three creatures, who sort of looked like a walking tree, spoke, <*"Four, definitely four."*>

It wasn't English, but was, instead, a thought that seemed to translate into our minds.

The creature to the tree's left, sort of looked like it was made out of rock, shook its head. <*"You are forgetting where she was when it happened. It is likely five."*>

The human-looking one, except he had to be eight feet tall and made of rippling muscles grunted out, <*"No known rune exists for that."*>

None of these three creatures seemed to notice we were there. Why in the world were we seeing this? It was then that I noticed a normal size person with her back to us. It was easy to miss her, considering how odd and big everything else was.

Professor Malton whispered, "I believe that's Ager Lucum, Captain Calvit's blade. I recognize it from a picture. I bet they're talking about how to repair him."

"Him? You mean the blade? Who are they?" I said, trying not to let the terror I was feeling take over.

"Blacksmiths would be my guess," suggested Professor Gass in wonder. "Perhaps makers of weapons of power? I've never seen any of these runes before."

The woman turned toward us. "And I suggest you don't experiment with them either," she said and waved her hand.

The blacksmith's shop faded away. The only difference was that she was now in the room with us as well.

"Hello, Vivian. It's nice to finally meet you. By the way, you don't need to keep standing on the circle."

Her voice, she was the woman in my mind. But now she was here. "Ma'am," I curtsied. "Thank you for your help, I—"

And I suddenly knew who she was and didn't know how to finish my sentence. She was practically the most famous person, ever.

I could feel the headmistress's commanding posture dominate the room again. "Whoever you are, Ms. Hampton is a student at my school and... oh, my God." Her voice trailed off. She had obviously recognized her as well.

Wanda's mouth was open in astonishment. Professor Gass took a step backwards. Professor Malton moved to the other side of me. Lord Grayson gripped my hand harder. How could they not know who she was? If you removed her red blouse and put her in a flowing white dress with a sword attached to her back, she would be...

I blurted out, "The Lady of the Lake. The last poem from the Tears of Avalon."

"Actually, I am experimenting with different names. Ianua was a bit hard to pronounce and didn't translate well. Today it's Alma. What can I do for you, Vivian?"

Wanda bounced while *eeping.*

The headmistress found her voice, "Milady, what is going on? My earlier comment still stands. Ms. Hampton is a student at my school."

The Lady of the Lake tilted her head. "Very well. The simple answer is what Cassandra asked of her earlier—dragon politics. Rupert, the dragon, is a friend of mine. Lucille, the other dragon is, well, related to me in an odd way. However, Hyancintho, the guardian dragon, lives much farther away. As Lady Cassandra is my voice, if Vivian agrees to follow her, it might help ease the tensions brewing between Rupert and Hyancintho. The other is what I suggested to Vivian before. She has the bardic voice, and therefore the Sight. It is possible she may see things which are of interest to me. That's it."

"So that rolling magic I felt coming from Amanda and Elaine," I said, "really is dragon magic?"

"Yes, Vivian. But an echo. And it goes both ways. If you can convince Elaine and Amanda to continue working together, it might influence Rupert and Hyancintho as well. Talking instead of fighting."

I felt the enormity of what she just said sink in. Me. Responsible for influencing dragons. But the Lady of the Lake seemed to be able to read my mind. "It's not all on you, Vivian. The same back-and-forth is being played out, mostly through Lady

Gawain, but others as well, including Cassandra and The Iron Dragon. Their goals are essentially the same, balancing their own lives while pushing the dragons toward working together. As dragons can be very stubborn, this is an uphill battle." The edges of the Lady's mouth turned up slightly. "I must admit, Lady Gawain's patience as she deals with the dragons is extraordinary."

"Milady," gulped out Wanda. "Can't you just tell them to play nice?"

Wanda's eyes went wide, and she immediately curtsied again. I don't think I had ever seen a curtsy that low before. But I was with Wanda, why wasn't the Lady telling the dragons off?

"If I did, other beings would be free to act in such a manner. There are a set of rules, which I agreed to sign, called the Accords. Which basically means, if I directly intervene without a task being demanded, others can as well. To break from that, would likely allow others an opening, and then, things would go very bad, very quickly. But let's talk about power and trust for a moment." The Lady of the Lake turned to the headmistress. "Ask your questions. But, per certain rules, you are only allowed three."

"I assume you are the person who talks to Vivian on occasion, what are your intentions with my student?"

"Other than nudging dragons, it is possible Vivian may see things that might be of interest to me. I am offering guidance only, as I noted earlier, to offer more, a service must be demanded."

"Suggestions," asked the headmistress, while looking at Professor Malton and Professor Gass. She seemed very frazzled.

Before they could say anything, Wanda blurted out, "Are Vivian's visions because of you?"

"Good question, Wanda," said the Lady of the Lake. "No, but the better answer is this. All Oracles have the Bard's voice. However, few know it. The training required to use it is intense and requires the right physical gifts which even fewer have. If it helps, imagine the universe as a near infinite set of vibrations, each showing a possible reality. Oracles can sense some of the stronger vibrations, and they interpret them as visions.

Understanding which one's will become real requires a great deal of training and, honestly, luck. As I said to Vivian, they change all the time. Attempting to see the totality of it is too much even for me. But the point is, the bardic voice and being an oracle are linked. It is all from you, Vivian."

"Vibrations of reality, Milady?" asked Professor Gass. "That almost sounds like string resonance."

"It is. But I am not a mathematician. Someone I know describes all matter as vibrations, so many that the numbers become meaningless. What causes the most complex disturbances in these vibrations are souls, free will. Imagine ten people each throwing a rock into the same pond at the same time. Some of the ripples will interact, cross over, be absorbed, and so on. But until the rocks are thrown, all an Oracle sees are the most likely ripples. This is a very simplistic example. Furthermore, the bardic voice has the ability to interact with those vibrations, albeit in a very small way. Hence why Vivian can share magical power with Wanda. She is tuning the magic around her, shaping it, if you wish."

The Lady of the Lake smiled. "I have time for one more question."

The headmistress nodded. "Ms. Hampton, I think you should ask it."

I bit my lip and looked at Lord Grayson, then Professor Malton, then finally Wanda. What did I want to ask? One question only. The first that sprang to mind was about Camillo, but the Lady of the Lake probably wasn't allowed to intervene. Besides, there was a master guardian maker coming in a few days. There was Terrance, and then...

I swallowed, curtsied, and asked, "Milady, that which lies below. Lady Cassandra thinks the original Merlin was trying to make a guardian. What has it become now?"

She smiled at me. "That, Vivian, is a very good question."

In a blink, the Lady was gone.

"I don't think I'm in any danger," I said to Lord Grayson. I couldn't believe I was trying to push him away, but for whatever reason, the man seemed to want to stand right next to me. Besides, Wanda would probably stomp on my foot later if he kept this up.

"Sorry," he said, and took a step to the left giving me some breathing room.

Wanda was getting better. She could cast the spell she wanted most of the time now. "I assume the burping sound is what you wanted?" I asked her.

She grinned. Then she concentrated and the light spell formed properly. The light was brighter too. With it, I felt that small drain again. Not much, but it was there.

"Do you think you could tune your magic so Sierra can cast as well," said Wanda in excitement, as she raced around inside of the spell circle holding out her glowing wand.

Working with Wanda was helping to calm my nerves. I had just spoken to the Lady of the Lake! My mind was still sort of numb. Reading the very dry wandmakers testing book helped to stop me from screaming. Part of me wanted to join Wanda and just run around the circle until the sun set.

The headmistress, Professor Malton, and Professor Gass came over from where they had been discussing the visitation. I broke the ring, and Wanda hopped across to join us.

"Rules," began the headmistress. "Don't discuss what occurred with anyone, and that includes you, Lord Grayson. There will be no speaking of what transpired down here."

Wanda came to a sudden stop. "That's not fair. Vivian's the best hero ever. Everyone should hear about it."

Professor Malton sighed. "No. And that's a hard no, Wanda."

"Ma'am," Lord Grayson protested. "I'm a reserve Realm Knight. Shouldn't the council know?"

"Play it out, young man," shot back the headmistress. "Let's say you do, what happens next?"

Lord Grayson swallowed and glanced at me. Then his face went white. "Oh."

"Oh. What oh?" I asked. "What are you talking about?"

"Vivian, the Lady of the Lake talked to you. In the council's eyes, your royalty now," said Lord Grayson. "They would probably ennoble you on the spot. But the reverse is true, there's a whole lot of bad going on behind the scenes right now. I could imagine assassins trying to kill you just to take you out of the picture."

"If word of this got out," said Professor Malton softly. "The school wouldn't be able to provide you with the protection you would need."

Lord Grayson turned his head away. "Do you trust all of them?" he said under his breath. "The Council. Damn."

Wanda stomped on his foot. "What are you talking about? Trust who?"

Lord Grayson let out his breath. "Terrance asked me a question the other night, and I didn't understand the significance of it until this moment." He met the headmistress's gaze. "He asked me, 'Do you trust everyone on the council?'"

Professor Gass's face went white. "Crap!"

"Are you going to hold your tongue, Lord Grayson?" asked the headmistress in a cold voice. "Yes or no."

"Yes," he said softly. Then he turned away and shouted out a string of profanity.

"Lord Grayson," I said. "Help me understand."

He turned around and got himself under control. "I took an oath, Vivian. A binding oath to Avalon and the Council. The council essentially represents merlin to the realm, the highest authority. What Terrance was asking me was whether I trusted all of them." He looked away and shook his head. "I never thought about it, in those terms before, until Terence asked me that question. I don't know what's coming, but the headmistress is right, if word got out that the Lady of the Lake spoke to you, gave you her time, you would be inundated—think the Second Coming.

But the other is also true. You would probably be dead within the week."

Oh. I wasn't sure what to think. My brain was freezing up. "I need to write a letter to Lord Winton." It was getting harder to think. "I'm just Vivian Hampton, a butterfly. I'm—" and then the world went black as every conceivable emotion hit me all at once.

Chapter 20

What's in a name?
-Shakespeare.

-The thought-

It took the thought in the ground most of the night to break through the first layer of magical locks. Just before sunrise, tendrils of light were able to wind their way through the rocks to touch the deepest warding stone under the tall building in the valley. Suddenly, a bit of its mind woke up. Past events were reviewed. The thought was certain the one who had called it was nearby.

It. Was that its name? Its voices had names. Memories surfaced; it was a general description. To have a name meant there was a purpose, a light. An odd sensation emerged within its vast matrix of light, a wanting. Before it had been reacting, now that a small part of its mind was awake, it began planning. To acquire a name, required a master to bequeath one. To find its master required exploring further, which meant pushing against the wards keeping the rest of its mind asleep.

Hmm. To break through the next set of wards took more knowledge than the thought currently possessed even with its expanded mind. The thought could sense the third warding stone just below this building. However, without the Pentwale keys or enough energy being applied to the warding stone, it might as well be on the next planet. It considered options. An idea occurred to it.

Would the voices it had collected over the years know? The thought asked them. Only a few knew what the word Pentwale meant. Ideas were discussed, but none of them understood the math or had broken this type of magical lock before. So, it prepared to wait in the hope that it would collect more power from the exposed warding stone. As always, it was very patient.

Then something happened that it did not expect.

The warding stone it was contemplating suddenly glowed with power. Furthermore, the thought recognized the magic signature. The person who had sung magic was charging the ward. Was this its new master calling out? In desperation, it attempted to break the next Pentwale lock to announce itself but couldn't. It pushed again, asking its voices to help, and for the briefest moment of time, it was almost there before the locks still holding it fought back. However, in that moment of time, the thought learned something. It discovered that the person who had sung magic was a young human female. But most importantly, it sensed the raw emotional power coming from this woman, power she was using to shape the magic around her.

The thought considered options. It could not reach the young woman yet, but perhaps one of its voices could. One that understood a song.

♫

-Vivian Hampton-

Pioneer Infirmary

"Vivian," said a voice. "Can you hear me?"

I blinked my eyes open at the request. Two blurry faces hovered just above me. I wasn't certain if I was looking at one person or two. At least colors weren't bleeding into each other this time. This day certainly seemed like a repeat from three days ago. The only things missing were the dragon and the pain.

"Is there one blurry face above me or two?" I croaked out. Then I felt the pain between my eyes.

Wow! *Well, at least the dragon wasn't here.*

"Will you two step aside," growled out a frustrated female voice. It had to be Healer Frenzia.

Okay. The blobs were two people. Blinking again, Lord Grayson and Jeremy's face vaguely came into focus.

"Hi," I said and winced at the pain behind my eyes. Last time everything hurt, now it was just behind my eyes. Was this a migraine? I never had one before and never wanted to again. "Could someone lower the light?" It seemed horribly bright.

"Ah," said a male voice out of my field of view. It sounded like Professor Gass. "I bet it's a backlash from the link with her snowman."

"Camillo," I immediately replied and winced again.

Lord Grayson and Jeremy were pushed aside. Healer Frenzia helped me sit up. "Here, drink this, child. It's the Mystil potion. Professor Reece brewed it up for us. Never heard of anyone using dried dandelion petals though."

As I sipped at the offered potion, the headmistress gestured at the main light globe and the lights in the room dimmed. My stabbing pain subsided considerably. That felt better. Drinking the rest of the potion, I could tell something was different. It didn't taste awful. Thank goodness for small things. Immediately my vision began clearing up.

I burped. *Great Vivian, I bet that looked dignified. Not.*

I swung my head at the giggle and saw Wanda sitting on the bunk next to me. "What happened?" I asked. Then I burped again. *Uh-oh. Was that from the potion?*

"Lord Grayson caught you before you hit the ground. The headmistress teleported all of us directly to a secret teleportation circle," said Wanda in excitement. "Then she did a second teleport to the infirmary. That was twenty minutes ago. Oh, and apparently Mrs. Rousseau contacted Jeffery and asked him to join us here."

"What happened to Vivian?" demanded Jeffery, in an angry tone.

I burped again and looked around. Someone was missing. "Where's Gail?" Before I started my second class, I checked up on her location via my wand. She had been in the infirmary like I asked her. Then added, "Where's Professor Malton?"

"Currently Gail is in my office, where I will be if you need me," said Healer Frenzia. She gave the headmistress a look I didn't understand and then pointedly closed the door to her office behind her.

Jeffery sat down at the edge of my bed. "What happened, Vivian?"

The headmistress cleared her throat. "Mr. Streatery. Ms. Hampton decided to ignore safety protocols and stepped on an active ring. She is currently suffering from energy backlash. Fortunately, I was there."

"Ma'am?" I said and swallowed. Then I burped again. *When will this stop?* "I'm sorry, but Wanda is very important to me." To hopefully divert her glare, I asked Professor Gass, "My link with Camillo is causing my light sensitivity?"

"If I'm right, it should fade soon," he said. "From what I know, bright light hurts your snowman. The creature is probably charged from the energy you absorbed, as with Ms. Hine and the other links. The extra energy had a path it could take and did so."

Lord Grayson sat down on the other edge of my bed, to the annoyance of Jeffery. "I bet that sensation of feeling lightheaded hit you hard. I was able to catch you before your head hit the ground."

"I should have been there," complained Jeffery.

To stop Jeffery from glaring at Lord Grayson I asked again, "Where's Professor Malton?" Then I burped yet again. I plopped back down on the bed in frustration; this was embarrassing. I think I would have preferred the awful taste instead of burping in front of my two boyfriends. My brain froze at that. *Stop it Vivian*, I thought to myself. Hopefully, my boyfriend, singular.

Lord Grayson was just a nice man; he is not my boyfriend. Besides, Wanda would be stomping on my foot for the next two weeks if I implied he was.

Then I felt like I might burp again but didn't. Hopefully that was it.

"Professor Malton is temporarily shutting down the dueling rings," said the headmistress coldly. "Every gargoyle has been fully charged. So is the library, including the restricted section. The absorbed magic from the dueling rings has nowhere to go for at least a few hours, if not longer."

Oh. I cringed. "Sorry, ma'am."

Jeffery's eyes went wide, and he took my hand. "Vivian, you did that. I knew you had more magic than Mina but wow!"

"Well," I said, then stopped at the headmistress's pointed shake of her head. Right, no discussing that the Lady of the Lake appeared.

"We were doing an experiment and, well, something, er, happened," I said, my voice trailing off. That sounded lame even to me.

"Oh," and Jeffery took his hand back, making me feel sad. I could tell he knew I wasn't telling him the whole story.

I bit my lip. "Are we still on for Friday night? I can tell you more about it then. Much of it is still blurry to me."

Professor Gass harrumphed. "That's an understatement." He stood up and bowed. "Headmistress, I need to write down some notes. I am sure we will talk about this later." He gave Jeffery a quick glance before leaving. "I assume we will be signing a unique document as well?"

"Jeffery?" I asked softly and reached out to touch his hand. Did he think I didn't trust him with the truth? That I was too powerful now? But all that extra power came from the Lady of the Lake, not me. Well, most of it had to. *I'm just Vivian Hampton, butterfly.*

"Of course, we are," he said. Then he leaned over to kiss me on my forehead, making me feel all tingly again. As he stood up, I think he glared at Lord Grayson. Lord Grayson, for his part, maintained a neutral expression.

"Thank you for catching me," I said to the man.

Jeffery grunted. "It should have been me."

Wanda giggled. "If they duel each other, my bet is on Lord Grayson."

"No dueling," I insisted, and burped again. Drat. "Am I allowed to leave?" My vision was back to normal, and that burp felt like the last one.

The headmistress motioned with her hand and the lights got brighter.

I winced and she immediately lowered them again.

"You will stay here until the effect wears off, Ms. Hampton. Ms. Hine may stay with you. Everyone else, out. When it is safe for you to leave, I want both of you in my office." From the headmistress's tone, we had better not take detours.

Jeffery kissed me on the forehead again before he left. Lord Grayson briefly looked away, bowed, and quietly left the room. The headmistress closed the door behind her. This left me alone with Wanda.

She bounced up while waving her wand. "Look at this!"

Her light spell went off correctly. Except now it was brighter. At my wince of pain, she immediately shut down the spell. "Sorry, I forgot. How long do you think it will be before your link with Camillo will settle back down?"

I pushed myself up, sat against the wall, and thought about him. Surprisingly, I could sort of sense him now and see out of his eyes. Terrance was laying down in a cave, for all the world he looked dead.

<*"Camillo,"*> I called out softly.

<*"I am here, Creator. Are you nearby? I can sense your presence."*>

<*"No. I am still at school. Once Terrance wakes, can you pass along a message for me?"*>

<*"Yes, Creator."*>

<*"I would like his help in a discrete matter. You may come too."*>

I felt Camillo ponder my request. <"*What does discrete mean, Creator?*">

Wanda giggled.

<"*To be diplomatic,*"> and stopped. He probably didn't know what that meant either. <"*To be kind, attentive and careful not to be overheard,*"> I said. <"*Thank you for being Terrance's friend.*">

<"*Yes, Creator, I will pass along the message. Is Wanda your friend? Do you watch over her as I do with Terrance?*">

Wanda's fit of giggles immediately stopped.

<"*Yes, Camillo, I do.*"> Then I broke the connection.

After a few seconds of silence, Wanda hesitantly asked, "Amanda's head of house is a dragon too."

I nodded and put a finger to my lips. I bet Healer Frenzia had spell trackers in here so she could check up on her patients remotely.

Wanda came over and sat down at the edge of my bed. "How come you didn't tell me?"

I pushed myself up and leaned into Wanda. Now that the excitement had passed of seeing three—well, gods, for lack of a better term—as well as the Lady of the Lake, I was beginning to feel very small. Also, it was impressed upon me that we were trying to get the two dragons to work together or at least not fight each other. I felt a small relief that it wasn't just me, but the feeling was short-lived. If people like Lady Gawain and others were doing the same thing, what help could I possibly be?

"I trust you, Wanda," I said and reached out to take her hand. "I'm feeling so lost. All I wanted was to do well in school, maybe have a boyfriend, and it feels like the rest of the universe wants other things for me. I don't know who Vivian Hampton is anymore."

"You're Vivian Hampton," said Wanda with conviction. "Amazing Hero. I've got your back." She grinned and nudged me. "I've got a crazy idea," she said excitedly. "What if she, you know, was trying to tell us something?"

Uh-oh. For Wanda to think her idea was crazy probably meant it was out there. But it was important to me that she felt included. I gripped her hand harder while nudging her back. "Right now, crazy might be our best option."

"Well," Wanda said and lowered her voice, so it was almost a whisper. "She," Wanda stressed, "said Lady Gawain was trying to get 'them' to work together too. Send Lord Winton a message through your wand to see if Lady Gawain could, well, be here when we put Amanda and Elaine in a spell circle together."

I stared at Wanda. "Yes, that's crazy."

Me, ask a high noble for help? I was certain Lady Gawain didn't even know my name, why would she.

Wanda nudged me right back. "Yep. So, are you going to do it?"

The headmistress blinked. "I want to make sure if I heard you correctly. You want to contact your benefactor so he can ask the third highest lady of Avalon to come to our school to be here when we put Amanda and Elaine in a spell circle together?"

"Actually, ma'am," I said, trying not to back up from her stare, "It was Wanda's idea. But I think it's a good one."

Wanda beamed at me.

The headmistress plopped down in her chair. Professor Malton started laughing.

"Ma'am," I said, "the Lady of the Lake pointedly said Lady Gawain was bearing the brunt of the two dragons. Could she have been trying to suggest this to us?"

Wanda bounced once. "Vivian is the best Hero ever."

The headmistress rubbed her forehead with both her hands, then looked at Professor Gass. "Thoughts?"

He shrugged. "I think I agree with Ms. Hampton. The lady might have been trying to tell us something."

Lord Grayson looked stunned. "If she does come, the security will need to be like nothing I have ever seen."

The headmistress just stared at me, then sighed. "Vivian, when you contact your benefactor, here's what I want you to say..."

Chapter 21

I would rather extend a hand of friendship.
-Arthur Pendragon.

-Vivian Hampton-

Pioneer School

Wanda and I completely missed music class which would have normally annoyed me. Well, that wasn't technically true, there were five minutes left. But what was the point, I couldn't sing again until I got my magic under control. A little part of me hoped—imagined really—it would be possible to make a girl snowman. Maybe Jeffery and I could go out on a double date then. I felt a tugging sensation on my arm and looked down to see Wanda's hand. Apparently, I had been about to walk into an instrument.

"I can always tell when you're thinking about Jeffery," teased Wanda letting go. "You get this far away look in your eyes."

The harp I almost bumped into played out a gentle string of cords. I instantly recognized the melody as a snippet from Handel's Messiah. I bet for the harp, that sort of translated into, *Watch where you walk next time.*

Wanda and I were almost at the gymnasium where I had asked Mina and others to gather. Yesterday it was empty at this time, I hoped it was again. Gail's predicament touched on some sensitive topics—dating between the social classes, political undertones from the Reece's Racoon Charter, and maybe even a spy who wasn't afraid to push people's minds a bit. I hoped Lord Thomas and the others were wrong. Imagining that my feelings might not be mine was very disconcerting. How Gail was feeling had to be worse. I was glad she was with Healer Frenzia right now. If it was me, I would probably be huddled in a corner.

"I wish we could skip ahead to Friday night," I fantasized. Jeffery and I would be sitting next to each other, enjoying dinner together. We would laugh about our week while the rest of the world passed us by for a bit. His head of house would have written back by then, thereby giving him permission to date me. The two of us would be an item. Not engaged but allowed to be with each other privately. I imagined our hands touching, then Jeffery leaning over to kiss me. I would...

"Yeah, me too," said Wanda, cutting into my fantasy. "Lord Grayson and I would be hiking to the next mountain pass. He's awesome."

I sighed as my fantasy evaporated in my mind, then cocked my head. Wanda should be shrieking in excitement right now. I was surprised she wasn't doing cartwheels down the hallway from what just happened in the headmistress office.

After I sent the headmistress's message to Lord Winton's wand through mine, I got back an immediate answer. That surprised me.

An illusion of Lord Winton appeared right in front of me. "Vivian, Kiera will pass along your idea to Lady Gawain. However, it may be several hours before that can happen. Expect a response this evening." Then his image faded away. I stood there feeling stunned at the audacity of what I had just done. Honestly, I hadn't expected an answer at all.

Wanda had her hands to her mouth. High-pitched *eeping* sounds were escaping between her fingers.

The headmistress looked down at her desk. "And so it begins," she whispered.

Professor Gass drained his coffee mug and stood up. "My bet is she's going to come. I need to work on the design for the outer ring."

Professor Malton's face twitched. "I think we should discuss the other matter first," he said, glancing at Lord Grayson. "If it's real, we need to have it solved before Lady Gawain arrives—should she decide to come, that is."

"Problem? What problem?" asked Lord Grayson.

Oh. That one.

"Professor," I said hesitantly. "I reached out to Camillo before the extra energy faded. He's going to ask Terrance to come visit me at school." At my words, I felt the tension in the room increase.

"What aren't you telling me?" demanded Lord Grayson.

Professor Malton sat down and looked at the ground. "Since the death of Lord Alerie and his daughter, some of the more conservative factions in chambers have gone quiet. This is very unusual."

"I was briefed on that," said Lord Grayson, crossing his arms. "But what has that got to do with Terrance? I don't think he cares about politics or political factions."

Professor Malton glanced at the headmistress. "Your call."

"Realm Knight," said the Headmistress formally, "an informal meeting occurred between Professor Gass, Professor Malton, Professor Holton, and me. We discussed the possibility that Lord Abner might have been *suggested* to involve himself with Ms. Gail. As you are aware, Lord Abner's head of house has not even hinted on which way she plans to vote on the Reece's Racoon Charter." The headmistress nodded toward me. "Apparently, early this morning, Ms. Hampton and her friend asked the same question."

Wow. If Professor Holton was involved, then the headmistress must be taking the idea seriously. She was a retired Realm Knight and currently head of House Coley.

"Why wasn't I involved in this?" demanded Lord Grayson. "It's my job."

"Young man," shot back the headmistress. "We have no official proof. If it's real, do you think this is an isolated event? Sorcerer Petotum doesn't care about a pigeon. He needs the entire flock."

Lord Grayson looked stunned. Then his face went a bit pink. "You don't trust me?"

"Just the opposite, young man," said the headmistress softly. "Think. Why did Sorcerer Petotum set it up so you were Terrance's apprentice? Furthermore, he arranged for the man—well, whatever he is—to get an extremely good wand outside of official channels. Think!"

Wanda reached over and gripped my arm in excitement.

Lord Grayson swallowed. "Sorcerer Petotum thinks this might go all the way to the top. He needs us to catch an officer in this hidden army. We're the unofficial spies. Off the books." The man suddenly bowed to the headmistress. "Ma'am, I think I'll take a stroll. It's a good day for a walk up to the mountains. I might even bump into a friend or two."

After he left, Professor Malton turned to me and Wanda. "This didn't happen, Vivian. I believe you were on your way to visit Lady Mina. Please don't let us keep you." Just as Wanda and I were about to leave he added softly, "Remember, Vivian, we might be wrong. Even if we aren't, I hope Lord Abner and Gail have a chance to talk it through. They're both people."

"How come you're not going all Wanda right now?" I asked my henchwoman. Lady Gawain, her hero, might be coming to our school. I still couldn't imagine it though. She was one of the highest ladies in the land. People went to her. Personally, I expected Lord Winton to tell me, well, to order Amanda and Elaine to take the teleportation circles so they could go to her. Lady Gawain would put them in a spell circle, aspects of the dragons would appear, and Lady Gawain would tell them both off. From all the stories I heard, she was kind but also very firm. I heard a rumor that she stared down Sorcerer Petotum on the wizard's council. She said yes, he said no. Somehow, she won.

Wanda stuck her tongue out at me. "I heard Lady Gawain has thousands of fans who practically scream themselves silly anytime they see her. I want her to remember me as Wanda Hine, a person with a brain."

"Good for you," I said. But I made a mental bet with myself that Wanda's self-control would likely last all of two seconds if she ever did meet Lady Gawain. Personally, I hoped I was wrong. Wanda really did seem to be taking my idea of redefining herself to heart.

Wanda stomped her foot. "You don't believe me!"

I was about to tell her that of course I did when the walls evaporated around me. I was having another vision.

I recognized Professor Vermis's office, having served detention there once last year. I had made the mistake of being snippy to Lord Seth where Professor Vermis could hear me. Wanda and I ended up spending two hours organizing magical ingredients that evening.

From the angle of the sun out of his windows, I thought my vision might be happening very soon, assuming it was today. Standing in front of Professor Vermis were Lord Seth, Lord Keith, and their respective henchmen. As with my other visions, I couldn't move unless someone moved into the space my perspective was from.

Professor Vermis leaned back in his chair, "The Hero has returned," he said derisively, looking at Lord Seth standing at attention in front of his desk.

"Professor, it wasn't my idea," complained Lord Seth.

"Yes, it was," shouted Lord Keith. "I was right there with you when you bragged to your grandfather about how you were going to get Elaine kicked out of school. *She's a nobody*, you said. Well apparently, she's not. My father is considering challenging your head of house to a duel, and this is all your fault. We even have a Realm Knight searching through our family's finances."

Lord Seth pushed Lord Keith away. "How was I to know that peasant was anyone important?"

Professor Vermis stood up and tapped the desk with his index finger. "And yet you acted without gathering all the facts and even convinced your head of house to make a formal challenge. If only your grandfather possessed a drop of wisdom and had reached out to me first. I would have instructed him to wait," said Professor Vermis disdainfully. "However, you and Lord Keith are in my house. An adjunct to a council member owes me a favor. With some carefully crafted words by your head of house, along with Lord Keith's, we might be able to get the audit downgraded."

"What about our seat in the lower chambers?" pleaded Lord Seth. "The vote is coming up in a week."

"I would suggest," said Professor Vermis, not quite rolling his eyes. "That you do everything in your power to keep your nose clean. The headmistress does have the ear of at least two council members that I know of. You might even try being helpful to the freshmen, as it is your job."

"Does that mean we still have detention for the next two weeks?" asked Lord Seth's henchman.

Professor Vermis pinched the bridge of his nose and closed his eyes. "Lord Seth, I am including your henchman in my previous statement about keeping your noses clean."

"What now?" asked Lord Keith.

"This is a school," said Professor Vermis, turning away. "I suggest heading to your next class. While you are doing that, I will be calling in my favor. Later this evening, I will brief the lot of you on where we stand."

Well, I was sort of relieved it wasn't Professor Vermis who pushed Lord Seth to file the complaint. But why was I seeing this?

Then just as the vision began fading, I noticed something odd. Jordon's shadow—Lord Keith's henchman—seemed wrong. It didn't move on its own, but his shadow looked off somehow, as if another person was there.

"Vivian," I heard from Wanda. "Are you having another vision?"

I blinked and my surroundings came back into focus. Wanda must have led me into a corner.

"I did and, well, I don't know why I had it. But there was something weird at the end."

"What was it?" asked Wanda breathlessly.

The bell went off and students began filing out of classrooms. "Let's get to the gymnasium," I said. "Tell you later."

♪♪♪

"Mina, you're wrong," I said emphatically. "This isn't your land where you can make a decree and it becomes law. Gail isn't your subject, she's your friend. We should be trying to help her."

Mina's boyfriend, Lord Thomas, moved to stand beside her. "We are helping her, Vivian. My mother has made arrangements for Gail to spend a few months on our lands. When this blows over, she can come back to school."

"And did you even ask if that is what Gail wants?" I asked, getting annoyed now. "She's not your subject either. We don't even know if either of them has been mentally pushed into their relationship. Regardless, they should be allowed to talk it out."

"Vivian," said Mina compassionately. "You're not a noble. You wouldn't understand. We're doing Lord Abner's family a service. We're doing Avalon a service. In a few months, Gail can come back to school. It's just the way things are done."

I could feel my anger beginning to rise. Mina was my friend; she had stood by me as I had stood by her. Now it felt like it all had been meaningless. No, that wasn't exactly true, more like, we were dolls in her playhouse. She liked us, and we could go about our imaginary day. But once we did something she didn't like, we got picked up and put where we "belonged."

When I suggested to Mina and Sierra we meet in the gymnasium during our free period, Mia was with them. Apparently she took that to mean she'd been invited too. From what I gathered, Mia passed the word to Amanda, Samantha, and Elaine, probably because those three had become the de facto leaders of the freshmen Orozco class. Along with them, Nathan, the senior head student for Orozco was here, and he had brought his henchman plus a few others. The same for Lord Thomas. Considering the number of people in the gymnasium with us, I was surprised we hadn't had a professor come to investigate why they were missing so many students. For the freshmen, this wasn't a free period.

"I'm the head girl of House Orozco," I growled out. "Not you. Gail isn't going anywhere unless she wants to."

Nathan took a step forward. "Actually, *I'm* the head student of Orozco," he clarified.

I gave him a hard stare. Where was he last year when we had to survive on our own?

"Well, I am," he reiterated.

His henchman whispered something to the effect of, "It's the Snowball Queen's show."

Nathan stepped back to stand with the others. I turned back toward Mina and crossed my arms. "Go ahead, convince me."

"Vivian, this is about Avalon," said Mina with a sad smile. She was acting like I was a freshman who didn't know anything. "You are my friend, but this is the right thing to do. Lord Winton made a good choice when he endowed you."

And there it was, in Mina's eyes, I belonged to Lord Winton. I was a subject to another noble. Mina reminded me I was just a commoner, and she was a noble. In other words, she outranked me. From her tone, I could tell she was trying to be kind. I don't think Mina had a mean bone in her body. But her underlying words were very clear: *back off, commoner. You're my friend, but this is about taking care of the nobility. Don't get in our way.*

"So, I don't get a voice?" I said trying not to shout and placing my hands on my hips. "Gail doesn't? You get to pick her up and toss her away? Hell, it's like you're channeling Lord Seth now."

Mina's eyes went wide, and she stumbled backwards into Lord Thomas. From her surprised expression, it was like I had slapped her.

Was this how all nobles really thought, I wondered? Commoners were just pretend people or cattle? Pat us on our heads like we were animals and, when needed, just lead us to a different pasture? Out of the corner of my eye, I noticed Wanda put her hand on her wand sheath.

Uh-oh.

I could feel the tension in the room spike. Wanda was outright challenging Mina. If they had a spell fight, my henchman would be flattened.

Lord Thomas partially stepped in front of Mina. "Draw it, and you're toast, Wanda. Back up and take your Hero with you."

"Hey, leave her out of this," Sierra protested and went to stand alongside Wanda. "She can't do anything to hurt you." Which was true, there were only three spells encoded into her wand and none of them were offensive spells.

Mina's eyes narrowed. Sierra was choosing a side, and it wasn't hers. "I stood by you, Sierra. Now you want to just throw it all away?"

An odd thought crossed my mind. Was that the reason Professor Malton paired Mina up with Sierra? Give the lady the lowest commoner of our incoming class? "Mina," I said, compassionately trying to defuse the situation. "Sierra is just trying to protect her friend. No one is throwing anyone away. That's why we're here, to help. Don't push us away."

For just a second, I thought my friend was back. Then Lord Thomas put a hand on Mina's shoulder and whatever struggle that was going on inside her disappeared; Lady Mina had resurfaced. "Lord Thomas and I must go," she said tartly. "Please excuse us."

As I was deciding what to say next, Sierra crossed her arms and pointedly moved in front of Mina. "Hell, I'm in the mole clan. The bottom of the heap. You taught me how to read. Vivian taught me—us—we were a team. Are you saying that standing together isn't important anymore? You're suddenly queen, and the little common girl should just go away so a noble's house isn't embarrassed? Should I just give up too?"

"Sierra," Mina said and reached out a hand. "This is about Avalon. Don't try to..."

"Don't try to do what?" spat out Sierra. "Think that I might have an opinion on the matter or that it might be worth listening to? Gail's my friend. She's yours too."

It wasn't just Sierra and Mina. Around the room, I could tell people were taking sides. Commoners were pushing back against nobles, and henchmen were challenging their Heroes. Everyone around us was staring between Lord Thomas and Mina to me, Wanda, and Sierra. *It wasn't a game anymore.* We were pushing against some of the basic tenets of Avalon: the nobility ruled, and everyone else didn't. Sierra, the lowest of us, had just intentionally blocked a noble.

There was a part of me that just wanted the tension to go away. *But was that the right thing to do for Gail?* I asked myself. Just give in and go back to the way it was? Forcibly separate Gail from Lord Abner so his head of house wasn't embarrassed. I was sure Gail would be treated well on Lord Thomas's family lands. I would make sure her homework got sent to her, perhaps even visit. And... it wasn't a vision but a memory. Wanda and I were sitting in Mrs. Rousseau's office, Wanda tapping her index finger to mime Gail wasn't wearing a contraceptive ring. Had Gail and Lord Abner been that involved already? Could they be having a child together?

Wanda bit her lip, glanced at Amanda, then extended a hand in friendship toward Mina. "What about a tea shop?"

Sierra blinked. Everyone else, including me, had some variation of "huh?" on our faces. What was Wanda talking about?

"I think I know what you're suggesting," said Amanda. "That's a good idea."

I turned just enough to face Wanda but kept Lord Thomas in my field of view. I had never seen the man this angry before. Like Mina, he had always been rather nice. Now I sensed he wanted to squish me into the ground. I wasn't certain, but it almost seemed as if he might be forcing Mina into a choice—follow him or else.

I hoped I was wrong. His house was politically more powerful than Mina's. Did he just expect Mina to follow him? Or worse, once they were married, would he do to Mina what they were proposing for Gail? Would Mina lose her voice as well? If so, was that what Mina wanted? I hoped not.

"What are you talking about?" I asked Wanda. But my eyes noticed something else too. Amanda was standing straighter and, well, projecting. She had transformed somehow, and I could clearly see the edges of High Lady Amanda.

"Well," said Wanda. "Avalon City has this tea shop, you know the one across from the bookstore, where nobles and commoners can talk as equals. Why can't our school have that as well? An agreed upon safe place where everyone can just talk to each other, without fear of repercussion."

I saw some heads nod at her idea. And a few frowns.

And suddenly I understood. This wasn't just about Gail and Lord Abner but Wanda too. And all commoners. If I walked away from Wanda's idea, I bet that vision I saw of Wanda leading a life controlled by others would be more likely to come true. I felt immensely proud of my henchwoman. It took a lot of courage to stand tall and talk instead of shouting at each other.

I took a step toward Mina and said quietly but firmly, "Wanda's right. We pick a spot and give Gail and Lord Abner the space to talk it out. But it's a safe space for all of us."

Amanda tapped the side of her wand sheath. "I bet my dad would support it too."

Lord Thomas groaned out, "Maker's nostril." He pointed at Amanda but addressed me. "Vivian, you're doing the commoners a disservice. If you think it's bad in school, it's worse out there. You're setting them up to fail."

I shook my head to clear it. Just stepping back and allowing the nobles to take over was so easy to do, it came naturally. It was almost ingrained. Wanda was looking to me for guidance. So was everyone else—including Amanda.

Was I going to back down or push back against Lord Thomas? My eyes found Amanda. Like the others, she was watching me, but only Wanda and I knew that she was really a high noble. Suddenly a kaleidoscope of visions expanded within my mind; they were all about Amanda and the person she could become. In a mental leap, I got it. This was a crux point for her. Yesterday, I asked her to trust me, and she did. There were so many possible paths I couldn't see them all. But there was one that stood out to me. She and Elaine were a bit older, laughing together and surrounded by friends, some of them commoners from our freshman class.

Amanda needed a push. If this was a crux point for her, so be it. It was time to push.

I took a deep breath and looked at Mina. "Gail's voice needs to be heard. So should Amanda's, Elaine's, and everyone else's. If we restrict who is allowed to speak, then Avalon has already lost."

Lord Thomas snorted. "Dammit Vivian, we're not the bad guys here. Whoever said that obviously doesn't understand how Avalon works."

My anger was nothing next to Wanda's. "The 'idiot' who said that," she said coldly, "was Lady Gawain. You're acting as if you belong in House Duke."

Lord Thomas was fast. Reg might have been faster, but I wasn't sure. But what I did know was that if I did nothing, this moment would be gone. I had my wand out and pointed at Lord Thomas just as his was coming up.

"Lord Thomas," I said in a flat voice. "I will fight you to defend Gail's right to choose. Maybe she chooses to go away for a while, but then it's her choice. She's my people. I'm her head girl and I'm the Snowball Queen. Gail gets a choice."

All my attention was focused on Lord Thomas, but I heard several people gasp out. Samantha said in a whisper, "Why are there glowing runes around Vivian's wand?"

"Because," replied Wanda with pride, "my Hero doesn't need to encode her spells. And that's a nasty one."

Then Lord Seth, along with Lord Keith, walked into the gymnasium with their henchmen. Immediately Lord Seth and Lord Keith pulled out their wands as well.

Chapter 22

I honestly don't understand how that young lady can function.

-Lady Gawain, speaking about the new merlin.

-Terrance-

I heard Darlene's voice in my dream again. Maybe my unconscious has a thing for older brunettes. Seconds later, another sensation swirled into my dream turning everything red—the scent of blood. With it came the purr of my hunger. It wanted to feed. This substitute brunette in my mind noticed me and ran down an alley. My hunger wanted to flow into darkness and take her. I pushed it down and turned away. Every time I consciously did so, I felt like it had less of a grip on me. I had an absurd hope it might die from pure starvation, but a person's nightmares were their own to deal with, as were anyone else's.

Darlene's voice came again, louder, almost desperate. Then I felt someone pushing on my shoulders.

"Camillo?" I mumbled out as I opened my eyes and sat up.

Darlene stumbled backwards, landing on a rucksack she must have brought with her.

"Terrance?" she whispered in terror. She had a hand on her wand sheath and looked ready to flee.

Immediately my ears picked up some people talking nearby, from the pitch, probably young ladies. I could feel Camillo's mental touch but very faint. He was at the edge of his range. So far, this had grown over the last day or so, but he had a limit. However, I didn't sense any immediate danger which would explain Darlene's apparent fear.

"Are you okay?" I asked her, standing up. Then I looked around in wonder. The free magic in the area was intense to the point the air was sparkling. Had the dragon returned? That would explain her apparent fear and the concentrated magic.

Darlene let out a sigh of relief and pushed herself upright. "Um, yes. When you opened your eyes, they glowed red for a second. I thought you might be—disoriented."

"Sorry," I said while dusting myself off. "I didn't mean to scare you. I'm fine. The redness was probably because I smelled blood in my dream." Then I cocked my head. The smell was still here, intense and coming from the rucksack at her feet. "You brought me blood?"

Darlene blew out her breath. "We weren't sure if you still needed blood, so Franklin gathered some cow and pigs' blood from the butchers. The preservation spell I cast on the mason jars should keep it fresh until tonight. When Franklin and I came up here this morning, we just expected to say hello to Camillo and drop them off. Then, well..." and she glanced toward the turn that led toward the cave's entrance while moving her hand through the air. Twinkling magic sparkled around her fingers.

"Is the dragon outside?" I asked. From the indirect sunlight bouncing off the walls, I could tell that it was probably late morning. So, I had gotten perhaps five hours of sleep. Camillo didn't like direct sunlight; he would avoid it if he could.

Were those young ladies' voices I heard from the dragon's harem? If so, the words they were using made them sound very educated. Not what I would have expected. Apparently two of them were having a spirited discussion on what made Camillo tick. Some of the concepts they were bantering about were downright complex.

Regardless, if the dragon had come again, I would have expected the tunnel I was in to have at least partially collapsed.

Darlene tensed up at hearing the rising pitch of one of the young ladies. Whoever she was, she was annoyed. Not angry, more pissed. Immediately the free magic in the area spiked again. Okay, so it wasn't the dragon. Who was out there? Then it dawned on me in one horrific moment that there was likely only one person who had that much magic about them.

"Please tell me it isn't her," I said to Darlene while closing my eyes.

"If you mean the new merlin? Yes, and she brought friends. But I think she's projecting from someplace else."

Oh joy. The new merlin was here. Well sort of. And apparently annoyed. I picked up the rucksack and headed toward the first turn toward the opening. Was the little moppet here for me or Camillo?

"Do you know why she's here?" I asked Darlene, while edging around the first corner. I wanted to drink from one of the mason jars in the rucksack just to calm my nerves. The last time I met her, it didn't end well for me. *Suck it up Terrance*, I told myself. *Letting fear rule me won't help*. Besides, if the kid wanted to kill me again, I would already be dead. What I wanted was to make sure Camillo was safe and get him out of there. I didn't get the sense Camillo was in danger, only that he was confused. He probably didn't understand a word of what the new merlin was talking about. *Sarah, that was her name.* It helped to calm myself down by thinking of her name instead of her title.

"Honestly," said Darlene, edging against the wall and staying just behind me. "I think she came here on a dare."

At Darlene's statement, something began clicking in my mind. Lady Elizabeth said she put what lies below off-limits to Sarah and Nenet. I bet the kid was using Camillo as a technicality to push back. She probably thought rules were meant to be broken and wanted to see what kind of backbone Lady Elizabeth possessed. From my brief interactions with Lady Elizabeth, Sarah was going to be on the losing end of that battle.

"Is one of the other young ladies with the new merlin a redhead? Stands like a queen and has a bracelet?" I asked and edged forward to glance around the corner; all clear, if you ignored the fact the magic about the place was growing stronger. The next turn would bring us to the cave's opening.

"Yes," whispered Darlene while staying just behind me. "Do you know who she is?"

"If I'm right, she's the Lady of the Lake's apprentice," I said. "I bet the new merlin is showing off. Lady Elizabeth said the two of them were frenemies."

I could feel Darlene staring at me. I was about to step around the final corner when I almost collided with the moppet's floating staff. Like before, it had a series of wands rotating around the top. Did it want to talk to us? Was it going to announce us? Destroy us? Who knew what the thing could do?

"Hi," I said. "I'm Terrance, and this is Darlene." Always good to be polite when introducing yourself to magical artifacts that could think for themselves and likely kill you.

<"I know who you are. I have a message for you from the lady.">

"Lady Elizabeth?" I asked uncertainly. I didn't think so though. If she wanted to talk to me, she could just pop in. Free teleporting for her was apparently not a problem.

<"No, creature. From the Lady of the Green Hand.">

Oh. Never had a goddess's agent talk to me before. "What's the message?"

<"O, while you live, tell truth and shame the devil!">

Darlene whispered into my ear, "Why is it quoting Shakespeare at us?"

"No clue." At least it wasn't trying to kill me, and it hadn't announced me yet either. Was the kid, the new merlin, even aware her staff was talking to me? Around the corner, the three young ladies were still arguing with one another about what made Camillo tick. Well, two of them were. The third, a young lady I heard called Tabitha, was getting increasingly distressed about being discovered by her father.

The wands rotating around the top of the staff slowed down. I almost heard the edges of a sigh from the thing. <"*Alas, I am constantly misunderstood. No, creature. I was referring to the preacher, Hugh Latimer. The demon wants all nine rings. The race has begun. You hold the first one.*">

Darlene gripped my arm. "Lady Cassandra doesn't hesitate to throw us into the fire, does she?"

I snorted. "Didn't trust her from the start." Then I replayed what Darlene just said: *us*. She was planning to see this through with me, and by default, that probably included her husband. Damn it, I didn't want my friends to face that kind of danger. I was built from a master thief, had exceptional powers which didn't come with a manual, and now owned, well, was permanently borrowing a core wand. My old self, well, who I was created from, would have seen having friends as a weakness. An unwanted distraction.

Darlene was a retired low-level sorceress turned librarian, and her husband was a former ground pounder in the army. Then there was Mrs. Capmond and the kid. I had the oddest group of people following me. And then there was Camillo; just thinking about him stirred something deep inside me. Last night he became aware his time with us was likely limited. He was going to melt, and all he cared about was being with his friends, with me. I wanted to scream at my doppelgänger about what a fool he had been.

I touched Darlene's hand. "Team."

I could sense Darlene smiling. "Franklin's going to want to name the team, it's a thing with him."

The staff just floated there. Did it want something else? Darlene edged forward to stand beside me to ask the staff, "Who is Tabitha and her father? The young lady makes it sound like her father is an authority figure to the three of them."

Good question. Didn't remember a Tabitha being in the merlin's group before. But I didn't exactly hold out my hand and introduce myself at the time. How she got mixed up with the new merlin and the Lady of the Lake apprentice is probably a story all its own. But the more information we had, the better.

<*"She is the only one of the three who has any common sense,"*> sniffed the staff. <*"Tabitha is the adoptive daughter of Captain Calvit, the sword bearer."*>

Aha. Pieces were falling into place. I bet the kid was at school and Captain Calvit got called away, and she used the unsupervised moment to show off. Before I could ask it a question, the staff floated around the corner. A niggling hope grew in me that Tabitha could stop the two other young ladies from blowing me apart.

I looked at Darlene. "Taking the plunge with me?" There was a small hope she would back out.

"Of course. But I'm terrified too."

"Amen," I replied, and we turned the last corner as a team.

Camillo was standing some fifteen feet inside the cave, staying just out of the direct sunlight. Yesterday had been cloudy; today was anything but. Unless the weather changed, Camillo would likely be staying in here all day.

Darlene was right, the three young ladies were projections. They appeared solid, but the outlines of their bodies shimmered. Having done a projection in my previous life—well, who I was copied from—I recognized the effect. Then it dawned on me where the new merlin was projecting from: Earth. The power to build, much less maintain this projection had to be tremendous.

The new merlin had her hands on her hips glaring at Nenet, who was glaring right back. I swear the space between the two of them was vibrating. The third young lady, I assumed Tabitha, was standing near Camillo, looking apprehensive.

Camillo turned to face me. "<*What does synthetic Somnium link mean, my friend?*">

Neither Sarah nor Nenet looked toward me and Darlene. They kept their focus on each other, almost daring the other to blink. Nenet pointed at Camillo without taking her focus away from Sarah. "You're confusing him, Sarah, like always. Besides, I'm certain you're wrong this time. I bet it is a convection energy transfer based on stored spirit pools."

Tabitha stomped her foot on the ground. "Both of you, stop it. You're not only confusing him, but we shouldn't even be here. My dad is going to be back any minute."

<"*My Friend,*"> I heard from Camillo. <"*Are these my friends too? Why are they so shiny?*">

That's when Tabitha noticed Darlene and me. "Hi," she said and blushed. "Did we disturb you? Sorry."

It took me a second to understand what she was implying. She thought Darlene and I had been together, and their sudden arrival had interrupted our play time.

Remember Terrance, I told myself. *Young teenage girls*. Be very calm, stay on safe topics. *Darlene came up to bring me some fresh blood and*, okay maybe not that detailed.

"I am Terrance, young lady," I said then bowed. "This is Darlene, and you didn't interrupt us. We came up to make sure our friend was okay."

Darlene stifled a laugh.

Nenet and Sarah broke eye contact with each other and swung their heads as one to stare at us. Sarah extended a hand. Her staff flew into her open palm. And suddenly, I felt as if all the free magic about the place was suddenly focused in on me, waiting for a trigger. Big gun, Terrance, little bug. Don't make any sudden movements.

Nenet's clothes shimmered, transformed into a flowing white dress. "I know you," she said, her eyes narrowing. "Are you here for round two?"

Make that two big guns targeting me.

Camillo pushed between the two of them to stand in front of me. <"*My friend. Why are they mad at you?*">

Tabitha grabbed on to Sarah and Nenet's arms. "Stop it! Both of you. He's not evil. If he was, I would know it."

What to do? Honestly, I was more worried about Darlene. I already died once, hated it. But I don't think Darlene would get the same second chance I did.

I slowly raised my hands. "What attacked you before is gone. A demon duplicated me from a master thief. It intentionally made sure all the emotional bits and pieces which make us human were left out. Once I reformed from being blasted by you, all those extra bits were there." I slowly lowered my hands. "I don't want to kill anyone or take your bracelet," I said, glancing at Nenet.

I bowed. "I assume you are Nenet, the Lady of the Lake's apprentice. Sorry for scaring you and your sister when we met before."

For a second, all three of them just looked at me. Was I about to be blasted into my next life? Camillo, still next to me, asked, <*Why is there such a strong song flowing from Sarah, my friend?*">

It was like a switch had been thrown. I was suddenly unimportant again. Nenet turned back to Sarah. "See I'm right, synthetic Somnium is just ridiculous. You've obviously lost your mind."

The new merlin slammed her staff into the ground and glared right back at Nenet. "Well, if I duplicate him, we could try to...."

"No!" shouted Tabitha. "Can't you see he's confused? Besides I bet my dad will be back soon from getting Ager Lucem repaired. And remember what happened when you tried to duplicate that other spell?"

"It wasn't my fault," demanded Sarah. "If we adjust the twelfth rune group by eight degrees, it should work this time. Probably."

Nenet rolled her eyes. "Pumpkins a mile away began animating, and you want to try that on the snowman? I'm with Tabitha. No way."

Sarah slammed her staff on the ground again. "It was just a first try. Besides, no one got hurt."

"No," reiterated Tabitha. "Sarah, we need to go."

Interesting. When Tabitha shouted, a faint ring of light, almost like a crown, formed around her head—then faded. But what was even more amazing to me was how fast those three young teenage girls could switch topics. I went from being targeted, to being ignored in the span of fifteen seconds. In other words, I was unimportant in their lives. To be that innocent again. It dawned on me that Lady Elizabeth and others were probably bending over backwards to give them the space to grow into themselves.

From behind me, Darlene gasped. "That looked like Guinevere's circlet."

<*"My friend, what should we do?"*> Camillo asked.

Well, at least they weren't blasting me with spells. Tabitha appeared to be the most levelheaded of the group, so I addressed her. "From what Lady Elizabeth told me, what lies under the mountain is off limits to your lot. Should I be calling her here now?"

Sarah's mouth opened in surprise, then her eyes narrowed. "Technically, we're visiting the snowman."

"Camillo," I immediately countered. "And with all the magic you're pushing around, don't you believe some of it might end up below?"

Tabitha stomped her foot on the ground and that same shimmering circlet appeared. "I told you this was a bad idea."

Nenet rolled her eyes. "Welcome to being Sarahed. You should get her to tell you the story about dragon's mount."

"That wasn't my fault. If you remember..." But her words were cut short by an elegant, commanding voice. Lady Elizabeth

Navartis appeared just to my right. But unlike the three young ladies who were projections, she was here.

"I said no, Sarah, and that goes for you too, Nenet."

"We're not really here, just projecting," protested Sarah. "Besides, we're visiting the snowman. So, technically I'm not breaking your rules."

"Camillo," corrected Lady Elizabeth. "How did you learn about him?"

Tabitha blushed. "Dad told us about him over dinner."

Lady Elizabeth sighed. "Sarah, Nenet, and this goes for you too, Tabitha. I'm going to discuss this with the Iron Dragon and Captain Calvit. Drop your projection, Sarah. I will be there shortly."

Sarah grumbled, "Fine."

Just before the three shimmering young ladies vanished, I heard Tabitha say, "See? I told you this was a bad idea."

And then they were gone.

Chapter 23

Shadow Bind. An evil necromantic spell which allows one to send their shadow out for reconnaissance, then merge with another person's shadow to take over their body.

-Spell structures, level six.

-Vivian-

Gymnasium, Pioneer School

There was a moment of surprise as Lord Seth, Lord Keith, and their henchmen walked into the gymnasium. They probably hadn't expected anyone to be here, much less to be suddenly targeted. I bet they were likely using the gymnasium as a shortcut.

It would have been nice if whatever controlled my visions would give me a heads up that things like this were about to happen. But we all turned toward the four of them.

From Lord Seth and Lord Keith's point of view, I understood why the two of them pulled out their wands. Along with me, Lord Thomas, and a few others, our wands were already out. Lord Seth and Lord Keith only knew what they could immediately see. Their reaction was from experience and past training. Besides, let's face it, they were House Duke. I bet we had all been targeted by them before. In my case, multiple times.

The silence was broken by Lord Seth. "Duke," he said haughtily, "as always, has the most house points. Make way for us."

Technically, he was right. The unwritten social rules of the school had the house with the most points getting precedence in the hall. It was a way of rewarding success. For the last seventeen years, no one gave way to House Orozco, we were at the bottom. Since we tied with House Duke in the snowball fight, there wasn't a definitive leader right now. It was an odd feeling, knowing we could push back.

I could tell some of my friends realized we didn't need to make way. Sierra and Wanda smiled at each other and clapped hands. Then Wanda turned back to Lord Seth and said with glee, "The adults are busy. Go play someplace else."

I inwardly groaned. *Not helping, Wanda*, I thought to myself.

Lord Seth's eyes narrowed. "We got three flags to your two. Make way."

Wanda pushed again, "Yeah, and you all ran away like scared little children when you saw the snowmen. It was awesome. You retreated, so your flags are ours. We win. Move along."

Lord Seth snorted and turned to me while raising his wand slightly. "Teach your dog some manners, Vivian."

Well, at least he wasn't casting yet. You take your successes where you find them. However, I couldn't let the dog comment go. Surprisingly, Mina got there first.

"I'm not in House Duke and Wanda has a voice. Grow up, Lord Seth. At least try to be polite." Mina gave Sierra a quick smile. That seemed to translate into, hey, thanks for being my henchwoman. Seconds ago, they were facing off against each other. Now, they had a common enemy. Sierra had reminded Mina of what it was like being the lowest. Then Lord Seth comes along and tries to do that not to just Mina, but all of us. For the first time, I really understood the saying "strength in adversity."

Instead of replying, a shimmering oval shield formed in front of Lord Seth.

Uh-oh, this was about to get ugly. Those around me who could cast shields did so as well. Samantha was right, Amanda was fast.

She had a shield up before mine even began forming. As the daughter of a high noble, I bet she had some amazing teachers.

Like before, my shield spell was amplified. It covered the front plane of my body and extended three feet on either side of me. Wanda edged herself to use the left side of my shield for cover. Glad I had a better wand now, and surprisingly, it almost felt cold to the touch. Was that because of Camillo? A question for another day.

Lord Keith looked nervous as he put his shield up too.

I bet he and Lord Seth started doing the math—it was six to one. Unless they had a secret weapon, they were going to lose. Besides, Nathan was a senior. I bet he knew some nasty spells.

Out of the corner of my eye, I watched Elaine step forward and cross her arms. "You need to apologize to Wanda. My lady won't like what you just said."

By now, everyone knew Lady Cassandra Altum was sponsoring her. This was the first time I knew of that Elaine had publicly made a statement. I bet she didn't understand that she just made a social decree. Roughly translated, check your tongue, or I will make sure my sponsor hears about it.

Amanda stepped forward to stand next to Elaine. Her wand was out but pointed at the ground. "I second that. Apologize."

Wow. Amanda's presence just expanded. I seemed to be looking at High Lady Amanda Lohort now. She wasn't hiding behind the anagram. That rolling magic which Samantha said she had seen from both appeared. *Okay, it's real. Wow.* But instead of targeting each other, the magic swirled together in a way I wasn't sure how to describe, except that it was focused on Lord Seth.

Mina, who was on the other side of me, whispered, "What's happening?"

It wasn't just her, everyone who had been watching Mina and I argue were now watching Amanda and Elaine standing together. If you have the Sight, you couldn't miss the rolling magic.

How to say this without giving anything away? I whispered back, "You know how Amanda liked Wanda's idea of having a safe place to talk? I really think you should consider it."

Wanda gave me a quick smile out of the corner of her mouth while watching Lord Seth.

The other piece to this was Elaine. She was an adept and strong one. She had flattened Lord Seth before. From her challenging tone, she was willing to do it again. It wouldn't surprise me if she had been called some things before and wanted to protect her friends from the same humiliation.

Amanda reiterated the demand. "Apologize."

Lord Seth's henchman urgently whispered to him. I caught the edges of, "Stay out of trouble."

I thought Lord Seth might spit on the ground, but he got his face under control and gave a brief bow. "Another time then. Luck only gets you so far." He began to turn away, keeping his spell shield up but angled in our direction.

Lord Keith let out a nervous breath and began to turn away as well. That's when I felt it, that same tingling sensation on the back of my shoulder but very intense this time. I wasn't having a vision; this was a warning. Something was about to happen. Only because I kept my focus on Lord Keith's henchman did I see it. His shadow shifted to look like a wolf. Immediately, the young man's eyes sort of glowed black for a second. Then he reached forward to nudge Lord Keith's wand arm from behind. The effect made it look like Lord Keith was about to cast.

I shouted, "Stop!" But it didn't help. All everyone saw was Lord Keith's wand move.

Spells went off instantly.

Lord Keith cursed, dived to the side, and got off a spell. His spell shield lit up as two spells impacted it. He got off another spell just as he rolled to a stop. Then his shield collapsed. It couldn't handle whatever Amanda had just shot at him.

Lord Seth was faster than his friend. He got off three spells as he dived to the ground. But his aim was off. One hit the top of my shield which glowed briefly. The other zoomed above Wanda's head while she dived to the side. The third struck the ceiling with a flash of light. A half second later, bits of stuff rained down on us.

While holding my shield spell in place, I watched Lord Keith's henchman, hoping I could see that shadow wolf again so I could figure out what it was. I did. It briefly morphed into a person, but I swear it wasn't Lord Keith. It was feminine looking. A memory in the back of my mind suggested I had seen the person whose shadow this belonged to. But things were happening too fast for me to put it together.

Things went very bad.

The shadow reached into Lord Keith's henchman's pocket and made a throwing motion. A split second later, the young man did the same. He had pulled out a small crystal and threw it toward us.

Amanda gasped out in alarm. "That's a spell bomb."

Oh. My. God. Who knew what kind of spell was in there? Spell bombs were expensive—and on the school's banned list. They were one-shot area-of-effect items. When activated, an impact would detonate the gem and the spell would be released. I had heard the shrapnel could cut like glass.

It was pure reflex on my part. I cast while trying to target the small crystal. But hitting something that small is hard. *Reminder, Vivian, getting some training in the dueling rings might actually be a good idea.*

Others did the same thing, but like me, they missed. Lord Keith got another two spells off, then he saw all the spells streaking in his direction. He curled up in a ball while covering his head. His henchman, however, was still standing. He blinked once and honestly appeared disoriented. Then his eyes went wide as he was hit with seven different spells.

Amanda got off another shot and missed the crystal. While I was screaming at Wanda and Sierra to get behind me, I pushed everything I could into my shield. Someone might get killed.

At my need for power, I felt Camillo's presence within my mind. It was a bright day outside. I doubted he was anywhere near me. Apparently our link went both ways. When I was charged, he got some of my magic. Why was he charged now? I had no idea, but a huge surge of magic flowed from him into me. A blue grid-like energy expended out from me connected with what looked like little snowflakes. This shield bubble grew, encompassing most of us. What in the world did Camillo come across which had that much power? Had the dragon come again?

Just before the little crystal hit the gymnasium floor, Elaine dived forward, caught it in midair, and threw it toward the back of the gymnasium. I cringed and put everything I had into this shield bubble. It expanded again. Wow, there was a lot of magic around Camillo.

Everyone watched as the crystal arced through the air. Then it hit the far bleachers and exploded.

It blew the bottom four rows of the bleachers to splinters. An intense pressure wave of energy slammed into my shield along with thousands of splinters of wood. Some of them were the size of wooden stakes.

I screamed at the force of the impact while trying to hold my shield bubble together. Falling to my knees, I was able to hold it for two more seconds before it fell apart. *Please, let no one be killed.*

Then it dawned on me what just happened as I replayed my thoughts. A part of my mind felt stuck. We would have all died. There was a circular thirty-foot wide section of the bleachers which was just gone. Mina was crying, Sierra was holding her. Others were stunned or crying. As I stood back up, it was only then I realized Wanda was holding on to me for dear life.

What brought me back was the growl, then the impact on the floor. Elaine had gotten up on her knees and that rolling magic from her looked very much like translucent fire. The impact was her fist slamming into the floor shattering the floorboards. Lord Keith was blubbering even as he pushed himself away, his back against the door. He seemed terrified at what she might do to him.

A part of me wanted to throttle him as well. But if she did hit him again, with all the magic surrounding her and focusing into a punch...

It wasn't a vision but an awareness. If Elaine lost control and hurt someone, it could haunt her for the rest of her life. I was only Vivian Hampton, but Elaine was in my house, and it was my job to protect her.

I shouted out, "It's a shadow of some kind! Light spells now." Then I cast the strongest light spell I could, targeting Lord Keith's henchman. It wasn't hard to hit him, he was frozen in place. He lit up, and I heard gasps from around me as a ring of blackness expanded out from him, then reformed ten feet to his left. Everyone could see the shadow wolf now. It growled at me, then ran up the wall toward the ceiling.

Well, I guess my vision had been trying to tell me something.

Lord Seth's eyes went wide. "What's that?" he blubbered out.

I screamed, "Do something *right* for change. Help us catch it." I tried to shoot the wolf shadow with a light ball but missed. The wolf easily dodged. It seemed to be able to jump from shadow to shadow if they were reasonably close together. Wanda and others caught on, and within seconds, other balls of light were being shot toward the ceiling.

But the wolf shadow was too fast.

Who was controlling that shadow? But more immediately, we needed to remove some of its hiding spots. To do that, we needed more light.

Lord Thomas shouted, "I bet that's what controlled—" He was cut off by his friends shouting back, "We get it."

More light, I thought to myself again. We needed light, or it was going to escape.

If it got away, Maker only knew who it would attack next. Also, I realized that its maker had just tried to kill Amanda *and* Elaine. I bet the rest of us were incidental to that. Someone wanted to remove Amanda. They knew who she really was. This was bigger than I thought.

Okay. More light. Well, I hoped the headmistress would forgive me.

I opened myself up and sang. Musical notes of light began appearing around the room. The shadow wolf attempted to jump into a shadow that had just disappeared. It backed up a bit and tried another path. Along with my glowing musical notes, my friends were still shooting balls of light. Even Lord Seth shot his own light spells. Then my song hit its peak, and the first rays of the morning light erupted into the room. The headmistress implied she could sense someone singing magic. Others had to have heard the explosion too. Well, if I was kicked out of school, it was for a good cause.

The shadow wolf dived off the ceiling toward the only shadow left in the room, under the balance beam. It seemed to be burning off wisps of darkness as it leapt.

Wanda cursed and ran toward the beam. She made a running leap and tumbled onto it. Wow, Wanda was good, I hoped she did make the gymnastics team. She got to her feet and swept her glowing wand back and forth, looking for movement.

Others, including me, moved closer to the balance beam and like Wanda held our glowing wands in front of us. The shadow under the beam grew smaller. Dammit, where were you?

Doors slammed open on both sides of the gymnasium, and I could hear people shouting. But all my attention was on Wanda. Where was the creature? Suddenly it pounced upwards landing in Wanda's shadow. I screamed at Wanda to run even as I watched the shadow wolf try to merge with her shadow.

Out of the corner of my eye, I watched someone streak past me and leap into the air. Lord Grayson grabbed Wanda in his arms, and the two careened off the beam, rolling to a stop on the mats.

Poof. Terrance appeared in front of the wolf. The wolf reared backwards, turned, and ran into the arms of Terrance's shadow.

"Now," said the headmistress, slowly walking toward the struggling shadow wolf. "Who is your master?"

Chapter 24

There is a rumor flying around Avalon that the Cursed Knight, Sir Galahad's Squire has taken an apprentice. Even as I write this, young ladies are purchasing candles to place on their windowsills at night. There is even a bet starting of which Lady the apprentice will visit first.

-Nathan Catexpil, Avalon Press.

-Terrance-

The snowstorm from last night had blown through. Now there wasn't a cloud in the sky. My hat, long cloak, and gloves helped to keep the direct sunlight from sapping too much of my strength. Camillo had tentatively moved into the sun hoping to follow us, but then quickly retreated into the cave. Since the inside of the cave was still charged with the merlin's magic, when Camillo moved, the air around him sparkled making him look for all the world like a snowman trying to catch fireflies in winter. There was a sort of ethereal beauty to it all.

<*"Can you ask the clouds to come again, my friend?"*> There was a longing in his words. The world was still new to him, and he wanted to see as much as he could before the spring thaw melted him down. Last night, as the two of us talked, I could tell he had begun to understand his time might be limited. While there was fear in his words, there was also an odd faith. My friend firmly believed his maker would come and collect his soul once he melted. As I was falling asleep, he asked, <*"My friend, will you*

put a candle above me after I have melted, so my creator will come and get my soul?">

What can you say to that but, "Of course my friend."

The blinding faith Camillo possessed still staggered me. But even more so was his faith in me. Just being this odd creature's friend made that warm glow inside me stronger. Then, I mentally stepped back as a realization struck me: I was the odd creature. No one really knew what I was, not even me. But every child already knew what Camillo was; he was the snowman that brought them gifts at Christmastime. And he had given me the greatest gift of all—he believed in me. After that sudden insight, it took me some time to fully sleep.

I bowed. "My friend, bringing the clouds back is something I cannot do. But I will return later today."

Lady Elizabeth had a faraway look for a second, then smiled. "Sorry, Camillo, it's going to be sunny for the next four hours."

Darlene raised an eyebrow. "Ma'am, you can sense the weather?"

Lady Elizabeth dimpled. "Short term only. It's from the Lady of the Lake's mantle, which got passed down to me. When I was younger, I always wondered how my mom knew it was going to rain."

Oh. Darlene's surprised expression probably mirrored that of mine. The initial authoritarian presence Lady Elizabeth had projected in front of the three young ladies was gone, but her casual comment about the Lady of the Lake reminded me that this amazing woman next to me was the highest princess of Avalon. I didn't get the feeling she was trying to create a social divide between us, rather, we could be ourselves standing next to her. Last night she opened the door just a crack by suggesting she was afraid of what she might become. Was she doing it again? Waiting to see if we would abuse her trust or pull away?

My chances of dancing with this woman were still probably that of a snowball in hell, but hey, we had a new merlin. Anything might happen. I would try to keep up the dialogue and see where it went. "Well, whatever I am apparently doesn't include a barometer," I said conversationally. It might have been my imagination, but Lady Elizabeth seemed to relax a notch.

Turning back to Camillo, I offered up a suggestion. "Why don't you stay here until the clouds come? Then head over to Mrs. Capmond's. I'll meet you there later today."

Once Camillo had moved deeper into the cave, an uncomfortable thought struck me. I turned back to Lady Elizabeth. "Ma'am, with the extra magic here, do you think what lies below will sense it?"

Lady Elizabeth looked back toward the cave. "Short of a sudden shift in the magical ground states, probably."

With a twist of her wrist, a small scrying ring formed above Lady Elizabeth's hand. Through it, Sarah and Nenet were still arguing with one another. Tabitha wasn't in the scene. After a few seconds, Sarah looked up and crossed her arms. The kid knew she was being watched. I distinctly heard the kid mutter, "It's like having three moms now."

Lady Elizabeth laughed and let the scrying circle break apart, then looked back toward the cave. "I only have a few minutes before I need to leave. Lord only knows what Sarah and Nenet will do next if they're left unsupervised for much longer."

As we walked into the full sun and turned toward the first switchback, our threesome quickly became a foursome. My shadow popped back into existence. It bowed to Lady Elizabeth's shadow and offered a hand as if trying to lead her into a dance.

"Leave the lady alone," I growled out.

I was ignored.

Lady Elizabeth laughed and shook her head. My shadow bowed again, then did a little tap dance.

Darlene smiled. "Ah, to be young again. But I still get a look now and then."

My shadow turned as if it had heard her. It leaned forward in expectation of a kiss.

Darlene shook her head. "Happily married."

As we rounded the switchback, the angle of the sun changed. My shadow took advantage of the opportunity. It moved to put its arm around Lady Elizabeth's waist. Shadow touching shadow.

I felt a surge of power and Lady Elizabeth's hand intercepted my shadow's left wrist. The runes on her dress had changed as well, becoming more complex.

"I said no," she said, forcefully. "Learn some respect."

When she let go, my shadow bounced backwards and cradled its wrist like he had been hurt.

What a showboat.

Lady Elizabeth rolled her eyes. "I didn't hurt you. But try that again, and I will."

It wasn't a threat but a promise. Then just as suddenly, she put a smile back on her face. "What do you know about Hugh Latimer?"

At her smile, those same conflicting urges came back in full force. I pushed the hunger down. It didn't get a vote. However, the man within me wanted to take a step closer to her. I pushed that aside as well. If I didn't respect this woman, she would turn her back on me. I am *not* my shadow or my hunger.

Darlene looked skyward for a second. "Honestly, I didn't even know he existed until the staff mentioned that he was a preacher from Earth."

I pulled out the ring and handed it over. "I remember reading a short passage about him somewhere. I believe he died some five hundred years ago. Burned at the stake, I think. That's the limit of my knowledge about him."

"So, there are eight other rings," murmured Darlene, staring at the ring Lady Elizabeth was examining again.

"I think we need an audience with Lady Cassandra," suggested Lady Elizabeth and handed me the damn thing back. "I'm beginning to think something went wrong, and she's wondering who to trust."

"Amen," I said. "But if the demon is involved, I'm not sure what good I would be."

We walked in silence for a few steps. Lady Elizabeth reached out to touch my arm, making me feel more alive than I had in some time. I wanted this woman to trust me, to believe she could be safe next to me. "Terrance, you're assuming it's the same demon. It might not be."

"Hmm, true," I said, trying to keep my voice steady. "I agree, we need some answers from that little minx. In the meantime, I can look through the school's library. You never know what might be there. Could we meet up tomorrow night and compare notes?"

Personally, I wanted to drop the ring at Lady Cassandra's feet and tell her to shove it you know where. But if working on the problem allowed me to spend more time with this amazing woman, I would take it. Demon or no demon.

Lady Elizabeth tilted her head and repeated, "Minx? As in, you like her or she's devious?"

Alarm bells went off in my mind. The woman was asking if I had an interest in Lady Cassandra. Trying to stay calm I said, "That young lady is devious. I personally think she's going to take over as the Iron Dragon once Doctor Cognitor has her babies. I don't like being treated as cannon fodder, did that already with a demon. Pass on round two."

The three of us, correction four, walked in silence for a bit. Well, my shadow never said anything which was a small blessing. Finally, Lady Elizbeth seemed to decide something and gave a small nod. "I'll try to free up some time. There are some unique sources I can check at the main library in Avalon City and other sources back on Earth."

My spirits rose. I felt like we were setting up a study date. Then remembering some advice from Mrs. Capmond about what a woman might appreciate, I took a chance. "If you find yourself with some free time, I'm hiking over to the next mountain pass this Friday."

I was surprised at my audacity and nervousness. I felt like a twelve-year-old who just worked up the courage to ask the prettiest girl in the room for a dance. I was in that moment where time stands still, and you wonder if she's going to laugh in your face, act like you don't exist, or just say no.

Lady Elizabeth didn't tense up or move away from me. That was a good sign, I hoped. She seemed to consider my invitation.

As we rounded the next switchback she said, "I do need a break from adulting. But I want to talk it over with my father first. I'll—"

And whatever else she was about to say was cut off by the screams.

"There he is!"

Franklin, Darlene's husband, was just around the next switchback apparently holding back eight or nine young ladies. His staff was angled in front of him, blocking their path. At the screams, he turned his head and chuckled. "Apparently there's a rumor spreading through town you're the cursed knight's apprentice. The young ladies want to, well, *introduce* themselves to you."

One of the young ladies in the back pushed herself forward. I recognized her as the barmaid's daughter whom I almost enthralled four nights ago. "I saw him first," she declared. "So, he should visit me first." She gave the other lady next to her a dirty look.

Visit first?

Darlene started to laugh.

Then I remembered the stories. Young ladies across Avalon would occasionally leave a burning candle on their windowsill at night as an invitation for the Cursed Knight to visit them. I had no idea if the man ever did, but the stories had to have started somewhere. Then I realized who was standing next to me, and those alarm bells in my mind began ringing again. And I had no idea what to say to Lady Elizabeth. Did a part of me want to visit these young ladies? Yes. But if I went down that path, well—and suddenly, another truth occurred to me. I liked walking with this woman, talking to her. Hoping she would be my friend as well. To sleep with these women would destroy that future.

Lady Elizabeth raised an eyebrow. "Were you planning to visit them from the shortest to tallest, or blondes to brunettes? Just curious. The apprentice to the Cursed Knight does have a reputation..." she concluded, "to live up to," while giving me a wicked grin. And, she said it loud enough for all the young ladies to hear.

In other words, it wouldn't matter what I said now. The merlin's guide just implied that yes, I was, indeed, the Cursed Knight's apprentice, without specifically saying so. Oh, she is one sneaky lady. Somehow, I will get her for that.

Like me, my shadow appeared stunned, then it rubbed its hands together while straining against our link to move toward the ladies.

The young lady next to the barmaid's daughter started jumping up and down. "I'm a blonde, I live on North Street."

Franklin leaned back slightly. "Am I letting her through? She seems rather, um, determined."

Lady Elizabeth mockingly curtsied to me. "I can see you're rather busy. Don't let me detain you from your important duties." And suddenly, she was just gone, leaving me to deal with the problem in front of me.

Three days ago, if this had happened to me, I would have been in heaven. Now, I just wanted to find a way out of this with some of my dignity intact. There had to be a legion of angels looking down at me and rolling in laughter. *Please, universe*, I thought to myself. *Give me an emergency.*

Then the alarm spell in my wand went off and an image of Lord Grayson appeared next to me.

"Terrance, there has been an explosion."

Be careful what you wish for.

As the ladies in front me began to fade away, I vaguely wondered if this was it. What's worse than free teleporting? Free teleporting without triple checking your math. Newtonian physics takes over.

Not that they ever left, but there's only one way to get the equations right and lots of ways not to. Then, you generally die. Most sorcerers and sorceresses won't try unless the two spots are on their lands and at the same altitude. Even then, most walk.

The beauty of teleportation circles is twofold: A team of people have checked the math, tested them, and some basic compensation is built into the ring. Step into the ring, a sorcerer charges the right rune and poof, you appear in the slaved ring. You don't fall on your face due to velocity differences or suddenly find yourself underground due to altitude changes. The farther the master and slave ring are from each other, the more compensation is required.

I don't think you could pick a worse free teleport than what I was doing. I couldn't see my destination and only had a vague notion of where Lord Grayson was from his sending. Oh, I knew he was outside of the school, toward the mountain, but that could cover a lot of territory. Then there was the altitude differential. I was at least a thousand feet higher than where he was. That might not sound like much until you consider that meant I was moving faster relative to him.

My last adjustment to the spell hopefully had me appear in the air versus underground. I always wondered, for those that got it wrong, was there a split second's awareness before they died that they got their math wrong or just blackness. Either way, death became their guide. Two bits please and don't fall into the water.

I had something to live for now, well, not die again, if I was honest with myself. Could I have children? If so, what would they become? That thought had to be because of Lady Elizabeth. Let's get past step one first: don't die again.

Would I have tried this with Darlene's loaner wand? Probably. I imagine I would have focused the spell, applied energy, and be center stage to having wooden shrapnel blow through me. Would that have done it? Kill me for good? Sort of the wooden stake through the heart?

The wand I picked out last night—correction, legally absconded with—held the energy matrix of the teleportation spell without any pushback and focused the spell quickly. It occurred to me as I began to materialize that I didn't know the upper limit of a core wand. Unlike the other wands in that rolling safe, there weren't any safety notes for this one.

Poof. I felt myself falling fast; the people on the ground were quickly getting bigger. Okay, not dead. Step one completed. Lord Grayson wasn't the only one pointing at me. Come on people, make room for the falling vampire. If I got swarmed by more young ladies, the Cursed Knight and I are going to have a talk.

I instinctively tried using my vampiric power to "appear" on the ground and discovered that, no, it doesn't work in the bright sun. Okay, change of plans. Better make it quick. I got the feather step spell off just before becoming a splotch on the stone pathway.

I landed in a crouch and felt the impact. Nothing broken but that hurt. Lord Grayson pushed through the crowd of people forming around me. "It happened fifteen seconds ago," he shouted and turned to run back toward the school.

I had to give the kid some credit. He teleported while running, thereby reaching the closest door in half the time. Doing the same, I ran in after him and began to feel my power returning now that I was out of the sun. "Where are we going?"

"Gymnasium," replied Lord Grayson without turning around. I could see magic gathering about him again, but there were too many people around us to free teleport again. The two of us turned left at a dead run with the kid in the lead. I only had a vague notion of where the gymnasium might be.

The double doors hadn't blown off their hinges, but they were warped to the point they wouldn't open. Two teachers were trying to lever them open. By now the headmistress and others had joined us coming from an adjacent hallway.

"Make a hole," I shouted and ran past Lord Grayson, almost time skipping. The teacher on the left saw me and got out of the way just in time. I hit the door with my shoulder and the hinges gave way. For a moment, I thought the roof of the gymnasium was gone. It was as bright as day in here.

Lord Grayson ran past me while cursing and, if anything, he picked up speed. About twenty kids had their wands out, each casting light, standing around a balance beam.

Wanda, Lady Vivian's henchwoman, was on top of it and, like the others, held a glowing wand.

"Wanda, the shadow is behind you," Lady Vivian shouted.

That's when I saw it. A shadow wolf stood on the beam. From it, little tendrils of blackness were expanding to merge with Wanda's shadow. Lord Grayson free teleported again at speed, he appeared in the air opposite the young lady and grabbed her. Both tumbling off the beam onto the mats below.

I felt an anger brewing inside me. Lady Vivian Hampton trusted me. I wanted to destroy that shadow, but it was our best lead. I was sure the wolf Lord Grayson saw the other night and this wolf shadow were connected somehow. *Well then, let's ask it some questions very impolitely.*

I poofed onto the beam just in front of the shadow wolf. Whatever expression it saw on my face made it rear backwards. Then it turned to run—right into the arms of my shadow. This time my shadow wasn't playing games.

"Now," said the headmistress, slowly walking toward the struggling shadow wolf. "Who is your master?"

Wanda untangled herself from Lord Grayson, then hugged him. The shadow wolf struggled to get out my shadow's grip. It was slammed headfirst into the balance beam. Good shadow.

"Oh, my gosh. I know where I saw it before."

All eyes turned to Lady Vivian. She had a hand to her mouth and slowly lowered it. Turning to me she added, "I saw it in a vision."

"Isn't that the kid whose family pissed off the Council?" I asked Lady Vivian.

We were still in the gymnasium. The headmistress and some of the other professors had blocked off the two entrances.

Currently, the headmistress was talking to someone through her wand. I bet it was someone from the Council. My shadow was no longer gripping the wolf. An older professor had cast an impressive glowing illusion of chains that had wrapped themselves around the shadow wolf. My shadow let go but hit the wolf for good measure. The shadow wolf struggled to break free, but the chains just tightened around it, making it fall off the beam.

"He almost, sort of, helped," murmured Lady Vivian under her breath.

Her henchwoman rolled her eyes. "He's still a putz."

Lord Grayson appeared as an illusion next to me. "You were right. There's a secret passageway in the restricted section in the library. That's probably how the werewolf got out the other night. We'll be up in a minute." Then his image faded away.

"How did you know?" asked the older professor who had cast the light chains. Interesting spell. Over a beer, I wondered if I could get him to show me the spell matrix.

I shrugged. "We were visited by a spirit the other day while down there. While they can go through walls, the wards in the restricted section are intense. Ergo, there had to be a path that the spirit had taken."

One of the young ladies in the group who helped in the capture took a tentative step toward me. "Are you really the Cursed Knight's apprentice?" she asked in excitement.

What to say. "He and I have spoken. But I'm not making any midnight trysts." Both statements were true. Hopefully my second statement would get passed around.

"So, what now?" I asked, partially turning away from the young lady. The hunger inside me wanted to enthrall her. Since I had used some of my powers, the hunger was stronger. It wanted to feed. I wished I had teleported Darlene's rucksack with me. But drinking blood in front of this group of youngsters would probably be frowned upon by the headmistress. Hopefully, cow or pig blood would satisfy my hunger. We would see.

"Terrance?" asked Lady Vivian hesitantly. "Thank you."

I bowed. "Thank you for finding the shadow." Without her, she and others would likely be dead, and our trail of breadcrumbs would have likely dried up. Avalon owed Lady Vivian something. Then, pointing to the glowing music symbols about the place. "Did you do that?"

She bit her lip, then nodded. "For whatever reason, Camillo was really charged with magic. My spells were amplified."

Ah. Well, hopefully through her link with Camillo, she drained some of the free magic in the cave. "He's a good friend to have," I said simply. I was about to add more when Lord Grayson and three others all but dragged a woman into the room. She was an older student and from the quality of her clothing, likely a lady. But what caught my attention was her lack of shadow. Interesting. So, she wasn't a shadow caster, but someone who could control her own shadow or knew a spell that could.

The headmistress walked over but didn't put her wand away. "I had an interesting conversation with one of your old teachers from Notir University, Lady Bell. You were murdered nine days ago."

Whoever Lady Bell was, attempted to shift into a wolf. Lord Grayson put his arm around her throat, exposing it, his wand shimmering into a silver dagger. "No one's in the mood to play," he said in her ear. "I know what you are."

Lady Vivian, Wanda, and others said a variety of surprised exclamations while taking a step back. I bet most of them had never seen a werewolf before. To their credit, most of them that had wands had them pointed at the werewolf. Lady Vivian surrounded herself with good friends.

"Now," said the headmistress, coldly. "Sorcerer Petotum from the wizard's council, plus a great many other Realm Knights will be here momentarily. You might consider making a deal."

"Lady Bell" shifted. Not into a wolf, but whatever illusion that she had held about her came apart. The woman now looked older and rugged. But what really caught my attention was her eyes. She was a killer, a believer in her cause, and she was prepared to die. "I will be dead before the Realm Knights can break past the mind shielding cast on me," she said with a laugh and spat on the ground. "You lose."

Lord Grayson looked like he wanted to twist her head off when he sucked in his breath. Every magical sense of mine was suddenly overwhelmed. The magic pressing down on us was significantly greater than that of the new merlin's projection.

Was she here, for real this time? From the looks around me, everyone else felt it as well, including those without wands. What was arriving?

Suddenly the rear wall of the gymnasium came apart in pieces like a giant hand had sucked it into the air. Looking down at us wasn't Avalon's dragon but a dragon that seemed to be made of formed water. The pressure wave of magical energy increased, as did my fear. Just being close to this gigantic creature brought forth ancient fears of being eaten. I wouldn't even be a snack.

<*"That may be so,"*> projected the dragon into our minds. Her voice was female, and from her tone, she was unhappy. To push back at this presence would be ludicrous. <*"But I can tear through the mind spell with ease. However, I promised a death knight that he had first go. You attacked a princess from his realm, and he does not forgive."*>

Next to the kid, the air shimmered and suddenly an eight-foot tall, armored black knight appeared. Thousands of little black glowing runes were written across his armor as if they made up a book. Lord Grayson moved aside as the knight reached down to put a massive, armored hand on the werewolf's head. Then the knight shoved his other hand directly into our prisoner as if she was made of mist. She screamed once. Her face went blank, and she began to talk in an expressionless tone. "My name is...."

Before she got too far, over twenty Realm Knights burst into the room from the far doors followed by Sorcerer Petotum and Lady Cassandra. I wasn't certain, but it seemed as if the dragon winked at her. The Realm Knights stared between the dragon and the knight. But it was Sorcerer Petotum who stepped forward. "Repeat the name again," he demanded.

Our prisoner repeated in that same monotone voice. "My pack was hired by Council Member Chandley…"

Sorcerer Petotum turned to Realm Knight Commander Bardot. "On my authority, arrest Chandley."

Chapter 25

The Accords were rumored to have been drafted after the fall of Lucifer. Essentially, angels and demons are not allowed to directly intervene on the middle plain unless they have been summoned and agree to a service. A full copy of the Accords is theorized to exist in the heart of the black section of the Houser Bank. I don't recommend visiting.

-The Guardian

-Vivian Hampton-

Infirmary, Pioneer School

"Take a deep breath, now let it out. Good. One more. Excellent." The master healer looked up at his spell structure hovering just above Mina's body. I had seen Healer Frenzia cast such a spell on me before, where it showed all my organs and other bits, but this projection was much more detailed. Along with five other healers, he had arrived minutes after the lot of us were brought to the infirmary. From the way they had been running, I bet they expected to see mangled bodies. Currently three of them were going from student to student, while the two older healers along with Healer Frenzia were behind a partition examining Lord Keith's henchman.

The master healer dropped his spell, then patted Mina's hand. "You're just in shock. Drink this and you should feel better in a few minutes."

Sierra eyed the glass of blue liquid. "I bet it's going to taste horrible."

A touch of a smile crossed the healer's face. "Well, they take away healer's licenses if we don't make our potions extra horrible for students."

Mina stuck out her tongue at him.

Wanda rolled her eyes.

He almost laughed, but then his expression shifted to concern as he glanced at the sectioned-off area. Turning away, he headed to the next cot.

Wanda whispered to me, "Sense anything?"

I shook my head, feeling very frustrated.

Mina was helped to a sitting position by Lord Thomas and Sierra. It made me feel good that the Sierra-Mina friendship had survived. Back in the gymnasium when they were staring down each other, I had been afraid that it wouldn't. As promised, Mina gagged while drinking the potion down. But her color started coming back. After a few seconds of deep breaths, she cried out, "I am so sorry. I have never fainted before."

Lord Thomas patted her on the back. "You were amazing." I noticed his casting hand was still next to his wand sheath though. Even though we were in the infirmary, some of the boys, and even Samantha, were still keyed up. When Nathan's henchman accidentally dropped a book on the floor, people spun around with their wands out, pointing at him.

Even one of the Realm Knights standing guard at the door had drawn his wand. From their sudden actions, they seemed to expect another monster might appear at any moment.

"Sorry," he said, slowly raising his shaking hands. "Don't shoot me."

Almost immediately after Sorcerer Petotum made his pronouncement, the dragon disappeared. The black knight did as well but not before he shattered the black gem the lady had worn as a choker. I had never heard of anyone who could crush a gem with just his fingers; I would bet money Elaine couldn't do it.

As it had shattered, a great burst of nauseating magic blew into the room, making us all flinch. But the swirling black energy never reached us. It was as if the little glowing runes across the knight's armor ate the spell. Then he gave a slight bow toward Amanda and was gone. The woman who had been pretending to be Lady Bell collapsed to the ground. I had no idea if she was alive or dead. That's when Mina fainted. She wasn't the only one.

The headmistress shouted, "I want my students in the infirmary, now!"

Lord Grayson picked up Mina. Six Realm Knights, with Lady Cassandra in the lead, escorted us. I wanted to ask her about a thousand questions, but I heard her say within my mind, <"*Not now.*"> From her tone, she was not happy. Once in the infirmary, she and Lord Grayson left us, but three of the Realm Knights stood guard just inside the door.

Healer Frenzia was overwhelmed, but other professors soon arrived, including Professor Vermis. Then other healers started arriving. The principal must have put out the call.

The only student we couldn't see was Lord Keith's henchman. Healers had separated him from us using several partitions.

Like Lord Thomas, most of the boys were still keyed up. Some were pacing, refusing to sit down. Nathan even tried challenging one of the Realm Knights, demanding answers. He didn't get a reply. But questions were thrown around the room. Why did the dragon come? Who was the black knight? Who was the woman pretending to be Lady Bell, and finally, who's the princess?

Why were some people looking at me?

"Sorry," Wanda said, backing up after bumping into me again. She seemed afraid to leave my side. A part of me wanted to curl up on a cot and fall over, but I had said the words last year. I was the head girl, an officer of the school. I went from cot to cot and offered encouragement where I could. Other than four cases like Mina, where their bodies went into shock when their own spells were overwhelmed, no one was physically hurt. But I still didn't know what was happening with Lord Keith's henchman.

At some point, Samantha, Elaine, and Amanda came over. Amanda looked around to make sure it was just the five of us. "I told them." Meaning she had explained she was really Lord Lohort's daughter. Not just a high noble, but a noble in another land as well.

Wanda bounced, "So, that black knight?"

"My sister told me about him the other day. He's some sort of death spirit. I understand his wife is a guardian fey dragon." Amanda held up her left hand indicating her ring. "She's the one who made this."

"Well, that makes you the princess," smiled Samantha. "Which means Elaine and I are your devoted subjects."

Amanda rolled her eyes. "Stop it. Six weeks ago, I was helping my mom repair magical books and having fun in the local wand dueling league. That's how Mom and Dad met. He needed an old magical book restored. The story I heard is during negotiating the cost, Dad made a snippy comment. Mom challenged him to a duel. After they were done, they kept on having fun. Nine months later, I came along. Next to my sister, I'm a *pretend* noble."

Elaine crossed her arms. "Well, I think you're awesome. Are we still going to face off in a spell circle? I don't want to fight you."

I nodded. "Yes, but you're not going to face off. I reached out to Lady Gawain. I hope through you two, the two dragons will appear. Lady Gawain will tell them off, ask them to play nice, and we all go about having a better day."

"It was my idea," announced Wanda happily.

"You know Lady Gawain?" asked Amanda excitedly. "My sister talks like she's the most amazing person ever."

I shook my head. "Lord Winton is marrying Lady Kiera. She's Lady Gawain's future sister-in-law. I just used the connection to suggest Wanda's idea. I'm still waiting for a response though."

We turned at the muffled exclamation from behind the partition. That didn't sound good. I wished I could see what was happening.

The five of us were silent for a few seconds. It was broken by Amanda. "While I might be *a* princess, I'm not *the* princess."

Samantha cocked her head. "Sure you are."

Amanda shook her head. "Think about it. Who just saved us? Called out the shadow and got us to fight as a team? Who builds magical snowmen in her free time, befriends the apprentice to the Cursed Knight, and reaches out to one of the two most impressive ladies of Avalon and suggests that they might want to stop by to yell at some dragons?"

I think my mouth was hanging open. "Oh, come on," I said sarcastically. "My life is a mess."

Samantha tapped her wrist with her wand. "Amanda does have a point."

Wanda blurted out excitedly, "And don't forget the Lady of—*ouch!*"

I stomped on Wanda's foot and glared at her.

"Huh, what lady?" asked Elaine.

Thank you, Wanda. I was saved by Professor Vermis, Professor Malton, Professor Gass, and Professor Reece as they came around the partition. Everyone in the room watched as they huddled up together. After a brief discussion, they pulled in Lord Seth, and surprisingly, me. Wanda wanted to come, but I shook my head.

Professor Vermis looked like he was about to say something but was cut off by Professor Malton.

"Vivian, when the young man tossed a spelled pebble at you the other day, do you think it was because he was being controlled?"

I looked up at all the professors and started to feel apprehensive. Even Professor Vermis seemed concerned. How bad was it? "Well, I had a vision right before it happened. I thought his shadow was odd, but I didn't really put it together at the time. Why?"

Professor Vermis looked away and growled out. "I didn't see it…" Then, looking back toward the partitions, he added, "The healers think his mind is fighting back. He's trying to regain control but is caught in some type of mind maze. It isn't going well."

Lord Seth blurted out, "The shadow is still here?" Others around the room turned to look at us. I stepped on Lord Seth's foot and glared at him. *Not the best thing to say right now.*

"No," said Professor Vermis. "This is more like a mind sickness. The shadow likely erected these blockades within his mind. I doubt if the young man has slept in days. What little strength he has left is being used to try to find a way out."

Okay, but what help could I be?

Professor Malton touched my shoulder, then withdrew his hand. "The healers are reaching out to someone they believe might be able to help, but it's a long shot. Even so, she is likely hours away, if not longer. Would you be willing to ask *the Lady* for help?"

Lord Seth cocked his head. "Huh? Which lady?"

Professor Vermis crossed his arms. "Explain. Another healer?"

"Vermis," growled out Professor Gass. "This is one of those times in life where it's better to shut up."

I gulped. "It's that bad?"

There was a short silence which told me everything I needed to know. "Let me see him."

Professor Vermis shot Professor Gass another dark look but stepped aside.

♪♪

The translucent medical charts hovering above Lord Keith's henchman shuddered, then started again. Did his heart just skip a beat? I didn't know what all the information meant, but just by looking at the young man lying on the cot, I could tell something was very wrong. His eyes were open but seemed sunken somehow, and they never blinked.

I looked up at the older healer sitting across from me. She had led the charge into the infirmary and started handing out orders. She had been with Jordon, Lord Keith's henchman since then.

"I am Healer Hochim, Ms. Vivian. We need some help, and we're running out of options. We have reached out to a young mind healer, but at best, she is hours away."

Now that I was sitting down across from her, that's when I noticed the four red crosses on her collar. She was the second highest ranked healer in Avalon. I have vague memories of my grandmother when I was young. What I remember most was the wrinkles around her eyes. Her voice control was amazing, but more than that, her eyes conveyed the emotions of the song: happiness, joy, sadness, rage, and madness. She could do them all. My grandmother could fill the room with her presence. More than anything, it was watching her that made me long to be a bard. The woman in front of me filled the room as well. I was both intimidated and awed at being in her presence.

Then my mind caught up with what Healer Hochim implied, she couldn't help him. "Ma'am," I asked nervously. "How can I help?"

She kept her eyes focused on me. "I've met the Lady before. Actually, Professor Gass has hinted you might know how to contact her."

"You want me to reach out to the Lady?" I bit my lip. "What happens if we wait for the mind healer to arrive?"

Healer Hochim didn't blink. "We think the attacker built contingency spells within the young man's mind. Essentially a death trap. The mind maze is shrinking. 'Leave no witnesses.'"

"So, if we wait for this other person?" I asked, but from Healer Hochim's expression, I already knew the answer.

"I am Lady Cassandra's guide, for lack of a better term, as she studies healing magic. So, I am aware of her unique association with this woman."

"But ma'am, I'm not a healer. How come you're not asking Lady Cassandra? Wouldn't she have a better chance of getting *her* to help?"

"She is performing her duties as Sorcerer Petotum's apprentice. As impressive as Lady Cassandra is, she cannot be in two places at the same time."

The diagnostic spell hovering above Jordon suddenly froze, then started again. The young man probably didn't have a few hours.

<*"Ma'am, what do you need me to do?"*> I thought as I mentally pushed through that connection in my mind to the Lady of the Lake. I was rewarded with an immediate answer.

<*"Vivian, I can help. But this goes far beyond providing guidance. For me to do this, I must demand of you an appropriate service, which you would then be bound to fulfill. Without that, others could reach across to their avatars and provide power without following the rules. Do you understand what you are asking?"*>

I wasn't certain why my conversation with the Lady wasn't private this time. But from the surprised expressions of everyone around me, they heard her too.

Professor Gass lowered his head and murmured out, "I didn't know what else to do."

Healer Hochim kept her eyes fixed on me. Professor Vermis's eyes had gone wide. But it was Professor Malton's guidance I sought. "Professor, she means—"

He sat down next to me and took my hand. "Vivian, this isn't your fight. My only guidance is if you decide to accept, you don't need to go it alone. We are here to help you repay the debt."

Without raising his head, Professor Gass nodded. Healer Hochim looked toward the other healer. "Back up a bit. If Vivian agrees, we're going to need some room."

The magical chart shuddered again. Almost all the little bits of light went to zero. There was another heartbeat, then nothing.

<*"Yes,"*> I said.

Suddenly the Lady of the Lake was here. Instead of a flowing white dress, which was how all the drawings depicted her, she wore battle armor. After pulling a glowing blue blade from her sheath, she touched the tip of it to the young man's head.

The chart of information blew apart into hundreds of sparkles. A shadowy blackness expanded out from Jordon's head which burned in the blue light of the Lady's sword. His body shuddered, then he took a breath. Then another. I put my hands to my mouth and cried out. He was alive.

Once the Lady sheathed her sword, I jumped up and hugged her. She seemed surprised but patted me on my back. I jumped backward to stand next to Professor Malton again. "Sorry, ma'am."

I had just hugged the Lady of the Lake.

"I am glad you called me Vivian," said the Lady. "There was a small chance the young man would have risen in three days—as a Malumbrus."

Oh. My eyes went wide. "Is he—"

"The blackness is gone. However, like anyone who has suffered an injury, his journey is not over. He will still need help if he is to have a chance at a full recovery."

Healer Hochim had risen to her feet. "The healer's guild will make sure he gets it. It is good to see you again, ma'am."

The lady tilted her head, then her expression darkened. "As you are about to learn, others around Avalon have been afflicted like this young man. This is all to further a particular person's goals. The young lady you hoped to contact today may be able to help them." Then she turned back to me. "So, Vivian, you asked me to save this young man's life." She twisted her wrist, a scroll appeared, and she tilted it toward me. "This is the service I am demanding of you."

I tentatively reached out and took the scroll.

The Lady of the Lake turned toward Professor Gass. "You initiated her request for a favor, young man. While Vivian had free will to accept or not, you nudged her toward this. Therefore, you bear part of the responsibility of fulfilling the obligation."

Professor Gass's mouth was hanging open. He looked like he was about to say something when the lady just disappeared.

Gone.

It was then that I noticed something was different. There wasn't any background noise from the main room anymore. Slowly turning around, just about everyone was watching us through the tatters of the partitions.

"See," announced Amanda. "I'm a princess, but not *the* princess."

Samantha snorted. "Next to Vivian, you and I don't rank."

Wanda ran in and hugged me, then bounced backwards. She blurted out in excitement, "Well, what does the scroll say? Are we slaying a demon, finding hidden treasure?"

I slowly unwrapped the scroll and blinked. I couldn't make sense of it. It had to be some kind of code.

Wanda grumbled out in frustration. "That's no fun."

We all turned at Lady Cassandra's voice. "Sorcerer Petotum is ready to begin the trial. He needs all of you as witnesses."

Lord Seth's henchman blurted out, "Whose trial?"

Lord Seth rolled his eyes and muttered something under his breath.

Nathan shook his head. "Mate. Your henchman is a bit slow on the uptake."

Chapter 26

Power challenges Power. It always does.

-Lady Gawain

-Vivian Hampton-

Gymnasium, Pioneer School

As we were being escorted back to the gymnasium, Elaine indignantly declared, "How come our dragon didn't show up?"

<*"What makes you think I did not?"*> we heard in our minds.

This was Avalon's dragon. But unlike when I had heard him before, he didn't sound exasperated, just firm. Also, still loud. <*"This is my planet, Elaine of Llamerel. I do not involve myself with the ebb and flow of human confrontations. Those battles never end. I care little about who is hunting for power this week."*>

No one other than the five of us acted like they had heard the dragon. Wanda spluttered out, "If it wasn't for Vivian, we would have all died."

<*"And you did not. Nor are you a child any longer. If you want to make a difference, then do so. After Arthur passed and Merlin retreated, Avalon began to regress. Then some four hundred years ago, the concept of the guilds was born and with that, battles. Historically, people in power do not want to relinquish that power. There are worlds where none of you would have a voice at all. If I stopped every infraction, attempted to*

right every wrong, then I take away your free will. But as Lady Vivian is learning, if you stand up and fight, there will always be those who fight back. That never ends. Everyone, including you, Wanda Hine, gets to choose. Even if you don't make a choice, you still have chosen.">

The dragon sounded much more philosophical than before. But something didn't add up. <"*Sir, you involved yourself when you learned about Amanda's ring. What do you want now?*">

The dragon didn't fully retreat, but I felt his presence pull back slightly. <"*Interesting, Lady Vivian. Very few ever ask me what I want. My eldest has become involved. If Hyanthio is willing to negotiate, my chancellor will listen to her. I assume Lady Gawain will be the intermediary?*">

<"*Yes, sir. I hope so.*">

Then I felt Lucille's presence in my mind as well. Since Wanda, Amanda, Elaine, and Samantha had varying degrees of surprise on their faces, they likely felt her mental touch too. <"*He almost sounds like an adult. It must be from hitting him on the head. I should probably do it again to make sure it sticks.*">

Avalon's dragon growled. It felt like my mind was vibrating. Then both presences were gone.

Amanda reached out a hand to Elaine. "Friends?"

"Friends," answered Elaine and the two shook.

I wasn't sure, but it looked like Lady Cassandra smiled briefly. Could she hear us and the dragons talk to each other?

Just before entering the gymnasium, Lady Cassandra turned to face us. "Most of your heads of houses are here. Sorcerer Petotum, along with the headmistress, created an information time recall spell. From the time the lot of you entered the gymnasium until you left has been crystal recorded. For those who feel up to it, you will stand with your head of house along with a teacher, to watch it being replayed. If you are asked any questions, do your best. Everything is being recorded at the trial."

The edges of the gymnasium were packed with people; I was surprised to see that the High Nobles, Senior Guild members, and the entire council were there. However, one of the Council members was standing in a circle away from the others. I had never met or even seen anyone from the Wizard's Council before. But I recognized them from pictures. Their portraits were prominently on display in the main hall.

The central area of the gymnasium was still the same. Random bits of stuff covered the floor, except where I had held my shield spell in place. Looking at it now, it was a really big area I had protected. Parts of the ceiling and back wall, which Lucille had lifted away, were now piled just outside the gymnasium. Realm Knights stood on them, keeping crowds of people away. I bet the mayor, reporters, and others were out there insisting on entrance.

I found Lord Winton and went to stand by him. He gave me a smile but put a finger to his lips. Wanda came over to stand with me. Her uncle, whom I had met once before, seemed a bit annoyed that she had followed me instead of going to him. But he came over and flanked Wanda. The only ones who didn't have a house family elder here were Elaine and Samantha. Both were escorted by a Realm Knight to stand next to the headmistress.

I wasn't sure what was going to kick this off, and I was a little apprehensive about everyone seeing me in the spell replay. *Was my hair a mess? Did I slouch? What if...* and let out a breath. *Elegant*, I thought to help calm myself down. Also, my mind kept on going back to the Lady of the Lake's scroll, which Professor Gass had taken from me to study. It had to be a code, but to what? My imagination had me studying the scroll at night with Professor Gass and Professor Malton, trying to break the cypher.

The silence stretched and suddenly a lady just appeared standing in almost the same spot I had been. Her green gown was stunning, and it looked like there were white runes slowly moving across it. From the exclamations around the gymnasium, others knew who she was.

I had seen this beautiful woman before. Oh my maker, she was, but before I could say anything, Wanda squeaked out.

"Lady Elizabeth Navartis, the merlin's guide."

She slowly walked toward Sorcerer Petotum and curtsied about fifteen feet away. Then turning around, declared, "My name is Lady Elizabeth Navartis, the highest princess of Avalon, Avalon's Lady of the Land, and eldest guide to the new merlin."

The stunning woman turned toward the ring holding Council Member Chandley. "The spell used to make that shadow amulet was very distinctive. Sorcerer Petotum was able to transmit the spell's signature to Commander Agave. Already eight other agents of yours have been apprehended in schools around Avalon. Realm Commander Othello and Bardot, with the assistance of the Calvit Battle School and the Prittle Knight School, have been very busy this last hour. You had a window where backs were turned, and you took it. Unfortunately for you, a bard, a junior reserve Realm Knight, and the apprentice to the Cursed Knight discovered one of your agents and by doing so, your plans began to unravel—a plan to kill as many as the young nobles whose families want to push Avalon forward."

The white shifting runes on Lady Elizabeth's gown froze for a second and turned red. Her voice darkened as she slowly walked to the ward circle holding Council Member Chandley. "Commander Agave is annoyed at you. She has formally charged you with treason, mind control, and attempted murder. The *only* reason you aren't in a duel to the death with her right now is because of the wisdom of my friend, Lady Gawain. Her exact words were, 'If I am to pick up the title, then I must believe there is a rule of law.' Avalon's laws state that if a council member has been charged, an immediate hearing must be held. You have been charged by Commander Agave, Council member Chandley. Do I hear a second to begin the trial?"

Sorcerer Petotum announced in a clear voice, "Seconded."

The other five council members nodded.

"So, let us begin," announced Lady Elizabeth, and she moved to stand between Terrance and Sorcerer Petotum.

Council Member Chandley rolled his eyes. He almost seemed contemptuous of the charges.

"Fools," he sighed. "You are on the losing side."

Sorcerer Petotum touched his wand to a blue gem hovering in front of him. "What you will be watching is the recording of a time recall spell. Anyone in this room is permitted to ask questions. When that occurs, I will pause the playback. Let us begin."

Then the entire central area of the gymnasium glowed a faint blue which faded away to reveal Wanda and me entering the room.

As Mina and I argued back and forth. I was surprised at my control. My back was straight, I wasn't reaching for my wand or raising my voice. I liked this version of Vivian Hampton; she had presence.

Wanda nudged me. "See? Elegant." For her comment, she got shushed by her uncle.

The first call to stop the replay was right before Lord Keith's henchman threw the spell crystal. Surprisingly, it came from me. As all eyes turned to me, I felt myself take a half step backwards.

"You'll be fine," said Lord Winton. "Go ahead."

I let out my breath and forced myself to step forward again. "Right there," I said, pointing to the young man. "If you pay attention, you can see his shadow shift to a wolf, then to that of a woman."

"Replay it," came Lord Navartis's commanding tone. Sorcerer Petotum twisted his wand around the crystal and the scene went backwards a few seconds, then advanced forward at a slower pace. There wasn't any sound, but doing it that way, it was possible to clearly see Lord Keith's henchman's shadow transform first into a wolf, then a lady, making a grab and throw gesture. Once the little crystal was in the air, the playback stopped.

Just about everyone was looking at it now. An older woman with white hair asked, "How did you know what to look for, young lady?"

Before I could answer, the headmistress did so on my behalf. "Ms. Vivian Hampton has recently come into her oracular abilities."

I wanted to cringe but kept my back straight at the murmurs around the gymnasium. "I saw it twice before in my visions. I didn't start putting it together until the shadow transformed in front of me though."

"Very well," said a council member standing next to Sorcerer Petotum. "Please bear in mind only certified oracles are allowed to present oracular evidence to the courts." He nodded at Sorcerer Petotum. "Proceed."

The next call to stop was right after the rear bleachers blew apart. Thousands of flying bits of wood froze in the air. Some of them had already hit my shield. Where they impacted, my shield lit up like little snowflakes. If you ignored the fact I was terrified, and we might have all died, it was rather beautiful. Without being able to pull magic through Camillo, my shield spell wouldn't have been nearly as large. Lord Winton put a hand on my shoulder and whispered, "I am very proud of you."

That one statement made me want to cry. I took his hand and squeezed it.

"What kind of shield spell was that?" inquired another council member, glancing my way.

Sorcerer Petotum coughed. "I believe it is a unique variation of Meupile's shield, with a bit of extra power thrown in."

"More than that," remarked Lord Navartis. "It's a damn good shield. What is that light rising from the floor in front of the young lady? It sort of looks like a sword."

I didn't see it at the time as I was concentrating with all my might. But now I could see it there—a glowing sword hovering in front of me.

Wanda turned to look at me in astonishment. Others were doing the same.

Lady Cassandra's voice rang out. "I suspect it is her mental focus. She imagines a sword, and with enough power, it takes form and acts as her focus. Her wand is enchanted. This allows her to create a secondary focus point, therefore bypassing the wand's upper limit."

"Ah. Ingenious," came that same older woman with white hair. Now that she had spoken twice, I recognized her. We had never met, but I had seen her picture before. She was the head of the Wandmakers Guild: Lady Keystone. I bet she had come up here to examine Elaine's wand.

"Fascinating. Let us proceed," demanded a council member.

The next pause was when Terrance appeared, and his shadow pinning down the shadow wolf.

"Who is this man?" demanded the oldest of the council members. "Is he a vampire?"

Terrance coughed, and everyone looked his way. He was standing just to the left of Lady Elizabeth. He bowed slightly. "I am Terrance, Council Member. I'm the Cursed Knight's apprentice."

Sorcerer Petotum sighed. "Hugh, if you bothered to read my notes, you would know this. The Cursed Knight and Terrance met up four days ago and came to an agreement. We drafted the man in hopes he could help. Besides, Lady Elizabeth had already indicated who he was."

Lady Elizabeth curtsied. "The Iron Dragon was there as well. You can't get any more official than that."

"Fine," growled out the council member. "But I want to meet him after all this is over."

Sorcerer Petotum twisted his wand, and the playback continued.

What can you say when a dragon and an eight-foot-tall black knight appear? All the murmuring in the room died away as the knight shoved his arm into the werewolf and the Lady Bell substitute began to speak.

♫

At the end of the replay spell, the area turned blue again, and the spell faded away.

"This has been recorded in five separate gems," announced Sorcerer Petotum. "I second the charge brought forth by Commander Agave to Council Member Chandley. Treason, attempted murder, and mind-control."

That's when I felt it. The tingling sensation on my shoulder started again, and like before, the room faded away.

I was still in the gymnasium. Everyone was here. If this was in the future, it could only be a few seconds from now. What was I supposed to notice? But that's when I felt it. Something very evil was slowly flowing into the ring holding Council Member Chandley. I watched in terror as red, glowing runes undulating like snakes expanded from the inner edges of the ring and wrapped themselves around the man. Instead of being terrified, the council member appeared almost euphoric, as if the man expected this to occur. I distinctly heard him say, "Master, it is time." At his words, all the runes making up the twisting red snake changed and became a demon. Then my vision blew apart, reformed, and blew apart again. It felt like three gigantic pressure waves of reality were competing for dominance. I was caught in the middle. *Oh maker, I bet this vision was going to come with a headache.*

I wasn't wrong. It took everything in my power to stay conscious.

The Thought

It had been able to expand tendrils of light up to the third warding stone; the one just under the floor where the young enchantress had sung light into being. Without the energy of her song, it had been prepared to lay dormant and consider options. While the warding stones weren't under its control, it could sense the locations of the other six now. Every time it touched another ward stone, a little more of it woke up. But this time, something else did as well. It could sense the young enchantress, but only when she had strong emotions. The problem was, it didn't understand them. Math was real, the sun was real, the warding stones were real, but these emotions the enchantress possessed were ephemeral. Were they important? In desperation, it asked the voices in its mind for help.

"She is consumed by fear," said one of its more powerful voices. Her image was that of an older woman with many wands. The woman had died up on the mountain cycles ago, and sensing her power, it had copied her, so her voice could be with him as part of his dreams.

"What is fear?" the thought asked back to this voice.

"While there are many types of fear. The young enchantress fears she and her friends will be no more. To go to sleep forever."

The thought understood sleeping. Most of its mind was still asleep. But this sounded different. "Do you mean die?"

Like fear, it didn't really understand death. When someone died, it copied them so it could remember their voice. What happened with the body and the other bits, it never even considered the questions.

"Yes, but stronger. To be destroyed. To never wake up again."

"I could copy her," the thought suggested. "Her voice would be with me then."

"True, but then she would not be able to sing anymore," said the old woman patiently. "Like me, her life song would have ended."

"I don't want her songs to go away," the thought said and was suddenly aware of an intense light growing in its matrix. It felt an emotion for the first time since it had reawakened. A longing, a fear of being alone again. And with that, a memory was unlocked.

Soon after the thought heard its first song, it had seen the old enchantress. She was standing next to a man with white hair and vast power. The thought could feel that they were happy but sad at the same time. It tried to reach out to her, this old woman who sang it into being. But the man cast a spell on a stone, and the thought felt part of its mind go to sleep. Why? Did it do something wrong? It tried to reach out to the enchantress again. But at each casting, more of it fell asleep. The last song it heard before the ninth warding stone was charged was the enchantress crying. "Be safe, my child," she said softly. "I hope you dream." And then there was darkness. The old enchantress, the one who had sung it into being, was right. It had dreamed.

Now with one of its warding stones uncovered, it could see the stars, and with more of its mind awake, it could measure time. It had been asleep for over six hundred years. It didn't really understand if that was a long time, but with that memory unlocked, it understood longing. Was this young enchantress the daughter of the old enchantress who sang it into being? If so, why was she afraid?

The thought considered the words of the voice it had just talked to. The young enchantress was afraid of going to sleep forever. Of never singing again. The thought knew that feeling very well. There was limited power in its matrix, but another emotion was bubbling up inside of it that seemed to amplify its power.

"What is this?" it asked the old woman with the wands.

"You are angry," she said. "Angry that something might cause this enchantress to sleep forever."

It considered her words. "Yes." And the thought also knew who it was angry at.

As always, the thought considered options.

♪♪♪

-Vivian-

I fell to my knees in disorientation. Lord Winton knelt down next to me. "Vivian, what's wrong?"

Wanda grabbed my hand. "I bet she's having a vision. A big one."

"Something big is coming," was all I could rasp out through the pain. I was so disoriented. The vision kept reforming, then fading. On the sixth iteration of this, my vision came apart as if a sledgehammer shattered it.

Well, at least the pain went away. Yeah.

Replacing it was a dragon. Avalon's dragon. And he wasn't in my vision. He was here.

<*"This is my world, demon,"*> came the dragon's powerful mental voice. Everyone heard it.

The room seemed to expand in all directions and with it came Avalon's dragon. A pulse of energy blew out from him almost causing me to fall unconscious. His massive head was angled down, looking at Council Member Chandley. Steam was coming out of his nostrils. From my vantage point, I was looking at his gut, and it was expanding.

We were all going to die!

<*"Shh,"*> came the Lady of the Lake's voice in my mind. <*"A dragon's presence is frightening. Especially an angry one, but there's something else in play here."*>

<*"Ma'am,"*> I thought back terrified. <*"See what?"*> There was a gigantic, pissed off dragon right in front of me. All my joints felt frozen in terror. Wanda was gripping my hand so hard that I thought she might crush it.

<*"What lies below. You called magic recently. It is responding. Now watch. This will become important later."*>

Only because the dragon was standing could I see Council Member Chandley beneath his legs. Those glowing red snakes made of runes twisted upwards inside the ring, and suddenly a sparkling outline of a demon appeared just behind the council member. It was the vision I'd had just a moment ago.

The demon grinned up at the dragon almost as if it was playing a game. <*"If you attack me, dragon, you will be the destruction of everyone here, including your precious mate. The man is mine. He called me and, by the accords, I am allowed to be here to take him. Then your precious people can live. Choose."*>

Seconds passed as the two stared at each other. The dragon's gut expanded even more. It was hard to formulate words in my mind. Even if Camillo had the energy and I recreated my shield against the dragon fire, I would be dead.

<"Ma'am,"> I cried to the Lady of the Lake, <"can't you do something?">

<"The man called to the demon. A service was offered. It is allowed to be here. But only to collect his agent. Only if he steps out of the circle, am I allowed to attack. The demon knows this. If I don't follow the rules, Vivian, others can break them as well. Pay attention.">

The dragon swung his head to look at Elaine. <"I do care about them, and that's what separates me from you.">

<"Then you are a fool,"> sneered the demon. <"A war is coming. While I am collecting generals about me, you do nothing but hide in the forest.">

<"Yet the demon lord you follow is but a ghost leaving you to stand on the target. Goodbye, demon.">

The demon bowed, then partially wrapped its wings around Chandley. Both began to fade as if they were moving away from us but not teleporting. Behind them it looked like thousands of red flames were pulling at them.

<"Now!"> I heard in my mind from the Lady of the Lake, and suddenly the demon expanded, warped, then screamed. A second later, it blew apart into millions of red glowing dots, each taking their own path to the red flames. A half second later, Chandley fell to the floor looking stunned. Then he blew up, reduced to nothing but a red mist within the ring.

<"Is the demon dead?"> I asked in terror.

<"No, Vivian. Short of dragon fire or a blade of power, they cannot be fully destroyed. But it will be a long time before that one can reform again.">

Oh. I felt some of my terror fading. <"Ma'am, about Council Member Chandley?">

<"Sometimes it's best not to ask,"> and she was gone from mind.

<"Apparently you need to add a fourth charge,"> said the dragon into our minds. <"Summoning demons.">

And he was gone. The gymnasium's walls glowed for a second at the backlash of energy.

Wow. No headache this time. Thank goodness for small miracles. Then I had an odd thought, was Camillo absorbing some of the extra power from me?

The Thought

The thought felt better. Most of its voices echoed a similar feeling of satisfaction. Whatever that creature had been, it hadn't belonged here. But for a moment, it could see inside the creature's mind, and it hadn't liked what it had seen.

With its anger abating, the power it could tap, receded. But the thought considered something. It had done it once. Could it do it again? The extra power it had tapped came from layers deep underground it had not been aware had existed until now. Its thought matrix had grown. Now it had merged with creatures long since dead, very big ones. Not bones anymore, they were a silicate of unstructured matter until the thought had sent tendrils of light into them.

It wondered; how big it was now? More importantly, was there a way to awaken this part of its mind?

For both, it had no answer.

It desperately wanted to talk to the young enchantress. Would she know?

Chapter 27

It terrifies me anytime Sarah plays with time dimension spells.
-Lady Elizabeth, the new merlin's guide.

-Terrance-

I looked out of the window of the tea house in the town and could see the top of the school if I squinted. Turning back to the man sitting across from me, I said, "So, apparently, I'm your apprentice."

"Seems to be that way," replied the Cursed Knight while leaning back in his chair.

"I haven't taken an oath," I objected. "What's to stop me from walking away from all this?"

He shrugged. "You chose to make a difference. That's oath enough for me. You can walk away anytime you want. However, if you start acting like others don't matter, the fight will be very short. You have free will, but so do I."

I looked around the corner shop. This was one of those places everyone knew about and could come in and get their favorite flavor of tea or coffee. It was owned by an older lady, who seemed a bit overwhelmed with so many customers this afternoon. A few regulars were eyeing us and had gotten up to stand against the wall to make room for the nobles. They had been coming in for the last five minutes—Lord Navartis, Lady Tartinelle, Lady Gawain, a few guild leaders, and others who had been at the trial. At some point, even Sorcerer Petotum came in, without his minx of an apprentice, and stood next to Lord Navartis. I bet she was avoiding me.

Outside, faces were plastered against the window, watching us.

"Are we waiting for someone else?"

"Three others, actually," replied the Cursed Knight and took a sip of his tea.

I wondered if there was a bit of blood in his tea? A few seconds later, the little shop's bell rang again, and I instinctually stood up. A handsome, fit man who radiated "leader" held the door open for two ladies, his wife and Lady Elizabeth Navartis. The sword at his hip gave it away. I could feel its presence as he walked into the room. There was a push at my mind as well. Not intrusive, just letting me know it. The Sword was here.

Captain Calvit nodded at the Cursed Knight, then me. He escorted his wife to our table and then sat down next to her. Lady Elizabeth Navartis sat down next to me and put her hand on mine. "I'm proud of you, Terrance. Thank you."

I slowly sat down and didn't move my hand. She kept hers on top of mine. I pointedly ignored the stare from her father. She would either decide to introduce me or not.

Three other teacups were brought over by the nervous shop owner. After she curtsied and asked if we wanted anything else, the Cursed Knight shook his head, and she retreated behind her counter.

All five of us took a sip of tea.

The Cursed Knight was the first to stand up. He drank the remainder of his tea. "The ladies of the Pioneer School requested that a place be established where those from all walks of life could sit down and talk without fear of repercussions." He turned his teacup upside down and placed it on the table in front of him. "I am the Cursed Knight and defender of Avalon, so appointed by the

Fisher King. I decree this is such a place. If anyone breaks with this, may all in Avalon turn on them."

Lady Elizabeth stood up as well, draining her teacup. "My name is Lady Elizabeth Navartis, highest Lady of the Land and the new merlin's guide." She put her teacup upside down in front of her as well. "I decree this is a safe place for those from all walks of life to meet and talk without fear of repercussions."

Captain Calvit and his wife stood up and said similar things, each putting their teacup upside down in front of them. Then all eyes turned to me.

I stood up, drained my tea. "My name is Terrance, the Cursed Knight's apprentice. I don't know what the hell I am. But I have people who gave me a second chance and friends. Should any desecrate this site, may all Avalon turn their backs on them." Like the other four, I placed my teacup upside down in front of me. Then my eyes went wide. All five teacups began to glow. An image of a young woman appeared on the table. I recognized her instantly—the new merlin. Gods was she young!

She turned around, seeming a bit flustered. I swear her clothes began to shift to that of a green gown right in front of us. "I hate it when that happens," she grumbled out.

Lady Elizabeth squeezed my hand. "Sarah, we talked about this. Sometimes you must dress the part."

"Fine!" the image of the new merlin grumbled. "My name is Sarah Cognitor, the new merlin. Gowns are stupid. I look lame in them."

The young lady got her frustration under control, stood straight and, just for a second, had some strength about her. Shimmering light began dancing up and down her gown as she tapped her staff on the table and announced, "I decree this site is a haven for anyone from any walk of life. If any break with this, may all Avalon and Earth turn on them."

At first it was the top of her staff; it began to glow. Then the wands rotating around the top of it began to glow as well. Arcing magic, looking for all the world like thousands of little lightning bolts, shot from the wands into her cupped hand. The young lady knelt and seemingly pushed the swirling ball of magic into the table. Magic shot down the sides of the table and spread through the floor. Suddenly the walls of the little shop glowed, and the people standing against the wall were farther away. The room had expanded.

Sarah stood up and looked around at what she had done.

"I think I'll call that my copy-and-paste spell. I just borrowed the framework of the spell from the tea shop in Avalon City." Then she grinned. "Can't wait until I try the spell on my bedroom."

Lady Elizabeth sighed. "Sarah. I don't think your mom would approve."

People around the room began clapping. Sarah blushed and curtsied. Then, apparently, she couldn't hold it in any longer. Looking skyward as if asking the gods for help, she declared, "Can I get out of this stupid gown now?"

Her image faded away, and we could still hear her shouting at someone.

Lady Calvit's wife broke out laughing. "That is so Sarah."

"So, who's our first customer?" I asked Lady Elizabeth.

The woman was still standing by me, and I wasn't going to waste the moment. See Terrance be a good boy.

"And here they are now," she declared a moment before the door opened.

Lady Vivian and her henchwoman, Wanda, were almost dragging a young man, who had to be a noble, and a young lady into the tea shop. Trailing them were several older people. From the looks, relatives of each and likely family elders. I gave Lady Vivian a nod, and she smiled at me but quickly turned back to help manage the entourage. After people sat down and tea was served, we moved away to give them some privacy.

"You know," I said to the lady running around and serving tea. "You might think about getting some help. Mrs. Capmond loves serving people tea."

The shop owner stopped, blinked, and seemed to consider my words. "Thank you, young man." She turned around and added in a whisper, "Do you like blood in your tea?"

I gave her a smile. "I prefer pig's blood, about a three to one mixture."

She thought about it and wandered off to help some others.

I turned toward Lady Elizabeth at her chuckle. "What's so funny?" I asked, almost afraid of the answer.

She tilted her head toward the shop windows. "Do I need to protect you this evening?"

After following her gaze, I groaned. Looking in through the shop window were those same young ladies I had met on the mountain trail early this morning. The lot of them seemed to be deciding if they should come in or not.

Taking a chance, I asked, "So about my offer on a walk."

"Let me introduce you to my father, Terrance."

Chapter 28

There are hundreds of street oracles in Avalon, they are akin to visiting a psychic on earth. Considering there is no official Oracles Guild, separating the charlatans from those with the gift can prove interesting. If the visions keep on getting "clearer" when more silver is offered, it's a good bet you're sitting across from a charlatan.

Those that have a stronger gift, generally don't advertise their services. Seeing the world from so many different points of view can be disconcerting. Powerful houses or prominent sorcerers will go out of their way to keep such individuals for themselves.

Guide to Avalon, 4th printing

-Vivian Hampton-
Stables, Pioneer School

I took a break from brushing Sunny, one of the new horses someone had donated to the school. He nudged me from behind, and I laughed. I knew what he wanted and fed him the other half of the apple. It felt surprisingly nice being alone for a change. Because so much had happened this past week, I had filled up half my journal. Dragons were taken care of, that had taken up six pages in my journal. Lady Gawain was even more impressive than I had imagined. She patiently let the dragons argue back and forth without flinching. She would make the occasional suggestion, withstand the backlash, and reiterate her suggestion. Eventually, they reached a place neither disagreed with. Lady Gawain had out argued two dragons. After their disagreements were settled, Elaine and Amanda hugged each other. I still don't know who the headmistress is going to choose as head freshman girl.

My new title took up five more pages in my journal: Lady Vivian Hampton Winton. A little part of me felt like I had a home with Lord Winton now. He wasn't my father, but I became a lady within his house. Once he was married, I would report to him through Lady Kiera.

Wanda had left two hours ago, hiking north along with Lord Grayson. I asked Camillo to go with them and he agreed. Watching a snowman carrying a parasol was one of the strangest things I had ever seen. Terrance was going in any case, so that made me feel better. I secretly wondered if Lady Elizabeth was going to pop in on him. Lord Grayson had been ordered to help settle any land disputes on the next mountain pass, along with mapping out the area—that's what he'd wanted Wanda's help with. Being a "Hine," she had probably learned how to map out an area by the time she was three.

I sat down and read the letter from my father again. Included with the letter was a picture—my father was standing with another woman, his girlfriend. I wanted to tear it up. She looked younger than Mother. My father's girlfriend was one of those cute, skinny women. But I had to remind myself not to instantly judge. My parents weren't with each other anymore. She might be a nice woman. But secretly, I didn't want to meet her. I think I was afraid of liking her.

Within his letter, Father had written that he was proud of me. That made me feel good, like he honestly wanted to reconnect. But I wanted just him, not this interloper. I stopped myself again. That was just stupid. Life moves on.

If Mother had found someone she liked, someone that brought her happiness, she had never written to me about it. I was looking forward to seeing her at Lord Winton and Lady Kiera's wedding. It was next weekend. Wanda and I were going to be fitted Monday evening after school for our new dresses. Then she and I would take the teleportation circles next Friday. I was looking forward to singing at the wedding. That was going to be fun. One of my plans was to ask Lord Winton if my mother could sing along with me. Mother and daughter together again.

"Penny for your thoughts."

I turned around and smiled as I noticed Lady Cassandra striding toward me. I blinked at the other woman accompanying her. She was about my age, shorter, with black hair and looked very fit. I didn't think she was a student at our school. Then I recognized her and curtsied. We had sort of met, briefly. She stood by Lady Gawain during the dragons' negotiations. Also, being one of Wanda's many infatuations, I knew a little about her. She was Lady Charlotte Fletcher, Lady Gawain's healing apprentice, and the Merlin's left hand.

She smiled and rolled her eyes. "I should be curtsying to you."

"That still makes me feel silly," I replied. Lord Navartis had knighted me. The knighting was real, but it was also a ruse to help hide that I was somehow associated with the Lady of the Lake. The lands Wanda were exploring were likely to become mine under Lord Winton's house. Which meant I was the one which ultimately got to settle land disputes. Anyone wanting to "claim" an area for working the land or settling would have to take an oath to my house. They would become my subjects. It would be my job to set the taxes, define the area, and so on. If Lady Kiera hadn't agreed to help me, I might have walked away from all of it. Currently, my only subject was Wanda. She had become my official right hand. That had been Lord Winton's idea. He negotiated with her head of house on my behalf. Later that night, I had just stared at my journal and at some point, started to cry. I wasn't sad, just overwhelmed and happy. Wanda had a future now beyond just being a baby-making machine. Instead of writing anything down, I just drew a picture of Wanda in my journal. I couldn't find the words.

Lady Cassandra made the official introductions. "Lady Vivian, let me introduce you to Lady Charlotte. I assume you would both prefer Vivian and Charlotte."

"Definitely," I agreed, and Charlotte curtsied again. I stuck my tongue out at her, and she laughed. Already I could tell I was going to like her. I just didn't know why she was here.

"What's this?" I asked Charlotte as she handed over an old book.

"It's one of my old master's journals," she replied. "Look at page ninety-seven."

I found the page. It was like a madman had written out complex mathematical magical equations in shorthand. The only thing I could understand were the three names at the bottom of the page. But only one of them was circled. Charlotte's.

"Why is my name there?" I asked.

Charlotte put her hands in her pockets. "I have the bard's voice as well. But compared to you, mine isn't very strong. Technically, I'm an oracle too, but all I get is the occasional immediate visions. Sort of duck-right-now type of thing. I bet you get some complex visions."

I nodded. "I just write them down and hope they make sense in the future."

Lady Cassandra chimed in. "I checked up on the third name. Kyle Tunson died in the Avalon war. Both of his parents were bards as well. I suspect he had the bard's voice too."

I flipped through the old journal. None of the notations made any sense to me. "Why would your old master care about the bard's voice?" I said and stopped flipping. I sort of recognized one of the equations. "I've seen this before," I said, turning the journal around in my hand.

Charlotte peered at the notes. "Okay, where?"

"From a scroll given to me by the Lady of the Lake."

Charlotte and I turned to stare at Lady Cassandra. What was going on?

"Ma'am," asked Charlotte. "What's happening?"

Lady Cassandra looked away and sighed. "Why did your old master want an apprentice with the bard's voice? I have some guesses but only that."

I looked toward the mountain. "Is it because of what lies below?" I asked.

"Maybe," said Lady Cassandra. "Probably, that's a part of it. But I bet there's more, I just can't see it yet. Neither can Lucille."

Charlotte pointedly stared at me. "What lies below?"

"I'm guessing here, but Lucille and Rupert think I'm right," said Lady Cassandra. "Your old master's grandmother was Merlin's wife, who also had the bard's voice. I can only imagine how old your master was. Centuries, likely. Anyway, from some sources of mine, Merlin's wife could call magic as well and was likely very powerful. I suspect she and her husband wanted to build a guardian, a thing strong enough to link up with the Houser bookstore. To do this, they created what lies below as an experiment. It's trying to wake up, but without the keys, which no one has anymore, it can't. The size of the thing is amazing. Lucille thinks its matrix is essentially dreaming now."

Charlotte stared at Lady Cassandra. "Lady Gawain introduced me to the guardian in the library. So, there's an experimental one under the mountain. Do you want it to wake up?"

Lady Cassandra looked up at the mountain again. "I could probably convince Sarah to figure out the right keys to unlock it. But she would probably begin playing with it. God only knows what would happen then. Personally, I have my own agenda."

"Which is?" I asked a little nervously. I was expecting to have a music lesson, not discuss guardians.

"I made a mistake," said Lady Cassandra bluntly. "And I'm having to make some hard choices."

Charlotte cocked her head. "Ma'am, what happened?"

"Alma let me take some things out of one of her secondary vaults. So, I could have some spending money."

Charlotte's eyes went wide, and my mind felt staggered at the thought. An item? Out of the Lady of the Lake's vaults? I bet there wasn't enough money in the world to purchase even a single item. "And?" I asked, intrigued.

"I made a deal with a dragon at the Houser bank. So, what I took out of the Lady of the Lakes vault could be stored safely. He assured me, all was in order. Within five minutes of Alma transferring what I asked for, almost everything escaped."

Charlotte's eyes had gone wide. "Is the Lady of the Lake mad at you?"

<"*Just the opposite,*"> we heard in our minds from Lucille. <"*She thinks it's hilarious. They are technically not weapons of power, so she doesn't really care. But to anyone else, including dragons, they are extreme magical artifacts. You couldn't buy one. That's what Cassandra is hoping to use what lies below for, to give the guardian something to do. Guard the items as we find them.*">

Oh. That made a certain sense in my mind. I still didn't understand why she was telling me and Charlotte though. Charlotte, for her part, was looking at me, and I could tell she just figured something out. "What am I missing?" I asked.

"The bardic voice. If Merlin's wife really had the gift. Would what lies below respond to you?"

I stared blankly at her, then cringed. "I am so not waking it up," I said. "Even if I knew how, which I don't, I wouldn't."

"I'm not asking you to, Vivian," said Lady Cassandra in a soothing voice. "As I said, only a small part of it is awake now. But it wouldn't surprise me if it tried reaching out to you. If it does, all I am asking is, on my and Lucille's behalf, ask if it is willing to guard some things. If it says no, the answer is no."

"Okay." That didn't sound too bad. "What will it look like if it does?"

Lady Cassandra shrugged. "I have no idea. All I'm asking is if it does, talk to it on my behalf. A no is a no."

"Um, ma'am," I said. "If it reaches out and doesn't want to help. What should we do?"

Lady Cassandra pursed her lips. "I'm hoping within Alma's cryptic notes she gave you, that we can find a way of putting it back to sleep."

Oh.

She clapped her hands, then rubbed them together. "So, the bardic voice, let me get a good warding circle up around us, and we can begin."

Five minutes later, I couldn't hold it in any longer. I broke out laughing. "I am so sorry," I said to Charlotte between gasps. "But that was horrible." She had sung out the morning light spell, the one I used earlier this week to corner the shadow wolf. Technically, she sang it correctly, but her voice control was, well, horrid.

"Well, it's not like I practice every day," she said, going red in the face. "You have a go at it then, Miss Perfect."

That stopped me. Somebody calling me Miss Perfect. "I'm sorry. That was rude."

Lady Cassandra jumped in. "Vivian, did you feel the way the magic vibrated around us as Charlotte sang out the spell? I'm going to increase the size of my warding circle a bit, but I want you to imagine a circle in your mind, smaller than mine."

"Okay, why?"

"From the notes I could find, step one is learning how to control how far out you are calling to the magic. Your voice travels pretty far. You need to learn how to control the size of your called spell."

Charlotte cocked her head. "My old master never asked me to do that."

A brief smile crossed Lady Cassandra's face. "You'll see why in a second. Vivian, the same song, please. Call the morning light, and like you did the other day, give it your all."

I took a deep breath, slowly let it out and did it again while imagining the sun peeking over the mountain. Then I began to sing.

Charlotte's eyes went wide. Like before, hundreds of glowing musical notes appeared in the air around us. Then the song hit its peak, and I could feel the magic responding to me, becoming part of the song. Night became day around us, and the imaginary circle within my mind blew apart, light slammed into Lady Cassandra's warding circle.

<*"Wow,"*> I heard from Lucille. <*"That some charge."*>

However, Sunny seemed unimpressed. He nudged me from behind and I gave him another apple. Charlotte giggled, placed her foot into his stirrup and jumped up to sit on his saddle. "However, I am Charlotte Fletcher, the merlin's left hand. Team leader in the

Calvit Battle School, and apprentice both to Lady Gawain and the mighty Bob," she said in a teasing voice while pointing her hand forward as if leading a charge into battle.

Sunny snorted and pawed at the ground. Translation, *so am I supposed to do something now*?

I gave him another apple and looked up at Charlotte. "The mighty Bob?"

Charlotte stood up on the saddle and somersaulted to land on the ground. She had a gymnast's body and amazing training. Wanda would have been impressed.

Charlotte put her hands in her pockets again. "Like Lady Gawain, he's very wise. Bob is the left hand of the Republic's President. I'm learning statecraft from him. Most of it is trying to survive the boredom, though, and still pay attention."

"Wanda would love to meet you. How are the healing lessons going?"

Charlotte rolled her eyes. "I stink as a healer, but somehow, Lady Gawain figures out a way to get through to me. She's awesome. Just being with her is like having the wisest person in the room training you. The woman never seems to sleep. I honestly wonder if she ever met my old master."

A sudden hope blossomed in my mind. "Would you be willing to help me figure out the wording in the land charters for me? I'm honestly lost and need help."

Charlotte reached out a hand, and I shook it. That felt good, Lady Vivian was making friends.

Lady Cassandra laughed. "Okay, enough chitchat. Charlotte, you need to learn how to sing better, which Vivian can help you with. My singing isn't any better than yours. And, Vivian, you need to visualize and control the area of your called spell. So, let's do it again."

♪♪♪

"How did it go?" asked Jeremy. He was waiting for me on the other side of the fence.

"It was surprisingly fun," I said and opened the gate to step through. Something was wrong. Jeremy didn't take my hand or move closer to me.

I could see uncertainty on his face.

"Your head of house said no?" I asked nervously.

He nodded. "Dad's thinking of pulling me out of school too. But it's not about you," he said hastily. "Gramps, my eldest, signed a contract to build several trading posts in Lady Gawain's lands. He wants to be one of the first merchant houses there. And, well, he asked me if I would want to run them."

"Oh. Are you happy?" I said nervously. Two minutes ago, I was imagining us kissing. Now I felt, I wasn't sure how I felt.

"Sort of. No one knows what's down there," he said excitedly and stopped.

I looked away. Here I was right in front of him, and Jeremy was already getting excited about going someplace else. My heart hurt.

"Can we still have dinner together?" I asked hopefully.

He bowed. "Lady Vivian, it would be my honor."

I still found it odd getting the occasional curtsy in town. I sensed Jeremy was nervous, but once we sat down together, he asked, "So why did Lord Seth's head of house vote in favor of the Reece's Racoon charter?"

I grinned. "Well, it was suggested by Sorcerer Petotum." And over dinner, we laughed as stories were told. I got to be Vivian with a hint of lady in there, and he was Jeremy. But a little part of me knew he was going away... and I couldn't have him back. At least not that way. But I remembered something Wanda told me that Captain Calvit had said once. "It is the stories that bind us together." I might become Lady Vivian, but Jeremy would always be a friend.

And that is what was truly important.

About the Author

By day **David Hochhalter** is an optical engineer who has designed some of the longest terrestrial systems in the world. Since he was given the 2:00am middle of the night idea brain instead of the 9:00am brain, he decided to try writing instead of reading technical manuals. Besides, imagining stories is more fun than reading about amplifiers.

Other Books by David Hochhalter and Tom Crepeau

Wandmaking 101
Wandmaking 201

Healer's Awakening
Healer's Journey
Healer's Love

Living Song
Dissonant Song

Made in the USA
Coppell, TX
18 September 2024